# ACKNOWLEDGMENTS

This book has been several years in the ma[...]
am indebted to my Edinburgh writing gro[...]
and listened to my groping attempts to fu[...]
emerged. Thank you, Tom, Marian, Kaye, Meyer, Fiona and Denise.

In the research phase, I was patiently and courteously helped by: Jean Whittaker and Olive Brown of the Mull Museum; the Ross of Mull and Iona Heritage Centres; the National Trust staff and volunteers at Duart Castle; the Writers' Museum in Edinburgh; Ruth Dickson, the daughter of one of the last lighthouse-keepers on Erraid; Helen Miller with the old diary she has preserved; Raymond and Sandra Train for a glimpse into life as a lighthouse child.

In the writing phase, thanks to *Moniack Mhor*, the delightful writing retreat in the Highlands; Meyer Averbuch, whose wonderful house, on Mull has nourished my writing on several occasions; and Cecilia Russell, who has so often made her much-loved house on Iona available – so many happy early-morning writing hours there.

In the first draft phase, my thanks go to all my readers-and-commenters: Rosemary, Peter, Caroline, Helen, Linna, Eluned, Susan, Carol, Marisa, Jean and Olive. Your comments, insights and encouragement were invaluable. In the final stage, my thanks to my patient proof-reader, Alex Thain, and my clever granddaughter, Megan.

For a wonderful week on Iona and Erraid filming the promotional video, and for producing the resulting film, my appreciation and admiration go to John Nowak. For their lovely welcome on a stunningly beautiful day in June and for their willingness to become involved in the film, my thanks and my love to Steve and Julia of the Findhorn Community, present day guardians and inhabitants of Erraid. I cherish a memory of sitting in their back garden in glorious sunshine, drinking tea, becoming friends and parting with hugs.

Finally, as always, my thanks to my family: my lovely, encouraging husband; my ever-interested and inspiring daughters; my grandchildren who keep me young; and my old dog, who was so often part of the research-phase excursions and sleeps sweetly at my side as I write.

### Erraid Song

*Come sit and I'll tell you of stillness and calm*
*Embraced in raw passion by saltwater arms*
*A fragment of Eden, alive in the charms*
*Of the wild tidal island of Erraid*
*Wind weathered old granite in pastel and grey*
*Holds sandy wee beaches in clear watered bays*
*Free scattered with islets, for seals at their play*
*By the smile of the island of Erraid*
*There's humble old trees on her*
*Bent at the knee for her*
*Huddled wee forests in secretive glens*
*Where peaty burns blether*
*Through fern and sweet heather*
*And sing all together, of seas that they'll blend*
*With birds they're a-whistle, reminding their friends*
*Of the song that's the island of Erraid*
**C. Liz Coley, 1991**

**This book is dedicated to Anne, my oldest friend,
who first suggested that we go looking for Erraid.**

4

# CHARACTERS

<u>**1924**</u>

<u>**The Galway Family**</u>   Robert Galway, born 1884
Maggie Galway, born 1890
Robert and Maggie marry in 1910
Their two children:
Liza, born 1911
Gerry, born 1914

<u>**The MacPhail Family**</u>   Lachlan MacPhail
his wife, Marion
their daughter, Catriona

<u>**The Other Lighthouse Families**</u>

1. The Campbell Family: Arthur and Bridie; their twin daughters, Kirsty and Allyson (11); their son Angus (8); and a younger son
2. Euan, married to Etta
3. Calum, married to Jenny
4. Thomas married to Kitty
5. Hamish married to Mhairi

<u>**The Schoolteacher on Erraid**</u>        Miss Joan Dow

<u>**The Neighbour in North Berwick**</u>     Mrs Helen Forsyth

<u>**2005**</u>

<u>**The young Edinburgh set**</u> :       Jen
Sarah
George

5

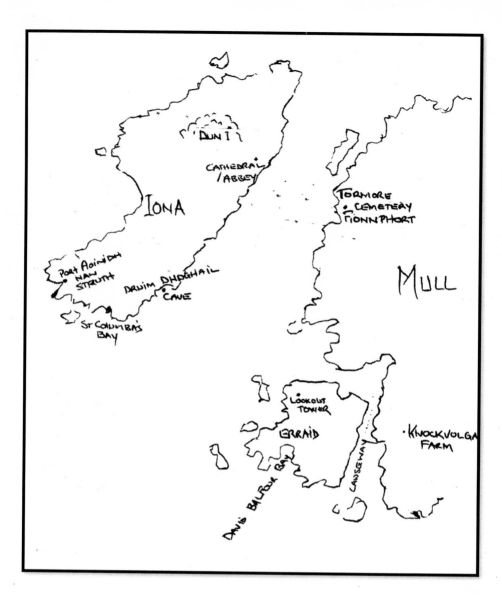

**IONA, ERRAID AND MULL**

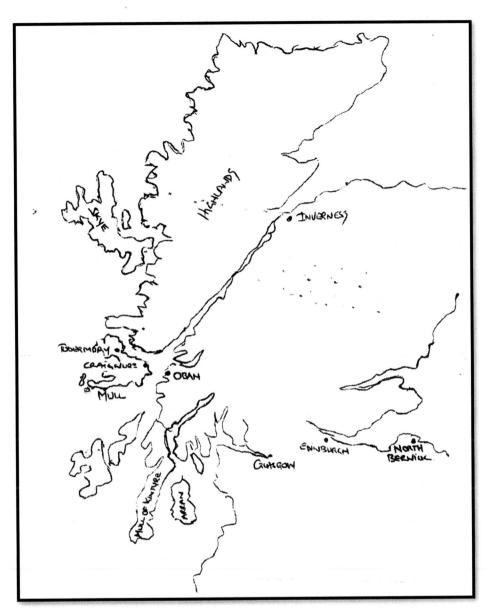

**SCOTLAND**

# PROLOGUE     2005

*To travel hopefully is a better thing than to arrive*

*Robert Louis Stevenson*

When they went looking for Erraid, they could not find it.

Sarah, ever the bookworm, had found a copy of *Kidnapped* in the holiday house and taken it off to bed with her. Next morning, she had pored over the map and pointed out the tidal islet which has a chapter all to itself in Stevenson's novel.

'Let's go to it,' she had pleaded. 'We're so close.'

It had looked easy enough on the map: just off the southern tip of Mull. They had set off on that hot June day, confidence as high as their summer holiday spirits. But, when they stood on the vast expanse of sand and looked at the rugged humps of coast all around, their confidence drained away.

They dropped their rucksacks on the white sand and gave themselves over to a spell of sun-worshipping. This week's holiday on the Hebridean isle was confounding all expectations. They had risen every morning for four days to cloudless skies. By mid-morning, the views were more like those from a Mediterranean cruise ship than from the garden of a holiday let in the West of Scotland: turquoise shallows shading to deep blues with the red and white sails of tiny boats peppering the horizon, white beaches, hazy blue hills and shimmering mountain peaks. And over it all, a sky so blue it seemed to throb with the white-hot power of the sun.

'We should have got the coordinates and brought a map and compass,' said George. He had been in the army cadets at school and liked to sound knowledgeable about outdoors things.

'Can you do that stuff?' asked Sarah, regarding him with new interest. Their friendship was based on shared membership of a city centre law firm in Edinburgh. The friendship was less than a year old and had been fostered by Friday night after-work drinks, extending into pub-crawls and merging into nights spent clubbing. It had been on one of these that the idea of going on holiday together had been drunkenly mooted and hailed as brilliant but, surprisingly, had lasted into sobriety.

'Doubt it,' replied George. 'Not any more. Could do once. Well, sort of.'

'Chancer,' murmured Jen. Sarah looked disappointed.

The sun rose higher. They were the only human beings on that great expanse of burning sand. A few sheep were immobilised, as if painted on to the landscape. An occasional bird hung in the sky.

'I'm going to find some shade.' Sarah had a redhead's intolerance to sun. The others too soon gave in before they fried.

They were sitting in an enclave of rocks, huddling into a tiny patch of shade, when they heard the sound. In the stillness of the afternoon heat, in the clear Hebridean air, it rang out, a high, sweet sound. They had heard the Iona Abbey bell each evening, its deep sonorous notes rolling over The Sound and reaching them as they sat in the cottage garden, chatting, laughing and drinking away their evenings. But this was very different. It had a melting, seductive quality as it drifted over the land and sea. Jen thought of the Lorelei, of the rocks which lay just off this coast, of the dozens of shipwrecks until the lighthouse had been built in the nineteenth century.

It rang and rang for a full minute; then it ceased. They tried to locate the direction it was coming from but this seemed to change. When it stopped, they were no nearer locating it than when it started.

They discussed it and marvelled, put forward a few suggestions, some plausible, some facetious, but, when the sound did not recommence, the topic ran its course and petered out. In the trek back across the beach and up the stony track to the car, discussions about the evening ahead took over. Beer supplies were running low and the one shop they would go near on the way home would be closed in half an hour.

They piled into the car, George driving. They met no other vehicles on the narrow, tortuous road back to Fionnphort. Their cottage was some three miles north of the village but they turned south down the hill towards the Iona ferry, stopping at the shop just as its owner was starting to bring in two sandwich boards advertising ice cream and newspapers. He greeted them cheerily, having made a nice profit off them in the past few days, but his expression sobered as they trooped into the little shop.

'A terrible thing, is it no'? A tragedy. You never look for such on a lovely summer's day like this. What can have made a body do a thing like that?' He shook his head as he put the two six-packs of beer into a plastic bag and took their money.

'What is it? What's happened?' asked George. 'We've just got back. We haven't heard.'

The shopkeeper regarded them mournfully. Jen felt an icy trickle down her spine despite her overheated body and the closeness of the shop.

'It was the wee motorboat that the folk on Erraid use for coming round here or going over to Iona. It went way off course and ran straight onto the Torran Rocks. One of the fishing boats saw it happen. The men say it looked like . . . like it was intentional.'

'Intentional? You mean . . .'

'It was going full speed, straight at the rocks. There's the buoys and the lighthouse. And perfect visibility. A calm sea. It couldna have been an accident.'

'Suicide? But who was it?'

'We've no' heard yet. The coastguards are out there now. But the boat will be smashed. Just bits o' wood floatin' - if there's anything left o' it at all. They'll have to wait and see where the body washes up. The Erraid Community folks – they take guests for retreats and the like - will ken which one of them is missing. The police will have been in touch with them by phone and Constable MacNeill will be going over there soon, I dinna doubt.' He paused in the act of opening his till to extract their change. 'Mind, they do say . . . every hundred years . . . and there's the legend o' the ghost . . .' He gave his head a shake as if to shake off a pestering fly. 'But that's all just nonsense, I expect. It's just a sad business.'

They left him still shaking his head, muttering 'sad, sad business', and walked slowly out to the car. On an impulse, Jen turned back into the shop.

'When did it happen?'

'What? Oh, it was just about an hour ago. No' much longer.'

'Did you hear the bell out at sea?'

His eyes narrowed. 'You heard a bell?'

'Yes, about an hour ago. Was that when the shipwreck happened?'

He made no answer but seemed to draw into himself as if regretting sharing so much with a mere tourist and Jen was forced to give up and respond to the insistent calls of her friends who were anxious to get back to the cottage and crack open the cold beers.

The sun still shone, the place was as beautiful as ever and they were still full of holiday sunshine but she felt only a creeping chill as she joined the others in the car. They drove home in subdued silence, for once not remarking on the stunning scenery or even on how much they were looking forward to the cold beers.

As they drew up at the cottage, Jen spoke into the silence. 'That bell we heard when we were on the beach out there. It must have been just at the time the boat was hitting the rocks.'

'Or just before,' put in George. 'A warning, maybe?'

'It didn't sound like a warning bell,' Jen said. 'It was more like . . . like it was luring the boat.'

11

'Like a siren, you mean?' said Sarah.

'Oh, come on, girls. This is a bit fanciful, don't you think? You'll be telling us next that the Lorelei is sitting out on those rocks, combing her hair,' said George.

Jen flinched, remembering her thoughts when they had been listening to it.

'There will be a perfectly commonplace reason,' said George, getting out of the car. 'You'll see. And it will have nothing to do with this poor bugger who saw fit to drown himself — or herself - this afternoon. Come on. Let's get to these beers.'


Jen drifted awake as fingers of light probed the curtains. She rose, slipped out of the little attic bedroom that she shared with Sarah, and crept down the narrow twisting staircase into a sun-filled kitchen. Already the day was filling with promise. As she waited for the kettle to boil, she caught a glimpse of a corncrake on the lawn before it darted into the long grass and emitted its cacophonous *crek, crek*. No one could miss the sound but a sighting was rare.

She carried her mug of coffee into the lounge and settled on the sofa with her laptop. As the computer booted up, she watched the sun begin to crown above the horizon. It was going to be another glorious day, their fifth on Mull. In two days' time, they would be heading back to the traffic-choked streets of Edinburgh.

The clock icon said six thirty-five. She had a good two hours before the others surfaced. Several websites carried photographs of wrecks all around the coast of Mull, many of them described as 'picturesque'. It seemed a callous word for what had once been a fatal tragedy.

She was so absorbed in her research over an hour later that she did not hear the morning noises of toilet flushing, kettle boiling, toaster popping, and crockery rattling as the household came awake.

'Checking your investments or the weather?' George strolled into the lounge, carrying a mug in one hand and a slice of toast in the other. 'Not that you need to do the latter.' He gestured to the east-facing window through which the sun was laying bars of gold across an old chintz sofa. 'Another scorcher, looks like.'

She raised a blank face from the laptop, slowly focused and stared at him without a word.

'What is it?' Sarah had joined George on the rug in front of her. 'What's wrong, Jen? What on earth are you reading?'

Jen looked up at them and drew a deep breath. 'I've discovered some weird stuff about Erraid. About shipwrecks near it. And about . . . Well, just really weird stuff!'


They clustered round her and peered at the laptop.

'Look – Duart Castle,' said Sarah. 'Where we went on Tuesday. "Ancient seat of the MacLean family" – yeah, we learned that. "1653: Shipwreck in Duart Bay . . . Cromwell's ships . . . Lady MacLean fled with her son to the south of Mull and tried to escape . . . shipwrecked on the Torran Rocks." Isn't that where the suicide was yesterday?'

'Yes.' George leaned over her shoulder. 'Scroll down. "Legend has it . . . one shipwreck with a woman and boy every century since . . . last one in 1925 . . . the story of that one was described by the Canadian crime-writer, Liza Connolly, in a TV history programme about the Jacobites in Scotland." Never heard of her. Have you, Jen?'

'Not until now,' she replied. 'But it seems she was there – well, living on Erraid then - and it had something to do with her family.'

'She'll be dead by now, surely?' said Sarah.

'It says she was born in 1911,' said George, 'so she'd be 94 now, if she's still alive. What's it got to do with you, anyway, Jen? Why were you looking so worried?'

Jen moved the cursor and hovered it over a small picture which had the strapline: 'Liza Connolly, aged twenty, when she first came to Montreal.' She clicked and it immediately expanded. All three looked at the young woman filling the screen. There was a moment of stunned silence. Then George and Sarah spoke together.

'Great God! That's amazing!'

'It's the spitting image!'

Amazing it was, indeed. The spitting image. The Liza Connolly of 1931 looked out at them, through 21$^{st}$ century technology, with the face, the expression and the very soul of Jen.


Details about Liza Connolly's life on Mull, before emigrating to Canada in 1931, were sparse. Jen spent the rest of the day trying to find out more about her and about Erraid.

She finally closed the laptop and joined the others as the shadows were lengthening and the aroma of barbecuing chicken could no longer be ignored by her rumbling stomach.

'Well, Miss Canada 1931, what have you found out?' asked George.

'Not a lot.' Jen flopped down on a sun-lounger. 'But I got one really useful bit of information. Well, two, actually: Connolly is - or was - her married name. She married a year after she landed in Canada. They had a good life out there, had two children, a boy and a girl. Then her husband died in the 1990s and – this is the second thing - she *left Canada and returned to Scotland.'*

'Did she come back to Mull? Is she still alive? Are you going to try and find her?' The questions came at her from both sides.

'I don't know. I don't know. I don't know.' She laughed. 'But I'll tell you one thing: I intend to find out. There's a story here, one that seems to run over centuries and end with Liza and her family. And I feel it concerns me too. There has to be a reason that she looks so like me; and why I've been brought here to Mull; and why we were on that beach so close to Erraid today; and why that bell rung; and why . . .'

George raised his can of beer. 'To Liza and Jen. May the best woman win!'

# CHAPTER ONE                    1924

*The thing had come so suddenly, like thunder out of a clear sky.*
*Robert Louis Stevenson, from 'Kidnapped'.*

The only good thing about Father's leaves was that they were always short – a week at the most – and then he would be off again. We all breathed a sigh of relief when he went, open and loud in the case of my wee brother Gerry and me, hastily suppressed and denied by my mother. Indeed, the only time I ever remember her smacking me was when I came right out with it as soon as he had gone: 'That's great! He's away again. Now we can all cheer up and no' think about him again for a long time.' A moment later I found myself lying face down across my mother's lap, my skirt raised and my knickers pulled down. Mother's hand was strong and work-worn. I never made such a remark again in her hearing, although I continued to think it every time he came and went. I also suspected that she thought it too. Maybe that was why she had skelped my bum so hard.

Father was a sailor with the Merchant Navy and was often away for as much as a year or more at a time. Long enough for the happy, even tenor of our fatherless life to seem permanent – at least to Gerry and me. It was always an unpleasant shock to come running in the door from school, looking forward to one of Mother's fruit scones, thickly spread with her bramble jelly, to find *him* sitting at the table, waiting for her to throw together a meal that would be enough to pacify him. She never seemed to know when to expect him; certainly she never warned us he was coming; she never had food prepared for him that first day; and her anxious face as she tried to concoct a satisfactory meal out of whatever happened to be in her cupboards set the scene for the rest of his shore leave. It was as if he caught her on the back foot at the beginning and she had to spend the rest of his leave trying to make up for it.

We lived in the gentrified seaside town of North Berwick. In summer, my mother worked in one of the large Victorian houses which belonged to wealthy Edinburgh families who came for three months of the year, seeking sea air and sea views. In winter, she was always at her sewing machine, her feet rhythmically working the treadle, one hand guiding material under the whirring needle, the other hand hovering over the shiny black wheel, ready to slow it down. She made curtains, sheets, pillowcases and simple dresses and blouses which she sold to one of the genteel draper shops in the town. We always had enough to eat, clean clothes and beds, new shoes when the old ones began to pinch. She reminded us often that we were 'among the lucky ones' and enjoined us to thank God for this in our nightly prayers and weekly trips to the dreary, cold Catholic church at the end of our street.

My brother and I did not see what was so lucky about our life. We had no experience of any other. We parroted the prayers and fidgeted on the pews, our young minds on more important things like envying a schoolmate her dolls' house or his collection of marbles.

Father flitted in and out of our life at infrequent intervals. Mother was different when he was at home: she smiled less and scolded more; she spent a lot of time in the kitchen cooking enormous meals for him and the rest of her time tidying up after him and cleaning our two-up, two-down terrace house. If it was a summer visit, she excused herself from her cooking job. If it was winter, the sewing machine lay idle. Everything revolved around father. He came and went as he pleased. Some days he went out in the morning and did not return till mid-afternoon or even early evening. As soon as he came in, he expected a meal to be ready and on the table by the time he had taken off his boots and washed his hands. If there was any hold-up, or if the food was over-cooked, he shouted at her and once he threw a plate of stew at her. She ducked but the brown patch remained on the wall beside the door, an unwelcome reminder of his unwelcome visits.

Then, when I was twelve, father got a new job and everything changed.

There came a shore leave that stretched into two and then three and then five or six weeks. Luckily, it was summer so Gerry and I took advantage of the long light evenings, romping on the beach and along the grassy cliffs above the shore. We came into the house only to eat and sleep, cocooning ourselves in determined ignorance of Mother's stooped shoulders, quavering voice and bruised face. If we heard Father's harsh voice raised in a snarling shout as we neared the house, we turned back and forewent our dinner or tea. Hunger was preferable either to watching him bullying her or to having his anger turned on us. I was so afraid of him that the one time that he noticed me enough to ask me where I had been and what did I think I was doing running about the streets in that state – I had been paddling in the sea and my dress was crumpled into a wet, sandy puffball above my knees, its hem still tucked into my knickers – I just stood there shaking and shivering, unable to say a word. If he had

16

not waved me away with a disgusted hand and let me escape to my bedroom, I would have added to my shame by wetting myself.

Gerry and I speculated about how long he was going to be there and why he had not gone back to his seaman's job. He certainly did not seem sick at all, eating vast quantities of food and spending hours in our back garden digging the plot over again and again, grunting like an animal as he put his back into the work. Sweat ran down his face and soaked into his shirt in great damp patches. He never planted anything, just kept digging.

One Monday morning – it was towards the end of summer, early September maybe – we came down to breakfast to find that he was not at his place at the head of the table.

'Is he awa' back on the ships, Ma?' asked Gerry as he sprinkled sugar on his porridge.

Mother shook her head. 'No, lad, he'll no' be doing that again.' She heaved a sigh.

'Why no'?' I asked, careful to sound as neutral as possible.

Mother did not answer. She was staring out the window and biting her lip. I thought I saw tears in her eyes. I tried another tack.

'When is he coming back, Ma?' Neutral as neutral can be. But I was anxious to know, all the same.

'In a few days, Liza, lass.'

'Is he . . .' But she flashed a look at us and bade us be done with the questions, on with our breakfast and off to school.

He was gone for five happy days but burst back in our lives with a vengeance the following Saturday. I was helping Mother peg out the washing in the back green when we heard him come whistling down the street, crashing open the front gate and staggering into the house. A moment later came the roar:

'Maggie! Where the hell are ye, woman? I got it! Got it, d'ye hear? Maggie! Damn ye, woman, where the bloody hell are ye?'

He went on bellowing and Mother went on pegging out the washing. I saw her fingers tremble as she pushed the pegs in and her lips were primped into a tight line but she gave no other sign of having heard him. I was trembling myself by the time we had finished with the washing. I wished I had the courage to go into the house with her to face him but, to my shame, I only ran to the bottom of the back garden, climbed over the wall and kept running until I had no more breath. By then I was on the beach and the violence of the crashing waves matched my mood and covered my sobs.

17

That afternoon, when Gerry and I, judging the coast clear and the house quiet, crept into the kitchen, we found Mother sitting alone at the table staring into space, twisting a damp handkerchief in her hands. But she turned as we came in and held out her arms.

'Och, bairnies, thank the good Lord I have you two. We'll have each other and that'll be something.'

As we stood awkwardly within her embrace, unused to such tactile demonstrations of affection, she told us that Father had been 'paid off' from the Merchant Navy and, these past five days, he had been away to Glasgow seeing about a job as a lighthouse keeper. He had been accepted and gone to Arbroath for four days initial training. Then he had been told where his first post would be.

'An' where's that, Ma?' I asked, hoping it was somewhere very far away.

'It's called *Dubh Artach*, Liza. It's off the west coast.'

'So when does he go? Is it soon?' Gerry made the mistake of sounding too eager. Mother thrust him from her and loosened her grip on me. She stood up briskly.

'We're *all* going. There's a cottage wi' the job. On a nearby island.'

Going! All of us! Leaving our home, our school, our friends, all the life we had ever known. We stared at her, our young minds brimming with questions and objections. Out of these, I found one that seemed to bubble up inside me and boil over.

'What island? Where is it? What's it called?'

'It's a tidal islet off the south-west tip of the Isle of Mull.' Mother sounded like she was repeating a lesson. 'It's called Erraid.'

The full realisation of what Father's new job meant did not at first dawn on us children. We thought only of what we were leaving behind, being unable to imagine our new future.

At school, I basked in unaccustomed interest from my schoolmates. I had just started on the last year at the local school. Along with the other girls in my class, I had discussed what we were all going to do when we left the following summer: into scullery service in one of the big houses; helping the chambermaids in one of the smart hotels along the front or in the home for disabled servicemen that had opened six or seven years ago during the war; delivering goods on bikes for the local shops; helping our mothers with laundry for 'the toffs'. I had thought to start learning dress-making and cooking from Mother, perhaps try and get a decent job in a big house like her when I had mastered them

When I announced that morning at playtime that I was going to be moving away from North Berwick, it was as if I had stolen a march on the others.

'Movin'? Where to?'

'A tidal islet off the south tip of the Isle of Mull,' I replied. I adopted Mother's didactic tone without any comprehension of what I was talking about. Fortunately neither did any of the others and they were suitably impressed.

Mr Chambers got to hear of it, however, and turned it into a geography lesson, after the fashion of teachers. We all looked at the fragmented coastline of western Scotland, at the hundreds of islands. The Isle of Mull was quite big, the Isle of Iona, off its south west tip, was tiny and Erraid was just a dot on the map. The Atlantic Ocean seemed impossibly vast, stretching away to the west.

'Next stop America!' said Mr Chambers cheerfully. Indeed, Erraid looked as if it could be easily tugged away from its tenuous hold on Mull and swirled away out to sea, like a speck of dirt clinging to the side of a basin, swept away by gushing tap-water and sucked down the sink drain.

He pointed out two lighthouses: Dubh Artach (Gaelic for Black Rock, he said) and - further west - Skerryvore.

'You will be following in the footsteps of David Balfour,' he smiled at me. 'But you, Liza Galway, won't be so stupid. You won't nearly starve to death because you don't know that there's a causeway over to Mull at low tide.'

Seeing my puzzlement, he elaborated. 'I was going to have the class read this fine novel anyway some time this year. But I'll give you your copy now so that you can begin reading as soon as possible. You will want to have read Chapter Fourteen before you leave for Erraid. It's quite a famous place – in literature, at any rate.'

He handed me a copy of *Kidnapped* by Robert Louis Stevenson. We had read *Treasure Island* last year. I had quite enjoyed it – it is a book and I love reading - but not as much as the boys did. I preferred stories about girls, like *What Katy Did* or *Anne of Green Gables*. But my interest was whetted and as soon as I got home that afternoon, I flicked through the pages of *Kidnapped* to Chapter Fourteen. It was called 'The Islet'.

I lay on my bed, face down, chin propped on elbows, and read the chapter. It did not make a lot of sense to me, lacking the story leading up to it as I was, but I devoured it. Then I turned back and began to read the book from the beginning.

I barely heard my mother calling me to come and set the table for our tea, two hours later.

19

# CHAPTER TWO

*I could hear the ticking of a clock inside.*

*Robert Louis Stevenson, from 'Kidnapped'*

THE ISLET. From the moment of reading chapter fourteen, it had assumed capital letters in my mind. Although it was never mentioned again, once David Balfour had found his thankful way across the causeway onto the Ross of Mull, for me that chapter was the pivot that the story turned on. Perhaps because, thanks to Mr Chambers' prompting, I read it first; more so, I think, because I knew I was going there to live.

At the risk of incurring his wrath, I plied my father with questions about Erraid, Mull, the Torran Rocks and shipwrecks. He was uncharacteristically patient, even showing me some maps, pointing out the lighthouse he would be working in and the other lighthouses in the area, Skerryvore and Rhins of Islay. *His* lighthouse, Dubh Artach, had been built about fifty years ago.

'The Torran Rocks - that's them that lie between my lighthouse and Mull,' he said, jabbing his nicotine-stained forefinger on the map, 'they were responsible for the death of many a man. One hellish winter in the 1860's, *twenty-four* ships were lost in a couple of months.'

'Did a lot o' people drown, Father?' My fascination overcame my fear.

He gave a bitter bark of a laugh that had me jumping back, mindful of his temper and its short fuse. 'More like too much valuable cargo going to the bottom of the sea. That's what mattered. The government didn't like that. Upset the trade back and forward from America, y'see. So they finally agreed to a lighthouse.'

'And David Balfour's father built it,' I said smugly, keen to parade my knowledge.

'Havers, lassie,' he said impatiently, 'who the hell is David Balfour? It was Stevenson built it. He built nearly all the lighthouses around there.'

'Stevenson? *He* built it! Fancy him being able to do that as well as write all those books.'

But my father's short spell of interest in me had expired. He waved me away and, lifting his jacket off the peg on the back of the kitchen door, strode away out of the house.

It was mother who put me right. She had been listening with half an ear and, when Father had gone, she explained that it was the author's father who had been the lighthouse-builder. Mother sometimes surprised me with the things she knew. Unlike Father, she remembered reading *Kidnapped* as a girl and knew who David Balfour was. When I spoke of Alan Breck and Uncle Ebeneezer, she screwed up her face in concentration and nodded slowly.

'The House of Shaws,' she came out with finally and was delighted when I endorsed this nugget from her memory. I began to remind her about the part that The Islet played in the story but Gerry came running in with a skint knee and a bloody leg. The moment was lost and never found again.

That month, as we packed up our life in North Berwick and prepared to head to The Islet, there were several such missed opportunities.

Like the time I woke one night with a desperate thirst.


The cap had come off the salt-cellar while I was shaking it over my 'champit tatties' at dinnertime. It had fallen straight into the mash, bringing a heap of salt with it. Mother had been for throwing the mash out and giving me some bread with my mince and carrots but father, his cruelty rising up to find amusement from my misfortune, had ordered her to sit down.

'It's nought but a wee bit salt. She's no' getting to waste good food.' Then to me, 'Just mix it in. Here . . .' he had leaned across with his own fork and mixed mince, tatties, salt and all into a grey mush. 'Eat that up. All of it.'

When I had protested, he had flipped his hand across my cheek and growled. It was but a light tap compared to his usual blows, but warning enough to cow me. Somehow I had choked the salty mess down, my gorge rising after each swallow and tears dripping off my nose to add their own salt to my lips. Ignoring a glower from him, Mother had risen and fetched me a large glass of cold water and I had gulped this between mouthfuls. As soon as I had finished, I had asked to be excused and Mother had said 'Yes, dear' before he could speak. I had fled to the 'wee hoosie' at the bottom of the garden and spewed the whole lot up. But I could not get the taste of salt out of my mouth for the rest of the day, no matter how much water I drank. Now, just two hours into my night sleep, the thirst was back. My throat felt sealed, my tongue a swollen weight in my mouth.

I padded downstairs on bare feet. The gas street light outside the front door shone through the pane of glass above it, turning the narrow lobby a ghostly greyish blue. As I glided round the newel post, heading for the scullery at the back of the house, I noticed a line of yellow light under the door into the Good Room. This chilly place with its heavy, padded chairs and scratchy horsehair sofa – always referred to as 'The Couch' – was seldom used. Occasionally visitors of importance, like the priest or the doctor, would be ushered in and left shivering while the best china was assembled on a tea-tray. Once or twice a year, the fire was lit. New Year's Day was the last time I could remember.

Who on earth could be in there at this time of night? Forgetting my thirst for the moment, I sidled up to the door and pressed my ear against it.

The voices in the Good Room were low and urgent. Female voices, I felt sure. I turned my head to see the old clock that hung on the wall behind me, between the bottom of the stairs and the front door. It was half past ten.

'Stop it, Nell. Ye're frightening me.' It was my mother's voice, suddenly shrill, making me jump.

'But ye need tae ken, Maggie. Forewarned is forearmed, is that no' what they say?'

I recognised the voice of Mrs Helen Forsyth, mother's steamie friend. They had been going together up to the municipal washhouse (everyone called it 'the steamie') every Monday morning ever since I could remember. Gerry and I had to call her 'Mrs Forsyth', of course, but Mother always called her 'Nell'. Father called her 'that nosy bitch' and occasionally something else, unrepeatable.

The voices dropped to a mutter again. I pressed my ear so hard into the door that the grooves round the panels dug into my head. I ignored the pain as long as I could and was about to give up when I heard Mrs Forsyth again:

'It's the back o' beyond, Maggie. The back o' bloody beyond. There's things could go on there and never see the light o' day. Terrible things.'

Mother's reply was fainter. I caught only 'superstition . . . stories . . .' and a nervous laugh.

'Please yourself.' Mrs Forsyth was sounding peeved now and I heard The Couch squeak as it did whenever anyone sat down or stood up. I hurried into the scullery for my glass of water and lingered behind its half-open door, hoping that Mrs F would be going out the front door.

The minutes passed and she did not appear. I heard Mother's voice raised again a few times but was too far away to decipher her words. Mrs F's voice, although also indistinct, was louder than Mother's and certainly seemed louder than it had previously been. I felt sure she was standing at the door, maybe even with her hand already on the handle. As soon as I moved, she would whip open the door and catch me.

Later, I wished I had made a run for it. If I had been caught, there was, after all, the cup of water clutched in my sweaty hand as alibi. But eavesdropper's guilt held me rooted to the spot.

I've no idea how long I stood there shivering, praying that Father would not come in through the back door into the scullery and find me. By the time, the two women broke up their conference and the Good Room door opened, I was a nervous wreck. They might have lingered in the lobby or on the doorstep but the sound of Father coming up the garden path at the back of the house, singing belligerently and off-key, sent them scurrying to the front door. When Mother turned from closing the front door on Mrs F, it was to the sight of me galloping up the stairs and Father staggering through the lobby towards her, bellowing obscenities.

He was a mean drunk and I paused for a moment, agonising, as always at that time, between standing with her against his vicious temper or saving my own skin. And I did the latter - as always at that time. I bolted upstairs, leapt into bed and pulled the blanket over my head in a vain attempt to muffle the clatter of chairs being flung to the floor, crockery and glass smashing, his shouts of ill-temper, her pleas and cries of pain.

If he hadn't come home when he did - he was often much later, which I knew from being awakened on other nights by similar sounds– I might have been able to ask Mother what Mrs F was doing in the Good Room at that time and even maybe find out what they had been talking about. She had been so much more open and talkative with me since the news of our impending move to The Islet had broken, treating me more like another adult, even a friend and confidante.


It was my last day at school because Mother had said I could have the next two days off to help her with all the last minute details. At the weekend we were setting off. Father called it 'setting sail'.

'Erraid ahoy! Everything shipshape and ready to go' he would say, with a belly-laugh and an exaggerated seaman's roll walk as he went off to the pub each day to meet his cronies, leaving Mother to get on with the packing and planning.

'Aye, aye, captain,' she would reply and give him a salute as he went off. She was always glad to see him go.

That day, I was late home from school as my school friends and I had said lengthy goodbyes, commemorating the past seven years with

23

replaying some episodes and escapades. Nostalgia, anticipation and apprehension jostled in equal measure in my heart. I had bid Gerry go on ahead with a couple of older boys who lived in our street and could be trusted to make sure he got home safely. To be sure he was nine by then and I had been looking after both myself and him by that age, but you know how it is with the youngest in the family – ever the baby.

When I came into the scullery, there was no sign of Mother. Nor was she in the living room. As I hung up my school coat on the row of pegs in the lobby, thankful that I would not have to wear it again as it had been too tight round my chest for months, I could hear Gerry talking to himself upstairs. Or rather, talking for several characters in some game he was playing. He was great wee lad for creating and living in a make-believe world, sometimes carrying on a story for weeks until it seemed as real to us as it was to him.

I noticed that the Good Room's door was ajar and presumed Mother was in there, packing up our small collection of ornaments, pictures and books. My mind on the bread and jam always ready for us when we came in from school, I went into the kitchen. But, as I sank my teeth into my 'jammy piece', a loud cry echoed round the house.

Of course, I was used to Mother crying out when Father was taking his foul temper out on her. But those were the natural cries of someone afraid in mind and suffering pain in body. This was a cry of such *un*natural terror and revulsion it made the hairs on the back of my neck quiver. Gerry's background chatter abruptly ceased so that the silence that followed was as sudden and shocking as the cry had been.

I found my feet and rushed into the lobby, colliding with Gerry who had come tumbling down the stairs. We locked eyes in a moment of questioning terror; then together, slowly, we pushed open the door of the Good Room.

Mother was on her knees in front of a box half-full of books. In her hands was a small, dog-eared volume. Its covers were a faded green; the title and the author's name on the front and spine were in old-gold lettering, smudged and illegible. She was holding the book at arm's length as if trying to ward it off. When she saw us, she dropped it, indeed almost threw it, on the carpet where it lay open, its yellowed pages fluttering.

'Are ye a' right, Mother?' Gerry found his voice before me but she did not reply, working to control her breathing and still her quivering lips.

'What's in the book? Is it something in that made ye cry out?' I moved towards it although some hidden force seemed to prevent me reaching out to pick it up. I nudged it with my foot, much as one would a suspicious, unsavoury object found in the gutter.

Mother did not answer nor did she touch or look at the book. She rose from her knees and shepherded Gerry and me out of the Good Room. When she eventually found her voice it was to bid me tidy away the bread and jam and Gerry to go and fetch more coal for the range from the bunker outside the back door. All attempts to open the topic of the book were stonewalled by a stream of directions about household tasks. I was no further forward in my enquiries by the time Father came home for tea at six, during and after which, as always when he was at home, we children had to be 'seen and not heard' until bedtime.

As I lay sleepless in my bed late that night, listening to the house settling around me, I pictured that little green-and-gold book lying open on the floor of the Good Room. Was it still there? What on earth could be in it that had so frightened Mother? Why had she not shown us what was in it? Or at least given us some explanation for her shriek?

I almost had the courage to creep downstairs to the Good Room and look for the book. Even if it was no longer lying on the floor, it would probably have been put in the box with the other books. I could steal it, carry it up to the safety and warmth of my bed and hide it under my pillow. Gerry and I could look at it together tomorrow in bold daylight. I envisaged myself doing this and several times got as far as sitting up and swinging my legs over the side of the bed but each time I halted and sank back.

It was not the memory of the sore slap Father had given my bare legs the last time he had caught me 'stravaiging about the house when ye've been put to bed hours ago' – that had been the night of Mrs Forsyth's visit to the Good Room when he had caught me in the scullery and belted me as I tried to escape. It was more a nameless dread, rooted in the horror of Mother's cry; in the sight of that book twirling its faded pages invitingly on the carpet like a spider twitching its web; in the look of frozen shock on Mother's face and her refusal to discuss, or even acknowledge the existence of, the book and the effect it had had upon her.

I heard the town clock strike three before I fell into a light, restless sleep. Two days later, we set off for The Islet.

# CHAPTER THREE

*To be feared of a thing and yet do it is what makes the prettiest kind.*
                    *Robert Louis Stevenson, from 'Kidnapped'*


Father went ahead to our new home to spend a few days with the man he was taking over from at the Dubh Artach lighthouse. Mother expressed hopes that this would also give Father time to make a list of anything that was lacking in the cottage that would be our home. He was coming back to Oban to meet us and conduct us on *The Lochinvar* to Mull.

'We'll maybe manage to buy some things in Oban,' she said. 'If it's any size of a place at all.'

'What sort of things? Ye ken there's very little money left now with me being idle these past two months' was Father's unpromising reply. 'Besides, ye've packed up enough rubbish and it's costing a small fortune to send it wi' the carrier. What more do ye need?'

They had been wrangling for the past fortnight about what he was allowing her to send and what he was making her leave. As she lost one argument after another, Mother became increasingly desperate. Father's insistence that the cottage would be furnished and, being smaller than our terraced house, would need less anyway did nothing to console her for the loss of almost all the contents of the Good Room, including The Couch and its fellow, The Sideboard. The loss of the heavy red velvet curtains had been a particular blow. It had taken her years to save up enough to buy the material and months of work to make them. She had to console herself with her pictures and knickknacks - and, of course, her books. She had fought hard to take *all* of her books in the teeth of Father's scorn and bullying, protecting them as bravely as she protected Gerry and me. I must have inherited my love of reading from her.

'Well . . .' Mother chewed her top lip for a moment. Then, bravely, 'we don't know what state the cottage is in. It might not have enough pots and pans or pillows or . . .'

'Enough!' Father crashed his fist on the table. The glass salt-and-pepper set in the middle of the otherwise empty table jumped out of its shiny chrome dish and toppled over. 'The cottage is fully furnished and equipped. The Lighthouse Board says so and that's good enough for me. There's no need for us to be buying anything new. Or taking anything else with us.' And he marched out, slamming the door as usual.

26

'How is it Father aye has money to spend in the pub when he says we've no much left?' Gerry had the folly to enquire. Mother rarely chastised him and to this day I never saw her lift a hand to him but she rounded on him then, her eyes flashing.

'And how is it a silly wee laddie like you has the cheek to say things like that about his father? You keep your smart remarks to yerself, Gerry Galway, or I'll tell him what ye said. Then we'll see how smart ye are. He'll wipe that insolent grin off your face.'

So fierce was her voice that neither Gerry nor I had the courage to point out that he did not have a grin, insolent or otherwise, on his face; nor that never in a million years would she report anything either of us did to Father. Her whole life was dedicated to shielding us from him, often sacrificing her own safety.


For Gerry and me, the excitement of the three train journeys, first to Edinburgh, then to Glasgow and then to Oban, and the opportunity these had given us for bragging and swaggering at school, had done much to alleviate the pain of leaving the familiar and the fear of the facing the unknown. The night before we left, Mother produced a special farewell meal, using up the entire remaining contents of her cupboards, so that we had a spread such we had never experienced before or that I have had since: round tins of baked beans with a chunk of pork in each one; flat, oblong tins of salty sardines, mashed onto bread and grilled; *champit tatties* smothered in grated cheese; a pot of pale yellow custard darkened with swirls of black treacle; heaped up piles of raisins and currants; and even – my favourite treat – a sticky greased-paper twist of glacé cherries. Mother always began hoarding the dried fruit in the summer so that by the end of October she could make the traditional fare for Hogmanay, giving it two months to ripen and become rich and juicy. She was famous for her 'black bun'. But this year we would be long gone by the time even Hallowe'en came.

'The Good Lord knows what we'll be eating this New Year,' she said. 'We'll be miles from any shops.'

'Maybe you'll be able to buy more stuff for making cakes in Oban and take it with us,' I suggested, hating to see her so sad.

'Aye, maybe,' was all she said.

Gerry cleared the table and I washed the dishes, just as we always did after tea. But nothing else was as always. Instead of saving the leave-overs from pots and the dregs from jars and packets as was our normal, thrifty practice, we were told to throw out everything that remained.

Only a small bag of oatmeal, a jug of milk, half a cup of sugar and a twist of tea leaves were to be kept for our breakfast. As I made a final trip to the big metal bin outside, which our house shared with two neighbours, Mother sat watching me with a pensive, sorrowful gaze.

'That's everything cleared away, now, Mammy. D'ye want me to do anything else?' I asked, wishing there was something, anything, I could do to put a smile on her face. I thought about the last time I had seen her smile. It seemed many months ago.

She shook her head and sighed. We went off to bed for the last time in the only home we had ever known, leaving her sitting at the table, staring at the empty cupboards. But later, before I fell asleep, I heard her go through the lobby and into the Good Room. It must have been bleak in there with no fire and the heavy, forbidding furniture no longer softened by ornaments, pictures and books. I did not hear her come out again although I lay awake for a long time before succumbing to sleep.


Next morning, the mood was very different. We were awake, those of us who had slept, - in my case fitfully and in Mother's barely at all by the look of her red eyes and the dark smudges under them – at five-thirty. It was still pitch black at the curtain-less windows. We had slept in beds without sheets or pillowcases for a week already, all our bed-linen having gone off with the carrier to Oban. Our feet clattered on the bare stair as we descended. Mother had lifted the runner and sold it, along with the red velvet curtains and the cushions off The Couch, to a neighbour. The bag of oatmeal made only three small bowls of porridge and there was barely enough milk or sugar. Mother made do with black tea unsweetened but Gerry and I just grimaced at the thought.

We all three packed our nightclothes, slippers and toothbrushes into the big hessian bag Mother had made for the journey. It seemed to be full of a great many other things but she closed down any line of questioning that we initiated and so we were none the wiser as we assembled in the lobby and faced the front door. We were solemn as befitted the occasion, Gerry and I overcome as much by the unheard-of possibility of exiting *by the front door* as by the solemnity of that farewell moment.

I was expecting Mother to say something memorable that we could all carry in our hearts and recall whenever we thought back to our North Berwick abode. And perhaps she might have. She was certainly drawing a long, slow breath like someone about to make a memorable statement.

But, before she could open her mouth, there came a sharp rat-tat-tat on the front door.

With a little *tut* of annoyance, Mother surged up the lobby to the door and flung it wide. Mrs Forsyth stood on the doormat, silhouetted in the lightening sky. She clutched a large book and as she stepped unbidden into the lobby, brushing past Mother, I saw that it was red plush, quite frayed at the binding and corners. She had a finger thrust into the book between pages and she let it fall open. I saw that it was a photograph album.

'I found it, Maggie. I knew I had it somewhere and last night, just as I was fallin' asleep, it came to me. I was up before my clothes and into the attic. Sure enough, it was there, in my grandfather's old trunk. It's been years since I looked in it – never had any cause to -  but, when you told me about goin' awa to live on that wee island place, when you said its name . . .' She paused to draw breath and Mother said 'Erraid' faintly and – I fancied – fearfully.

'Aye. That's it. My grandfather's folks were from the islands. He used to sing to us in Gaelic when we were bairns. No so much singing, just a sort of chanting. "Mouth music", he called it.'

'We have to go, Nell. We'll miss our train.' Mother began to shepherd us towards the open door, trying to push past Mrs Forsyth's considerable bulk.

'But, Maggie, look at this. Look!' She turned the book around and thrust it at Mother. I was not tall enough to see the page properly but I made out a large piece of newspaper stuck to the page. It had a photograph and some print beneath it. There were two figures in the photo, one tall, one small – a parent and child perhaps, I thought.

Mother tried to keep going but Mrs Forsyth blocked her way, lifting the album higher and higher until it was almost under Mother's nose.

'It's one of those boys! Like I told you. This is proof that it's real. It's no just a story or a superstition like you were makin' out.' Mrs Forsyth was craning over the album and staring fiercely into Mother's eyes. 'Don't tell me you're still goin' to go? Take these precious wee bairns to a place like that?'

It was the first I had heard of Mrs Forsyth considering Gerry and me to be 'precious bairns'. More often we had had the rough side of her tongue and even the occasional attempted skelp as we charged through her garden, chasing each other, tangling ourselves in her washing as it blew on the line, sometimes streaking it with dirt as our muddy hands clutched at it for balance.

Mother pushed Gerry in front of her and tugged roughly at my arm. I was standing on tiptoe, trying to see the photograph. I even did some tugging myself – at Mrs Forsyth's elbow, hoping she would lower the album. So it was that the four of us straggled jerkily out through the front door, not unlike the lines of inebriated men you sometimes saw issuing forth from the pub on a Friday night – except that we were not singing or laughing.

Once we were all four outside, Mother let go of Gerry and used both hands to jerk me away from Mrs Forsyth. I let go of the old busybody's elbow so suddenly that she tottered and dropped the album. I strained away from Mother, thinking my chance had come to see the photograph, but the album tumbled on the two steps that led up to our door and closed itself as it came to rest in the short path to our front gate.

'Now, look what you've done!' cried Mrs Forsyth. She sounded furious. I wasn't sure whether this was at me for tugging her elbow or at Mother for wrenching me away and causing me to pull her off balance.

'I'm sorry, Nell.' Mother spoke loudly, a tremor in her voice. 'We have to get away to the station. The train to Edinburgh won't wait for us and if we miss it, we'll miss the one to Glasgow and then the one to . . .'

'Here, ye stubborn, silly woman!' Mrs Forsyth had swooped down with surprising agility for a lady of her ample proportions and snatched up the album. She thrust it at Mother. 'Take it! Take it! It'll be more use to you than me. There'll likely come a day when ye'll need to look again at that photo.'

But Mother was already at the gate pulling it open and pushing Gerry and me out on to the pavement. The last time I ever saw Mrs Forsyth she was standing on our front path, still clutching the red plush album, shaking her head. As I looked back, I waved a goodbye but she did not return it.

The first train was late and we shivered in the early morning drizzle as we stood on the platform. North Berwick station was one of the smartest in Scotland as befitted one that regularly played host to the Edinburgh gentry who came to spend time at their seaside holiday homes. Late September as it was, the flowerbeds were still immaculate displays of colour without a weed in sight. The roses were particularly beautiful, I remember.

At last we heard the chug-chug in the distance and, as it rounded the long bend into the station, we saw the pillar of steam, seemingly immobile in the still, damp air, and heard the rasp of brakes escalating into a long scream. We were sharing the platform with several formally dressed men, bound for a day's work in the banks and businesses of the capital. As the train finally shuddered to a halt, they stood back to a man, allowing Mother to proceed to a door of her choice. She acknowledged their courtesy with the slightest inclination of her head and shepherded Gerry and me forward. Mother had a natural dignity that never left her though it was to be sorely tried in the months that lay ahead.

My memories of the journey to Oban are punctuated less by the changes at Edinburgh and Glasgow than by the surprises that Mother produced from the hessian bag. Our spirits had been lowered by the meagre breakfast, the strange altercation with Mrs Forsyth and the damp, dismal wait for the train. We might have been disposed to dwell sadly upon what we were leaving behind and fearfully on what lay ahead. But, on the first short journey to Waverley Station, as soon as were settled in a carriage, each at a window seat, she opened the bag and drew out two brand new pads of white paper and two packets of colour crayons. We exclaimed in delighted surprise. Our Christmas stockings always held such delights but the last ones from nine months ago were long since used up. We forgot our gloom and fell to sketching, Gerry, of course, drawing the animals he loved, everything from next door's cat to the tigers and elephants he had only ever seen in books. I have never been much of an artist but, at that time in my short life, I loved creating patterns and would start in the centre of the page and build up an intricate web which gradually spread over the paper. Sometimes it took me the best part of an hour to cover the whole of the page. We were still absorbed when Mother bade us give her back our pads and crayons for now as the train was drawing into Waverley.

The enormity of that place! The soaring height of its dirty glass ceiling, the press of people scurrying hither and thither, the noise of steam engines shrieking and loudspeaker announcements bellowing incomprehensible bulletins every few minutes. Gerry and I cowered, he clutching mother's skirts and me wishing my great age of twelve did not preclude such comfort. We had half an hour to wait there in a crowded 'ladies waiting room' where a girl about my age was pushed off her seat by the woman sitting beside her to create a space for Mother. Again that dignified nod to both girl and woman as she took it. Gerry and I were left standing but again the magic bag yielded comfort. This time, we were handed lollipops, their round heads wrapped in bright yellow paper which we tore off gleefully; then stuffed the heads in our mouths after mumbling our thank-yous to Mother. For herself, she took out a

31

macaroon bar, covered in coconut and nibbled it daintily. The three of us bonded in sugary escapism from our strange, frightening environment.

The hour-long journey to Glasgow gave us a tiny set of snakes and ladders. We played three games: I beat Gerry first time; Mother beat me second time; and Gerry beat Mother third time. I think she managed to let him win although I could not work out how. She and the dice must have been in league.

The terrors of the huge Glasgow Station were tamed by three greaseproof-paper parcels which proved to contain cheese and pickle sandwiches. From the bottomless bag, Mother produced a bottle of her homemade lemonade and three straws. We took turns at sucking the fizzy treat between mouthfuls of sandwich. And so the time passed and we were on the last leg of our great adventure.

This was the longest part and we were growing tired. The final gift from the bag was a book for each of us, *The Jungle Book* with illustrations for Gerry, *The Railway Children* for me – these two were brand new – and a dog-eared volume of *Jane Eyre* for mother. Mother and I read happily and would have done so for hours but Gerry soon tired of words and asked for his pad and crayons again so that he could try drawing some of the scenes and animals he had been reading about.

And so it was that we went west and west again, into the beautiful county of Argyll. From time to time, I lifted my head to marvel at the mountainous grandeur of the scenery, so different from the plains, hills and seaside resorts I was accustomed to. I had thought Berwick Law a fair height of a hill but I saw now it was but a pimple.

As we entered the last half hour of our journey, we laid down our books, first Mother and then me, and stared out at the unfamiliar landscape. Occasionally our eyes flickered into a meeting, almost long enough to register our mutual dread, but slipping away before it could be given life by so much as a nod.

The feeling of the train beginning to lose speed was a clutch at my heart that I saw mirrored in her jaw tightening and her hands shaking as she began to gather in our books and crayons to consign them once more to the hessian bag. We saw Father standing on the platform as soon as the train drew to a halt.

# CHAPTER FOUR

*There's many a lying sneckdraw sits close in kirk and stands well in the world's eye.*
*Robert Louis Stevenson, from 'Kidnapped'*

Our first sighting of *MV Lochinvar* was not as impressive as I had expected. Perhaps my first experience of the huge stations in Edinburgh and Glasgow had used up my store of wonderment. The sturdy little boat with its black hull had a workaday aspect that banished any glamour my imagination had invested her with. Mr Chambers had shown us pictures of some of the packet steamers that operated in the Clyde and I had imagined a great yellow funnel with a black top. *MV Lochinvar* had only a small funnel painted the same orangey brown as the rest of its superstructure. Mother had said we were to have high tea aboard as we sailed to Mull but I did not see where such a thing could happen.

Gerry had also seen the packet steamer photographs. 'Where's the big funnel?' he demanded. 'Why has it only got that daft wee thing?'

Father was pleased to parade his lately acquired knowledge. 'She's no' a steamer like those old-fashioned things on the Clyde. *Lochinvar's* motorised. She doesn't need a big funnel. That's what MV stands for: motorised vessel.'

'What about our high tea? Where will we go for that?" Mother voiced my own doubts.

'It's bigger than it looks. There's a dining saloon down below. You get a fine wee meal there, rice pudding an' all.' Father was enjoying the superior knowledge gained from his recent journey back and forth to the Isle of Mull.

The boat suddenly gave a deep growl and a shudder shook its two masts, causing the flags aloft on them to flutter. The growl became a roar and then settled to a steady throb. Part of the side nearest the quay seemed to split off and fall slowly towards the shore. It settled with a rattle on the quayside. Gerry and I watched amazed. We had never seen a ship lower its gangplank before. There had never been anything like that in the little harbour at North Berwick.

'Come on.' Father began to stride along the quay towards it. He seized Gerry's hand and began some kind of man-to-man talk about the difference between steamers and 'MVs'. I could not help smiling to myself as I saw Gerry attempting to nod up at him knowledgeably, as if he understood a word of what Father was saying.

'I know I could have carried a few more bags of dried fruit,' Mother was saying fretfully. There had been time in Oban, between our arrival at the train station and the hour of *Lochinvar's* departure to do a little food shopping on the busy main street. Father had been vague about what was available in the nearest shop on Mull, impatiently assuring her that he had already bought enough food to be going on with and had stocked the cottage on Erraid for our arrival. Mother looked sceptical but did not argue, only reminding him gently of the time of year and the impending black-bun-making season. Still regretting the loss of her hoard, she had wanted to replace as much as possible in case the island shop was lacking in refinements like candied peel, glacé cherries and currants. But Father had limited her purchases strictly.

'We've to get ourselves off *Lochinvar* and into the boat to get to the pier at Craignure. Ye don't want to be burdened with any more bags when you're doing that,' he had said. She had managed to stow a surprising amount of stuff into the hessian bag all the same. It truly was a magical bag, seeming to have endless capacity both to take in and give out. I fantasised that it had no bottom and, deep down, I felt sure we would have our black bun for Hogmanay.

About a dozen other people were beginning to form a straggling queue at the foot of the gangplank. We joined them.

'Look!' Gerry pointed to several grey sacks being loaded though a hatch at one end of the boat. 'What's in them?'

'That's the mail,' said Father, nodding importantly, still enjoying his role of educating the ignorant. He had a fair swagger about him as he nodded familiarly to several of the people in the queue. He made no attempt to introduce them to Mother but, as the queue finally began to move, a tall, thin woman forewent her turn to board the gangplank and waited for us to reach it. She had jet black hair, scraped back so severely into a bun that not even the skirling wind that whipped along the quay was able to ruffle a strand. It might have been painted on to her head. The long, grey gabardine raincoat fell to her ankles. When we came up close, I saw she had beautiful bone structure and fine eyes. But her expression was haughty and forbidding: I felt a sudden chill that had nothing to do with the sharp onshore wind.

'Good afternoon, Mr Galway. I see you have been as good as your word and brought me two new pupils.' Her voice was strong and very flat. I had heard the chatter in the queue, tuning in with some pleasure to the soft lilt of the West Highland accent, but this was not a voice that had anything in common with that. 'And this must be your wife. How do you do, Mrs Galway. I am Joan Dow. I am the teacher at Erraid School. Your husband spoke with me last week and enrolled the children.'

'I told her Liza was twelve and not in need of any more schooling,' Father, incredibly, sounded somewhat shamefaced as if embarrassed to be caught out in some weakness. 'But Miss Dow persuaded me that Liza should have another term or two. I thought, since there will be little chance of her getting a job here, at least until we get known on the island, she might as well . . .'

He tailed off, becoming aware, as I had already been for several seconds, that Mother was staring at Miss Dow with a very strange expression on her face. Miss Dow met Mother's stare coolly, lifting her chin so that she could look down her long nose.

'What are you doing at that school?' Mother's voice was rather hoarse. She sounded fearful. 'You're not a teacher!'

'For God's sake, Maggie! What are you saying? Of course, Miss Dow is a teacher. She's an important member of the community. Everyone in the south knows her.'

I remember thinking what a strange expression 'in the south' was. Later I came to understand that those who lived in the south half of the island felt themselves to be quite apart from those 'at the other end'. Tobermory at the north end might as well have been the North Pole to inhabitants of Bunessan and Fionnphort at the south end. Craignure where we were bound on *MV Lochinvar*, was border territory. In a few short weeks, father had absorbed this fundamental fact of life on Mull and taken on the parlance of a south-islander.

By now we were the only people left on dry land and a shout from a crewman on the vessel alerted us to the fact that the gangplank was about to be raised. We all five of us hastened to board, Father still remonstrating with Mother while she continued to look distracted, Gerry and I holding each other's hand, closing our eyes as we stepped on to the plank, clattering up it as fast as we could, holding our breath until our feet felt the wooden deck beneath them. Miss Dow had gone first, turning immediately at the crewman's shout and seeming to skate up the gangplank in a trice.

Father and Mother began to argue in low voices as we took our seats on the wooden benches provided on the deck for passengers. I was torn between trying to hear what they were saying and watching the preparations for casting off into the grey, swelling sea. Already, I was beginning to feel queasy and to fancy the cheese and pickle sandwiches of several hours ago were making an unwelcome comeback in my mouth.

'. . . know what I saw . . . definite resemblance . . . too much of a coincidence . . .' That was Mother, sounding frightened but determined.

'. . . bloody, stupid ideas . . . comes of reading these old books . . . listening to that half-wit next door . . . doesn't have enough to bother her . . . trying to make herself important . . .' That was Father, riding some of his favourite hobby-horses.

'. . . don't want the children having anything to do with that woman . . . do some lessons at home with them . . . old enough to leave school anyway . . .' Mother's voice had begun to tremble. She was pleading. I heard Father's response loud and clear to that. Everyone on the boat did.

'They'll go to school with Miss Dow. I've enrolled them. And that's an end to it. I won't hear another word about it. Not another bloody word.'

He had stood up and he leaned down, thrusting his face at Mother, one hand gripping her arm tightly, squeezing hard. I had seen those bruises before, always in the same place, always four round marks on her outer arm and one big smudge on the soft inner arm. I saw the other passengers look and look quickly away, averting their eyes. And I saw a quick smile, a feline smirk of a thing, chase over Miss Dow's face.

Father turned abruptly and strode up the deck to the rail at the back end. He ducked his head into his jacket and I saw the flare of his Lucifer lighter, the one he had brought home from the war. As MV *Lochinvar* began to pick up speed, the rolling motion became more pronounced and the bile in my throat would be quelled no longer. I rushed over to the side and, gripping the rail, I threw up several times. The wind whipped the vomit back and matted it in my hair. Mother was at my side at once, producing a bottle of water and a small towel from the magic bag and cleaning me up in her efficient, fuss-free way.

As she wiped the tears off my cheeks, she was looking over my shoulder and I saw her face harden. When she had completed my makeshift ablutions, I was free to turn and see what she had been looking at. Father was still standing at the back end of the boat, still smoking, but there were two cigarettes glowing now. There was no mistaking the gaunt, grey figure that stood beside him.


In a few minutes, we were summoned to descend to the dining saloon. I shuddered at the thought of food and pleaded with Mother to remain on deck. The thought of going down into the belly of this heaving, rolling monster terrified me. I imagined the waves sweeping over the rails and the water pouring down the narrow, steep stairway.

36

'I'm frightened,' I wailed, my teeth chattering. Gerry was tugging at Mother's coat, happily unconcerned about the danger of being trapped below deck and meeting a watery end. He was thinking about food, as usual, and was obviously not suffering from sea-sickness as I was.

'Now, Liza,' began Mother sternly, 'get a hold of yourself. There's nothing to be afraid of. If you don't feel like eating anything, you don't have to. Maybe better not, in fact. We don't want you throwing up in the dining saloon. Best let your stomach settle. But you *have* to come downstairs with us. A little drink of water will revive you. Come along!'

She held out her hand and I rose from my miserable huddle against the side of the boat. I knew better than to argue with her when she spoke in that tone and, besides, Father was now striding down the deck towards us.

'Time for high tea,' he declared. 'All included in the ticket price. This way.' He seized Gerry's hand and the two of them went to join the little queue that was forming at the top of the stairs. Mother put a consoling arm round my shaking shoulders and drew me gently across the deck.

I staggered, light-headed, convulsive shivers racking my body. I felt deathly cold. Other passengers overtook us and a few cast sympathetic glances. I must have presented a pathetic sight indeed. I had quite forgotten Miss Dow until I heard her flat, nasal voice behind us.

'Fresh air is the best thing for her, Mrs Galway. Take it from me. I have done this crossing with many sick children. I am not going below myself. She can stay up here with me while you and Mr Galway have your tea.'

The offer – it sounded more like an order, really - took both Mother and me by surprise. Mother half-heartedly protested that she couldn't possibly impose and she was sure I would be all right in no time.

'Nonsense! Off you go! Here comes your husband to fetch you.'

And Father took command, roughly lifting Mother's arm from my shoulders and steering her away toward the head of the stairs where Gerry was hopping impatiently from one foot to the other.

I was left alone with Miss Dow, not sure if this was any better a fate than drowning below deck. She stooped to link my arm and in this way she half marched, half dragged me over to a bench. I put up no resistance. I was too weak and shaky but, even if I had been my normal wiry self, I doubt if I would have tried. There was nothing in her action of the friendly support that usually accompanies the act of linking arms. It felt like the grip of a vice. Like, I imagine, what it must feel to be arrested by a determined policeman and marched off to the cells. I threw a despairing glance over my shoulder and caught Mother's eye as she, being likewise frogmarched by Father, did the same. We shared a brief moment of helplessness. I did not know it then but a chilling pattern was being set for the future.

'Fortunately, I was not planning to eat aboard today as I had a large lunch in Oban. I was visiting one of my aunts there and she always insists on feeding me ridiculous amounts of food. She gets so few visitors nowadays; she takes it as a rare opportunity to revive her culinary skills.' Miss Dow spoke as if addressing a public meeting. She was used to a classroom of children with no option but to listen. When I made no reply, she sat down on the bench and pulled me down beside her.

'This can be our opportunity to become better acquainted before you take your place in my school. Tell me about yourself, Liza. What do you like to do? What are you good at? What were you studying before you left your last school?'

My mind went blank but not in a confused, involuntary way. Rather this was a shutter that came rattling down, a shield behind which I consciously retreated. Every instinct told me to fend this woman off. I stared at her and she stared at me. Mutual antipathy reared up between us. I felt threatened. It was inexplicable but very real. And, strangely, I knew that she felt the same.

'Come along, child.' Her voice was sharp, almost squeaky, betraying her fear. I found the courage to stare her down.

'I said, come along.' She had herself in check now, the schoolteacher expecting obedience. But I was not her pupil - yet. I huddled into my coat collar and turned my shoulder away from her. If I had had the strength, I would have leapt up and run – or at least stood up and walked – away from her. Even the perilous below-stairs dining saloon would have been preferable. But I did not have that strength and I was trapped.

She made several other attempts to trick or bully me into response but I maintained my silence. My shield withstood the assault and, when Father, Mother and Gerry reappeared some forty minutes later, it was still intact.

'You look better, dear.' Mother hurried over to reclaim me and *The Dow* (as I began to think of her) rose and nodded haughtily.

'As I said, fresh air is the best medicine. And it gave me a chance to become acquainted with my new pupil, did it not, Liza?' Her eyes bored into me, daring me to challenge the lie.

'Good,' said Mother uneasily. I could tell she was as little enamoured of the woman as I was and I felt a rush of grateful relief to have her adult support. It gave me the strength to stand up and take the hand she stretched out to me and even to smile bleakly at her.

Father pulled Gerry over. 'More important, Joan,'- Mother looked startled at the Christian name – 'to get to know my *son*. I have high hopes for him. High hopes indeed.'

Gerry tried to look like a high hope and failed as both Father and The Dow looked down at him, Father with an interest and pride than I had never seen in him before, The Dow with a speculative gleam in her sharp eyes. My heart quailed for Gerry and my resolve never to darken the door of Erraid School faltered. My wee brother might be going to need my protection.

# CHAPTER FIVE

*The sound of (her) voice went through me like a jar.*

*Robert Louis Stevenson, from 'Kidnapped'*

After what seemed like hours to me, the island loomed through the soft, misty air, no more than a blurred black hump at first, like a sleeping animal, but getting bigger and gradually resolving into the contours of rugged, mountainous land. We saw a ruined castle on a promontory jutting out into the sea. It was nothing like as grand as Edinburgh Castle which I had first seen when Mother and I had gone up to the city on the train for an afternoon.

'That's Duart Castle.' Father, in didactic mode again, broke into my reverie. I noticed he made sure Miss Dow heard what he was saying. 'Belongs to the Clan MacLean. It's a bit of a ruin and was empty for many years but the present Chief of the Clan bought it in 1911 and he's set on restoring it.'

'Why did he have to buy it?' Mother asked. 'If it belonged to the clan already, I mean?'

It was The Dow who answered and her voice was harsh, strangely bitter. 'I'm afraid the MacLeans of Duart backed the losing side against William of Orange. They fought and lost at the Battle of Inverkeithing in 1651 and later in the Jacobite uprising of 1689. Their estates were confiscated in 1691. Before that, they had owned the castle for over three hundred years.'

I looked up at her sharp profile. 'Three hundred years,' she repeated and there was a kind of anger now. I saw the muscles in her jaw twitch and, sensing my glance, she turned slightly in my direction. But it was not at me that she looked. Her eyes travelled instead to Gerry who was staring in fascination at the castle. I saw her gaze sharpen and once again take on a speculative look. Predatory, even, I fancied.

I felt a tremor go through my body which, though still cold, had stopped shaking. The word, 'Jacobite', reverberated in my body. I had heard it before, of course, and I had my recent reading of *Kidnapped* to flesh out the dry bones of history classes at school. It had assumed an aura of romantic, doomed adventure. But what I felt now was quite different, immediate and personal, underpinned with a drumbeat of dread.

Her eyes, steel grey, expressionless now, swept over me and then she turned away and moved to the prow of the boat to join the other passengers who were gathering to watch the Craignure pier coming into view.

'Time to land soon. Make sure you have all our belongings,' said Father. 'Look, son, here comes the boat to get us.' He took Gerry's hand and pulled him towards the prow. I had never seen him so forthcoming with Gerry, indeed to either of us, and neither had Mother. She looked torn between pleasure and bewilderment at this turn of events.

We all watched the boat that was being rowed out to meet us. It looked very small beside *MV Lochinvar*, very low in the water compared to the sides of the big boat.

'How in the name o' God do we get ourselves down into that?' wondered Mother and I echoed her apprehension, visualising a flying leap or swinging rope.

But, in the event, the descent was accomplished with remarkable speed. Everyone else on *The Lochinvar* was obviously well-used to the manoeuvre and calmly clambered backwards down the metal ladder that was slung out from the ship to land onto the boat. Strong male arms assisted at both ends of the ladder and there was cheery, familiar banter, scraps of news exchanged, even a couple of social dates arranged. The Dow went ahead of us, seeming to glide down the ladder in the same way she had gone up the gangplank in Oban. She ignored the male arms held out to help.

Gerry was so keen to show off his bravery that he almost jumped on to the ladder and caused it to swing out and clatter against the side of the ship with a loud clang. Four strong seamen's arms steadied him and the ladder as he was admonished: Tak' yer time, wee fella. Ye'll end up in the waves if ye go on like that.'

Looking down into the small boat, I saw The Dow watching anxiously until, not a whit chastened, he clambered down like a monkey and leapt off the second last rung into the boat, causing it to sway and earning him another rebuke from the crewmen.

'Thinks he's a seasoned seaman already,' said Father, sounding pleased. He even waved down to Gerry who waved back grinning. I did not like this conspiracy that seemed to be getting up between Father and Gerry. It did not include me. Gerry and I had always stood together against Father but something had happened on this short voyage to change that. Something that involved The Dow, I felt sure.

I was so preoccupied with these thoughts that I forgot my fears and had made my own descent before I knew it. All the passengers waited

41

and watched a sailor hurling sacks of mail and a few larger parcels down into the boat. You had to hope there was nothing fragile in either sack or parcel. And then – startling sight! – a sack swung out from the side of the ferry on a grappling hook, a sheep's head poking out of the taut hessian. The head looked enormous, great curling horns, black, slobbery mouth open and drooling, yellow eyes rolling. I heard a man say with cheerful satisfaction: 'He's a fine big lad. He'll do the business!' Several other men laughed and few of the women tutted and made shocked faces. I had no idea what they were talking about.

With all the passengers and cargo transferred, we were ready to go. The crewmen fell to their task and soon the oars were slicing through the waves. It took but minutes to cross the bay and reach the pier.

Dry land again! I felt ready to weep with relief.


As we neared the Craignure jetty, the behaviour of our fellow travellers underwent a change: their subdued, rather dour manner faded as a buzz of chatter escalated; smiles became broad, laughs became loud, arms were linked, backs were slapped and snatches of singing broke out. It was as if they had survived some kind of ordeal or danger or as if they had been away for years and this was some kind of miraculous, long-awaited return. Tuning into some of the talking and singing, I realised it was no longer in English. As their island home drew nearer, their natural language had reasserted itself. I did not speak it then but I recognised it: Gaelic – the ancient language of the Celtic people, which I knew was discouraged and never used in formal places and situations. Like schools, for example.

I glanced up at The Dow, expecting her to disapprove but, to my surprise, she was smiling and nodding amiably to several other people. That smile transformed her face, softening its severity. Yet it was not the smile of shared pleasure and comfortable belonging such as I saw on the other faces around me. Joan Dow smiled as a queen to her subjects, indulgent and condescending.

A woman called out something across the boat to her and she replied. The woman laughed and The Dow looked at the girl who sat at the woman's side, a sturdy, square-faced girl about ten or eleven who pushed her head down into her scarf and shuffled her feet, clearly embarrassed at being the object of their attention. I surmised that she was one of The Dow's pupils and mother and teacher had shared a joking reference to something school-related. I felt sympathy for the girl. It is more hateful than adults ever realise to be used as material for their complicit banter, to have to listen to it and even to be eyed up during it, but to have no right of reply. I always hated it myself and especially between teachers and parents, those twin pillars of power in a child's life. I tried to catch the girl's eye in hope of signalling support and solidarity but she went on staring intently at her shuffling feet as if willing them to carry her away from her humiliation.

The singing, which had been patchy and uncoordinated, grew in volume and unity as the jetty came close. I recognised the melody if not the words. By the time the boat was nudging the fender of huge rubber tyres that hung around the jetty, it sounded like a conducted choir, as good as anything I had ever heard in church or at a school concert. I watched the sacks of mail and parcels once again being thrown, this time on to the flagstones of the jetty. Mother went first, Father behind her, holding Gerry's hand. I was left to fend for myself. A gaggle of people awaited MV Lochinvar's arrival. As the twenty or so passengers began to disembark, handed over the gap from boat to shore by a stalwart crewman, I became distracted, watching for another sighting of the airborne ram.

'Well, lassie, are ye fur comin' off or are ye wantin' a job wi' us?' The crewman was holding out his hand, smiling but impatient. I felt the slight push of the remaining passengers behind me and reached for the big, calloused hand. As soon as my feet touched solid ground, Father's hand was on my shoulder, but not a kind, paternal hand such as Gerry was holding. This hand was heavy and threatening, broad fingers stabbing into my bones, bruising my flesh.

'Pay attention, Miss. We've enough to be doin' getting ourselves off the boat and on to the bus without lookin' after a great muckle lassie like you. Ye've been a big enough nuisance already.'

He punctuated his words with painful, pinching squeezes. I tried to wriggle out of his grasp but only made my plight worse as his grip tightened. He shook me free at last and I slunk over to Mother's side, tears spilling down my reddened face, tears of humiliation as much as of pain. All the other passengers had witnessed my shame but worst of all, The Dow had been standing at Father's side. And now her smile was a satisfied smirk. I saw her take Gerry's other hand.

Thus it was we first set foot on the island of Mull, already split into two factions: Mother and I; Father, Gerry and The Dow.


My first impressions of the island were not good. Even if I had not been still weak from sea-sickness and miserable from Father's rebuke, I

43

doubt if that first sighting would have lifted my spirits. Craignure, which I had been imagining something like North Berwick, with shops and traffic, a street of smart houses along the front, people bustling about their business, was nothing but a few houses spread along the foot of a precipitous hill that rose almost straight out of the sea. Shading my eyes against a burst of late afternoon sun, I could see no one on the short strip of road that ran in front of the houses. What life there was seemed entirely concentrated on the arrival of *MV Lochinvar*. About a dozen people had congregated at the street end of the jetty and as each person from the boat stepped on to the island, he or she was greeted with a handshake and a Gaelic greeting. Each greeting called forth a reply that was clearly part of some ritual. I looked doubtfully up at Mother and saw my dismay reflected on her face. We might have been castaways washed up on the shores of some far-off, undiscovered continent, so far from home did we feel.

Father and The Dow, by contrast, walked briskly towards the welcoming party, Gerry almost running between them to keep up. The Dow went first, dealing rapidly with half-a-dozen handshakes, tossing the Gaelic greetings back in sharp staccato that made it sound like a different language from the one the islanders were speaking. Then she gestured to Gerry and spoke in English:

'This is Mr Galway's son. *Gerrard.*' She brought the full form of his name out with a triumphant flourish. From that day to this, I never heard her call him anything but that. 'He is *nine* years old.' She made it sound as if this fact was of considerable significance and, indeed, I saw a couple of the women there nod gravely and exchange knowing glances.

Gerry tried to look important but only succeeded in looking what he was – a confused, tired little boy who did not know where he was or what was expected of him. And he was missing his mother and sister, who, although standing only a few paces behind him, might as well have been miles away.

It was then Father's turn to pass along the welcoming line-up. I watched in amazement as a jovial fellow exchanged hearty handshakes and answered the Gaelic greetings. He clearly was not yet word-perfect for his attempts called forth giggles from the women and guffaws from the men. This was not a man I had ever met; this was not the father I knew. Mother, however, simply shook her head and met my startled look with one of rueful resignation.

'My wife and daughter,' Father was declaring, waving his hand grandly at us. The welcomers beamed with open curiosity at us. Mother did us proud by graciously nodding to each of them, accepting their handshakes and replying a firm, English 'thank you' to each Gaelic greeting. I am afraid I let the side down and incurred further displeasure from Father by refusing to move forward and staring miserably at my cold feet, which were standing in a seawater puddle. He might have turned back to fetch me and woe betide what might have befallen me then. He was not above giving me a thrashing there and then in front of them all. But Mother, ever alert to our safety when he was around, was at my side in a trice, bending down to link arms and pull me quickly past the line-up. I heard her say 'Sea-sick, poor lassie. First time in a boat' and the sympathetic murmurs of the kindly islanders.

The ferry-bus was waiting. It was nothing like the buses I had seen in Edinburgh. It was small, painted a dirty cream with fat red mudguards which had not prevented its sides and windows being liberally splashed with blotches and streaks of dark brown mud. It was already chugging out a column of odorous, black smoke from its rear end as if it might take off any moment without the passengers it had come to meet. The red mudguards shuddered and rattled. I looked up, curious to see the driver who was gunning the protesting engine. I expected some ancient worthy to match the filthy, rickety vehicle. Not so. As he sprang down, leaving the engine still labouring noisily on, I saw a tall, upright fellow of about thirty-five years, wearing only a white shirt and flapping tie above his coarse tweed trousers. He seemed impervious to the snell sea-breeze as he bent to his task of stowing his passengers' bags into the hold at the side of the bus. I liked this man at once. There was about him an air of confidence and kindly good humour. He made me feel safe and that was no bad thing as I prepared to face the next and, I prayed, last leg of that endless journey.

The only other passengers were the woman and her daughter from the boat. The five of us – The Dow already seemed an inevitable part of our family group – were seated in the bus waiting for several minutes before they began to saunter up from the welcome group where the mother had been blethering and the daughter had been engaged in some kind of solitary game that involved a lot of hopping up and down the flagstones of the jetty. The driver seemed in no hurry, lounging against the side of the bus, sucking at an unlit pipe. As the knot of people began at last to break up, several gave him a greeting and a handshake as they passed. Gaelic again, but I did make out the word *Lachlan* several times and guessed that must be his name.

When the woman and girl left the diminishing group and began to make their way to the trap, he shook the dottle out and thrust the pipe into his sporran.

45

'Catriona!' he shouted and ran towards them with his arms open wide. The girl at once picked up speed and the two met in a crushing embrace, he lifting her clean off the ground and swinging her round in dizzying circles before setting her down, still keeping hold of her hands as she tottered worse than men coming out of the pub on payday. The woman said something - it looked like a playful mock rebuke – and he held out an arm to draw her into a charmed circle that tugged at my heart in a way I barely understood. I heard Father say something I did not understand in a sarcastic tone to The Dow and saw her lift her eyebrows and give a thin smile in response. Mother was leaning forward, attempting to talk to Gerry who sat wedged and unresponsive between Father and The Dow, so she saw nothing.

The threesome reached the bus with more banter and laughter. At last, just as Father was about to lose patience and contravene what I would learn were two island rules – that there was never any hurry and that blethering with other islanders always took precedence over any other activity – mother and daughter climbed into the bus and settled themselves on either side of the two facing benches that constituted the passenger seating, the mother beside me and the girl, Catriona, squeezing in beside The Dow. Lachlan stamped on the pedals and eased the long gear stick forward. With a squeal of the tyres on stone and several farts of black smoke, we were off.

And that was how I first met the MacPhails of Tormore who were to play such an important part in my tale.

# CHAPTER SIX

*With my stepping ashore I began the most unhappy part of my adventures.*
                                    Robert Louis Stevenson, from 'Kidnapped'

I had looked at a map of Mull, at Craignure and Erraid and the distance between them. Compared to the rest of our journey, I had thought it no more than a short hop. But I had not factored in the difference between speeding on a train or even sailing on *MV Lochinvar* to bumping along narrow, winding roads in the boneshaker ferry-bus, stopping periodically to open and shut huge, rusty gates which marked farm boundaries. As soon as we cleared the last straggling houses of Craignure, the road deteriorated into little more than a track in places, often with a column of sprouting grass and weeds up the middle. It was so narrow that meeting anything coming in the opposite direction was an event that took quite some time and a lot of shouting and hand-waving to accomplish. Once, Lachlan had to get down from the bus and tramp away round the bend to tell the pony-and-trap waiting there to come past as the 'passing place' on his side was a great deal wider.

The bus swayed and bumped but the pace was so slow that it created a soporific rhythm. Gerry was soon asleep, tired out by new experiences, sea air and a hefty high tea. He lolled against The Dow, somehow finding a place to pillow his head on her angular frame. She did not yield to create comfort for him but nor did she recoil. She simply looked over his head and smiled that strange, smug smile at Father.

'Here. Let me take him. He'll be heavy, leaning on you like that.' Mother attempted to assert maternal rights. She leaned across with the intention of pulling Gerry on to her knee and cradling him as she was wont to do when he ran crying into her arms after a painful scrape or frightening dream. Unfortunately, the bus lurched to an abrupt halt as Lachlan sighted an oncoming cart, slammed on the brakes and swerved into the passing place. Mother was catapulted into The Dow's lap and had to right herself with embarrassed apologies. 'I'm right sorry, Miss Dow. I hope I didn't hurt you.' Her hair was coming undone under her hat and her face was flushed.

The Dow, in contrast, looked prim and cool. 'Please don't concern yourself, Mrs Galway. The boy is fine where he is and it would be wrong to disturb him.' Gerry had bounced a little and muttered under Mother's onslaught but he subsided easily, drooping a heavy head deeper into the crook of The Dow's arm.

'For God's sake, Maggie, settle down and stop fussing. Ye've no need to be carrying on like that. The lad's fine where he is.' Father weighed in with his special brand of scathing disgust and Mother gave up. I slipped my hand into hers, thinking to comfort her, to assure her of *my* loyalty in the face of Gerry's treachery, and was rewarded with a squeeze. The bus resumed its slow, uneven pace.

It was now almost half past five and the light was beginning to fade. I saw bleak, scrubby moorland on all sides with no sign of life other than the occasional buzzard hovering overhead. Once, a huge bird swooped out of the sky and plunged into the bracken. There was a chilling squeal rising to a terrified shriek, immediately and completely cut off. The bird rose with the hapless small creature dangling from its talons. Lachlan braked a little and pointed. 'There he goes. Now, is that no' a grand sight for yer family on their first night? The golden eagle, our island's largest bird. A magnificent sight, d'ye no' think?' He turned round as he spoke to catch Father's eye and the bus lurched alarmingly.

'Bunessan would be a better one, Mr MacPhail. Just attend to your driving and get us along the road,' said The Dow sounding every inch the schoolteacher and I hoped he might tell her where she got off, speaking to a grown man like that. To my surprise and despair, he only nodded and mumbled 'Aye, ye're right there, Miss Dow. But Pennyghael's only a wee mile along so we're near half-way to Fionnphort.'

Mother and I had studied a map of Mull, lent to me by Mr Chambers, my old teacher, but the place names, spoken now with full Gaelic intonation, did not sound at all like what we had read them to be.

I whispered to Mother that I was hungry. Indeed I was ravenous. Now that sea-sickness was a distant memory, my healthy appetite had returned. I had thrown up most of my lunch overboard and my stomach was growling.

'Is there an inn or a shop at the next village? Can't we stop and buy Liza something to eat? The lassie'll be getting' faint if she doesn't eat something soon.' She addressed Father but it was Catriona's mother who answered, speaking for the first time.

'There's no inn, it's only a tiny village, but there's a post office shop. It will be closed now for the night but I daresay Mrs Cameron, who runs it, will open up and sell you something when she sees the situation.'

She smiled kindly at me as she spoke and my spirits lifted.

'Thank you, Mrs . . . ?' said Mother. 'That's good of you.'

'Marion,' said our benefactor. Marion MacPhail. Lachlan . . .' she nodded to the driver's back, '. . . is my man and this is Catriona, our girl. She's ten, near eleven.'

'And my Liza is twelve,' said Mother, as if that clinched some kind of deal as perhaps it did for the two mothers fell to blethering about the cost of kitting out growing girls and other such topics. Catriona and I eyed each other shyly and said nothing. But she smiled and wrinkled her nose from time to time in a way that made me copy her involuntarily. She had a springy thatch of red-gold hair which seemed to grow in all directions but its colour was the only feature that linked her to her mother. Marion MacPhail was a beautiful woman, with exquisite features, creamy, lightly-freckled skin, full lips, high cheekbones and startling turquoise-blue eyes. Her daughter was plainer with heavy brown freckles spattering a broad nose and fat, pouchy cheeks. Later, I would notice her slate grey eyes and come to see a certain steadfast beauty in them but that day I took no notice of such fine details. I was too busy wishing the 'wee mile along' to be covered as quickly as possible so that I could appease my hunger.


It never occurred to either Mother or me that there would be more sailing before we reached our destination. Father had sent a postcard telling Mother only to get the three of us to Oban where he would meet us and we would all board the ship for Mull. Imagine my horror when we stumbled out of the bus at the hamlet of Fionnphort and were led by Father down to the sea and a small boat which was tied to a large black bollard by a thick rope.

At Pennyghael, the good Mrs Cameron, a stout lady enveloped in a brightly flowered, wraparound apron, had not bothered with opening up the shop. She had simply appraised the situation in a glance and invited Mother and me to come into her cottage which was attached to the little shop. There were obviously only two rooms, the one we stepped straight into, combining all the functions of kitchen, living and dining rooms and bedroom. What was left for the back room to do, I could not guess. Later, I would discover she took in paying guests, hikers and cyclists during the brief summer season. She made me a large sandwich with ham and cheese and gave me an apple and a little bar of Cadbury's chocolate. Mother's offer of money was waved away with a gust of laughter as if she had simply cracked a good joke. We found ourselves being shooed out of the cottage and on to the bus before we had time even to thank Mrs C properly. It was our first taste of Highland hospitality.

Gerry spied the chocolate bar at once and began whining that he wanted one. Before either Mother or Father could silence him, The Dow had opened her large black handbag and taken out a bar which was larger than the one Mrs C had given me. He smirked as he tore off the wrapper and it seemed to me that The Dow smirked too. I was too immersed then in consuming the food to care but later I would remember that smirk and add it to the pile of resentments and suspicions that I was amassing around this strange woman.

We had at last reached journey's end - at least for the bus which ran its daily service between Craignure and Fionnphort for locals living in between or tourists heading to the sacred isle of Iona which lay one mile across the Sound by way of a small motor launch. But now we learned that the only way to get to Erraid and our new home was by sea. The bobbing little motorboat belonged to the National Lighthouse Board and was provided for the six lighthouse families to make the trip round the coast of Mull to Fionnphort when necessary. A burly man sat in the stern beside the outboard motor. He wore a nautical jersey with the NLB crest and motto on a pocket over his heart. One of Father's fellow lighthouse keepers, clearly. He waved to Father and Lachlan as they unloaded our bags from the bus and stood up to take them into the boat.

'But what about the causeway?' said Mother. 'On the map . . .'

Father was already in conversation with the man in the boat but making no move to introduce him to Mother. It was The Dow who answered, cutting across Mother in her frosty voice. 'There is no vehicular access to Erraid, Mrs Galway. Indeed, there is only the roughest of pedestrian access. A mere track across moorland and sand. The causeway can be crossed on foot when the tide is out but you will often get your feet wet.'

'I see . . .' Mother was dismayed and I knew she was thinking about being trapped and unable to flee from Father when he was in his worst rages. In North Berwick, she had been able to lose him in its winding streets and find sanctuary in a shop or the library by day, or a tenement close at night. I had been about to voice my fears that Mrs Cameron's lovely sandwich might end up in the choppy waters but this new fear, so plainly written on Mother's face, superseded seasickness qualms. I shared her horror at being trapped on the tiny islet with no way of getting off it except by hiking over moors and beaches or alerting the whole community by requesting the boat. As we were handed down into the boat by Lachlan and Father, I remembered reading in a history book at school about the French penal colony on Devil's Island and I pictured Mother and me as prisoners on our way to serve our sentence there. This fanciful notion served at least to distract me from my heaving stomach and I managed to hold on to Mrs Cameron's good food after all.

I envied the MacPhails who did not have to go on to Erraid. They lived on their croft at Tormore, a mile or so north from Fionnphort, near an old quarry which had closed down some eight years ago, lacking men to work it during the war and, sadly, after it too. Lachlan shared ferry-bus driving duties with another man who lived up 'at the other end' and they farmed their croft well with bees for honey, a goat for milk, plenty of freshly picked vegetables and all the fish that Lachlan could catch. All this I had learned from listening to Mother and Mrs MacPhail on the bus journey. From Catriona herself, in a brief, shy exchange towards the end of the road, I learned something more important: although she should have gone to the school which served the Fionnphort and Bunessan catchment area, she came instead to the school on Erraid. Lachlan did not like the Fionnphort schoolmaster – something to do with 'politics', she thought – and had once almost come to blows with him.

'It was outside the kirk on a Sunday morning, too.' Catriona giggled. 'Ma was mortified. She dragged him away just in time.'

After that, Catriona, then aged eight, had been taken away from that school and sent to the one on Erraid, which had been set up for the children of the lighthouse keepers. It had been low on pupils that year and glad to have her.

I did not know what 'politics' meant but I was pleased that there would be a 'kent face' at school and it did not occur to me to ask how she got there each morning as I did not then understand the difficulties of getting on and off the islet. Now, as our boat rounded the southern tip of Mull and chugged towards a small stone pier, I realised that she must be brought by sea. Lachlan must surely have his own boat. There was something comforting about this, a sense that we would not be quite so cut off. Catriona would be our daily link with the outside world. I could not have known then just how important this link would turn out to be.

The sun was setting behind us as we scrambled out of the boat and set foot at last on the islet. I had been looking forward to this moment for weeks, ever since reading *Kidnapped*, and now, travel-weary and sea-sick as I was, it was still a magical moment. The west-setting sun was painting a warm amber glow over a heathery slope which led up to a small ruin. Large chunks of grey stone lay around it, transformed into things of beauty by the amazing light. There was an exhilarating scent on the breeze – bog myrtle, I would discover in time – and I could see tiny splashes of pink, red, violet and blue peeping out between nooks and crannies everywhere, even between the concrete edges of the pier. I raised my eyes to the block of grey-granite, single-storey houses further up the hill and saw the pink-orange wash of sunset sliding down the pitched roofs to reveal black slates and soft billows of pale grey smoke puffing out of the six chimneys. Suddenly, unexpectedly, I felt at home. More than that, I felt that I had *come* home. As if I had lived here sometime in the past, been exiled and homesick - and had at last come back. My feelings of dread and my fancies about penal colonies melted away as I succumbed to the islet's charm.

'Good, they've seen to the fire. I did ask them to but I'm never sure how much they listen.' It was The Dow again, with her forceful, fault-finding voice. I wondered if she ever said anything good about anyone or anything encouraging. It did not bode well for her manner in the classroom. 'Ah! Here comes the reception committee.'

I had been bending down to fasten a loose buckle on one of our bags but something in her sarcastic tone made me look quickly up. Running down the hill was a gaggle of women and children. I counted more than a dozen children old enough to attend school plus a clutch of toddlers and several babies in their mothers' arms. There was even one woman with the curved-back, large-belly look that I knew meant a new baby coming soon. How the baby got in there or out I had not yet discovered but I had observed the sequence of events quite a few times in my friends' mothers. I had been too young to notice or remember when Mother had been carrying Gerry but I sometimes imagined what she must have looked like. It always made me feel tender and protective towards them both and now, seeing the pregnant woman in this back-of-beyond spot so far from civilisation as I had only ever known it, I felt a rush of concern bordering on dread. The evening light seemed no longer warm and beautiful but unreal and threatening, a lure to the unwary, false reassurance in a place of doom. I shivered.

Around me, however, flowed a tide of good cheer and chatter. The women, all five of them, surrounded us, bidding us welcome, asking how our journey had been, where we had come from, what our names were and a swirl of other, friendly queries. Older children ran round the perimeter, chasing and calling out to each other, while toddlers strained at the end of their mothers' arms, tugging at the hands that held them. A baby I had not noticed because it was tied to the mother's back by a big, paisley-pattern shawl, woke up and began to bawl. Immediately, two

52

others joined in. It was bedlam, but jolly, friendly bedlam and, after the cold company of The Dow for the past six hours, Mother relaxed and expanded into smiles and willing replies.

But where *was* The Dow? Father and the other keeper were tying up the boat and getting ready to shoulder the bags, Gerry was now being firmly held by Mother's hand and tugging away from it just like the toddlers. I looked around but could see her nowhere. She had melted into the landscape, it seemed, and no one was interested or caring, not even Father who clearly admired her or Gerry who had lapped up her attention on the journey.

We were borne up the hill towards our new home on the chattering tide. By the time we reached it, the third house from the right in a row of seven, Father and the boat man had dumped our bags at the door and gone off somewhere. Mother looked vaguely round for him and began to ask where he was.

'Och, the men'll be away having a dram together,' said one of the women. 'My Euan's shore this month as well – that's him was on the boat – and Jenny's Calum will be with them. Up at the lookout or the ruined cottage no doubt. Keeping out of the way till all the work's done, as usual.'

She laughed and held out her hand. It was large and red and I noticed that the nails were bitten to the quick. 'I'm Etta – Henrietta, really, would you believe?' She laughed again. 'Posh sort of name for the likes of me. My mam was in service and got fancy notions when she was expecting, so I was told.'

Mother grinned. It was the first smile I had seen on her face for weeks. 'I'm Maggie. My parents weren't so original.'

'Come on. Let's get you settled. We put the fire on a couple of hours ago so it should be cosy.' Etta flung open the door. 'Welcome to Erraid!'

# CHAPTER SEVEN

*If these are the wild Highlanders, I could wish my own folk wilder.*

*Robert Louis Stevenson, from 'Kidnapped'*

My first impressions of our new home were favourable. It was spacious and well furnished, even to the shining brass pots and pans which twinkled as the oil lamps above the fireplace were lit by one of the women.

For sure, it seemed smaller than our North Berwick house but, in fact, it had the same number of rooms: two bedrooms, a sitting room and a kitchen/living room with the standard bed recess where the man and wife of the family slept. Perhaps it seemed smaller because it was all on one level whereas, in North Berwick, Gerry and I had slept upstairs. I did not like the thought of Father being so close at night but hoped that it might at least mean he would not vent so much of his bad temper on Mother. Surely the thought of his children only a few yards away would restrain him? And then, there were all the other lighthouse families so close by and known to each other, men he had to work alongside, and their wives, in this tiny community of six families. Not to mention The Dow. The seventh house at the far end of the row was the schoolhouse and she lived a short distance away in a detached cottage. Any noise of shouting and swearing from him, any cries of pain and fear from Mother, would be heard – or heard of - by everyone. I allowed myself a little cautious optimism.

In North Berwick, Mother had kept herself to herself as far as possible, only the determined Mrs Forsyth making any inroads into the terrain of neighbourliness, if not actual friendship. She had held her head high and refused to meet the pitying eyes of the other women in our street or at church, firmly rebuffing any attempts to befriend her. As a young child, I had simply thought that was her way, that she was uninterested in having friends or joining any of the groups and societies that other women enjoyed. By now, I had begun to realise that she was deeply ashamed of her abusive marriage and could only cope with it by maintaining a dignified isolation.

But here she would have no hope of such a strategy. Before our first hour on the island was up, we had met all five of the other wives – Etta, Jenny, Bridie, Kitty and Mhairi. To me, in my tired, over-excited state

54

that first night, they seemed all of a pack, interchangeable, like a gaggle of geese and just as noisy. As time went on, this impression barely changed. I thought of them as 'the wives'. Never as 'the mothers', oddly enough.

They crowded into our kitchen without invitation and took turns in telling mother about the life of a lighthouse family on Erraid, all the while making themselves at home, taking the big copper kettle out to the covered spring that ran along the back of the houses, setting it on the range to boil and proudly displaying a basket of provisions to which they had all donated some essential. Mother made a small show of protesting – one of our bags did in fact contain all the things in their basket and more - but was stoutly informed that this was a lighthouse tradition: that new families were always welcomed to a lighthouse community in this way.

While the women settled down around our table to enjoy what Mhairi, the only true Highlander and Gaelic-speaker among them, called *a strupak*, the children raced through the other three rooms and all over our garden, talking nineteen to the dozen about life on Erraid as Gerry and I could expect to find it. We were showered with promises of playing on beaches, fishing in rock-pools, hiding in caves and gathering wild flowers and by warnings about getting sucked into bogs, missing the tide and being stranded on the wrong side of the causeway or having to wade across and arrive home soaked and shivering. We tried to tell them that we were used to beaches and rock-pools, to keep our end up as it were, but they were not interested. This was a well-worn track for lighthouse children, one that they coursed for every new family who came to wherever they happened to be. It was the child's version of the welcome basket and the gossipy tea-party that was going on in the kitchen for mother.

In time, I came to understand that lighthouse families moved around so often – every three years on average – that these customs had evolved as a way of making them feel as close to long-stay residents as they were ever likely to become. The arrival of each new family meant the previous new family moved up the ladder and could now join in the welcoming ritual and the false feeling of permanence it gave.

Of Father, there was no sign, nor of the other two men who were 'shore' that month. It was their last free weekend as all three of them would be heading out to 'the rock' on Monday morning to begin another four week stint. Mother learned this from the wives since father had not thought to tell her anything about the job or the way of life - he had been too busy trying to impress The Dow - and I saw the lightness of relief in her face as soon as I came back into the kitchen.

'Have they all gone, Mother?' I looked around warily, half-expecting a wife or a child to be hiding in a corner.

'Aye, I think so, Liza. Come and help me to put away this food and then we'll get the beds made up,' said Mother. She smiled sympathetically as I sighed.

'I ken it's been an awful long day and you've no been well for some of the time but the sooner we get organised, the sooner we can all get some rest. Where's Gerry?'

'I think he went to the lavvie.' I replied without thinking, using the word the other children had used when they had shown us the wooden hut in the far corner of the front garden.

'Liza Galway! Since when did we call the toilet by that coarse name? Just because we have moved to the middle of nowhere is no reason for you to start talking like a guttersnipe.'

'That's what *they* all called it,' I defended myself.

'And, if *they* all threw themselves into the sea, would you do that as well?'

I was saved from answering this difficult question by Gerry bursting into the room screaming. He was clutching his grey flannel short trousers which were open round the waist and his white shirt flapped down to his knees.

'There's a monster in the lavvie,' he screamed and rushed at Mother, burying his face in her skirt. It took us several minutes to get a coherent story from him. Just before the last neighbouring child had gone, Gerry had said he needed the toilet and been shown the hut which was by now in almost total darkness in its shady corner. He had been about to come in and ask for a lamp or a candle when the other child, a boy called Malcolm, a year younger than Gerry, had called him 'a feartie' and dared him to go without a light. Everyone here went to 'the lavvie' in the dark, he boasted, even if it was in the middle of the night. Lamps were for sissies. So Gerry had screwed up his courage and settled himself on the wooden seat in the damp, dark hut, all the while talking to and being answered by Malcolm, which was reassuring. Then, Malcolm had stopped replying and the silence had grown until Gerry became frightened. He was just concluding his business when something came hurtling through

56

the tiny window, thrusting open the wire mesh casement and landing on Gerry's bare bottom as he bent down to pull up his trousers. As he screamed and jerked round to throw it off, the creature emitted a piercing yowl, leapt up and struck out, leaving a long trail of blood on Gerry's thigh. He had wrenched open the door and fled in the state of undress we now saw.

It did not take a genius to work out that Gerry had been tricked. His 'monster' had undoubtedly been a cat – the scratch on his thigh, once the blood was cleaned off it, bore testimony to that – thrown in through the window, possibly by Malcolm, possibly by another child in league with him.

'The poor cat. It must have been terrified,' I said.

'So was I,' said Gerry, glaring at me.

He turned to Mother. 'Are you going to tell Malcolm's father? He should get belted for this.' His hysterics had shrunk to snivels and hiccups as the need for vengeance replaced terror.

Whether Mother would have agreed to this course of action or not we never found out because at that moment Father strode in. He was laughing as if at a recent joke and, when he saw Gerry still clinging to Mother, he laughed all the more.

'A monster in the lavvie! A monster!' he roared. 'You've given us all a good laugh the night, my lad. That'll go down in the ship's log. They'll be telling that one for a few years.'

Still chuckling – a most unusual sound from him – he went over to a drawer and took out a packet of Woodbine cigarettes then reached down into the bottom of the kitchen dresser to retrieve a half bottle of whisky.

'The lads and me are making the most of our last Saturday night before we go out to the rock on Monday. There's no drink allowed out there so we're stocking up.'

He paused at the door and glanced round proudly. 'It's a fine house, is it no', Maggie. I've done well for you and the bairns.'

He looked at me. 'Mind you give your mother a good hand to get settled in.'

'Yes, Father.'

'And you, Gerry . . . Mind you watch out for monsters. Especially when your arse is bare.'

His laughter could still be heard as he tramped away along the path that ran between the row of houses and the front gardens.

57

I think Gerry was too young or too upset to realise exactly what Father had said but Mother and I knew. Gerry had been set up and cruelly ridiculed, not just by one mischievous boy, but by a whole gang that had included three grown men, one of whom was his own father.

I wondered what The Dow had heard and what she would think of Father now.


The next morning, making my way back into the house from the lavvie (I would try to remember to say 'toilet' when Mother was listening but I knew better than to set myself apart in this way when with the other children), I heard a rhythmic *tramp, tramp* of feet coming along the path between houses and front gardens. I ran into the house to watch from the kitchen window and was astonished to see all last night's rag-tag-and-bobtail gang of children marching sedately along the front path in pairs. They were all soberly dressed: the boys in white shirts and black short trousers, grey socks well pulled up to knees, black shoes shining and grey caps firmly rammed on heads; the girls in pale blue or pink striped dresses, knitted cardigans in dark blue or red, white ankle socks and black T-bar shoes. In their hair, ribbons of various colours, tied into large bows.

At the front of the line, two of the wives, smart in matching skirts and jackets with felt hats, led the way. The other three wives, equally smart in dresses, jackets and hats, brought up the rear. They were all singing a slow, solemn song but not one I recognised. Some of the children looked up towards our window and I waved to them but none of them returned the wave or gave any sign of having seen me.

'What's going on?' It was Mother, coming sleepily into the kitchen, her hair spilling down her back, a crocheted shawl half covering her long white nightdress. She joined me at the window, stared out for a moment and then exclaimed:

'O Mother of God! I forgot all about this. They told me something about it last night but there were so many of them all talking at once and I was that tired . . .'

'What is it, Mother? Are they all going somewhere? It looks like a funeral procession!'

I had seen a few of those going through North Berwick, although not with anyone singing.

'It's the Sabbath. We're in the Highlands now and we've to do what Highlanders do on the Sabbath. It seems the Lighthouse Board are keen on us joining in with local customs and they like everyone to go to church on Sundays. Ach, I wish Robert had told me. I'd have set the alarm clock but we were all that tired last night and I just thought . . . I mean, I haven't seen a Catholic church anywhere here . . .'

'For God's sake, woman! Hold yer tongue about Catholic churches. Do you want to get us all lynched?' It was Father, striding into the room and pushing his way between us to see out of the window. The back end of the sedate crocodile was now making its way up the hill and out of our sight. He whirled round and pushed first Mother and then me towards the door.

'Get yourselves dressed – properly, mind – as fast as you can. And get Gerry up and into his Sunday best. We need to be up to the big bothy before the minister arrives.' He rushed back to the window and leaned into the glass to peer down at the pier. 'I can't see the boat. Euan or Calum must be away to fetch him. Quick!'

'A minister? You mean a *protestant* minister? But, Robert, we're Catholics,' cried Mother. She sounded as baffled as I felt.

'Not any more we're not. This is Presbyterian country. I'd never have got the job – certainly never have got posted here – if they thought I was a left-footer.'

'But . . .'

'Just bloody do it!' roared Father. He strode across the kitchen and rammed the flat of his hand into Mother's chest. I scampered off before he could turn on me.


Quarter of an hour later, unwashed, un-breakfasted and wearing the nearest approximation to our Sunday best that we could unearth from bags not yet fully unpacked, the four of us followed the path so recently trod by the decorous line of women and children, although we did not attempt to imitate their musical accompaniment. The path snaked uphill for about half a mile and, lifting my eyes I could see The Lookout, the small white tower at the top of the hill. Some of the children last night had talked about going there to 'talk' to their fathers when they were on shift, out on *Dubh Artach*, the 'Black Rock' lighthouse. They had winked when they said this but refused to tell me what they meant by 'talking'.

It was a fine, still morning, the sky like Milk of Magnesia, the air soft, like a damp caress on my face. A weak sun was straggling through pale, puffy clouds and the intoxicating scent of herbs and flowers rose around us as we bruised tiny plants beneath our feet. In the sky, birds hovered immobile and I fancied the islet was holding its breath as every living thing waited for the arrival of the minister. We passed a narrow, peaty burn blethering its way to the sea and I felt like reproving it, reminding it that this was the Sabbath. We none of us spoke a word nor needed telling to be quiet.

As we climbed, the sound of the singing grew stronger, drifting over the islet and out to sea, slow, measured and mournful. It was hard to reconcile it with the chattering wives and wild children of the night before.

Father kept turning back to see if the boat carrying the minister was coming and, sure enough, just as we rounded a bend in the track and saw at last the big wooden bothy, he exclaimed: 'That's them coming in now. Euan and Calum are both with him in the boat. Come on. Let's get ourselves inside.'

The door was slightly ajar though not quite enough for us to enter. Father tugged at the big door and a grating squeak announced our arrival. Two of the children in the front row began to giggle and were *shooshed* by a tall, thin woman in a tartan skirt, white blouse ruffled at the neck, long green cardigan and a boater trimmed with green ribbon. The Dow in her Sunday best.

Mother led the way tentatively up the side of three long wooden benches to the back. There was some space in the back row and we squeezed in. The singing seemed to be in a foreign language. Gaelic, I guessed, and the tune was quite unknown to us.

The bothy grew hot and airless and I was on the point of giving in to drowsiness when the door emitted its screech again. The singing faded to a halt and soon we heard the minister begin one of the longest prayers ever. I was beginning to feel faint, having had nothing but a mug of bedtime cocoa since the Pennyghael sandwich yesterday afternoon. We stood, singing incomprehensible songs or listening to incomprehensible prayers, for well over an hour. Gerry fell asleep and almost tumbled into the girl in front of him. Mother grabbed the tail of his jacket just in time.

The minister climbed up into a makeshift pulpit (three boxes piled on top of each other with a two-step metal ladder at the side). For someone able to make so much pompous noise, he cut an unimpressive figure, being short, fat and bald. He wore a black suit, black shirt and white dog-collar and seemed to be bursting out of all three. His sermon lasted so long - we had, at least, been allowed to sit down for it - that a foot-shuffling campaign got underway, calling forth sharp *tuts* from the adults and suppressed giggles from the children. The Dow did not tut. She simply looked in the direction of the shuffling, noted the children in the area and turned back to the minister. I felt again that sense of being trapped in an isolated place where every little deed or word – and maybe even thought – was known to all. This was a wild, beautiful and, in many ways, entrancing place but there was inescapable menace here too.

Presbyterian service or not, I bowed my head and said three silent Hail Marys though I could not have articulated what I was praying for, Protection, perhaps. But from what?

## CHAPTER EIGHT

*One thing they couldnae kill. That was the love the clansmen bore their chief.*
*Robert Louis Stevenson, from 'Kidnapped'*

A pall hung over the island. Mother took her cue from the wives and
kept us indoors all day. Father spent the afternoon preparing his kit for
departure and packing a food box that made serious inroads into our
supplies. If Mother was worried we would be left without enough to eat,
she kept her thoughts to herself and pandered to his every whim. He had
been out to Dubh Artach a couple of times already for what he called
'induction and orientation' which meant we heard at length about what
his job would entail: how he would have to be winched in a 'breeches
buoy' – a sort of harness seat – onto the rock as there was no landing
stage; all the delicate and expensive equipment he would be looking after;
how the wicks of each paraffin lamp had to be trimmed to exactly three-
eighteenths of an inch; how the reflectors were cleaned every day and
polished with a soft linen rag and Spanish white chalk, which was the
most finely powdered kind. He went on and on about details we barely
understood and we eventually ceased listening. I think now that he was
probably excited and nervous about his first real shift and kept himself
talking to hide this. And I think Mother knew this and humoured him.
But that day I was conscious only of acute, restless boredom, confined to
the house for a reason I did not comprehend, baffled by the air of
repressiveness that hung over all the houses and sick of the sound of his
voice. In the end, about half past three, I snapped.

'I wish ye'd get away to yer precious lighthouse and leave us in peace!'
As soon as the words were out of my mouth, I regretted them. And I was
still regretting them the next morning as my well-skelped buttocks
pressed into the hard wooden form in the school. Father was so angry -
and perhaps glad to have something to vent his tension on - that Mother
literally had to drag me off his knee as he belaboured my backside with
the leather sole of his slipper. She caught a few of the blows on her own
hands and arms but stood her ground until he gave in. Only because he
had no more time to waste on me, he said. I spent the rest of the
afternoon crying and sulking in my room, emerging only after he had left
at five o'clock and having to be coaxed by Mother to eat my tea.

'Will you never learn, Liza?' she said sadly as she dished scrambled eggs on to toast.

Now it was Monday morning and the misery of the Sabbath was over. At nine o'clock on the dot, The Dow marched in and the school day began - after a chorus of 'Good morning, Ma'am' - with the Lord's Prayer. Gerry and I stopped as always after 'and deliver us from evil'. Fortunately, the other children were chanting so loudly that our 'Amen' was not heard as they carried on to add 'for thine is the kingdom, the power and the glory, forever and ever' before proceeding to a resounding 'Aaah-men!' Gerry turned his head from the middle form, where he had been placed, to catch my eye and we shared a look of amusement. It seemed that nothing, not even the familiar 'Our Father' prayer, was the same here.

The prayer was followed by a psalm, led by The Dow, who had a deep, strong singing voice. It was not something Gerry or I had ever sung before, He hung his head and muttered God knows what; I held my head up and moved my mouth and jaw muscles as if singing lustily but without emitting a sound.

Finally the tallest boy in the class went out to the front and stood holding a huge book. It had rich maroon covers and marking ribbons in a variety of colours hung out of it at various places. When he lifted it to read, I saw 'Holy Bible' embossed on the cover in thick gold letters. I had only ever seen one like it in church. Even the one in the bothy yesterday, which the minister had read from, had not been as large or as ornate. The boy read slowly for several minutes, enunciating each word clearly, never making a mistake.

'Thank you, Earnest. Now, children, sit down and take your slates out. You have ten minutes to write about what Earnest has just read to us. The children on the first bench may draw a picture, although I would like to see a few words from the seven and eight year-olds as well. The children on the middle bench will write at least two sentences; and the back bench at least a hundred words. Get on with it.' Stately as ever, she glided over to her desk, sat down and took out a gold pocket watch, setting it on the desk in front of her. Ten minutes it would be, not a second less or more.

I pulled out a slate from the shelf under the form, copying the other children's actions, and took a matchbox with three pieces of chalk in it out of my skirt pocket where Mother had put it this morning. But I had no idea what I was going to write. I had heard the reading, of course, but had been too overwhelmed with new impressions and events to process any of it. Earnest might as well have read a recipe for Irish Stew for all I had understood or retained. Glancing at Gerry, I saw he was in the same boat except that he was about to cry. I could see his lower lip trembling and a hand rubbing his runny nose. I had to do something to avert this crisis. Gerry was a bit of a cry-baby for his age and no amount of Father's sporadic attempts to toughen him up had had any effect – indeed, quite the reverse. But I hated the thought of him being labelled here as such from the start.

Perhaps those three Hail Marys in the bothy yesterday were beginning to take effect for, before I could think of anything to do, The Dow called out: 'Would the new girl and boy come up to my desk, please. I need to enrol you officially. You are excused from the bible exercise this morning.'

We sprang up with alacrity and made our way to her desk. Gerry stumbled as he crossed the floor at the front, either because he was partially blinded by unshed tears or because his shoelace was coming undone, probably a bit of both. He managed to avoid hitting the floor but only by landing in her lap. The class erupted into merriment, glad of the distraction from the book of Hezekiah.

'Be quiet, all of you, at once.' Her voice was like a whiplash and there was instant silence and a semblance of getting back to work. Gerry righted himself awkwardly and mumbled a miserable apology as she rose to her feet.

'It is no matter, Gerrard. It was an accident and neither of us is hurt. Here, put that foot up on my chair. You will have another fall if we don't tie that lace properly. Can you do it yourself or do you need help?'

I felt rather than saw the astonishment on the faces of the other children. It was her tone of gentle kindness which was so amazing. I had only known the woman for two days but I knew as well as the children who had been in her class for years that this was totally out of character. And yet . . . I remembered how she had been with Gerry on the journey. Perhaps not *quite* totally.

What was it that she saw in Gerry that she did not see in the other three or four boys of his age? Or in me, his sister? He seemed to have the power to change her from a frosty schoolmarm into a motherly woman. I continued to muse on this until we were released into the playground - a small, rough field with a pile of boulders at one end and a high gate at the other, both good for climbing on and jumping off, as the show-offs among us were soon demonstrating.


'Well, what's the school here like?' asked Mother, ladling out our bowls of midday broth. 'What kind of a teacher is Miss Dow?'

'Narky, too strict'.

'Nice. I like her.'

Gerry and I spoke at the same time and Mother raised an eyebrow.

'She favours the boys, then? I couldn't help noticing the difference yesterday between how she was with you and you.' She nodded at each of us in turn.

'Not *boys* in general. Just me,' said Gerry smugly.

I heard Mother catch her breath and a strained, anxious look replaced the teasing smile that had been on her face. She stood up abruptly.

'What nonsense! Don't make up stories, you silly little boy.'

'It's true,' insisted Gerry. He turned to me. 'Tell her, Liza, You've seen it. You know you have.' He was on the verge of tears and I rushed into my peacemaker role as usual.

'Well, no wonder. You're such a lovely boy, so handsome and clever. Who wouldn't prefer you to those other rough boys?'

'You see, Mother. It *is* true. Liza says so.'

But Mother did not reply. She had her back to us as she stood at the sink but I could see a faint reflection of her face in the window. She was biting her lip.

By tacit consent, we spoke no more about The Dow but the feeling of discomfort and the sense of danger that she evoked in me, especially with her attitude to Gerry, had grown just a tiny bit more.

When the bell for afternoon school to commence was rung, rather than we children filing in to the classroom (which had been created by making the two bedrooms and the lobby between them into one big room), The Dow came out and joined us. She wore the long, grey overcoat again with a pair of short wellington boots and a headscarf tied over her hair. None of the other children seemed surprised so I presumed this must be what normally happened after the midday-dinner break.

'Find a space,' commanded The Dow. 'Stretch out your arms. No touching anyone else. Hurry, please.' We obeyed. 'Now stand with your feet wide apart. Arms still out. Then jump and close feet and arms, open feet and arms, close, open, close . . .'

She demonstrated, largely, I thought, for Gerry's benefit, since all the other children were familiar with the routine and I simply copied them. Gerry alone looked clueless but he got the hang of the jumping scissors movement when he watched her. He could have looked at any of the other children and copied them but he did not. He had eyes only for The Dow. And she for him. It was as if a thin thread stretched tight between them, thin but strong – and getting stronger every day.

After twenty jumps, she called a halt and bade us get into pairs. I made a bee-line for Gerry but was intercepted by Catriona. 'Hello, Liza,' she said. 'Remember me? Shall we pair up?'

In truth, I had forgotten all about the MacPhail family in the welter of new impressions and excitements over the past two days. I felt a rush of pleasure to see her.

'Catriona! Yes, of course. But where were you this morning?'

'Da had to go up to Salen to pick up some bit for the boat's motor. It was supposed to have been dropped off with the mail at Craignure on Saturday but there was a mistake and it got taken round to Salen. So he had to drive up there this morning for it and then fit it on the boat before we could sail round. Ma wrote me a note for Miss Dow.'

'Why'd he not go yesterday?' I asked, unthinking.

'On the Sabbath?' she laughed. 'Well seeing you're a lowlander!' And I blushed at my folly.

I looked over to see if Gerry had found or been chosen by a partner. It was no surprise to see that it was The Dow herself who had him by the hand as we began our afternoon ramble. The weather had changed, the sky had cleared and the breeze had freshened. We swung our arms like soldiers and marched briskly until we ran out of path and then we scrambled through the heather up a hill and down to a sandy cove where we examined seaweed, rocks, plants and shells, all the while listening to a stream of information from The Dow. Grudgingly, I had to admit she knew her stuff and made it interesting. She was, in fact, an excellent teacher. If only she did not have this fixation with Gerry.

We stayed in the cove for about twenty minutes when she bade us find our partners again and head back to school. 'And don't forget all I have

66

been telling you. I shall be testing you on it when we get back.' A few brave children let out audible groans and she immediately rounded on them. 'And you will be writing out some bible verses for an extra half hour after school finishes for the day.'

Catriona and I exchanged grimaces, thankful that we had not been unwise enough to let our own feelings show.

'Did you like David Balfour's Bay?' she asked as we made our way down the hill. 'I love it. In fact, I think it's my favourite beach in the whole of Mull.'

'David Balfour's Bay? Is that what it's called?' I paused as light dawned. 'Oh, is that the place in *Kidnapped*? Where David was shipwrecked ashore and thought he couldn't get off the islet because he didn't know about the causeway?'

'Well, it's the one Robert Louis Stevenson had in mind when he wrote that chapter. It *is* only a story.' Catriona laughed at my reverent tones but I ignored her.

'Oh, I wish I had known when we were there!' I turned and looked wistfully back up the hill but the bay was out of sight now. 'I'm going to go back as soon as I can.'

'Well, we have a walk every afternoon at this time so we'll probably go back there quite soon. It's one of Miss Dow's favourites. Sometime next week, maybe.'

But I knew I would not be waiting that long. David Balfour's Bay was calling me and I could not resist.

'Read, please,' said The Dow. '"The Clan Gathers Again" – that's your title, is it not? Come along, then.'

I was a good reader, both silent and out loud, often top of the class. I loved books. But I had never before read a newspaper – they were for grown- ups. The broadsheets of The Scotsman and The Glasgow Herald had been passed around and each child told to take a page. The smaller children were working on a list of words from a dictionary, making them up with Lexiko tiles, copying them on to their slates. The middle form, where Gerry and Catriona were, had another list and were looking the words up in the dictionary and copying down the meanings. My form, the top one, had been given the two national newspapers to work on. Our task was to choose a headline and prepare to read aloud the article underneath it. The other six children in my form had all set to the task confidently, obviously used to it. I had not, wasting time dithering between headlines and trying to scan the pieces to get a sense of what they were about. With the result that, when The Dow had called 'time' and requested that each child read out their headline for her to write up on the big roll-down blackboard , I had not yet made up my mind. I ended up blurting out the first one that caught my eye.

The readings began. The first was about a court case in Edinburgh and, after it had been read out, The Dow asked us all to say what we thought about it, to describe the case in our own words and check how much we remembered about details like names and places. It was interesting and quite fun. As the other five readings proceeded under The Dow's guidance and encouragement, we became sharper about noticing details and better at discussing the stories. Once again, I thought what a good teacher she was. There was a funny one about a cat that had made its way from Dumfries to Airdrie after a family moved house; a sad one about a baby abandoned on the doorstep of a big church in Edinburgh; and a couple of boring ones about the aftermath of the war with Germany in France – that was a constant topic in the news then. That left two headlines to go, which was when the Dow turned to me.

I took a deep breath and began to read from the Glasgow Herald. *'Duart Castle on the Isle of Mull, which has been a ruin for the past hundred years, is under new management and bidding fair to become a fine stately home again. The twenty-sixth Chief of the Clan Maclean bought it over a decade ago and began restoring it but had to stop the work during the war due to shortage of men to do the work. This has now resumed and plans are afoot for another Gathering of the Clan MacLean next summer. One was held in 1912 when the castle was still a ruin but the Chief, Sir Lachlan MacLean, hopes it will be in a much better state for the second twentieth century gathering.'* I paused for breath and plunged on, warming to my task and beginning to enjoy it. *'Duart was the proud home of the MacLean Clan Chief for over three hundred years, but the Clan supported the Jacobite cause against Oliver Cromwell and later against William of Orange. In 1653 . . .'*

'Stop! That's enough. We'll move on to the last reading.'

I looked up in surprise, as did all the others who had been finding this bit of local news more interesting than all the other pieces. 'But the next bit is really good, Ma'am,' I pleaded. 'I've read it and there's this Lady MacLean who . . .'

'I said enough!' she snapped and turned to the girl sitting next to me. 'We will have your piece now, Betsy. At once, please.'

'Can we no' talk about Liza's story, Ma'am?'

'Imagine all the people from that Clan meeting up after all those years. I bet some of them had to come from Canada and America and . . .'

'Can we go and see the castle some time, Ma'am? It would make a great local history trip.'

'We're aye learning about English Kings and Queens. It'd be good to do some Scottish history for a change. Aw, go on, Ma'am. Please!'

The others weighed in excitedly. The story had caught their attention, even the half of it that I had been allowed to read out. And what they were all saying made sense. Why not learn about the history on our doorstep? In North Berwick, Mr Chambers had been a great one for taking pupils to see historical sites in nearby Edinburgh. In my last class, we had had several bus trips into the city and walked around it, learning about statues, buildings and the Royal Mile which Mary Queen of Scots had traversed between Edinburgh Castle, which had been full of her hostile, protestant lords, and Holyrood Palace, where she had felt safe to practise her Catholic religion. I had loved those trips, lapping up the stories and legends, imagining the feelings and the conversations of the historical figures.

So I was about to add my own plea to the others' efforts but stopped when I looked at The Dow. She had gone very pale, even her eyes seeming colourless. A shaft of late afternoon sun through the window caught her head and made her hair seem almost white and her skin translucent. She looked as insubstantial as a wraith as she rose from her chair, which she had earlier carried to the back of the room to be beside our form, and glided to the front of the classroom. She motioned with a shaking hand for one of the boys to bring her chair back to her desk at the front and, when he did so, she sat down slowly.

'What's wrong with her?'

'What did we do? Or say?'

'Is she no' well, d'ye think?'

We whispered amongst ourselves, more cowed than we would have been if she had shouted at us. There was something in her demeanour that made us all uneasy, even a little frightened. But, abruptly, she snapped out of her trance and began briskly checking the work of the first and second forms, ignoring us completely, so that we sat feeling uncomfortable and unsure what to do until the big clock on the wall struck four and we were released.

# CHAPTER NINE

*When I suffer in mind, stories are my refuge. I take them like opium.*
*Robert Louis Stevenson*

That night, I unpacked my copy of *Kidnapped* and re-read for the umpteenth time the chapter about David Balfour being – as he thought – stranded on Erraid. I tried to picture what he had gone through. There had been no Dubh Artach lighthouse then, so no row of houses for families, no big bothy for religious services, no pier to come and go from and no lookout to send or receive messages from. And not a single living soul as far as David could see. He had been shipwrecked on that beautiful beach on the west coast of the islet where we had just spent some of the afternoon. Between that beach and the causeway on the east coast was a rocky, heathery hill, not very high but enough to obscure the one from the other. David had trekked all over the islet looking for food and shelter but had neither found any sign of habitation nor realised that, when the tide was out, the creek could be easily forded. *Kidnapped* is set in the second half of the eighteenth century, shortly after the Battle of Culloden which finally annihilated the Jacobite cause, and I wondered if there had truly been no one living on our islet then.

'Have we any history books, Mother?' I asked as we sat down to our tea the next day.

'Well,' she replied, 'I did bring all my books but most of them are literature rather than history.'

'What's the difference?' demanded Gerry through a mouthful of bread and jam.

'Don't speak with your mouth full,' she replied automatically but I could see that she was thinking, mentally sifting through her books for ones that could be classed as historical.

'History is true stories and literature is made-up ones,' I told him.

'Like lies? Is lit–ra–yure just lies?' He turned to Mother who was still musing on my question. 'Are your books all just lies, then?'

She made no answer but shook her head with an indulgent smile.

'There's a difference between telling lies and telling stories. You ken that fine, Gerry. Stop pestering Mother. You're just looking for attention.' I was sharper than I meant to be and his face fell, his bottom lip pouting. But I wanted help with my quest to understand the history – the true story - of this daft wee scrap of land that we had ended up on

71

and with the feelings it engendered in me of wonder and delight alternating with dread and danger. I felt compelled by a need to know that I could not explain, not even to myself.

'What kind of history is it you're after?' asked Mother, pouring herself another cup of tea.

'Stuff about here – Mull, Erraid, Iona, Duart, the Jacobites, The MacLeans . . .'

She was silent for a moment, her face a shuttered frown. Then she gave a strained smile.

'Hold on, missy!' She held up her hand. 'That's an awful lot of things you're wanting to ken about.' She gave a small, forced chuckle.

'Is it? It's all round about here. I read in the Glasgow Herald that the Chief of Clan Maclean is restoring Duart Castle and . . .'

'Oh, la-di-da!' Mother seemed to seize on the diversion gratefully. 'Reading the Herald now, is it? Quite the young lady.'

I explained about The Dow's use of the two Scottish broadsheets with the pupils in the oldest form and she expressed grudging approval. Like me, she did not like or trust The Dow but we were both admiring of her teaching methods which were surprisingly progressive in such a backwater as an island school for less than twenty lighthouse children.

Mother promised to have a look through her books and shooed Gerry and me out of the kitchen as she had bread to make. Our appetites, sharpened by the sea air, had made short work in two days of both the loaf she had brought from Oban and the one in the wives' welcome basket.

'Can we go out to play? Please?' wheedled Gerry and, after a glance at the sky and an order to put on our old boots and old jackets (it seemed that even here, with so few people to impress, we must still keep our school clothes and shoes in good condition), Mother agreed. Her belated cry to remain within calling distance was ignored and we hoped she would assume that, ironically, we had not heard it.


Gerry charged off to find the friend he had made – an eight-year-old boy in the fifth house along the row. He always preferred pals younger than himself. I ignored the gaggle of girls who were playing a skipping-rope game down on the pier and, copy of *Kidnapped* under my arm, set off up the hill to The Lookout. It was a steep, short climb to the small, circular, white tower. It had been erected, so Father had told us, when the Dubh Artach lighthouse was being built, mainly for the purpose of looking out to the rocks through a telescope and judging whether materials and men could be shipped out and landed, if further building work was going to be possible that day or if the wind, waves and weather would once again frustrate their purpose. It had been a long slow business building a lighthouse on a rock in the middle of the wild sea and in frequently wild weather. Thinking of this now, as I climbed, I stopped to thumb the book I was carrying till I found the account of the shipwreck on the Torran Rocks, those very hazards that our lighthouse had been built to help sailors avoid.

*. . . the tide ran very strong . . . it was strange to see three strong men throw their weight upon the tiller and it, like a living thing, throw them back . . a sea so huge that it lifted the brig right up and canted her over . . .*

The Lookout was still used nowadays by the keepers to check conditions out on the rock and decide if it was safe to take the men to and from it. I had heard the children talking about communications between the rock and the shore from The Lookout but I wondered how they did this. Waving flags, perhaps, or flashing lights. It was all quite mysterious and rather magical. I hoped I would get to see it or even have a go myself, although I had no actual desire to contact Father. Out of sight, out of mind, had served me well as far as he was concerned for years and it had been as much of a relief to me as it obviously was to Mother to learn that he would be away from home every second month of the year.

Today, I had a different purpose: I had an inkling that The Lookout might have been erected on the very spot that David Balfour described as his makeshift 'home' for the four miserable days and nights he passed on Erraid. When I reached the door into The Lookout, I paused and dipped into *Kidnapped* again.

*I had become in no way used to the horrid solitude of the isle but used to look round me on all sides like a man hunted. . . I could catch a sight of the great ancient church and the roofs of the people's houses in Iona; and, on the other hand, over the low country of the Ross of Mull, I saw smoke go up, morning and evening, as from a homestead . . . I used to watch this smoke, when I was wet and cold and had my head half-turned with loneliness; and think of the fireside and the company until my heart burned.*

Poor David Balfour. My heart was wrung with the pathos of it. It had been so the first time I read chapter fourteen but now, standing in the very place, I was almost overwhelmed. No matter that, as Catriona had so pragmatically pointed out, it was only a story. It was as real to me then as the events and trials of my own life this past month. Erraid was no longer the bleak uninhabited place of Robert Louis Stevenson's imagination; it had houses, families, a school and church of sorts, a pier, a motorboat and a resident schoolteacher. But, as I opened the door and skirted round the big telescope to look out upon the view, the very one so poignantly described by Stevenson's wretched young hero, I was seized by a powerful conviction: Erraid was once again to be the starting point for an escapade that would create a story worth the telling. A story that I would be at the heart of.

On the large rock just outside The Lookout, I sat and looked across The Sound of Iona. Just as in *Kidnapped*, the ruins of the ancient church could be clearly seen and smoke was drifting from the scattered houses on the isle of Iona. Between it and Erraid, the sea that was presently surging in and out of Erraid Sound, the narrow sandy passage between Erraid and Mull, filling it up and cutting us off for the next five or six hours, flowed out to merge with the ocean.

Our early afternoon walk today had been to this causeway, when it was still fordable (wearing the wellington boots we had been told to bring) and we had walked over it to pick wild flowers and gather shells on the beaches 'over there'. I had learned the names of the birds that thronged the shore there – oystercatchers, curlews, shags, guillemots and many more. On returning to the classroom, we had been shown pictures in The Dow's big book of birds then set to drawing and labelling them in our own jotters. While the lowest form had been given crayons to draw as many of the birds as they could, the middle form had copied out whole paragraphs and each been given one bird to learn off by heart and recite later.

My form had been given the task of writing in our own words about a bird of our choice. Today, it had had to be factual but tomorrow, the afternoon writing task would be to make up a story concerning our bird. Once again, I had to admire the way in which The Dow handled the job of teaching children of all ages in one room and how she wove one activity into another so cleverly. I was already loving the afternoon outings and looking forward to many more before winter closed in. Catriona told me that indoor exercise and activities replaced our walks when the weather was bad. She was looking forward to that, she said, for, although – or maybe because – she had been born and raised in the Hebrides, she did not much enjoy the 'trailing about' and preferred the crafts and drama which apparently replaced it in winter. For me, I was lapping up the opportunity to explore Erraid and learn as much about it as possible. I resolved that, if Mother's library did not yield what I was looking for, I would overcome my dislike and distrust of The Dow and ask her. I was sure she would be a fount of knowledge.

I had not given any thought until now to the isle of Iona. On the map, it simply looked as if the mapmaker had dropped a mistaken blob off his brush whilst painting Mull. Mr Chambers, bless him, had pushed a lot of information my way in the last few weeks at my North Berwick school. I recalled stuff about St Columba coming from Ireland in a coracle and setting up a rough and ready monastery; medieval Scottish kings being buried there; Viking raids and monks being massacred. As I stared mesmerised across the sea at what Mr Chambers had called 'the faery isle', there came to me a clear memory of a picture, in one of the books he had insisted on loaning me, of strange, priest-like figures in robes standing in a circle. And underneath a caption. Something like . . . *'Iona is a thin place . . . the veil between the natural and the supernatural . . . Druidism is believed to have flourished . . .'*

What were Druids? I knew nothing of them. Something else to find out. It felt important although I had no idea why.


Lost in my thoughts, I did not hear the sound of someone coming up the hill to The Lookout and the screech of the door opening caught me unawares and set my heart jumping into my mouth. There was no reason that I knew of why I should not be here – I had heard of no rules of prohibitions – but for some reason I felt guilty as if discovered in an illegal activity. I even briefly considered crouching down in front of the trolley that supported the telescope and hoping to go unseen but quickly ditched this idea. The Lookout was altogether too small to enable one occupant to hide from another.

The entrant was a man whom I had not met before. He was small and wiry with a red curly beard, a rather greasy cap rammed over red, curly hair and a pipe emitting fragrant smoke rammed in his mouth. He did not seem at all surprised to see me.

'You must be Liza Galway,' he said, covering the distance between us in one stride and sticking out a big, calloused hand. 'How d'ye do? I'm Arthur Campbell. I met your father last week when he came out to the rock.'

'How do you do, Mr Campbell,' I replied carefully. He must be one of the keepers whom Father had relieved on Sunday afternoon. I was always wary of meeting anyone who had met my father first. Mother was the same. We could never be sure what impression Father had made for he could be charming and hail-fellow-well-met one day, argumentative and bad-mannered the next.

'He's going to make a fine keeper, your daddy is,' said Mr Campbell. 'Just the sort of man we need in the service. Knows the sea and knows how to handle her. She's a hard taskmistress and merciless on anyone foolish enough to think they can get the better of her.' He eyed me keenly. 'Are you much of a sailor, yourself? Has your daddy taught you how to handle a boat?'

The idea of Father doing such a thing, expending the time and patience that would be required on one of his children, was as foreign and unlikely a notion as the thought of calling him 'daddy'.

I shook my head. 'I get sick. I was awfy unwell on the big boat from Oban.'

'Now, is that not a pity?' said Mr Campbell. 'A sailor's daughter shouldna be getting seasick. You'll have to learn the tricks to avoid it. Get your daddy to tell you about those.'

I smiled awkwardly. This man's assumption that Father and I had that sort of relationship was making me uncomfortable, as if I was about to be caught out in a lie. I edged round the other side of the telescope. 'I have to go. Mother will be needing me.'

'She a fine woman, yer mother.' He suddenly grinned as if something funny or pleasing had struck him but he only repeated 'A fine woman!' and, for some unknown reason, he broke into a cackle of laughter. I could still hear it as I ran down the hill and through the old quarry where lay sharp-edged pieces of granite, all shapes and sizes, piled against and on top of each other. Catriona said that all sorts of small animals lived in the holes and passageways created by these remnants of the quarrying days when the lighthouse was being built. Mr Arthur Campbell had unsettled me and, whereas I strode confidently through them on the way up, never giving a thought to any rodent population, now I was sure I heard rustling and squeaking and caught sight of a long tail sliding into a cavity. Other children had told of wildcats living there and said I would hear them caterwauling in the night. With my nerves jangling, I raced on and down at last to the path leading to the houses.


When I got back to our house, I found Mother sitting at the table which was littered with books. She was holding a book in one hand and some screwed up paper in the other. She looked up with a start and a smile. A forced smile I thought. I noticed that the book in her hand had faded green covers with old-gold lettering and it was my turn to start.

76

I was transported back to that day over three months ago when Gerry and I had been eating 'jammy pieces' in the kitchen of our North Berwick house after school. I heard again Mother's scream from the Good Room where she was packing books and other possessions ready for our move to Erraid. I saw her kneeling on the floor, holding in her hands a small, dog-eared volume, its covers a faded green; the title and the author's name on the front and spine in old-gold lettering, smudged and illegible. She had been holding the book at arm's length but when she saw us, she had thrown it down on to the carpet where it had lain open, yellowed pages fluttering. Then she had pushed us out of the Good Room and refused to talk about the book.

I approached the table eagerly but quickly saw that, unlike that book, the writing on the cover of this one was quite clear.

'I've been sorting through my books, Liza, dear, to see if there was anything about this part of the Hebrides or about the Jacobites like you asked for. I've only found this one so far but it could be what you're looking for. How about you make chips for tea while I finish here? Mind you wash your hands first, though. If they're anything like you're knees, they must be filthy.'

I glanced down surprised and saw that my knees and calves, where my long socks had slipped down were covered in muddy smears and criss-crossed with scratches. Such had been my absorption in my quest as I scrambled up to The Lookout, I had not noticed what the boggy terrain and the gorse were doing to me. I washed my hands and used the sink cloth to rub the worst off my legs. As I threw potatoes into the sink and set the chip-pan on the stove, I called over my shoulder,

'Do you ken a man called Arthur Campbell?'

She did not reply at once, being deep in reading, but Gerry, coming into the kitchen just at that moment, immediately and enthusiastically cried:

'That's my pal's dad. He's a great mannie. He was showing Angus and me how to get a fishing rod ready and how to tie on the bait. He's promised to take us both fishing this Saturday. I *can* go, Mother, can't I?' He tugged at her arm, frustrated that she had not so much as looked up since he had come in.

'Aye, of course,' she answered distractedly. 'That's fine, Gerry . . . nice for you, making friends so soon . . . Listen to this Liza!' She held up the green and gold book and read:

'*Where the Sound of Mull meets the Firth of Lorne, a towering castle grows out of a high crag and commands the channel between the island and the mainland. Jutting out from the end of a peninsula on Mull, it claims a proud position from which it has resisted attack since the mid-13th Century. This is Dubb Ard (Black Point), known today as Duart Castle, seat of the Clan Chief Maclean. The MacLeans are descended from Gillean, a 13th Century warrior, who was related to the Kings of Dalriada, and this heritage can certainly be seen in the history and character of the Clan.'*

She looked up. 'Is that the sort of thing you're after?'

I almost snatched the book out of her hand, ignoring the fact that my own hands were wet and a couple of 'tattie peelins' clung to the back of one.

'That's great, Mother. Can I have this?'

'Well, yes, you can have a loan of it but only if you promise no' to get it wet and stuck with bits of tattie.'

I paid no attention but held the book in my wet hands and read aloud:

*The 16th Century began with disaster: in 1513, Clan Chief Hector Maclean of Duart, along with the flower of the Scottish nobility, died fighting the English at Flodden and his successor, Lachlan, was murdered ten years later. But whereas Hector's demise was tragically illustrious - at least according to the sorrowful song, The Floo'ers o' the Forest - Lachlan's was more like a fitting end for a cruel brute. When his wife, Catherine Campbell, failed to produce a son and heir, he assuaged his frustration by abandoning her on a rock which would be submerged when the tide came in. He reported her death to her Campbell kinsmen. 'Drowned in a dreadful accident', said he, shedding a few crocodile tears. But they knew better: Catherine was alive and well, having been rescued by fishermen and conveyed to her brother, the Chief of Clan Campbell. Summary clan justice was exacted from the luckless Lachlan: he was 'dirked in his bed' on a visit to Edinburgh shortly after this (1523). 'Lady Rock', where the terrified Catherine passed several frantic hours, can be seen to this day at low tide from the battlements of Duart and an old etching hangs in the castle depicting the poor woman before she was rescued. We can imagine the etching's look of despair and terror being replaced by one of vengeful glee: she certainly had the last laugh.*

I jumped up and down in excitement. 'I knew there would be some great stories. Oh, I wish I could go and see Castle Duart.'

'We saw it from the boat when we were coming into Craignure,' said Mother.

'I mean walk around it, not just see it in the passing.' I remembered Father pointing it out and The Dow explaining something of why the present Chief of Clan MacLean had had to buy it. But it was a hazy memory. I had been so seasick and miserable that I had not retained much of what she said. Something about three hundred years and Jacobites. I had a sudden picture of her face as she spoke and heard her angry tone. Then she had looked over at Gerry in a strange way. Yes, this was definitely the sort of information I was after. Castle Duart was the key or at least one of the keys to the mystery that I had sensed the moment I first saw the Dow and had become bigger and stronger with every day that I spent here.

I commandeered the book which was entitled 'Tales and Legends of the Highlands and Islands' and secreted it away from Gerry's inquisitive paws, hiding it between my mattress and my bedsprings, before returning to my kitchen chores. I could barely wait for bedtime and would be sure to take a candle with me tonight so that I could read as much as possible before I fell asleep. So it was not till much later that I realised that there were several pages missing. They had obviously been torn out rather than simply fallen out because their jagged edges were still poking out of the book's spine.

# CHAPTER TEN

*The rightful heir to an estate now starving on an isle at the extreme end of the wild Highlands.*                    Robert Louis Stevenson, from 'Kidnapped'


Our first week on 'The Islet' passed slowly. By contrast, the weeks that followed seemed to tumble upon one another and in no time we were looking forward with apprehension to Father's return and dreading him being 'shore' for four weeks. But those first few days were so full of new experiences and so many mixed emotions that each one seemed more like a week than a day.

Gerry began to make friends – one really good one in particular who would last for many years – and so, much more surprisingly, did Mother. Perhaps it was having Father out of the picture so soon after our arrival that gave her the chance to put her own stamp upon the image that the wives conceived of her; perhaps it was the remoteness and inaccessibility of Erraid that drove her to overcome her usual reticence; maybe both. In any event, I was surprised to find one or two of the wives frequently sitting in our kitchen when I came home from school in the afternoon. I would hear their chatter and laughter as I walked along the path towards our house and marvel. It was so far from the homecomings I had known in North Berwick and it made the two places seem even more miles apart than they are.

For myself, I did not find the making of new friends so easy. The posse of three of four girls around my age seemed already a well-formed clique. They were not openly unfriendly but neither did they encourage me to become one of them, letting me hang at the outer edge of their circle. Sometimes they would ask me about my family and my last school, questions that required factual answers, but never anything about me as a person, my likes, dislikes, hobbies and thoughts. It was as if they opened a small slot to grant me access, a slot of their own designing. I could then choose gratefully to mould myself into it. Or not - it was up to me, it was all that would be on offer. Of course, I accepted gratefully – what alternative was there? But it was not the real me in that slot and I felt isolated, all the more so as I watched Gerry and Mother settling in so well.

So it was that I turned more and more to Catriona, albeit she was almost two years younger than me and not in the same form. She too had struggled to make friends, the fact that she left Erraid as soon as school was over each day clearly being a big obstacle. On that tiny islet in that tiny community, everyone was constantly thrown together without respite. Catriona only dipped in and out of the cauldron of claustrophobic relationships which gave her both an advantage and a disadvantage. She was spared most of the gossip and rumour, the judgement, speculation and conspiracy. But she also lacked any real friends and she opened up like a flower to my tentative overtures.

And, so it was from her that I learned about the ghost of Erraid.


We were walking together on the Wednesday afternoon of the third week, this time crossing Erraid Sound and continuing on up a steep, rocky climb to the farm of Knockvolgan on Mull. Here the farmer's wife came out to meet us with a big tray of freshly baked scones which disappeared into seventeen hungry mouths. The farmer took us to see the hay stored in the small barn for winter cattle feed and spoke about the work that goes on in a farm in September, harvesting late crops, getting the big barn ready as winter quarters for the cows and spreading turnips over the fields to feed the sheep when the grazing would dry up.

Catriona and I had begun chatting on the climb up and took only slight interest in the farmer's agricultural lecture. I had been telling her about the book Mother had given me and recounting the legend of Lady Rock.

'Aye there's a whean o' stories about Duart,' she said, puffing a little as we climbed, for she was chubbier than me and The Dow was setting a brisk pace, appearing as always to glide rather than walk like a mere mortal. 'The best one I ever heard – I think it was Ma that told me - is about the Lady MacLean who escaped when Oliver Cromwell sent five ships to capture Duart and put a stop to the MacLeans supporting the King.'

'Which King was that?' I asked as we reached the top of the climb and saw the others thronging around the tray of Knockvolgan scones.

She did not reply immediately, distracted by the smell of the scones, but later, as the others settled on hay bales to listen to the farmer, we found a corner away from them and she resumed.

'Well, the English had beheaded their King, Charles was his name, and Oliver Cromwell was in charge. But in Ireland and Scotland, lots of people, the MacLean family at Duart included, didn't want Cromwell. They wanted a King again. There were battles: one at Inverkeithing where Hector, the Chief of Clan MacLean was killed – his brother, Alan became Chief after that; and the famous one at Killiecrankie where they say a soldier leapt right over the river. Cromwell got so fed up of them that he sent five ships full of soldiers to Duart to put a stop to it.'

'And what happened?'

'The Duart folk were lucky. There was a terrible storm the night the ships arrived and they were all sunk in Duart Bay, right below the castle. A lot of the soldiers on them were drowned but some got off the ships and climbed up the cliff to the castle, with murder in mind.' Catriona lowered her voice to a sepulchral whisper. 'But Hector's widow, Lady MacLean, and her son escaped and fled south, down here, right on to Erraid.'

'What happened when they got here? Did the soldiers catch them?'

'Nearly. Lady MacLean and the boy had to take to the sea in a wee boat to escape them. But it was foul weather and the boat hit the rocks. No lighthouses then. It broke up and sank.'

'What happened to her and the lad?'

'Drowned, poor woman. Her body washed up on the shore at Tormore, where I live. Her grave – what's left o' it - is still in the wee cemetery there.'

'Was the boy drowned too?'

'I suppose so. But they never found his body.' Catriona let her voice sink to a quaver. 'They say she is still looking for him.' Her eyes were wide and slightly bossed. 'That's *The Ghost of Erraid*. Still seeking, still calling for him. Wanting to find him and take him to the graveyard to be with her.'

I shivered although it was hot in the barn, stuffy with the crush of children and stacked straw. 'When does she come? Is it often? How do we know when she's coming?' I was breathless with excitement, desperate to know more.

'We never ken exactly when she's coming. It's no' like at any set time. But we ken when she's on her way.'

'How?'

'There's a bell, a bonnie, tuneful bell, that rings way out at sea and, sure as God, there'll be a boat wrecked on the Torran Rocks that day.'

'But what about the lighthouse? Is that no' why it's there – to stop that happening?'

'Aye, you'd think so. And the keepers hate the ghost for that very reason. It's like she gets one over on them.'

I was quiet for a few moments, digesting the information. Then I asked the question that had been lurking at the back of my mind from the very beginning of her story.

82

'How old was the MacLean lad, the one that escaped with the ghost?'

'Well, Liza, she wasn't a ghost then.'

I wriggled impatiently. 'Ach, you ken what I mean!'

Catriona laughed and conceded: 'MacLean's only son was nine years old. Nobody ever found out what happened to him. His body was never recovered.'

I did not reply or thank her. My head was buzzing with all this new information. The Dow called us all to order then and it was time to get into our ragged crocodile formation and begin the descent to the causeway before the tide came in.


It was an unusually mild, dry autumn on Mull that year. Greenhorns that we were, we took it for granted. On Mondays, Mother hung out lines of snow-white washing in the top half of the long front garden and watched with housewifely satisfaction as it fluttered, horizontal and flag-like, in the brisk wind. She soon discovered that the wives were in tacit but deadly serious competition to be the first to hit the drying green on wash day. Some yardstick, agreed but never referred to, measured the whiteness of table linen, shirts, petticoats and drawers. Nothing was ever said but every wife scrutinised her neighbours' washing lines and compared them with her own. Mother claimed she had watched one of the wives take all her washing back in and reappear with it an hour later, after presumably subjecting it to more hot water rubbing on the washboard and more cold water rinsing in the rain barrel at her back door.

Mother was scornful. 'Ye'd think she'd have better things to do. Her washing was fine as it was. Ye'd think we were living on some grand country estate instead of the back of beyond without so much as a decent road to walk on. What does it matter anyway? Who's going to see it?'

The wives' obsession with 'doing the brasses' also earned her scorn. The NLB supplied brass pots and pans and each front door had a brass doorknob and threshold strip. The wives were frequently to be seen on their hands and knees rubbing the knob and the strip till they shone and indoors the pots and pans received the same effortful care. Mother declared she could see no point in any of it. She unpacked her own cooking pots, cast iron and black with years of use, and put the brass ones away under the bed. I was given the task of 'doing the door brasses' and took it very seriously at first, trying literally to outshine the wives, but I soon grew tired of it and had to be reminded – not by Mother who did have better things to do, like writing up the journal she had decided to keep and reading anything she could get her hands on – but by the other girls at school who did the same chore and had imbibed their mothers' intensity.

Mother and I were later to find out exactly why we should have taken the wives' excessive house-pride more seriously and modelled ourselves on it; but that moment of truth lay in the future. To be sure, the wives told mother all about the 'snap inspections' that the NLB carried out and the standards expected in the houses they provided  but Mother just laughed and said she didn't need any man telling her how to run her home. The wives were exaggerating, she said dismissively - to me, not to them.

I soon devoured 'Tales and Legends', particularly enjoying the gory ones like Mull's headless horseman who, they say, can still be seen riding in Glen More, where he lost his head in battle. A man called Oran, probably a Druid, having been buried alive on Iona, was found still alive when the grave was opened a few days later but immediately reinterred for blasphemy because he said he had seen Hell.

Druids cropped up in quite a few tales, several connected with Iona, but the references were vague.  They were, said *Tales and Legends*, the keepers of 'the ancient wisdom' and they guarded it with their lives. They wrote nothing down because they believed that the very act of writing gave precious knowledge away so they had left behind only tantalising half-clues: clusters and lines of big standing stones; circles of small stones atop hills and mounds. I resolved to try and find some of these. A trip to Iona would be a good place to start. It cropped up time and again and began to assume an aura of magic for me. Maybe Catriona would be able to help. I thought of her setting off in her father's boat at the end of each school day, slipping round the coast to her home. It would be but a short trip across the Sound of Iona for that wee boat. She had probably been there lots of times.

I read about Iona's 'street of the dead' and shivered as I thought of walking along it but it was a delicious shiver, such as one gets while anticipating a scary fairground ride. Medieval kings had been brought by ship to be buried on Iona. The royal corpses had been carried to their resting place along this cobbled walkway. Maybe Catriona had already walked it! The more I read, the better I wanted to know Catriona and her family. They could be the key to finding out. Exactly what, I could not then have said but that did not make my growing compulsion any less.

84

My fascination with Druidism was whetted by the sparse references which hinted at powerful priests, dark practices and superhuman courage.

'Do you ken much about the Druids?' I asked Mother.

'No, Liza, I do not,' she replied shortly.

It was the Saturday of the fourth week, two days before Father was due back and she was doing a huge baking of bread, scones, shortbread and oatcakes. She was also preparing to make bramble jelly from berries picked by the three of us the evening before. I had come back from The Dow's afternoon excursion with tales of blackberry bushes hanging with ripe fruit and Mother had immediately instigated a foraging expedition. We had come back in the twilight with hands and arms scratched by the thorny bushes and bitten by the persistent 'midgies'. The berries had been boiled into a sludge which was now draining through a big felt poke (known as a jelly-bag) which was tied to a pole suspended between two chairs. Underneath the poke, Mother's big jam-pan was catching the slow drip of deep purple liquid which would be boiled with sugar for several hours and then decanted into glass jars and left to set. The resulting jelly would be absolutely delicious spread on toast or scones. My mouth was watering in anticipation.

'What do you want to ken about them for?' she asked as she rolled out the scone dough and handed me the circular cutter. This was one of my favourite jobs and I forgot about Druids for a moment as I carefully planned out how many scones I could get out of the dough, lightly imprinting twelve circles on it before starting to press the cutter through. Once the scones were in the hot oven, I was sent out to fetch more washing up water from the rain-barrel and set the bucket on the stove to heat. Mother gathered up the utensils and bowls she had been using and dumped them in the big sink. Then she lifted the simmering kettle off the hob and made a pot of tea.

'Well?' she prompted me. 'Why were you asking about Druids? Have you been learning about them at school?'

I hesitated, trying to think when my interest in them had begun. 'I've been up to The Lookout a few times . . .'

'Have you?' she interrupted. 'What for? You've not been sending messages to Father, have you?' Some of the wives had offered to take her up there and show her how to send a semaphore message out to the lighthouse but she had not taken them up on it yet. Unless there was a particular reason to contact Father, she said she saw no need and I guessed she had no desire. The thought that I might have done so seemed to alarm her, possibly because it would highlight her own lack of communication, and I hastened to reassure her.

'No, of course not. What would I do that for? I just like going up there. I think it's built on the spot that David Balfour spent his miserable few nights on – you know, in *Kidnapped.*'

She looked blank for a moment then nodded. 'Oh, aye. Are you still reading that?'

'I've read it a few times but the chapter about Erraid is really interesting now that we're here. All about the shipwreck as well – right out there where Father's lighthouse is now.'

'Your father will be home on Monday morning,' she said as we sat down to drink our tea and wait for the scones to bake.

'Aye.' I replied cautiously, keeping my voice neutral. It was a couple of years ago now but I had not forgotten the spanking she had given me for saying how glad I had been to see the back of him at the end of one of his Navy leaves.

'I wonder what he'll find to do here for a month.' She stirred sugar into her tea.

'Have ye no' asked the other wives?'

'Not really.'

I guessed that she had simply avoided talking about him at all, which was understandable but had left her facing his first month 'shore' with no idea as to how it would play out.

'Ach, they're bound to have things they have to do,' I said. 'The Lighthouse Board wouldna' pay them just to do nothing for a whole month.' An image of Father with time on his hands and enough money to buy strong drink hung in the air between us. It had been bad enough in the months after he had been made redundant from the Navy and before he had landed the lighthouse job but, at least, he had had very little money to spend. Now he would have a month's pay in his pocket.

She gave me a wan smile. 'Let's hope you're right, Liza.' It was the nearest I had ever heard her come to admitting to the kind of family we were – a family living in fear of the drunken, violent bully that was its head. It emboldened me to say:

'There are no shops here. He won't be able to buy booze.'

Even as I said it, I knew it was stupid. There were shops at Fionnphort and Bunessan, general stores which sold everything and certainly whisky and beer. The men had their boat, the very one which had brought us to Erraid on our arrival and which took the men back and forth from the lighthouse. I had seen it leaving and arriving at the pier here many times over the past month. Supplies of alcoholic drink would not be a problem. I remembered the half bottle of whisky Father had taken from the kitchen cupboard that very first evening and the wives' talk of the men 'making the most of their last evening before another month out on the rock'.

Mother made no reply, her tight-lipped expression closing the conversation down. 'That's enough! Don't let me hear you speaking about your father like that again.' Her voice was sharp but I was no longer the ten-year-old who had understood only that speaking the truth about Father would earn me a walloping; I knew now that she was as afraid as I was and desperate to hide it - from me, from other adults and even, to some extent, from herself. She rose then to take the scones out of the oven and Gerry came running in on cue to begin whining and wheedling until she gave in and allowed him a hot scone.

'Share it with Liza,' she ordered him. 'That's all you're getting just now. The rest are for next week when Father is home.'

As I ate the piece of scone which Gerry reluctantly tore off and handed to me, I reflected that I was no further forward in my quest for knowledge about the Druids.

# CHAPTER ELEVEN

*My vanity got the heels of my prudence.*

*Robert Louis Stevenson, from 'Kidnapped*

In the event, our fears about Father proved unfounded. He arrived back on Erraid on Monday mid-morning while Gerry and I were at school. It was play-time and the cry went up among the children.

'Shore! Shore!' they cried. 'Here comes the shore boat!' And we all rushed from the playground down to the pier to greet the three men. The children of the other two men – there were seven in all – flew at their fathers joyfully. We watched as the men swung the smallest two up into their arms and held out hands to the others. Our father stood for a moment looking awkwardly at Gerry and me; then an embarrassed smile crept over his face and he held out his hands to us. I could not remember ever actually holding his hand although I suppose there must have been times when I was very small. But I did not want the other children to think that we were any different as a family and I could see that Gerry was wondering what to do so I took Father's hand. And strange it was to find my small hand inside his big one. Not altogether unpleasant; indeed it set off a strange yearning in me.

We walked in procession back up to the houses where the wives were all waiting. The men let go of hands and put the tinies back down on to the ground so as to be free to greet the women, opening their arms and gathering their wives in for hearty kisses. Once again, Father was obliged to behave as the other two men did or else seem the odd man out. So it was that I saw him embrace Mother in a creditable show of affection. A strange sight indeed. I rolled my eyes at Gerry and he burst into giggles which fortunately went unnoticed as The Dow appeared at the school end of the path, ringing the hand bell to summon us back to lessons.

Later, when we went home for midday dinner, we found Father sitting at the table looking as relaxed and affable as I could ever remember. Mother too seemed more at ease than I had ever seen her in his presence. She was flushed, her hair coming loose from its bun, auburn tendrils curling around her face and down the back of her neck. She had an excited, girlish air.

'Come away in, you two.' She spoke a little breathlessly as if she had been running. I noticed that one of the buttons on her blouse was undone and her petticoat hung down in a white scallop of lace below her black skirt.

'Wash your hands,' she said unnecessarily since we were already pouring warm water into the basin from the big steel jug that sat in the hearth. She began ladling soup into bowls, serving Father first. He took up the breadknife and cut four slices off a big, crusty loaf. The smell of the soup made our hungry mouths water and we hurried to sit up at table. Gerry was about to pick up his spoon when Mother hastily recalled him to his manners.

'When you're ready, Robert.' And Gerry remembered that we must always wait for Father to start eating.

To our surprise, he bowed his head and muttered something unintelligible, ending in what sounded like 'our bodies' use.' Then he picked up his spoon and we could follow suit a few seconds later.

'What was that you said, Father?' asked Gerry, always unable to contain his curiosity.

'That was grace before meals, you wee ignoramus,' replied Father. 'We say it out on the rock before every meal.'

'Are Euan and Calum right God-fearing men, then?' asked Mother, passing him the butter.

'Ach, it's more of a lighthouse thing,' he replied. 'The NLB expect all their keepers to be God-fearing, as you put it. So it's just become second nature. Besides,' he added, spreading butter thickly on the heel end of the bread, 'if you saw that lighthouse sticking up out of the rock and the sea raging around it, you'd be keeping in with the Almighty as well. The sound of the wind tearing at the window and the waves lashing right up against the door on a dark night is enough to drive any man to saying his prayers. "No unbelievers on the rock". That's what they say.' We were to hear the phrase 'on the rock' a lot from then on. Said with proud bravado, fear just below the surface

He paused to chew bread and sup soup for a few moments then resumed. 'I thought I was used to the sea but I've aye been in a fair-sized ship and moving through the water. It's no' the same somehow when you're stuck in a wee tower on a rock in the middle of the ocean.' He shuddered. 'There was a bad storm in the second week. I never got a wink o' sleep even though I was first watch till midnight and could have had eight hours sleep after that. It was like the wind and the sea were trying to tear the lighthouse off the rock.'

'That's like the story of the Lady of the Rock,' I said and earned a warning glance from Mother. Interrupting Father *and* talking at the table

89

when he was there: I was courting a double risk. But it seemed there was no end to his good humour that day.

'What story's that, Liza?' he asked. It was so unusual for him to speak my name except in anger that I was momentarily distracted and did not answer.

'Tell your father what the story is,' Mother prompted me, nodding her head and flashing her eyes by way of warning me not to rile him.

I began to relate the story I had read in *Tales and Legends* but I was nervous now, totally unaccustomed to the role of storyteller in his presence and anxious in case I was taking a liberty that would lead to retribution. As I stumbled through the tale, he quickly lost interest and cut across me, returning to his own exposition of life on the rock, describing in boring detail their daily tasks and routines. Mother maintained an attitude of admiring interest but Gerry and I fell to wondering if there would be second helpings of soup and looking forward to the fragrant, fruity steamed pudding that was sitting on the warm plate of the stove beside a big jug of custard.

There came upon our home then an atmosphere that I had never known. We – Mother, Gerry and I - had expected a routine similar to his Merchant Navy days: peace and good cheer when he was away; violence and misery when he was at home. Except that he would be at home more often and for longer periods. The realisation that he would be away every second month had initially cheered Mother as she had been under the depressing apprehension that, as a lighthouse keeper, he was to be coming home at the end of each working day. For the mercy that he had been at least posted to a rock lighthouse, where wives and families could not accompany the men, she was as thankful as I was. Without his black shadow over our lives, we had all settled quickly into life on The Islet. But the month had slipped by and our sunshine was about to be eclipsed once more. We all three held our breaths and tiptoed around him for the first few days but gradually we began to hope that he had changed.

The signs were good. He and the other two men who were his co-workers, Euan and Calum, had clearly formed a friendship. This was something of a miracle since they had to spend four weeks in such close proximity and without any other human society. The wives were full of tales of men falling out and fighting, of the NLB inspectors having to take measures to discipline them and even move men on to other posts if they could not live and work together on the rock. One of the wives, the mother of Earnest who had done the bible reading on our first Monday morning in school, spoke bitterly of having to leave Shetland just as she was making a really good friend because her husband and one of the other keepers had twice come to blows out on Muckle Flugga lighthouse. The second fight had been so bad that the other man had fallen – he insisted he had been pushed – off the rock and into the sea. He had been thrown a line and pulled back on to the rock by the third keeper on duty with them but had lodged a serious complaint with the NLB who had dealt with it by splitting up the warring keepers and sending them both away to other lights.

Mother and I, listening to this story, had feared that Father would follow this path too. But instead he seemed to have bonded with Euan and Calum and taken rock life in his stride. He boasted of learning to cook and demonstrated his new skill by making a fine pot of stovies and a loaf of soda bread. He had learned several new card games which he attempted to teach Gerry without much success. I watched and listened in on one of these sessions on an evening in the second week of his 'shore' spell.

'I dinna understand,' whined Gerry. 'How can I no' play that card?'

'It's the wrong suit. I've told ye that. That's a club and we're in diamonds just now.'

'But they look the same.'

'No they don't, ye stupid laddie. This one's black and this one's red.'

'So I could play *this* one then? It's red.'

'No. That's a heart. I just told ye: we're in diamonds.'

'But . . .' Gerry was near to tears. Father had no skill as a teacher and his explanation at the start had been brief and largely incomprehensible to Gerry. And he was rapidly losing patience which was making Gerry more nervous and less likely to think straight.

'I ken what to do,' I interrupted. 'I understand what the game's about. Let me play.'

'No!' Gerry did not want to give up this rare bout of attention from Father, however confused and frightened he was. 'You're just a girl. You can't play cards.'

'What nonsense!' Mother entered the fray. 'Ladies have been playing cards for centuries.'

'No they haven't,' Gerry pouted. 'Father learned this one out on the rock from Euan and Calum. *Izza* man's game.' He sniffed noisily and wiped his nose on his sleeve.

'Where's your handkerchief?' asked Mother automatically, coming over to the table. 'Let's start a new game. I'll help you, Gerry. Liza can take a hand as well and we'll see if she's any better than us.'

I held my breath, wondering if Father would accept this takeover, but he acquiesced easily and the four of us spent the next hour playing gin rummy while the rain battered on the dark windows and the fire crackled in the grate. Father and Mother tossed teasing quips across the table, challenging each other, sharing jokes, smiling and laughing. For the first time ever, I had an inkling of why they had married each other.

I had understood the game perfectly well from Father's explanations to Gerry but I was so entranced by the rare delight of feeling part of a safe, loving family that I did not concentrate so it came down to a needle match between Father and Mother. Of course, he won. Mother was not yet so taken in by his new persona that she would risk having him lose. But it was a close-run thing which made his glee in carrying the victory all the greater and he went off for his nightly walk round the islet laughing.

'I'll be back soon to collect my prize,' he said, winking at Mother as he lifted his oilskin coat off the peg. And he tramped off, out into the wet, blowy night.

'What prize is that, Mother?' asked Gerry. 'Father never said there was a prize.'

'Aye,' I said. 'I'd have tried harder if I'd known. What is it?'

'How should I ken?' replied Mother. 'Now, you two, off and get ready for bed. I'll have your cocoa ready in ten minutes.'

I remember noticing that she had a funny sort of giggle in her voice and her cheeks each had a hectic spot of red.


It was not until the Friday of the third 'shore' week that a cold draught blew in upon our cosy domestic scenario. Two things happened on the same day that changed things. Two bad things – and both of them my fault.

Father had been out all day on the boat with Euan and Calum. 'Going fishing,' he said, although there was not much of a catch to show for it when he returned. They left shortly after the bell had been rung for the start of another school day and did not return until twilight. We were well into November now and it was getting dark by four o'clock. Mother had been spending the afternoon along at Bridie's, Angus' mother's house. Gerry and Angus were now practically inseparable: they sat together in school, they stuck together in the playground and they spent almost all their free time together. They were kindred playmates. Together they created a cast of characters in a make-believe world and would often carry on the same game for days, talking for the characters in a range of voices, creating sets as carefully as any stage director and endlessly discussing the plot, changing the ending again and again. They had now produced several ongoing scenarios and plots which they picked up and progressed from time to time. There was never any chance of their plaguing adults with the timeworn complaint, 'I've got nothing to do'. As a result, they were indulgently left to get on with it. And, because the boys were so often in and out each other's houses, the mothers too became friends.

Gerry and I had been told to stop at Bridie's house on our way along the path after school. We were greeted by the smell of hot gingerbread – Bridie had been trying out one of Mother's recipes – and, of course, nothing else would do but that all we children sat down round the table to sample it. Angus' twin sisters, who were in the form below me, squashed me in between them and his wee brother and all six of us began rehashing what had happened that morning.

One of tinies had got out of his house unnoticed and followed the older children along the path to school. The last house in the row before the schoolhouse had a big, black dog called Seamus, a noisy creature rather terrifying to see and hear but well known to be harmless. Seamus had also wandered out unnoticed onto the path and, as was his way, begun to bark and leap up and down, seeking friendly fun but terrifying the tiny, who let out a piercing scream and commenced wailing and shrieking. Before any adult could come out to see the cause of the commotion, The Dow's dainty little marmalade cat, Ginty, who often came to school with her, shot out of the schoolhouse and was on the dog in a flash, hissing and spitting, lethal claws unsheathed for action.

It had been a great sight: the ball of orange fur flying through the air and landing on the broad black back; the startled dog quickly changing from barking to yelping as the feline claws sank through his coat into the back of his neck; the two animals careering along the path like horse and jockey in a race. The noise escalated: the tiny screaming; the dog yelping; the cat meowing; the children yelling encouragement to the animals; the wives rushing out of the houses, shouting at the animals and the children; The Dow appearing and ringing the school handbell with extra vigour. It was probable that the good folk of Knockvolgan farm heard and maybe even the crofters on Iona.

It had been brought to an end by the dog finally managing to shake off the cat and disappearing up the hill, still whining loudly. The cat, having executed a perfect landing from its whirling ejection off the dog's back, padded haughtily along the path, striped tail erect and twitching, acknowledging the cheers from the children as a queen to her subjects.

The Dow had called them in, as soon as she could make herself heard, and the excitement was over.

We were, all seven of us, recalling the event, everyone chipping in their own experience of it, vying for adjectives to describe the two animals and things to compare them to, with much laughter and talking over each other, when Mother suddenly stopped mid-sentence and stared at the kitchen door. One by one, we subsided and followed her gaze. Father was standing in the doorway, still wearing his oilskins and holding his rod from the fishing trip. How long he'd been there I do not know but it was immediately clear that he was not happy. I saw at once in his face the mean, dangerous man that I was only too familiar with.

He did not say anything. He did not have to. Mother rose at once, catching my eye and pulling Gerry up with her. Before the astonished Bridie, with the gingerbread not yet eaten and the tea in our cups still hot, she ushered us smartly towards the door.

'Thanks, Bridie,' she called back over her shoulder as she squeezed past Father and got all three of us out of the house and onto the path before we had time to protest. Not that I would have but Gerry still lacked a proper sense of self-preservation as far as Father was concerned. We almost ran back to our own house as if Father was actually chasing us although he was not. He did not need to.

We fell into our kitchen and Mother at once bade us to go to our rooms and make ourselves scarce. I hesitated, not wanting to abandon her, but she chased me out of the room before he came in. I did not go to my room. I stayed outside the door in the lobby and listened.

'. . . getting your feet under the table with the wife . . . carrying on with her man . . . slut, whore . . . '

These last two words were punctuated by a rattle of crockery and a crash. I guessed Father had thumped on the dresser.

'. . . got such an idea . . . never dream of . . .' That was mother' voice, bewildered and panicky but indignant too. Then, quite clearly, 'Where have you got such an idea, Robert?'

I pressed my ear to the door; then fell back horrified.

'Your own lassie told me. Liza kens what's going on.'

With horror, I remembered walking up to The Lookout with Father the day before. Lulled by almost three weeks of patience and even kindness from him, I had told him of my last visit there, of the David Balfour connection and of Arthur appearing.

'Aye, Arthur's a fine man.' It seemed Father had decided that everyone and everything connected with the lighthouse was fine. 'Did he say anything to you?'

94

# CHAPTER TWELVE

*I can think of nothing but . . . the trouble it is like to bring upon quite innocent persons.*
                                    Robert Louis Stevenson, from 'Kidnapped'

For the second time since arriving on Erraid, I prayed for protection. But this time I made myself quite clear to the deity. Besought with guilt for my thoughtless revelation of Arthur's remark about Mother, I begged for some kind of intervention that would check the rising tide of Father's jealous rage. Mother's denials and protests were as much about trying to *shoosh* him for the sake of the neighbours as to save herself from injury. They were having little effect, indeed he was warming to his subject and – I knew the signs only too well - working up to striking her when three sharp raps of the brass doorknocker on our front door cut across his ranting.

He stopped mid-phrase, checking his angry pacing, and it seemed as if the house ceased rocking, like a boat suddenly becalmed in a stormy sea. A woman's voice bit into the silence.

'Maggie! The inspector's here. His boat just came over.' A woman's anxious voice coming now from the door that led out to the back yard. I turned to see one of the wives coming into the passage. Before she could say any more, however, the doorknocker sounded again. The wife rolled her eyes at me, put a finger to her lips and shot out the back door.

I was now thoroughly frightened, the escalating noise of the doorknocker a drumbeat to my confusion and fear. I bolted into my bedroom and cowered there, listening to Mother's shaky voice as she confronted the source of the noise. Then I heard Father sounding hearty and cheerful again, like the person he had been since the start of his ore month. A third voice, tinny and precise, chimed in.

The doorstep exchange was over quickly but it had a remarkable effect. Mother and Father turned back into the house talking now in us collusion, as if putting aside their strife to confront a common . After a few minutes, I judged it safe and crept through to the .

at was that about?' I addressed my question to Mother but it was who replied.

was a man from the NLB. Says he's come to do an inspection. arrived – in the dark, would you believe? He's staying the night 's family. He'll be doing the inspection in the morning.'

'He said you're going to make a fine keeper,' I replied and saw Father's gratified smile.

'Anything else?' Father was liking these remembrances.

'I told him I got sick on the boats and he said I was to ask you to learn me some tricks.'

'What kind o' tricks?'

'To stop me getting sick. He said a sailor's daughter shouldna be getting seasick. Do you ken some tricks like that, Father?'

Father frowned and said nothing. Anxious to recapture his good mood, I remembered something else that Arthur had said.

'He said Mother was a fine woman.'

Father checked his stride and turned his gaze full on me. 'What's that? What did you say he said?'

'He said Mother was a fine woman,' I repeated and added, for good measure, 'He said it twice and he laughed after he'd said it.' As Father continued to stare at me, I grew nervous and began to babble. 'Wasn't that a nice thing to say about Mother? He seems a nice man. And his wife's nice too. Gerry's palled up with Angus so we see a lot of them. The whole family's really nice . . .' My twittering had petered out.

Father had said nothing beyond advising me to find another adjective. '"Nice" four times! Miss Dow would expect better from you, Liza.' Then we had reached the tower. Father had shown me a few semaphore moves so that I would be able to send a message out to the rock n time he was on duty.

All talk of Arthur Campbell and his family had been over. I' expended. Subject closed. Or so I had thought. Now I realise' horror that my innocent prattle was having awful consequences.

Mother had dropped into one of the fireside chairs. I saw that she was a strange colour, her face waxy and rather yellow, like a tallow candle. The hand she put up to smooth a strand of hair from her brow was shaking. I hastened to reassure her.

'We'll be fine, Mother. I polished the doorstep and knocker a couple o' days ago. And everything else is . . .' I glanced round the kitchen. Apart from a couple of chairs askew and some shards of broken china on the floor beside the dresser, it looked fine indeed to me.

'What are you talking about? What's the NLB man come for?' Alarm was writ plain on Father's face. The flush of angry jealousy was fading, leaving small streaks of red on his high cheekbones.

Mother said nothing. She leant back in the armchair, closing her eyes and letting her head loll against the antimacassar.

'What's going on? What's this NLB man here for?' repeated Father. Then, a thought striking him, 'What've you been up to while I was on The                                                                                           Rock?'

He took a step towards Mother and, without thinking, I sprang between them. 'It's just a thing they do to everyone . . . every house, I mean. They don't let any of us ken when they're coming. We heard the other wives talking about it.'

'What for?' Father narrowed his eyes as he switched his focus from Mother to me. 'What are they looking for?'

'It's all right, Robert. Honestly. Don't worry.' Mother's words came out in jerky puffs. 'It's just to make sure . . . looking after . . . stuff they've given us . . .' – she waved a hand round the room – '. . . keeping the houses clean. . . ..Like Liza says . . . nothing to worry about.' She flashed me a grateful smile and I glowed, realising that I was actually intervening in a fight between them at last.

Father too looked round the room, trying to see it with an inspector's eye. But he had no yardstick for this kind of scrutiny and quickly gave up. Mother continued to lie back in the chair looking quite sickly. The uneasy silence that fell was punctuated by the loud tick of the 'wag at the wall' clock. Not NLB issue - a family heirloom. So Mother had said as we had wrapped it up and put it in a box for transporting to Erraid.

A rap on the window made us all jump. The head and shoulders of either Euan or Calum – I hadn't yet quite distinguished the one from the other. The man made the well-known gesture of crooking his elbow and raising his cupped hand to his mouth. Father seized the diversion and was out of the house in a trice, slamming the door; but not before he called out: 'Get this bloody house spick and span. Not a hair out of place! God help the pair o' ye if we fail this inspection.'

97

I saw a surprised look on the man-at-the-window's face, perhaps at the swear word, perhaps at the threat. Then the two men were gone to wherever they went to drink and play cards. To the shelter of The Lookout maybe, or in the lee of the walls of the old ruined cottage. Gerry came wandering in, one sock at half-mast, school jacket buttoned up wrongly and, for some reason, his school cap on back to front. The sight of him galvanised Mother as it always did.

'Look at the state of you! Go and change out of your school clothes and wash those dirty hands. And your face,' she added as light from the lamp fell on him. 'You too, Liza.' She turned to me and I swelled with pride at the gratitude in her smile, the guilt of my indiscretion over Arthur feeling less acute.

'Will I put on my "dirties" apron? Are we going to be cleaning?'

'No, we are not,' she said with a defiant tilt of her head. 'Inspection indeed! I don't need any pipsqueak pen-pusher from the Lighthouse Board showing me how to run my house.'

'But Father said . . .'

'And what does *he* ken about keeping a house clean? All he ever does is make a mess of it with his socks and drawers flung on the floor and his cigarette ash everywhere.'

She was brave was Mother – when Father wasn't there. I just hoped she knew what she was doing. I resolved to give the door brasses another wee bit of Brasso and some elbow grease anyway before tomorrow morning.


The second bad thing to spoil our temporary respite, which was, as I have said, also my fault, came hard on the heels of the row about Arthur's compliment to Mother.

Father came back in time for 'tea', which was what we called the meal at half past five. It was a lesser repast than the midday dinner, usually eggs of some kind followed by scones or pancakes with jam. I was sitting at our open front door polishing the brass doorknob and knocker as if my life depended on it – at least my life on Erraid, which suddenly seemed precious and under threat – when I saw a green felt hat, anchored by a large hairpin, bobbing along the top of the high wall that ran along the bottom of the front gardens. It belonged to The Dow. She wore it most days now, as winter turned the weather wet and windy. She was obviously striding along the path which ran behind the wall and led up towards The Lookout past the ruined cottage. I carried on with my polishing but kept an eye on the wall to see if and when she came back.

She did not but Father did. I dropped my tin of Brasso and the old vest, which was ending its days as a polishing rag, into the cleaning basket and hurried into the house.

We ate in almost silence, only Gerry unaware of the tension, immersed in one of his imaginary worlds. Father did not wait for a second cup of tea that night but, to my relief, headed out once more as soon as he had eaten. Once again, he bade us get the house up to inspection standard. Then he was gone again. We heard him begin a cheerful, tuneless whistle as he tramped off along the path.

I did not think any more about either Father or The Dow that evening. Mother, for all her bravado, was nervous about the impending inspection and decided we had best make some acknowledgement of it. I was put to black-leading the range and Brasso-ing the knobs of its four little doors while Mother changed the bed linen and polished the furniture. To our surprise, several of the wives dropped by – each for a short time alone, as if they had organised a sort of relay race – and offered to take on a task.

'The first visit's a bugger,' said Bridie, who was the first to call. 'He tries to put the fear o' God in ye so ye'll run around like a hen wi' its head cut off before he comes all the other times. An' he picks on the daftest things. Finds something new every time to carp about. It's a right pain in the arse.' Bridie's salty language was part of her charm, her rich Irish accent masking the impact, covering any crudeness. She produced a damp chamois leather from her apron pocket and fell to cleaning the windows, inside and out. 'Ye'll need to give the outsides another rub over in the morning. He never starts until nine so ye'll have time.' The permanent sea-spray that blew in the wind and hung in the early morning mists coated everything with a patina that attracted dust and trapped tiny insects.

Mother and I were, at first, rather affronted by the implied insult to our housekeeping standards but there was no stopping the wives and we soon saw that, rather than being a barrage of criticism, this was sisterly solidarity in action. As Bridie said, 'We're no' letting any damn man get the better o' us.' Only Jenny, Calum's wife, did not come. Her job was to entertain the inspector and keep him out of the way until our house was ready for his fault-finding eye.

Of Father, there was no sign and we were glad of it. The wife who had called at the back door with the warning about the inspector and who had possibly heard Father shouting those horrible accusations at Mother – I think it was the one called Kitty – came and did her stint without any mention of Father. Mother held her head up and quelled any curiosity or sympathy by sheer force of dignity and tacit denial. The wives

99

would be no more allowed to express negative opinions of Father than Gerry and I were.

As I slipped down to the bottom of the front garden at nine o'clock for my pre-bedtime visit to the 'lavvie', I again saw the green hat bobbing by, this time in the opposite direction and this time without its hatpin and slightly askew. Shortly after that, Father came home and I hurried off to bed. He liked Gerry and me to be 'off the floor' by nine o'clock in the evening. Although I lay with ears cocked for further unpleasantness, I heard only a low rumble of voices in the kitchen and eventually I drifted off to sleep.

Mother had us up with the lark. No Saturday lie-in for us. It was a dark, dingy sort of morning, one of those November ones that make the birdsong dawns of spring seem mere wishful thinking. I would not have believed there was anything left to dust, wash or polish but she set a new standard that day. Even as Gerry and I sat supping our porridge at the table, she was rubbing away at its legs and brushing the carvings on them with an old toothbrush.

'Where's Father?' asked Gerry. 'Is he no' having to get ready for the mannie coming as well?'

'I gave him his porridge in bed,' replied Mother, turning her attentions to the range, brushing away invisible particles of ash.

Gerry threw a glance in the direction of the green chenille curtain that screened the bed recess. 'What for? Is he no' well?'

'He's fine, Gerry. I just wanted to get breakfast over quickly and he didn't want to get up that early. He'll be up soon.' She spoke with emphasis as if asserting it could make it sure to happen. 'Now, finish up your breakfast and get ready to go out.'

'Where to?'

'Just out to play. I want you two out of the house before the man comes.'

'What for?'

'So that I can get the last minute jobs done and know one of you won't undo them again before he comes.'

'What sort of jobs?'

'Making your beds, tidying the shoe-rack, sweeping the floor . . .'

'And don't forget to do the outsides of the windows again,' I chimed in. 'Mind what Mrs Campbell said.'

'I'm not forgetting, Liza. That's your job this morning. Take the shammy out with you and just keep it till he's finished the inspection.'

'Why is it called a shammy?' asked Gerry.

'How would I know? Get on with your porridge. I'm clearing this table in two minutes whether you've finished or not.'

'Is it because it's like a kiddy-on thing?'

'What are you talking about now?'

'Like when we say something's a sham, no' the real McCoy. Is it a sham for a duster?'

'I don't know, son. Now please . . .'

'But Miss Dow said we can only learn if we ask questions. Is it a sham for something else then?'

'Oh, Gerry. I . . .'

'Stop pestering your mother like that.' Father burst through the chenille curtains like an actor on cue. His voice, always rough, was like a dog's bark first thing in the morning. He strode across the floor and gave the side of Gerry's head a sharp flip as he passed on his way out to the 'lavvie'. Gerry squawked as if mortally wounded, although, as 'thick ears' went, it had been pretty mild. He also dropped his spoon into his bowl. He had eaten most of the porridge and only some grey, speckled milk remained. It splashed over the table and on to the floor. A few tiny lumps slid down one of the recently tooth-brushed legs.

'That's it.' Mother seized both our bowls, although I still had over a half of mine to eat. 'Get away out NOW! No arguments. Coats on, hats and gloves too – it's damp this morning – and OUT to play. Liza, don't forget the shammy. Leave it in the toilet when you've done the windows. No, wait, he might inspect in there as well, or need to use it . . .'

'I'll put in round the back behind the rain-barrel. Dinna panic, Mother. The house is like a palace. You'll pass with flying colours. Bound to.'

'Who's panicking?' squeaked Mother.


There were no other children around and Gerry was still sulking about his thick ear when I finished cleaning the windows. Once I had returned the ladder to its place beside the spades and rakes in the wee shed and put the 'shammy' behind the barrel, I took his hand and dragged him, still snivelling, along the path and out to join the track that led up to The Lookout. The damp air was settling into a fine, soaking mist and I wanted to get some shelter. Who knew how long the inspector would be in starting or how long he would take?

The morning mist was beginning to clear and allow what little sunlight we would have that day to break through. Gerry and I trudged up the hill, he still snivelling and dragging his feet, me just wanting to warm

101

myself up by the effort of climbing. I kept my eyes on the ground, picking our way over the marshy terrain, skipping from boulder to boulder to avoid deep patches of muddy water. Gerry almost slipped into the mud a few times but I dragged him on impatiently, ignoring his whining.

'What are we going up here for?' he demanded more than once. I gave him no reply. In truth, I was not sure myself. It was not simply for shelter from the cold and damp – I could have got that from any of the wives or even gone into the big bothy where community meetings and the Sunday services were held – but rather a feeling that there was some reason that I must go to The Lookout that morning. Within a short time, we were at the door.

'What are we going to do?' asked Gerry. 'What have we come awa' up here for?'

I did not answer. Then, for some strange reason, I knocked on the little door.

'Is there someone in there?' whispered Gerry, catching my trepidation. 'Is it a ghost?' he added fearfully. I remembered how he had hung back the other times we had come here, once or twice with Mother and once on a school excursion when The Dow had spoken about the building of the two lighthouses. I had covered myself in glory that day by knowing who had built them and the connections with Robert Louis Stevenson and *Kidnapped*. The Dow had bidden the other children, who had heard the story several times before, not to answer her questions and had directed her steely gaze upon me. She rarely paid me any attention, reserving it all for Gerry. It was my moment of triumph. I had recited the story of poor David Balfour on Erraid and had even gone on to describe his adventures on Mull before he and the Jacobite, Alan Breck, had found a ship to take them over to the mainland. The Dow had cut me off quite quickly. 'Just so, Liza. Yes, that's quite correct. Thank you.' It was clearly not in her vision of things to have me as the centre of attention. But I remembered my triumph with a smug glow.

Now I pushed open the door and thrust Gerry inside, warning him not to touch the telescope. I did not want any trouble, not with Father in his current mood. The tiny, round room smelt musty and the floor was gritty with sand and dried mud. The three small windows revealed swirls of clammy mist shot through with occasional arrows of watery sunlight. It was bitterly cold and, when I closed the door, the cold seemed to intensify so that it felt as if we were in an icehouse.

'I'm awf'y cold,' whined Gerry. Can we no' go back home?'

102

I shushed him at once, instinctively, as if someone nearby was listening and, in truth, there was an eerie sense of a presence in the little room that morning. Quite different from the other visits I had made. It no longer felt like the friendly, fascinating place where I had sat re-reading my favourite chapter of *Kidnapped*.

'What have we come up here for, Liza? Can we no' go down to Angus' house? Mrs Campbell will let us stay there 'til the inspector mannie goes.' Gerry tugged at my hand and I almost gave in. There did indeed seem to be no point in freezing up here. The imperative that had driven me to drag Gerry up here this morning was slipping away.

Then my foot struck something on the floor, something hard that skittered over the boards and fetched up against one of the legs of the telescope. I looked down to see a hatpin and, when I bent to pick it up, I knew at once that it was The Dow's. I remembered the green felt hat bobbing first one way, and then later the other way, along the top of the garden wall last night. I also remembered that the hat had been askew on the way back and lacking its hatpin. I picked the pin up and put it in my pocket. As I did so, I saw two cigarette butts, stubbed out and kicked under the bench that ran around one side.

# CHAPTER THIRTEEN

*A thunder bolt seemed to strike me. I saw a great flash of fire and fell senseless.*
*Robert Louis Stevenson, from 'Kidnapped'*

I gave in to Gerry's whines and let him pull me outside and back down the hill.     'We're no' goin' to Angus' house, though,' I warned him.

'Why no'? I want to go and play with him. How can we no' go there? I want to . . . I want to . . . I want . . .'

'Stop it!' I halted and turned to face him. 'Do you want Father to get angry again? You saw how he was yesterday when he saw us all sitting together at their table.'

'But why? What's wrong wi' visiting their house. We've been doin' it for weeks. I want to . . .'

'Shut up!' I exploded. 'We're no' going an' that's final.'

Gerry burst into tears and I had to half-drag him down the rest of the hill.

'Let's go an' see Seamus. Maybe we can take him out for a walk.'

This was an inspired idea as Gerry loved the big dog and he and Angus had featured him in several of their games. Seamus had the sweetest of tempers and had even permitted the boys to drape him with 'robes' and put a cardboard crown on his enormous, sleek head. It had lasted all of one minute until Seamus had spotted a passing rabbit and leapt off in pursuit, barking like mad. But the boys had easily incorporated this into their fantasy game.

I threw a glance at our house as we passed it but the door was closed and there was nothing to see. I thought I heard men's voices – Father and the inspector, presumably – but I did not falter in my brisk progress along to the last house before the school. Seamus was tied up on a long rope in the front garden, gnawing at a bone. He leapt up, barking a welcome when we approached him, and the door of the house was opened quickly by one of the wives – I think it was Jenny, who had had the 'NLB mannie' as an overnight guest.

'How is it goin' wi' the inspector?' she asked.

I shrugged. 'I don't know. We were put out o' the house afore he came. We've nothing to do. Can we take Seamus for a walk?

She consented; so we untied the dog and set off with him. 'Let's go over to Davy Balfour's Bay,' I suggested and Gerry was happy to agree so long as he got to hold the lead all the way. The rain had eased, the mist had lifted completely and the sky was a pale, pearly blue with the hint of a rainbow. I judged it would be fine over at the bay for a few hours.

We walked briskly, Seamus setting the pace, towing Gerry, and soon we were there. He and Seamus took to cavorting along the shore line, dodging the waves of the incoming tide. I sat on a rock and thought. What was the meaning of the hatpin and the two cigarette butts in The Lookout? Had Father and The Dow met last night up at The Lookout? It was surely *her* hatpin but were the cigarettes from Father's pack?

'Ye're looking awf'y sad, Liza. What's wrong?' Gerry flopped down panting beside me. Seamus lolled his big tongue and drooled on my feet. I snatched them away and stood up.

'I'm no' sad, Gerry love. Just thinking – ye ken, puzzling, trying to work something out.'

'What? Tell me. I'll help ye work it out.'

'No It's nothing to do wi' you. Come on. Let's go back and see if the inspector has finished.'

But he was not so easily put off. He could be worse than Seamus with a bone. He narked and persisted all the way back and eventually, in irritation, I told him.

'But why would Father and Miss Dow want to go up to The Lookout together?'

'They didn't go together. I think they maybe met up there though.'

'But why?'

'I don't know. That's what's puzzling me. And it might no' have been Father at all. Might have been one o' the other men.'

'Can we no' just ask him?'

'No! Absolutely not! Ye're no' to say a *word* about this to him. Promise me.'

He promised, obviously enjoying being in on the secret, nodding his head vigorously. 'I won't say anything to him, Liza.' He added a phrase that he and Angus had been using a lot in their games lately. 'Yer secret's safe with me.'

'It had better be,' I warned him.


When we returned Seamus to his bone in the garden, Jenny told us that the inspector had left. 'He came back along to collect his wee valise about half an hour ago and Calum's away takin' him up to Salen in the boat so he can catch the ferry.'

'Did we pass?' I asked fearfully.

'I dinna ken, lass. He wouldna have said to me anyway and I've no' seen your ma and pa yet to ask. Yer door has been shut ever since he left.'

I did not like the sound of that and we proceeded cautiously along the path to our own house. As Jenny had said, the door was closed and I could see nothing or no one at the window. I tried the handle carefully but the door was locked.

'How can we no' get in?' demanded Gerry. 'I'm starving. It must be dinner time by now.'

He made to knock but I caught his fist before it could make contact with the door. 'Patience! Let's wait and see if . . . Oh my heavens! Look out!'

I snatched his arm and dragged him sharply away from the house as the window exploded into a shower of splintered glass. I felt needle-sharp rain on my face and cried out again. 'Oh my heavens!' Then something heavy struck me full on the chest, knocking me off my feet. I went over backwards, still clutching Gerry's arm and pulling him on top of me. I felt rather than saw another missile flying over my head, thankfully missing it by a few inches.

I lay winded on the path, aware of Gerry struggling to his feet and screaming like a banshee. A moment later, I was aware of a woman's voice telling me to lie still until I felt able to get up. I thought it must surely be Mother but, as the fog in my brain cleared, I saw that it was Bridie Campbell. She was cradling Gerry in her arms, murmuring incomprehensible endearments – Irish stuff, I supposed. Then the whole row of houses seemed to erupt with women, children, dogs and even a couple of curious cats. Within moments, Gerry, Bridie and I were surrounded but of Mother or Father there was no sign.

I sat up and accepted a hand from one of the wives to pull myself up. I was recovering from my shock now and could take in the sight of our kitchen window completely smashed and three cast iron pots lying among the broken glass.

'Oh, no,' I whispered. 'Oh, no. The pots under the bed. The brass pots. We forgot about them.' I began to weep. We had worked so hard to make everything perfectly spick and span. But we had completely forgotten the NLB-issue brass pots which Mother had consigned to a hiding-place under the bed while she unpacked and installed her own favourite cast iron ones. The inspector had no doubt homed in on the missing brass pots, wanting to see how shiny they were. After more than a month gathering stour under the bed, they would surely be dusty and

106

dim. We had failed the inspection and Father was furious. Furious to the point of throwing the cast iron pots out the window.

'Where's Mother?' I jerked myself out of the clutches of a clucking wife and lurched unsteadily toward the door. If Father was angry enough to smash the pots through the window, what might he have done to Mother?

Even as I raised a hand to hammer on the door, it flew open. Father's hand shot out and pulled me into the house, thrusting me behind him and striding onto the path to snatch Gerry from Bridie.

'Get away home the lot o' ye!' he yelled. 'Have ye nothing better to do than stick yer noses in where they're no' wanted?' He made a menacing step towards the gaggle of women and children and they backed away. He dragged Gerry by the hand, almost lifting him off the ground, and threw him into the house. I was still cowering in the lobby but I grabbed Gerry and bolted up the short passage into my bedroom. I shut the door and dragged a chair up under the handle. Then I put my arms round the hysterical Gerry and we fell on my bed, sobbing together in a tangle of wet coats, muddy boots and rumpled blankets.


A long time seemed to pass but perhaps it was just our fear and hunger that made it seem so. The house was full of a heavy silence, as if it too held its breath, unable to imagine what would happen next. My mind was full of a hateful image of Mother lying on the floor in the kitchen, injured, bleeding – or worse. At last, I saw the door handle turn and the chair under it scraped forward a little.

'Liza! Gerry! What are you doing? Let me in.' It was Mother sounding anxious but quite steady. She was not lying on the floor, at least.

I thrust Gerry behind me and crept to the door. I leaned on the chair, closing the door again. 'Has he gone?' I whispered, despising myself for the coward I was.

'Aye. Calum came back in the boat from taking the inspector to Salen. He took your Father away somewhere.'

'But . . . Is he coming back?' I was crying now as much from shame as from fear. She had faced his rage alone while I hid like a rabbit down a hole. He had gone and I was still holding back from going to comfort her.

'Open the door, Liza.' Mother's voice was stronger now, more like her usual confident self when dealing with Gerry and me. 'This is nonsense. Come out of there at once.'

I obeyed of course. Twelve years of firm upbringing saw to that. As soon as I had dragged the chair away, Mother was in and over to the bed to scoop Gerry up from the tangle of bedclothes where he lay wide-eyed, face streaked with snot and the channels that his tears had made in his dirty face.

'Look at the state of you! My poor wee lamb. Liza, go and get a bucket of water and put it on the stove. This wee fellow needs a good wash.'

'But . . .' I glanced fearfully out into the lobby. 'Is Father outside? Is he still angry?'

Mother glared at me. 'Will you do as you're told at once, Liza?' Then, softening, seeing perhaps the signs of tears on my face too, 'Your Father's still out with Calum. I think they've gone fishing. He'll no' be back for a while.' She shooed me gently out of the room and towards the back door. 'The bucket's out there beside the rain barrel. Quick now.'

And that was all the discussion I could get from her about the incident. She served us bannocks and cheese washed down with hot water – she was a great believer in the health-giving properties of warm, boiled water – while we waited for the bucket to heat. Then she undressed Gerry, lifted him onto the draining board and gave him a thorough wash. I was given a jugful of the hot water to take into my room and use at my washstand. It was as if Mother was trying to wash away the trauma and the public shame of it all.

Yet I could see no signs of injury or abuse: no bruises or cuts on her face, no limp, no grimaces of pain as she used her arms and hands. If Father had vented his spleen on her as well as the iron pots, he had left no marks. For this, at least, I was thankful. Father had let the whole world – or, at least, the whole of our little world – see his foul temper but we might yet manage to hide his cruelty to his wife and children.

I had barely finished my ablutions when I heard a male voice in the house. My heart leapt in fear but I quickly realised that it was Euan, the other 'shore' keeper that month. I crept shyly along the lobby and stood listening at the kitchen door.

'Thank you very much. How very kind.' Mother was at her stateliest. 'I can't think how I came to overlook the brass pots. Entirely my fault, of course. Robert was so disappointed, you know, and he lost his temper for a moment. Quite unlike him. It's just that this job means so much to him . . . to us all . . . '

'Dinna fash yersel', Missus Galway. I'll have yer window patched up in no time. A bittie wood to keep the weather out for jist now. When Calum and yer man get back, I'll tak the boat round to Bunessan. There's a yard there'll give me a sheet o' glass. It'll be good as new in a day or two.

Cannae do it tomorrow, it bein' Sunday, but it'll be first on ma list Monday morning.'

'And what . . .' I could hear the strain in Mother's voice. 'What will the NLB say about it? This will surely be the last straw after we failed the inspection?'

'Och, cheer up, lass.' I could hear the sound of glass tinkling on to the floor and guessed he was removing the remaining jagged glass around the edges of the window. 'Whit makes ye think ye failed the inspection? There's never any family does that. Been twelve years in this job, four lights, never heard o' such a thing. I reckon you'd have to be doin' a lot worse than sticking their damned brass pots under the bed.'

'But the inspector was so unpleasant about it. I was sure we'd failed. So was Robert.'

Euan snorted. 'Damned wee dictators! That job only gets done by jumped-up sissies. I'd like to see them out on the rock in the middle o' winter wi' a Force Ten blowin'. Na! Ye've nothing to worry about. Ye keep a bonnie hoose, anybody can see that.'

'But the window!' wailed Mother and I sympathised so much with her at that moment. We had come through the dreaded inspection after all, only to shoot ourselves in the foot with the smashed window. It was too cruel.

'What about it?' Euan was shouting now above the noise of hammering nails into wood.

'Won't the Board be furious? It's wanton damage to their property.'

'They might be if they knew,' said Calum simply. 'Who's goin' to be tellin them? Ye'll no' find anyone here to do that. Rock families stick together. The last thing anyone here would be doin' is clyping to the Board. Set yer mind at rest, lass. Could ye hand me up those nails now?'

I wanted to rush into the room and throw my arms round Euan. He seemed to me like some kind of magician. A wave of his wand and all our problems were gone. Well, some of them, anyway. The worst ones – for the moment.

Calum, too, obviously had a touch of magic about him. He brought Father back later in the afternoon, the two of them seeming in good fettle, joking and laughing as they handed the boat over to Euan who set off immediately for the yard in Bunessan. Mother welcomed Father back calmly, armed with the good news of our escape from seeming disaster. She made no reference to the window and had a fragrant, mouth-watering stew cooking in the largest brass pot. The iron pots were now the occupants of the under-the-bed space and the brass ones had been polished to gleaming gold by Mother and me.

'We were worrying ourselves about nothing, Robert,' she said with an over-bright laugh. 'The others' – she avoided mentioning Euan by name – 'tell me that no one ever actually fails an inspection. The inspectors just act severe to frighten us.'

'Aye, that's what Calum was saying as well,' he agreed, sounding quite amiable. Nothing to worry about.' And he suddenly lurched across the kitchen towards her. She cowered instinctively but he only ducked her under the chin and gave her a smacking kiss on the lips.

'Maybe cause for a wee celebration. What d'ye say, Maggie, my bonnie lassie?' He took a half bottle of whisky out of his pocket and waved it in her face.

'He's drunk,' I thought anxiously. He was an unexploded bomb when drunk.

'Get a couple of tumblers, Liza,' said Mother and I obeyed quickly. I left them there then, celebrating their near-miss in the inspection, carefully ignoring the boarded-up window. I crept out of the house into the darkening late afternoon. Gerry was along at Angus' house and I was sorely in need of some solitude. I took my torch and headed up the hill towards The Lookout.


I had been up here so often that I surefooted my way in the falling darkness without once needing the torch. The three small windows all faced out to sea so I was quite unaware, until I pushed open the door, that there was a candle burning inside. I got such a fright that I almost dropped the torch.

'Ah, Liza, I thought it might be you. In search of some solitude, my dear?'

Her words echoed my thoughts exactly but, far from feeling comforted, I only felt exposed. I had come to consider The Lookout as my sanctuary. I could leave the house and be up here in less than ten minutes, when not encumbered with Gerry, and had done so almost on a daily basis for the past six weeks, rarely finding anyone else in it and only occasionally being interrupted. While Gerry was off playing with Angus, and Mother assumed I was with some of the other girls, I would be here in my hidey-hole, sometimes reading, sometimes just gazing out to sea, lost in thought and weaving stories in my head. Once I had tried looking through the telescope but I was not really tall enough and I was afraid to start adjusting it. On a clear day, the lighthouse could be glimpsed, a hazy finger bisecting the south west horizon. I loved the sense of being above the rest of the world, part of sea-and-sky immensity.

'Sorry, Miss,' I mumbled and made to back out again.

'Ma'am, Liza. Not Miss.'

'Sorry, Ma'am.'

'Come in, child. You have as much right to be here as me. Indeed more, if occupancy rates over the last two months are anything to go by.'

I was not sure of her meaning but the 'come in' was as peremptory and compelling as every order she gave. I stepped into the candlelight and stood in the centre of the little tower just behind the telescope. She was sitting at the end of the bench as close to the window as was possible.

'Close the door.' I did so and returned to my spot. She regarded me thoughtfully. 'How are your father and mother?'

Was it my imagination? Was their more emphasis on the word 'mother'?

'Fine, thank you, Miss . . . I mean, Ma'am.'

She regarded me thoughtfully for a moment, as if toying with me, and I squirmed under her gaze. It was really intolerable to be made to feel as if I was at school, called out to the front to be grilled over some misdemeanour and being made to wait while she decided my punishment. And in The Lookout – *my* Lookout, as I had come to think of it – of all places. Now I would never feel safe here again. She had spoiled everything. I felt my intense dislike of her, which had been instinctive from the start, rise up to choke me.

'What are you doing here?' I burst out. 'What are you wanting?'

She did not answer, only looked out the window and pointed. 'Do you see that pinprick of light going on and off? Do you?'

'Of course,' I replied irritably.

'Do you know what it is?'

'Of course,' I said again, even more irritably. 'It's the Lighthouse. It's the reason we're all here.' My impatient tone implied her question was a stupid one and she swung round to stab a long, slightly crooked finger at me.

'Don't play smart with me, young lady. Remember who I am.'

Some devil was in me. Perhaps because of the strain of the day's events, I was angry and reckless. 'We're not in school now. You can't tell me what to do. Not up here.' I swept a hand around the tiny room, meaning to encompass the whole panorama of sea and sky.

Her eyes widened and she rose from the bench to loom over me. 'I am your teacher on Erraid whether in school or out, whether during school hours or not. You had better apologise for that insolence or you will be sorry.'

I primped my mouth into a tight line as if to stop any word of apology escaping. I tilted back my head and stared her down.

'Your Father shall hear of this. He will know how to bring you to heel.'

'Him!' I spat out the word. I think it was a kind of backlash from the shame I had felt because of my craven behaviour, hiding behind a barricaded door and once again leaving Mother to face his fury alone. I was on the cusp of adulthood, able now to appreciate what she was going through but unable to help her, afraid even to try. But I was not afraid of The Dow, I suddenly realised. 'He's nothing but a drunken bully. Gerry and I . . .'

She was on me in a flash, gripping my shoulder and shaking me. 'Has your Father hurt Gerrard? Was he cut when the window broke over him?' Her eyes bored into me and I saw fear and – could it be? - pleading.

'What's it to you?' I said. 'What do you care about our family? Why can't you leave us all alone?'

'You impertinent . . ! Your Father will . . .'

'And when will you be telling him?' I was out of control now, beyond discretion or self- preservation. 'Will it be at one of your cosy wee meetings with him up here?'

For a moment I wondered what the sharp crunch was and where the ringing soud in my ears was coming from. Then I realised that she had slapped me across the side of my face so hard that I had fallen back and cracked my head on the door.

# CHAPTER FOURTEEN

*They broke before (me) like water, turning and running and falling, one against another in their haste.*

*Robert Louis Stevenson, from 'Kidnapped'*

'Liza! Liza! Wake up, for goodness sake.'

I half-opened my eyes and saw a shimmering blur that gradually resolved into my wee brother's face.

'Come on, Liza, wake up,' he repeated. 'Mother's fair worried where you are. She sent me out to look for you. It's near bedtime. We've got to get back before Father comes home or we'll catch it. Come ON!'

He shook my shoulder and I groaned as a sickening pain surged through my head. It seemed to come from the back of my neck and sweep through my mouth up to my eyes so that my vision blurred still more. A fierce wave of nausea gripped me and, turning my head away from him, I vomited half-digested bannocks and cheese on to the floor of The Lookout.

Gerry sprang back to avoid it and staggered into the telescope. It hit him a painful blow between the shoulders. He yelped and burst into tears.

Habit dies hard. Quickly wiping my mouth with my sleeve, I struggled to a sitting position and held out my arms to comfort him. He made a wide circle round to my other side, avoiding the vomit, dropped to his knees and snuffled miserably into my shaking embrace. I closed my eyes and let the dizziness have its way for a minute while I massaged his sore back and murmured words of comfort. After a while, the awkward position began to give me a sore back as well and that, mixed with the stench of sickness in the small space, brought me to my senses. Pushing him gently from me, I got slowly to my feet and took control of the situation as best I could.

'Go back down to the house and tell Mother I was  . . I've been . . . tell her I've had a wee accident.' Something stopped me saying what had actually happened although it was becoming quite clear in my memory as the dizziness receded. The exchange with The Dow, her violent reaction to my reference to her meeting Father up here, these were not things I was ready to divulge, especially to Mother. That, at least, I could protect her from. 'Get her to bring something to clean up this mess.' I gestured at the stinking pile on the floor.

'But I've hurt my back,' he whined. 'I dinna feel like going away down there on my own.'

'Well you'll have to. I would come with you but I need to stay here in case anyone else comes up and wants to get in. They'd likely stand on it, maybe slip and hurt themselves. I've got to stay here to warn them.'

'But . . .' He began to wail again.

'Just GO!' I pushed him out of the door. Then, 'NO! GO!' as he tried to come back in.

I was frantic now to get past this hideous moment of fear and embarrassment, to be on the other side of it, back down the hill and safe at home. I was trembling and very close to tears myself. He did, at last, start to make his way back down the hill.

It was raining lightly now, that fine, soaking mist that is such a speciality of The Hebrides, and I was shivering as much from shock and pain as from cold and wet. Even so, I could not bear to be in The Lookout any more. It was not just the stench. The place itself, which I had so grown to love in the short time we had lived on Erraid, had become a place of horror for me. I was filled with hatred for The Dow who had sullied it with her bullying and bad temper. And it was the place of their trysts, she and my Father meeting there behind Mother's back while he pretended to be going for just 'a wee walk round the islet before bedtime.' He had been doing that regularly, I realised now, thinking back over his 'shore' month. Perhaps I was not quite old enough to comprehend fully the implications of his behaviour, but I knew that repeated clandestine rendezvous with another woman were no way for a married man to behave. 'Poor mother,' I thought. 'Poor, poor woman.'

It was not, however, a 'poor woman' who appeared over the brow of the hill some twenty minutes later. Mother was raging at me with the fury that often follows anxiety and fear, once they are relieved.

'What the *hell* are you doing up here at this time of night? And all on your own! No wonder you had an accident. It's pitch black tonight.' As if to emphasise her point, the lighthouse darted its far-off beam on the horizon, swooping once and then gone. 'Have you no sense at all, you stupid, wicked girl?' She had our big rubber torch with her and she shone its yellow beam on my face. 'What happened? Where are you hurt?'

'I fell. I must have tripped over my shoelace . . . hit my head on the wall . . . or the door . . . not sure.'

'And if I hadn't asked Gerry where you might be and if he hadn't known to look here – good wee lad that he is – you could have been lying here the whole night. Frozen to the floor by morning.'

I thought it unlikely. I would surely have come to of my senses of my own accord eventually and at least tried to make my way back down. But I said nothing, judging it best to let Mother's anger run its course.

'And you've been vomiting, Gerry said?'

'I couldn't help it. As soon as Gerry touched me - he sort of shook me - it just came out. I couldn't stop it. I'm sorry.' My eyes filled with tears again.

She abruptly changed her manner and now her relieved anxiety took a different course. She gathered me into her arms and let me have a few moments of hiccupping and sniffling against her comfortable bosom before bidding me sit on a nearby rock while she cleaned up my mess. I saw now that she had brought a bag containing a small shovel, an old newspaper, two beer bottles full of soapy water, an old towel and a metal can of Jeyes Fluid. Within a few minutes, she had removed all traces of my misdemeanour and The Lookout smelled only of the powerful disinfectant. The bag now contained an unsavoury newspaper parcel, two empty bottles, a sodden towel and the remains of the Jeyes.

'Let's go,' she said brusquely but not unkindly. 'Just pray we get back before your Father does.' We both prayed hard as we scrambled down the rough path.


Gerry and I were both abed when Father came home that night and no more was said by either parent about the inspector's visit. Nor did Mother mention my escapade at The Lookout. But Gerry was another thing altogether. There never was a boy to whine and wheedle like him and he had such a nose for information that was being withheld. Monday morning found him still pestering me about what he called 'the real story' of what had happened at The Lookout on Saturday night

'For heaven's sake,' I burst out as we walked along the path to the house for our midday dinner, 'can you no' leave me alone?'

'No' until you tell me who hit you.'

'No one hit me. I fell. I've told you a hundred times.'

'And I've said I dinna believe you a hundred and one times. You're a liar, Liza Galway.' And he began to chant: 'Liar! Liar! Breeks on fire!'

A few of the other children, walking ahead, heard him and slowed their pace to join in, although they had no idea what I was supposed to have lied about. I was scarlet with embarrassment and annoyance by the time I reached our house and hastened through its door, pulling Gerry in behind me and slamming it.

I thought that was an end to it but, to my horror, when we returned for afternoon school, I found the three children who had been taunting me were telling The Dow about it. I had kept my head down all morning, avoiding her eye, not even volunteering to help out with the first form which I usually liked to do. She, for her part, had ignored me completely.

'Miss Dow's going to find out what you've been telling lies about,' said Kirsty, one of Angus' sisters with lip-smacking righteousness. 'Aren't you, Ma'am?'

'Aye, go on, Ma'am. Ask her! Ask her!' cried the other two and children coming into the classroom, took up the chant without the slightest idea what they were supporting.

The Dow looked over their heads straight at me, no doubt noting the bruise on my cheek and the pallor which had persisted despite a day of what Father called 'mollycoddling' when I had lain abed till dinnertime, been excused from attending the church service in the big barn and given only light, nourishing food and much kindness from Mother.

I met The Dow's stare boldly, facing her down just as I had done in The Lookout the night before. She was the first to look away and turned to shooing the three tale-telling girls to their seats. She was kinder to me that afternoon than ever before, much kinder, given that she had previously passed me over in favour of Gerry. Perhaps she had begun to hope that I intended to say nothing about her attack on me and to realise that I intended to keep my suspicions about Father and her a secret.

Gerry was not for giving up and he began to renew his attack when we were back home, this time with Mother present, at the tea table. Desperate to keep the truth from Mother, I hissed at him when she briefly went out of the room to fetch a letter that had come that day. 'Shut up, Gerry, for pity's sake. I don't want to talk about it, not in front of Mother.'

He seized his advantage. 'Well, promise to tell me when she's no' here, then. Promise!'

Hearing Mother's footsteps, I said 'All right. All right.'

'Cross your heart and hope to die! Go on. Or else I'll tell her you've got a secret.'

'Cross my heart,' I said desperately. 'Now, ssshh!'

Mother came back in holding two sheets of thin, ruled paper covered in copperplate writing. 'Look, you two. A letter from Mrs Forsyth. You remember her from North Berwick?' She sat down and began reading out the letter to us, quite unaware of Gerry's smirking anticipation.

Mrs Forsyth had written mostly about goings-on in North Berwick, cheerful, chatty gossip that washed over me in my preoccupied state. It was only towards the end of the letter that the tone changed. She moved on to asking Mother how we were getting on in our new lives.

'Have you seen anything of the Ghost of Erraid? Remember that photo I showed you? The boy and . . .' Mother's voice trailed off and she shuffled the pages together quickly, folding them roughly and stuffing them back into the envelope.

Gerry had stopped listening very quickly and turned his attention to spooning surreptitious mouthfuls of jam. My own attention had been minimal but now I pricked up my ears. The Ghost of Erraid! Those were the very words that Catriona had used when she told me about Lady Maclean fleeing from Cromwell's soldiers and escaping with her son in a boat from Erraid. I tried to remember what Catriona had said: something about them being drowned, a bell ringing, the ghost of Lady Maclean still looking for her dead son. And I suddenly remembered the sepia photograph of adult and child in the album that Mrs Forsyth had been so keen to show Mother on the morning of our departure. I saw again the album tumbling down the steps, even as I tried to see the photograph, and closing itself as it landed on the our path.

'I know about that ghost,' I said excitedly. 'Catriona told me that . . . '

'That's enough, Liza,' said Mother sharply. 'Get on with your bread and jam.'

'But I know. . . '

'I said enough! Gerry, leave that jar alone at once. Look at your face. Come here and let me wash that jam off it. You look like a tinker's bairn.' She rose quickly and, snatching a startled Gerry off his chair, whisked him over to the pail of warm water that stood on the stove. 'Get those dishes cleared off the table, Liza. Quick, smart, now.'

I could only obey, recognising the tone she used when she was not to be argued with.

I was spared having to make good immediately the promise that Gerry had wrung out of me as Angus appeared at the door with his usual 'Is Gerry comin' oot to play?'

Gerry hesitated, looking at me hopefully, but I turned away and busied myself washing our cups and saucers. Mother shooed him out with the usual stipulations about coats, boots, gloves and one of the wee rubber torches, supplied by the NLB, that were our constant companions in winter. It was now pitch dark by four o'clock with none of the cheerful gas streetlights that we had known in North Berwick.

I mooched through to my bedroom and buried myself in a book. This was the time when, up until yesterday, I would have slipped out, taking my own wee torch and my book, and made my way up to The Lookout. But I could not face it today and did not know if I ever could again. If Mother wondered why I was keeping to the house, she did not comment, perhaps thinking I was still feeling a little tired and weak after my 'fall' two days before.

But I could not escape my nosey little brother for long. Worse still, by the time the moment of revelation came, he had already shared a garbled version of events with Angus and it was not one but two persistent little boys who accosted me when I came out of 'the cludgie' (as Angus called it) at the bottom of the garden an hour later.

'Tell us now, Liza,' demanded Gerry.

'Aye, go on,' said Angus, his eyes saucer-wide in his freckled, snub-nosed face.

'I didna say I would tell *him* as well.' I was only playing for time, of course, since I knew Gerry would tell Angus anyway. Those two were as thick as yesterday's cold porridge.

I tried desperately to think of a story that would fob them off. 'Well . . .'

'It's to do wi' Miss Dow, isn't it?' said Gerry. 'I saw the way she was looking at you in class. *No'* looking at you, more like. An' you were *no'* looking at her the same.' He saw at once from my expression that he had hit the mark and pounced. 'I was right, Angus. I telt ye. You said it wisna about Miss Dow but I *knew* it was. That's a penny ye owe me.'

'You've no' been gambling with each other?' I said, appalled and diverted from my other worries. 'Father would leather you if he found out. You know he hates gambling.'

Father had always been scathing about any of his pub pals in North Berwick who 'threw good money after bad' on horse or greyhound racing. I think, perhaps, there was family history of past disasters brought about in this way.

'I'm just jokin', he said hastily, with a quick glance at Angus which I interpreted to mean: 'for pity's sake, don't tell her'.

I saw a lifeline and grabbed it. 'You're lying, Gerry Galway. Whose breeks are on fire now? Wait till I tell Father.'

'I'm no' lyin'. I'm NO! Tell her, Angus.'

'Are you a wee liar too? And a gambler? Wait till I tell *your* father. And the minister.'

Angus stood for a moment looking from one to the other of us, chewing his lip and hopping from one foot to the other. Then he gave a yelp like a cornered puppy, spun round and ran away up our path and back to his own house.

'Now look what you've done, Liza! Ye've scared off my best pal. I hate you. I'm going to tell Mother all about you and your rotten secret.' He made to copy Angus' flight.

'Oh no you don't!' I grabbed his arm and yanked him back. 'You say one word to Mother and I'll tell Father you and Angus have been gambling.'

'It was only a penny,' he wailed, the ready tears squeezing out of his eyes.

'And it'll only be Father's belt for you,' I said grimly.

He stared at me as if I was a stranger, as indeed I was to him at that moment. Never before in his short life had his doting big sister been so severe and determined. He was used to winding me round one of his grubby little fingers. The idea that I would be the cause of him being on the receiving end of Father's belt had no framework in his experience or understanding.

'You wouldnae,' he whimpered.

'Aye, I would.'

'I dinna believe ye. Ye wouldnae.' More tears, now being joined by snot.

'You say one word to Mother about what you *think* happened up at The Lookout last night and I'll be whispering in Father's ear before you can say . . .say . . . "Jack Frost".' This was an expression much used by the wives on Erraid.

'But I want to ken what happened.'

'Is it worth getting belted for?'

He squirmed and snivelled but there was never any chance that he would opt for risking Father's anger. He lapsed into sulks, muttering that he would find out somehow, see if he didn't, and then I'd be sorry. I tried to put my arm round his shoulders and heal the breach that had opened up between us but he shrugged me off and ran away along the path to Angus' house, no doubt to call me some horrible names but reassure Angus that their shady little bet would not be earning them some fearful retribution after all.

I went back into the house and began to help Mother with our high tea preparations. Father had come in and was sitting dozing in the chair by the fire. Mother put her finger to her lips to prevent me waking him and we worked in silence, relying on mime to communicate.

119

I was mightily relieved that my secret was, if not safe, then at least out of immediate danger. I was, of course, still left with the conundrum of what was going on between Father and the Dow. Was it simply some sort of betrayal of Mother, some sinful dalliance? Or was it in some way connected with The Dow's strange, intense interest in our family, especially Gerry?

'You'll cut yourself with that knife, Liza, if you start daydreaming while you're chopping potatoes.'

I started at Mother's urgent whisper. Father stirred and muttered, making us both freeze, but he subsided into wheezy snores again and we resumed our tasks, me paying more attention to the chips I was preparing for the big frying pot.

# CHAPTER FIFTEEN

*He said this as if he had been Charlemagne and commanded armies.*
*Robert Louis Stevenson, from 'Kidnapped'*

After the alarms and excursions of the weekend, the rest of Father's last 'shore' week seemed uneventful. Gerry nursed his grievance over the threat to tell Father about his gambling - if such a silly wee bet could be called that. I was certainly not about to disabuse him of the notion that Father would see it as such. He sulked for the best part of Monday and Tuesday, shrugging off olive-branch offers of half my weekly portion of dolly mixtures and an extra story at bedtime. But his resolve was crumbling by Wednesday and gone by Thursday. I dared to hope that he would forget all about it.

How I wished I could do the same! I watched Father covertly and The Dow openly, waiting for more signs of their clandestine relationship but Father was out of the house a great deal that week, often not coming home for his evening meal, which Mother plated and kept warm for him, till eight or nine so there was no way of knowing if he was meeting her between the end of the school day and his return home. I could hardly go snooping all over Erraid with my wee torch looking for them, even if the weather had not taken a turn for the worse. We were having our first taste of a Hebridean winter, not bitter cold like we had known in the eastern lowlands of Scotland, but wet and wild. The sky changed hourly, it seemed, great scudding banks of black, heavy clouds building up of a morning, turning to thrumming downpours of an afternoon, occasionally mellowing briefly into a stunning rainbow before the relentless darkness fell for another sixteen hours.

If I had not been so preoccupied with my uncomfortable suspicions and speculations, I might have noticed that Mother was not herself. It was Father who drew my attention to it.

'Come for a wee walk with me, Liza, before you go back to school,' he said suddenly on Friday as we finished our midday dinner. He rose, lifted his jacket and cap from the peg on the door and jerked his head at me. I was not quite finished scraping the last of the jam and custard off my plate but I heard the peremptory note in his voice and hurried to fetch my own coat and scarf from the fireguard where Mother had put them to dry - it had been raining heavily by eleven that morning. My heart began to thump as I followed him out. I ran over in my mind the terrifying possibilities: The Dow had told him about our encounter at The Lookout and my accusation about her and Father meeting there; or he had realised that there was nothing going on between Arthur Campbell and Mother and was going to accuse me of making up stories about them; or . . . Only the fact that he had called me outside gave me hope. If he had been intending to belt me, he would not have taken me outside, I felt sure of that. He would not want to give his fellow-keepers or their wives any more ammunition for gossip, not after the inspection day fracas.

'It's about your Mother,' he said abruptly. 'I want you to look after her while I'm away on the rock.'

'Look after her,' I repeated. 'Why? What's wrong with her?' I thought suddenly of the way Mother had been sitting down much more than usual this past week or two. She hadn't been eating much either. I had a picture of her pushing her plate aside or rising to scrape the food into the slop bucket. In fact, she had done that at dinner just now and she had simply shaken her head when I had offered to put out her porridge this morning. I could not recall her eating breakfast at all that week, I realised. 'Is Mother ill? What's wrong with her?'

There was rising panic in my voice. If anything happened to Mother, we would be left with only Father to care for us. It did not bear thinking about.

'No, not ill, Liza. It's not anything that will last.'

'She'll get better then?' I said keenly. 'Better soon?'

He gave a short bark of a laugh. 'Oh, aye, she'll get better. That's for sure. But it'll no' be right away.' He laughed again.

I could not see anything amusing about Mother being ill, short time or not. Even for Father, it seemed incredibly callous to find amusement in the fact of his wife being ill.

'What's so funny?' I demanded, angry now and impetuous. 'How long will she be ill for?'

He hesitated and I had time to fear that my sharp questions might be considered 'setting up cheek' and bring about the usual punishment of a clout round the head. But he stopped in the path – we were almost down at the pier now – and turned to look at me thoughtfully. I stopped too but did not turn to meet his eye, just stared nervously at the seagulls perched on the boat bobbing against the stone pier. He suddenly shot out a hand and I flinched but he only put it on my shoulder and turned me to face him. His eyes raked over my face, appraising me, as if judging me fit for some task. Then he nodded and dropped his hand.

'You're not a bairn any more, Liza. You'll be a young woman before long.' It was the first I had heard of it. He still treated me like a child to

122

be ordered about and skelped into submission. 'Your Mother is going to need you. She's . . .' He swallowed and looked over my head, working his lips. He put up his hand and pulled at his nose. 'She's . . .'

'She IS ill!' I burst out. 'Really ill. That's what you're trying to tell me, isn't it? Is she going to die?' I was shouting now. The screaming gulls overhead echoed my terror.

'NO!' he shouted above both me and the gulls. 'She's no' going to DIE. She's going to have a BABY!'

The world stood still. The boat froze mid-bob, the gulls arrested mid-scream. Father's face was a mask, mouth paused on the words. Six words. I heard them playing over and over in the motionless scenario. *She's going to have a baby.* Mother was pregnant.


Gerry and I were going to have a brother or sister. The thought drummed in my head for the remainder of that day, the implications tumbling over each other as my mind darted hither and thither between simple practicalities like where 'it' would sleep – would it be Gerry or me who would have to share a bedroom? And areas of unfathomable ignorance like what would happen when the time came for 'it' to be born. I had a hazy memory of suddenly being sent to live with my Granny and Grandpa Paterson on a sort of tiny farm near Perth. Mother called it 'a smallholding' on the rare occasions she referred to it. I had been homesick and miserable despite Granny's efforts to cheer me up and even more miserable when I came home a week later to find Mother sitting up in bed with a baby at her breast. But my jealousy had soon turned to wonder as Mother introduced me to my new brother and to pride as she delegated little tasks to help take care of him. Father was away at sea so I had felt more like the other parent than a mere three year-old sibling. I grew up very fast in Gerry's early months and, by the time he was toddling, I had become the doting older sister. Together, Mother and I had produced the clingy, babyish nine-year-old who so irritated Father.

But what had happened before I was sent to Walnut Grove, the Perthshire smallholding, and what happened to Mother when I was there, these were mysterious areas that she and I had never talked about. Of course, I had a sort of theoretical grasp on 'the facts of life', as I had heard grown-ups describe it. Several of my North Berwick classmates had been farm children and they talked about animals mating and calves, lambs and piglets being born. I knew vaguely – if I had allowed myself to dwell on it – that the creaking bedsprings, the rattles and bumps, the snorts and muffled cries from Mother and Father's bedroom were something to do with those facts but I hated to imagine my parents behaving like the animals our farm-bred schoolmates had described. I suppose I could have equated Father with a rutting ram or bull but I could no more imagine Mother engaged in such an act than I could have pictured her lifting her skirts and flashing her bare bottom in church.

As to how the conception of a baby actually resulted from this animal act, so unthinkable to my childish mind when related to my parents, how it grew to become baby-sized and got born, of all these fundamental processes I was desperately ignorant. I had seen pregnant women and knew the impending baby was growing inside them as they grew fatter and fatter but how and where it grew, and how it got out, were complete mysteries. Even the farm girls had been a bit vague on the details, using words I did not know. Or rather, words I did know - like labour and delivery – but could not understand what they meant in that context. Of other words, like breech, forceps and still-born, I had no understanding at all.

Father seemed to think, however, that he had discharged his responsibilities. I had been told of Mother's pregnancy, I had been ordered to look after her. Job done. With one last stern look, he abjured me to mind I 'didn't let her lift anything too heavy' and strode off to hail Euan who was coming down some way behind us. I stared after him bewildered until the bell for afternoon school recalled me to the need to get myself back up the path.

Our afternoon excursions had now ceased for the winter and the hum of activity in the classroom, as we set to a new Friday afternoon indulgence called 'crafts', covered my inattention. Instead of the dreaded knitting for the girls – in my case more time was spent unpicking and re-knitting until it resembled a dog's dinner – we were set to making Christmas decorations.

'Only four weeks till the Christmas Party,' announced The Dow. There was a whoop of glee from the older children and wriggles of excitement from the tinies. She frowned and sharply bade them pay attention while she outlined what each form would be making. But no amount of schoolmarmish repression could dampen their excitement as each form was given a box of materials. The red and gold paper, the glittery tinsel, the bright threads, the sheets of coloured card, the pots of glue, jars of paint and bundles of scissors – it was like fireworks being set off as the children's response to the boxes crackled and fizzed in the steamy air of a damp November afternoon.

The other girls in my form were keen to tell me all about the Christmas Party and I must have been a sore disappointment to them in my distracted state, as they vied to impress me with the details.

'We all get taken on the boats round to Fionnphort,' said Catriona. 'My Dad brings his boat over and we go in that as well as the NLB one. Even so,' she giggled, 'it's a fair squeeze.'

'Aye, and then the wee bus run back and forward to their school until we're all there,' said another girl. 'There's folk from Iona and Bunessan and Pennyghael and Pottie and . . .'

'You can see the Christmas lights in Fionnphort School all the way across the Sound. They have a big tree waiting to be decorated – that's what we're making these things for – and there's candles and paper chains as well.' The speaker dipped her brush into a pot of sparkly gold paint and applied it to a fir cone.

'The food is great!' enthused one of the boys. Tinsel and candles were of secondary interest to him. 'All the mothers bring stuff. Tons of it. There's black bun and cream cakes; cheese straws and meat pies; jellies and tarts.' His eyes shone as he pictured the spread.

'There's music and dancing after the food,' Kirsty Campbell chimed in. 'Fiddling and a couple o' squeezeboxes. And Miss Dow played the piano last year.'

'Games as well,' added another boy. 'Like musical chairs and statues. And races. Prizes for the winners. I won a stick o' rock last year at the egg-and-spoon race.'

'I like the singsong at the end,' said Catriona. 'Folk always do the same things. Everyone's got their party piece. Dad aye does 'My Love is like a Red, Red Rose'. He looks at Mum while he's singing and she goes all red and tells him no' to be a big sap. But we can all see she likes it really.'

'I like the bairns' singing better,' said Kirsty. She turned to me. 'The schools practise something and we all get our turn. It's like a competition to see who's the best. Iona school were amazing last year. Remember, Catriona? What was it they sang again?'

'The Skye Boat Song. They did wee trilly bits and harmonies. First in Gaelic and then in English. It was beautiful. All the mothers were greeting.'

'We finish up with community singing. Christmas carols, mostly. We'll be practising them here soon, ready for the night.'

They all looked at me expectantly now, waiting for my reaction.

'It's at *night?*' I grasped at one bit of information in among the deluge, realising I must show some interest. 'I was imagining an afternoon . . . I suppose.'

'That's the best bit,' declared Kirsty. 'We dinna get back to Erraid till near midnight. All the wee bairns are sleeping on the boat back and have to be carried up the path.'

'Remember the crib that Bunessan School brought last year. They'd made the figures and the animals out of paper mashy and painted them. They had real straw in a big box stood up on its end. Mary and Joseph were . . .'

'And the Baby Jesus!' Kirsty almost swooned. 'He was lovely. Awfy sweet. Made me think of our Angus when he was wee. I just love babies, don't you, Liza.'

'No!' I snapped. 'I canna be bothered wi' them.' I turned away from their surprised stares and, snatching up a pair of scissors, I fell to slicing red ribbons and curling them into fronds, working so fast and with such a sour expression on my face that they turned away. Out of the corner of my eye, I saw them make faces at each other.


Mother was baking when we got home after school. She was flushed from the heat of the oven, with a smear of scone mixture on her cheek. She looked up and smiled as we came in. I am not sure what I expected. My new knowledge of her condition heightened my perception and I stared at her, seeking differences, perhaps even looking for a reassuring sign that Father had been wrong. She met my eye and held it. Perhaps she blushed but I could not tell under the flush already on her cheeks. She was first to look away but I knew in that moment that she knew that I knew.

Gerry filled the gap, unconscious as always of any interaction that he was not part of. 'Guess what, Mother? Just GUESS WHAT?' He did not wait for her to try but rushed on, his voice rising to a squeak of excitement. 'There's going to be a Christmas party over at Feefort. All of us get to go, you as well. There's going to be pies and jellies and sweeties and games and prizes and  . . .' He ran out of breath and I took the chance to cut in.

'Calm down,' I said repressively. I was finding it hard to care about anything that afternoon other than Father's bombshell. 'Take your boots off before you make the floor dirty and hang up your coat.'

'Goodness, Liza, don't you sound grown-up!' laughed Mother. 'Anyone would think you were the Mother here.' She came round the table and began helping Gerry out of his boots. 'This sounds exciting, wee man. Tell me more.'

Something about her casual air, her refusal to acknowledge the momentous fact that was sitting in the middle of our kitchen like an elephant, goaded me beyond discretion.

'How can you just carry on like nothing's changed?' I demanded. 'When were you going to tell me? How are we going to cope with a newborn baby here? How can I take care of you when I don't know what's going to happen? How could you do this behind my back? *He* won't be here and he wouldna help anyway. It'll be all down to me! And I ken . . . I ken . . . *bugger all* about having babies. Especially in a back o' beyond place like this.'

My voice rose and shook as I fought tears. Truth to tell, I had worried myself into a state of near hysteria. Father's command – tossed off as if it was nothing more than an extra little job added to my workload – to 'look after your Mother' had weighed on me all afternoon until it felt as if her life was hanging by a thread and it was in my hands. I was, quite simply, terrified.

'Liza! What kind of language is this? Since when did you use words like that in this house? Go to your bedroom at once. I'll bring soap and water to wash your mouth out. It's a good job your father isn't here. He'd skelp the living daylights out of you for swearing. And you'd deserve it.' Then, as I just stood glaring at her, 'Did you hear me? Go! At once!'

She took a step towards me, eyes flashing and nostrils flaring. My fear boiled over and I gave a whimper and charged across the kitchen, heedless of the dirt my own boots were shedding onto the spotless floor. I flung myself into my bedroom and collapsed on my bed in a storm of tears.


'What is all this about, Liza?'

Mother had been sitting on the end of my bed for several minutes and this was the third time she had asked this question. The first time, she had gone for sounding slightly amused; the second puzzled and rather anxious; now there was more than a hint of irritation. 'Answer me, please, Liza. At once.'

I burrowed still further into my pillow and wriggled in embarrassment. Mother lost all patience and took a firm hold of my shoulder, pulling me up and swinging me round to face her. 'Well, what *is* this all about?' Her hand on my shoulder was like a vice and I could not twist out of it. I fought to find the words.

'Father told me that you're . . . you're going to . . . going to have . . .' I choked on the last, crucial word but Mother did not supply it.

'Going to have what? Come on, Liza. Spit it out.'

'You know!' I burst out. 'You ken fine. Oh Mammy, what are we going to do? How will we manage?'

'Manage what?'

Something boiled over inside me. 'Having a baby here! Father says I've got to be the one to look after you while he's on the rock but I dinna ken what to do. I dinna even ken what happens when a bairn gets born. What if I dinna look after you properly and you get sick? Maybe even die? And the bairn as well? Father will kill me if that happens. And what will happen to me and Gerry? Who'll take care o' us? Oh, Mammy . . .' – it had been years since I called her that, not since I started school at age six – '. . . What will Gerry an' me do if you die? I dinna want to be left with just Father.'

Mother considered this outburst for a moment then she smiled. 'You're not being logical, Liza. You say that if I die, Father will kill you. Then you're worrying about being left with just Father to care for you. You can't have it both ways.' She regarded me teasingly but saw my bewilderment and relented. 'Come here, you silly lassie.' She put her arms round my shaking shoulders and pulled me into her embrace.

'Yes, there is going to be a little brother or sister for you and Gerry but, no, I'm not going to die. Why would I do that? Have I no' had two fine, strapping bairns already?'

'But Father said I was to look after you,' I wailed. 'What did he mean, then? What does he want me to do?'

'Dear knows, Liza, dear knows. Likely his conscience troubling him. It wasn't supposed to happen. I told him to . . .' She stopped suddenly, as if realising to whom she was talking. 'But it'll be fine,' she concluded briskly. 'Just fine. No need for you to look after me. Now dry your eyes and come through for a scone before they're cold.'

And that was all I could get out of her. Attempts to re-open the conversation in the week that followed only elicited impatient *tuts* and shakes of her head. Maybe I should have been reassured but I felt that I was between the devil and the deep blue sea: between Father's strict though baffling instructions and Mother's rebuttal of any need for them.

One thing was clear: this was not the time to be airing my suspicions about Father's secret assignations with The Dow at The Lookout. I might not feel able to do anything positive towards 'looking after' Mother but I could at least refrain from adding to her burdens.

# CHAPTER SIXTEEN

*The nothing of childhood put some fetters on my boasted free will.*

*Robert Louis Stevenson*

Among the children of Erraid, it seemed as if there was now only one topic of conversation: the forthcoming Christmas party. Neither Gerry nor I had ever been to one. On the east coast of Scotland at that time, Christmas was barely celebrated. Workplaces like mines and factories all remained open and no one expected so much as a day off. Children might get a small present, perhaps an apple or an orange wrapped in silver paper, and we had always gone to mass on Christmas Day. But parties were reserved for New Year's Eve – Hogmanay, we called it – when everyone stayed up till midnight and saw the New Year in with a dram of whisky for the adults and raspberry cordial for the children. Then there would be feasting, singing and dancing into the early hours of the morning. With Father away at sea, Mother, Gerry and I had usually joined the party in Mrs Forsyth's house for a little while until Gerry needed his bed. Other children were put down on top of piles of coats or they simply huddled sleepily into corners, forgotten and ignored. Mother had not approved of this, however, and we were always back in our own beds by half past midnight.

The Christmas party in Fionnphort sounded altogether different and much more fun, at least for us children. The date was set: the twenty-second of December, the Saturday after the school term finished. Gerry and I were soon caught up in the hum of anticipation and preparation. Father's second 'rock' month would be over by then, he would be back with us on the previous Monday. But even that discouraging thought could not dampen our spirits.

Then something even more exciting happened. About a week before the party, Catriona handed me an envelope addressed to Mother.

'What is it?' I asked. 'Where did you get it?'

'It's from my mother.'

'Why? What's she writing to *my* mother about?'

But she only grinned and bade me be sure to give it to Mother. I fingered and fumbled at it all the way along the path but it yielded no clue as to its contents. Indeed, it felt as if there was nothing in it. I was in a fever to get back to the house and watch Mother open it. Gerry and

Angus were dawdling behind, deep in conversation. I left them to it and burst, breathless with running, into the house.

'Look, Mother! Catriona gave me a letter for you. Open it and see what's in it.'

Mother was cleaning the brass oil lamps. An old newspaper, covering the table, was littered with a can of oil, a tin of *Brasso*, trimming scissors for the wicks and two smelly polishing rags. She looked up and regarded me dreamily. She was always a great one for losing herself in thought whilst engaged in dull, repetitive tasks. As I advanced, thrusting the letter at her, her gaze sharpened.

'Where's your brother?'

'He's just coming. Go on, open it, it's addressed to you.'

'Put it on the sideboard. I'll look at it later. Now go and make sure Gerry's coming.'

'But . . .'

'Liza. I said GO. NOW.' She turned back to the lamps. As I still lingered, hopping from one leg to another in an agony of impatience, she picked up an oily rag and said, calmly, 'Do as you're told, Liza, or I won't open the letter until tomorrow morning.'

I opened my mouth to protest but was saved from such an unwise course of action by Gerry and Angus bursting into the room, falling over and landing in a tangled heap up against Mother's feet. They tried to rise but fell back into a worse tangle with screeches of hysterical laughter. I saw that Gerry's right ankle was tied to Angus' left with a dirty bit of rope. They had been practising for the three-legged race which was to be one of the games at the Christmas party. The playground was full of children doing this during play-times, that and the egg-and-spoon race, using potatoes as eggs.

Mother, however, had not seen the rope, nor did she have my insight into current play-time activities. She jumped to her feet and shouted over the racket the boys were making.

'Stop this hooliganism at once. This is a house not a playground. Look at the mess you're making!' The floor was covered in mud, grassy streaks ending in squishy dollops. 'Stand up, the pair of you.'

The boys attempted to obey but were still unsteady with laughter, quite unable to find the careful balance needed to rise as one. The more they tried and failed, the more they laughed and the more unsteady they became. Mother looked over the mad pair and met my eyes.

'What on earth is wrong with them?' she asked me, shaking her head.

'They're tied together. Practising for the three-legged race.' I reached across the boys and handed her the precious letter. 'You open this and

I'll sort them out.' It seemed a fair bargain and, after a moment's hesitation, she nodded.

'You win, smarty-pants,' she conceded. Then she rallied. 'Mind, if you hadn't left Gerry on the path, they would never have got up to this nonsense. I've told you always to make sure he comes straight home. *And takes his muddy boots off at the door.* 'Oh, all right . . .' as the boys began to fall over and shriek again, 'Here. Give me the letter. You see to these two scamps. I'll tell you what it's about once you've cleaned the floor.'

She drove a hard bargain, did our mother.


'Well, for heaven's sake, what *does* it say?' I could not keep the exasperation out of my voice. Father would have given me one of his 'thick ears' for daring to speak to a grown-up like that. Mother had more subtle ways of bringing me to heel.

'If you speak to me in that tone, milady, you'll only have to wait longer. You need to be taught patience. And manners.' She set me yet another task, this time to take the kettle out to the spring and fill it, while she cleared away the oil lamps' paraphernalia and threw a cloth over the table. Further impatient demands from me earned me three more tasks and, by the time I had mastered my tongue, the table was set, the treacle-and-raisin loaf was buttered and milk had been decanted, from the big pitcher in the cold box attached to the outside back wall, into the small jug. This time, I managed to bite my tongue and remain silent until the tea was poured and we had begun eating. Mother opened the envelope with the pretty paperknife she always used, a wedding present from a cousin, so she had told me. It contained one flimsy sheet, folded once. Through the back of the thin paper, I saw several lines of copperplate writing.

I was pressing my lips tightly together to stop my questions bursting out through them. I must have looked quite strange because Mother laughed and said 'All right, Miss Impatience, here's what it says: "At Catriona's request, I invite Liza to come to our home after the Christmas Party and stay for two nights. She will be most welcome here. Lachlan will bring her home on Christmas Eve. I hope you will give her permission to do this." It's signed "*Kind regards, Marion McPhail*".'

Mother looked over the letter at me. 'Isn't that most kind of Mrs McPhail? I expect Catriona gets lonely, being an only child. We'll have to ask your father what he thinks. He'll be home on the 17th so there will be plenty of time to let Marion know.'

131

'But I want to go!' I burst out. 'How can ye no' just tell her yourself that I can. Why do we have to wait for *him* to come back? He'll stop me going. He hates any of us enjoying ourselves, you ken that.'

I was close to tears. My heart was racing with excitement. I had never been invited anywhere in my life and the idea of spending two days with Catriona at her home was thrilling. And I was so delighted to be asked – actually invited in a proper letter. The idea that Father would have to be consulted and have the power of yea or nay over such a delectable treat was horrifying. Nothing good or happy ever came from involving him. I was as good as doomed to bitter disappointment. Didn't Mother know this? How could she be so stupid or so cruel?

I begged and pleaded. I wept and howled. I lost my temper and snatched the letter from her, declaring I would write an answer myself and forge her signature. Finally, I was sent to my room for the evening and given only a bowl of cold porridge while the savoury aroma of cheese on toast drifted through from the table.

At bedtime, Mother came and sat on the end of the bed and waited for my apology. I had cried myself out by then and wanted only to be back in her good books. Once I had found a few stilted words to beg forgiveness for my behaviour, she spoke quietly.

'If I gave my permission now, your father would find out as soon as he came home. He would likely be so angry that this decision had been taken behind his back that he would instantly forbid it. If we wait until he has settled back home and is in a good mood, we will have so much more chance of a favourable answer. And with things as they are just now,' she rested her hand briefly on her stomach and I remembered with a guilty start that she was pregnant *and* that I was supposed to be taking care of her, 'he will possibly be more amenable than usual to anything I ask him. Just give me a chance to find the right moment. That's what I was going to say, Liza, before you flew off the handle.'

'I'm sorry, Mother,' I whispered, this time sincerely. 'I shouldn't have upset you like that. I'm meant to be looking after you, not causing you more trouble.'

'I don't need looking after, Liza. I've told you that. Just you look after yourself, especially that temper and that tongue. Thank your lucky stars your father wasn't here to see that performance. You'd have had something worth crying about.'

She was right. Contrite and shaken, I thanked her and settled down to sleep. But an hour later, I was still awake, staring at the frame of moonlight silver round the black blind on my window, fretting over the three weeks that lay between now and Father's return, agonising over Mother's chances of persuading him to agree.

'Well, what did your mother say? Has she written an answer for mine?'

Catriona pounced on me as soon as I walked into the schoolroom next morning. Her slate-grey eyes were sparkling with excitement and I realised she was looking forward to my visit as much as I was.

'She said . . .' I felt a flush of shame heat my cheeks. How could I admit that it was not up to Mother, that there was every chance that Father would put a damper on her lovely plan for no better reason than because he could, that we had always to plot and scheme to circumvent his cruelty? I thought of the MacLean family as I had last seen them on the journey from Craignure. Was that really only two months ago? I pictured them on the pier that day: Lachlan rushing to meet his daughter, scooping her up and spinning her round; Catriona, dizzy and tottering when he set her down; Marion shaking her head at him in mock rebuke; and the three of them drawing together into that circle of love that had so tugged at my heart. What chance was there that Catriona would understand the kind of family I came from?

'Well, is it fine? Will I tell Ma? Och, Liza, we're goin' to have a great time. Da says he'll take us over to Iona on the Monday - that's Christmas Eve - if the weather's fine. If we go first thing once it's daylight, we can have a few hours there before he brings you back here.'

She beamed at me with such innocent friendliness that I could find no way to disappoint her. The promise of a trip to Iona sealed my helplessness. I was longing to go there and find out more about the Druids. The suspicion that they were somehow implicated in the mystery of The Dow's obsession with Gerry and Father's obsession with her had not left me. It had only been forced on to the back burner by my recent worries about Mother's pregnancy. I felt my determination to solve it come back in force at the prospect of exploring the ancient, sacred isle.

'Of course, it's fine, Catriona. I'm looking forward to it. Tell your mother that mine will be writing to her soon.'

She hopped and skipped with delight, her thatch of unruly, red-gold hair bouncing wildly. 'Hurrah! I can't wait for the party and now it's even better.' She undid the knot in her school tie and pulled it off her neck. 'Come on, let's practise our three-legged.'

Thus was I mired in the deception of my best friend, this carefree, wholesome girl who knew only the bright and loving side of family life, and, because I wanted nothing so much as to be like her, I pushed my

133

problems to the back of my mind. A minute later we were rolling on the ground, helpless with laughter, just as Gerry and Angus had been the day before.

My forthcoming visit to the MacPhails' home, as well as endless three-legged practising, drew Catriona and me closer than ever. With school afternoons now being spent in 'handwork' – knitting and sewing for the girls, wood-carving and Meccano constructions for the boys – the two of us would huddle together over our messy efforts, whispering and giggling. If The Dow noticed, she said nothing. I was still being accorded a long rein since our altercation up at The Lookout. My bruises were fading but my leverage against her was not, at least not yet.

Catriona and I both hated handwork and looked with some envy at the little metal strips, plates, wheels, axles and gears that the boys were assembling into working models of machinery, using tiny nuts and bolts. It looked a lot more interesting than the wool tea cosies and cotton aprons that the girls were attempting to make.

Some of our whispered conversations in class, as well as several open discussions in the playground, centred on the promised trip to Iona. I was remembering my conviction a few weeks ago, while gazing from The Lookout over to the sacred isle, that finding out more about it was important in my quest to understand The Dow's obsession with Gerry. I listened to Catriona naming places that all rang chords of memory from some of my final lessons in the North Berwick school. 'St Columba's Bay' spoke of the sixth century monk coming from Ireland in a coracle and setting up a monastic community; 'The Street of the Dead' of medieval Scottish kings being brought from the mainland to be buried in the ancient cathedral's graveyard; 'Martyrs Bay' of monks being massacred as they went on to the beach to offer a peaceful welcome to marauding, murdering Vikings. And, importantly, 'St Oran's Chapel' spoke of the Druids and Mr Chambers' picture of strange, priest-like figures, standing in a circle, pale robes flapping in the wind. He had said that some people believed St Oran was the last Druid on Iona.

'Is it true that Iona is a thin place?' I asked her as we took a breathless break from three-legging one morning at play-time. 'You know, like they say about the supernatural being closer there?'

'I ken what a thin place is, Liza. I've aye known. You've only just learned it.' She grinned. 'Sassenach!' she teased. It was what Gaelic-speaking highlanders called the English-speaking lowlanders.

'I ken about the Druids,' I parried. 'My teacher back in North Berwick told me how there were lots of them on Iona long ago.'

'Oh, aye . . . The Druids . . .' Catriona's face took on what I thought of as her 'fey look'. I was about to question her more but the bell rang, summoning us back to the classroom for the second half of the morning. Later that day, under cover of our handwork huddle, I picked up the topic but she was vague and mysterious. I eventually concluded that she knew very little about them, had simply absorbed their aura of Celtic, medieval mystery without any hard fact or even a decent legend.

'But there must be stories,' I persisted at the end of the afternoon, as we packed away our scraggy, half-knitted tea-cosies into our linen lap-bags.

She shrugged. 'I can ask my mother and father. Or *her*.' She indicated The Dow who was standing at the door bidding each child good-bye with a dry nod. 'I bet she knows loads.'

Before I could stop her, she strode up to the teacher. 'Excuse me. Ma'am. I was wondering if you ken anything about Druids. We're goin' over to Iona with my Da on Christmas Eve and . . . 'She stopped as The Dow made a quick, slicing motion in the air with her right hand.

'That is a very big, very serious topic, Catriona. Once you start finding out about the Druids, you can become lost in their history, their legends. They flourished in this area long before even the time of Christ. They were immensely important.' Her eyes began to burn in her thin face. She might have been talking to a whole roomful of people hanging on her every word. 'They belong to a far-off, very different era. A time when the veil between the natural and the supernatural was often pierced, especially on Iona.' Her voice quavered. 'You can discover things that you wish you never had. But there is no going back.'

She suddenly became aware of me, hanging back but well within earshot. Her face changed instantly, losing its dreamy intensity and sharpening into its customary severe expression.

'Get off home, now, the pair of you,' she snapped and turned on her heel to march back into the classroom and begin clearing her desk for her own departure.

Catriona and I exchanged startled glances. Catriona seemed about to turn back and press The Dow for more information but I grabbed her arm and dragged her out into the lobby and pushed her towards the front door. I could not have explained why I was so determined to get away from The Dow but the urge was too strong to be ignored. I had had it before, several times since coming to Erraid. It was like an overwhelming sense of self-preservation.

Only when we were out on the path, and she was about to turn off to meet Lachlan's boat as it drifted into the pier, did I mutter, 'Sorry, sorry . . . I just didn't think we should . . . She was being so funny . . .'

'We'll talk about it tomorrow.' Catriona had seen her father's boat.

'Mind and ask your folks about the Druids,' I shouted after her as she ran down the hill to the pier, waving to Lachlan in response to his upraised hand. There was a dry cough behind me and I knew without turning that I had been overheard by The Dow.

# CHAPTER SEVENTEEN

*There fell upon me a blackness of despair, a horror of remorse and a passion of anger.*
*Robert Louis Stevenson, from 'Kidnapped'*

The short winter days slipped by and the end of our first term at Erraid School approached. I put to the back of my mind for the moment my suspicions about the relationship between Father and The Dow and my questions about her fixation over Gerry. To be sure, there were several small incidents that proved this was not lessening, so much so that he was dubbed 'teacher's pet' by some of other boys. The appellation was not meant to be a compliment, of course, but Gerry, used to being treated as Mother's pet at home, simply took it as his rightful due. He thought nothing of slipping his hand into The Dow's any time they were walking along the path side by side, a situation she engineered frequently, even if it was just for a few moments whilst going in and out of the schoolhouse. Whenever the class was given tasks to work on and she was circulating to see how we were faring, she would spend longer with him than any other child, bending over him, murmuring in his ear.

As to myself, she largely ignored me, keeping comments on my work to a neutral minimum. Occasionally, I would look up and find her eyes resting on me in a brooding, calculating way but she always looked away immediately.

After my shameful behaviour over Marion MacPhail's letter, I put my mind to the task Father had entrusted to me - looking after Mother. She did not make it easy, since she refused to think of herself as needing looked after, so that my offers of help were often refused and my expressions of concern brushed aside. I stuck to it, though, and gradually she let me do little things like fetching a box for her to put her feet on when she sat down of an evening and filling up the fireside basket from our outside peatstack. She even asked my help to tell Gerry about the baby.

'It's going to be such a shock for the wee man,' she said as we worked side by side at the kitchen table chopping carrots and turnips for the soup-pot. It was late afternoon one day during the last week of Father's away month and Gerry was playing along at Angus' house. 'I need to tell him soon. Before Father comes back. He might . . . well, you know how

. . . how impulsive your father can be. And he'll be thinking I've told Gerry a while ago. I said I'd do it right away, as soon as he left for The Rock. I keep meaning to but I'm worried the wee man'll see it as shoving him out of the way. I mean, he'll still be *my* baby, of course, just not *the* baby.'

'He's nine, Mother. He's not been a baby for a while. Maybe it's time he grew up. Actually, I think he has, quite a lot, since we came here.' I realised, as I spoke, that this was true. The island was such a safe environment, with everyone knowing everyone else and the smallness of it creating a comfortable boundary, that Gerry had much more freedom here. Angus had been good for him, too, being a confident, jolly wee lad, well versed in island life and lighthouse family ways. The Campbell house was a second home for Gerry now and the four Campbell children like extra siblings. His fears about settling into a new school has dissipated quickly under The Dow's favouritism. He was no longer the babyish boy who had run screaming out of the lavvie on our first day.

'Do you really think so? I hope you're right, Liza. Although I'll miss my wee pet if he becomes too grown up.'

'I doubt if there much chance of that,' I said drily. I was aware of a growing impatience over Mother's infantilising of Gerry. In the past, I had accepted it and even thought it rather sweet. Indeed, I had largely colluded with it. But, now there was to be a new baby, a real one with all its real needs and demands, there was no place or time for a nine year old boy being also treated as one.

But I could see that she was fretting about telling him, all the same, and, in my capacity as her chief carer and protector, it behoved me to take this burden off her.

'Do you want *me* to tell him?'

'Would you? Oh, Liza, dear, that would be such a relief.'

'I'll do it tonight. I'll do his bedtime story and tell him then.'

'You're a treasure.'

I glowed with pride. At last, I was doing something that pleased both Mother *and* Father.


Predictably, Gerry's reaction centred on what it would mean for his own little life.

'Will I have to share my bedroom with it? Will Mother have to go away to have it? Who'll look after us?'

I reassured him as best I could and Mother went to him then and hugged him, assuring him he would always be her favourite. Then, assuring me later that, of course, she did not really have a favourite: she had just said that to console him. For a wise woman – which she was in so many other ways – she was remarkably misguided in her relationship with her son.

Angus was the one who helped the most. When Gerry told him in a lugubrious voice about the baby, the next morning as they walked along the path to school, his friend slapped him on the back and congratulated him. Angus was probably imitating what had happened to his own father when the news of his mother's last pregnancy had broken in the community. He no doubt thought it was what men did to each other in this circumstance and he announced it to the other lads as soon as they congregated in the playground to wait for the school bell. The other lads took their cue from Angus and there was much hand wringing and back slapping. The effect was like magic on Gerry. He swelled with pride as if he had actually had a hand in the anticipated happy event. No first time father-to-be ever looked more pleased with himself. I blessed Angus and so did Mother when I told her.

Thus I was feeling fairly confident about Father's return. I had done my best to make life easier for Mother and she was looking well. Her nausea had lessened to just half an hour in the early morning, she had roses in her cheeks and a smile in her eyes again. He would be pleased with me and getting his permission to stay with the MacPhails for two nights should be easy. I was feeling happier than I had been since before we left North Berwick. Looking back, it seems incredible that I had forgotten, or at least shoved to the back of my mind, the fact that I had already told Catriona I had permission.


'Look what I've got for you!' Catriona's freckled face was lit up with the pleasure of giving me something that I had expressed a wish for. The sweetness of this was not lost on me and I loved her all the more. But my delight at having a friend and confidante such as I had never known before was quickly surpassed by my excitement when I saw the article she was holding out. It was a small, slim book, its covers a faded green.

I felt my heart constrict – was this going to be the same as the one that Mother had seemed so afraid of? I took it into my grasp almost fearfully and stared down at it.

'What's wrong? Is it no' what you were wantin' after all?' Catriona looked taken aback, as well she might for I was frowning and holding the little volume at arm's length as if it could contaminate me.

'What's wrong?' persisted Catriona. 'Is there something wrong with it? I told my Da you were interested in Druids and he went up into the attic specially to get that book for you. And he says he'll show you the Druid places on Iona when we go over on Christmas Eve.'

I looked down at the book. The title and the author's name on the front and spine were in old-gold lettering and quite clear to read: '*The Druids of West Scotland.*'

'It's perfect. Just what I was looking for. It's only . . . I was thinking about another book, just like this one. My mother had it in our last house but I've not seen it since . . . since we came to live here.'

'What's so special about it?'

I had no answer to that and mumbled something about just wanting to see what was in it.

'Well, these wee green books are all part of a set. Da has a whole shelf of them, all about the West o' Scotland in the past. Maybe the book ye're so desperate to find will be among them. But why not ask yer ma if she brought it? Or what it's called?'

'Yes, I will,' I said but knew I would not. 'And thanks again for this.' I hugged the wee book to me now, feeling reassured.


It was not an easy book to read and, despite my interest in the subject, I struggled to find information I could understand. It was written in a dry, scholarly style with much referring to and quoting of other sources and historians. I stuck to my task, however, sneaking a new candle out of the cupboard to replace the wee stub that was all I usually got to take to bed with me. When the house was dark and silent, Mother and Gerry sleeping sweetly, I lit the new candle and huddled the bedclothes round my shoulders as I sat up to read.

My nerves were severely tested for it made ghoulish reading in the flickering light, with the winter wind howling across the Sound and keening round our little row of houses. The Druids were an ancient sect, going back possibly to the time of Moses and the Egyptians. The powerful Roman Empire, attempting to conquer Britain, had come up against the Druids. These were clever, civilised people, wise in the ways of nature, entrusted, so they believed, with the sacred task of preserving and honouring their ancient tradition and culture. They wrote nothing down; part of their task was to keep it a close secret and hand it down by word of mouth only to the next generation of Druid priests.

Perhaps because of this, many legends and myths had grown up around them. By the time the Romans were trying to conquer Northern England

and Scotland, Christianity had taken hold in the Roman world and Druids were seen as heathens, their religious rituals as demonic practices. In particular, the Druids were labelled child murderers because there was evidence of their practising human sacrifice.

The writer of my little book tried to be fair and play this aspect down since he was of the opinion that the Druids had only very rarely resorted to this practice and then only in dire straits when they needed their gods to come to their aid immediately and effectively. As they were hounded to extinction by the zealous Christians, the Druids were possibly driven to human sacrifice more often and more openly so that this aspect of their culture achieved disproportionate publicity. And, then again, said the writer drily, it *does* make a very juicy bit of scandal.

With eyes red-rimmed and out on stalks with the effort of reading by shaded candlelight, I gave up at last and let the book slip to the floor as I blew out the candle and slipped into a uneasy sleep. Druid priests, like the ones pictured in the sketched illustrations, strode through my dreams, always fleeing, always being chased until their backs were to a wall, when they would turn round waving great meat-cleaver weapons. In one dream, a child no older than Gerry was dragged by his hair into the circle of priests who spread out their white robes in a circle of concealment around him. I was pulling at their arms, trying to penetrate the circle, but I could not. I woke with terror in my pounding heart and it was some time before I became calm enough, telling myself that it was all just made-up stories from long ago, to slip back into sleep.

I remember vividly the weekend before Father came home. His team of keepers was due back from The Rock on Tuesday morning, exactly a week before Christmas Day, and the ensuing week was to be full of happy events. Mother, Gerry and I were in high spirits on Saturday as we decorated our cottage with red-berried rowan sprigs and prickly holly. Gerry and I had searched all over the almost treeless islet until we found a single but beautiful rowan tree over near David Balfour's Bay; and Mother had crossed the causeway to buy the holly from a cart that had come all the way out to Knockvolgan Farm to sell Christmas greenery to the lighthouse families.

School was to end with a concert on Friday evening and each form had been practising one Gaelic and one English song to be performed to all the parents in the big bothy. Catriona's form were dancing as well – the Hebridean Weaving Lilt, which depicted a loom at work, the dancers being the 'shiftin' bobbins'. My form, all three of us, were attempting the

141

Eriskay Love Lilt in Gaelic, at which I was becoming quite proficient since so many of my classmates spoke it, or more often a hybrid that was half-Gaelic, half-English. In English, we were all singing from the tartan-covered 'Burns Songbook' that I remembered from my North Berwick school. My favourite was 'Whistle an' I'll cam tae ye my lad' but sadly my form had been given 'Flow gently, Sweet Afton' which I had never much liked. Apparently, The Dow had been prevailed upon last year to give a solo and had enthralled them all with a sad, Jacobite lament. 'She's got the voice of an angel, my mam said,' Catriona told me. 'She had all the women greetin' and the men blowin' their noses.' I tried to reconcile this affecting image with the sharp schoolmarm who manipulated Gerry and ignored me. Truly, the woman never ceased to surprise.

Saturday was the big party at Fionnphort for all the schools in the area, starting at six o'clock and going on throughout that evening and even into the next day, if the stories were to be believed. What was left of Saturday night I would be spending at Catriona's house, going to the kirk over there with them on Sunday and staying on till Monday, Christmas Eve. And, of course, to cap it all, there was our trip to Iona with Lachlan before he brought me home that day and his promise to show me the Druid sites on that ancient, sacred isle. My cup was fairly running over and I had never been happier, certainly not since we came to Erraid.

'Is Catriona still wanting you to go and stay after the party?' asked Mother as we fashioned a holly and mistletoe wreath for our front door. 'Her mother's not changed her mind?'

'Of course not,' I replied. 'Catriona and I are really looking forward to it.'

'Well, remember your father has to . . .' She was interrupted by Gerry falling off the step-stool – again - this time banging his shin and bursting into tears. Of course, I know now that she was going to say 'your father has still to give his permission' but I was surfing a wave of excited expectation and gave no thought to her unfinished sentence.


Tuesday dawned fine and bright. Mother looked especially well that morning, her lovely face enhanced by a soft rose bloom, her eyes clear and her smile sure. She was feeling confident for once about Father coming back into our little fold. The cottage was looking beautiful, all the Christmas food preparations were well in hand, Gerry and I were settling down well at school and she was settling down well with the other wives. They were all delighted about the forthcoming baby and had taken her even more under their wing. My terrors about Mother giving birth –

whatever that would entail – in this back-of-beyond place had been assuaged by their explanations and reassurances. There was even another lighthouse baby due before ours – Kitty, I think the wife was called - and so we would have the chance to see how the arrangements for the birth would work out. I sang lustily that afternoon as we practised our songs for the concert and not even a chilly look from The Dow did anything to lower my spirits.

The first inkling of calamity came as soon as the schoolhouse door was opened to let us out at the end of the afternoon. The exodus always took the form of a disciplined crocodile with the little ones going first and my form last. As soon as each child crossed the threshold into open air, he or she would let out a whoop of glee and charge around like a caged animal newly escaped, especially in winter when we had been indoors all afternoon. It was a kind of daft tradition that had grown up and we all played the game.

About half of the children had 'escaped' and we could hear the cries of freedom from them, when a man appeared in the doorway and started pushing his way in, thrusting children from the third and fourth forms out of his way quite roughly. Two of them banged their heads together as he shoved them and they yelled in sudden pain.

The Dow often let us make our own exit while she finished collecting her books and belongings. She had us so well trained and was sure enough of her discipline to know we did not need her eye upon us all the time. The yell from the head-bangers was the first she knew of the man striding up the short corridor to the schoolroom. I was at the very end of the line and so I realised the cause of the commotion up ahead at the same moment as The Dow did. And we both recognised the man at the same moment. It was Father.

'Robert! I mean, Mr Galway. Whatever is the matter? What are you doing here? And why the hurry?' It was the most agitated I had seen her for some time, since that night in The Lookout, in fact, when I had taunted her with my knowledge of the goings-on – whatever they were – between Father and her and she had slapped me so hard I had fallen, hit my head and passed out. 'Do you wish to speak to me? Is it about Gerry's or Liza's progress?' She sounded calmer now, in control, the schoolmarm in her own territory.

All the remaining children had arrested their exit and some of the previously freed ones were starting to come back in to see what the hold-up was. As Father thrust the last of Catriona's form out of his way and reached mine, The Dow called out: 'Carry on, please. Out you go. All of you.' Reluctantly, the children obeyed, casting curious glances over their shoulders, sorry to be deprived of ringside seats at such an interesting event. I moved to follow, assuming that he had come to see The Dow and feeling quite shocked at his brazenness. I wondered if he had even been to see Mother yet or whether he had come straight off the boat and up here to see *her* first.

'Now, Mr Galway, if you want to discuss anything, why don't you come into the schoolroom? Is Mrs Galway with you? Is it about Gerry or Liza?' She was putting a lot of effort into covering up what was actually going on, I thought, a little amused at the game they were playing even while I detested it for Mother's sake.

But Father had stopped short of the schoolroom door and was ignoring the Dow. His eyes were fastened on me and I saw with a spurt of fear that they were snapping with anger. He shot out a huge, calloused hand and grabbed my arm. The other hand gathered my two pigtails in it and twisted them viciously. This way, he propelled me in front of him towards the outside door. It happened so quickly and was so unexpected that I had no time to resist or protest. I was outside before I knew it and being frogmarched along the path to our house. I tried to turn my head to see his face, to get some clue to what was going on in his mind. My eyes rolled in my head like a panicked horse and I caught glimpses of my schoolmates lining the path like a guard of honour, staring avidly.

Before we reached our door, Mother came running towards us, her floury apron flapping around her. Gerry had run ahead to tell her what was happening, I supposed. But Father simply pushed her aside, just as he had the children in the school crocodile. He marched me up the path and through the open door of our house. Only then did he let go with a final shove. I fell on my hands and knees and a sharp kick on my behind jerked me forward and brought my shoulder up against the wall with a painful crunch.

'You bloody little snake in the grass,' bellowed my father. 'I have to be told by someone else's wife that my own daughter is going to be gallivanting about and staying away from our own home *overnight!*' This last word was said with such emphasis it might have signified a capital crime.

In a flash, I remembered my casual reassurances to Catriona about her Mother's invitation and remembered too that Mother had said we must ask Father's permission before we replied. She had known how he would react to such a decision being taken without reference to him. But, of course, the MacPhail family knew nothing of such terrors. One of them must have been speaking to Father already about the invitation, before

Mother had had a chance to present it to him in her careful, well-timed way.

My castles in the air collapsed. My Christmas dreams were in ruins.

# CHAPTER EIGHTEEN

*You took me for a Johnny-Raw with no more mother-wit or courage than a porridge stick.*                    Robert Louis Stevenson, from 'Kidnapped'

I was prepared for a thrashing – if it is ever possible to be prepared for such a terrifying prospect. There was no fight in me then. The humiliating march along the path, watched excitedly by all my schoolmates - except Catriona, thank goodness, who always left first as she had furthest to go - had taken all the pride and rebellion out of me. I squirmed with humiliation, not only for myself but for him too and for Mother who would have somehow to live this down. It was not that other fathers did not wallop their children sometimes. In those days, it was the norm. It was my father's ugly, unbridled temper, and his vicious behaviour when the temper had him in its grip, that set him apart. He cared for nothing and no one then. He must let fly no matter where he was or who was witness. It was never enough simply to overpower and physically abuse whoever was the butt of his temper; the mean streak in him was not satisfied until his victim was mentally humiliated and cowed as well. I huddled into the wall, curling up and concealing my face like a frightened hedgehog. I could hear myself pleading, the same four words over and over. 'No, please, Father, please.' Through my terror, I hated myself for sounding so abject and I hated him. How I hated him! I think, if I had had a weapon of any kind at that moment, I would have tried to kill him.

He bent down and took hold of my pigtails again, pulling me to my feet. I smelt whisky and beer on his sour breath. With his other hand, he twisted my left arm up my back and propelled me forward. 'Get into the kitchen, you little bitch. I'm going to teach you . . .'

'Robert! Stop that! Leave Liza be.'

I heard the voice and supposed it was Mother come to attempt my rescue. A fresh terror washed over me. He would turn on her, harm her, maybe even harm the baby. Gritting my teeth against the searing pain it caused in my scalp, I pulled my head round.

'Get away, Mother, Get away. He'll only belt you as well . . .'

The words died in my throat even as he let go of my hair and my arm. The woman standing in the doorway was not Mother: it was The Dow.

146

The sudden silence after the hubbub of his shouting and my screaming felt like suspended animation. No one moved. The mantelpiece clock ticked and the peats in the fire shifted. Then Father took a step towards her, opening up a gap in the kitchen doorway, and I saw my chance. I darted round him and pelted past The Dow. I think she must have jumped aside to let me out for I had no memory of any contact with her. I cannoned down the path straight into Mother who was just turning in at the door.

'Liza, lass, what on earth is going on? What have you done to put your father in such a rage?'

For answer, I buried my face in her apron and howled.

'Have you children no homes to go to?' Mother turned on the gawping gaggle of my classmates behind us. 'Off you go now. All of you. At once.'

They obeyed reluctantly, muttering to each other, some even giggling, though what there was to laugh about I could not imagine. Mother knelt down and took my face in her hands. Then, unaccountably, she too laughed.

'You're a bonny sight, Liza Galway. You've flour all over your face and hair - it's even on your eyelashes - and big, dirty streaks down your cheeks. You look like a guiser on Guy Fawkes Night. Here . . .' She turned the hem up and used the other side of the apron to scrub at my face. I had come to the end of my howling sobs and was at the hiccupping, snivelling stage.

'I'm sorry, Mother.' *Sniff.*

'What for? What is it that you've done?'

'I told Catriona' – *sniff* - 'to tell her mother that it was all right for me to go and stay with them' – *sniff* – 'after the Christmas party. Father must have heard about it before he got back here.' *Sniff.* 'He's flaming mad. He says he going to . . . '

'Oh, Liza. Will you never learn? Did I not tell you to wait and let me ask your Father when he came home? What did you have to go and jump the gun for? Now your father's in a bad mood and him not five minutes back with us.'

She sounded about ready to howl herself and I added guilt to my woes.

'Sorry,' I whispered again. 'Sorry, sorry . . .'

'Well, it's done now and we'll have to try and sort it out. Come on.' Mother was brisk, sounding a lot more confident than I knew she was feeling. I tugged on her arm to stop her heading up the path into the house.

'Stop, Mother. You can't go in . . . yet.'

She hesitated, considering. 'You might be right, Liza. Might be better to give your father time to calm down. Maybe one of the other men will come along and see him first. Take his mind off things. Then, later, we can talk sensibly about all this. Not,' she fixed me with a stern eye 'not that I am going to plead your cause and ask him to let you go. You've been caught telling a lie to Catriona and her mother. I don't want him to leather you – you're getting too old for that now and he doesn't know his own strength – but you'll have to be punished in some other way. No overnight visits to the MacPhails for you, my girl. You'll be lucky if you get to the Christmas Party at all.'

If I had had any tears left, I would have wept again but I had to make do with screwing up my face and quivering with misery. And in this state, Mother dragged me by the hand along to the Campbell house where, of course, Gerry was ensconced at the table, enjoying milky tea and fresh-baked mince pies with the rest of the Campbell children.

I had been about to tell Mother that The Dow was in our house with Father but some devil of revenge was in me, I think, and I said nothing. I had been on Mother's side completely in the whole business of Father and The Dow, ready to do whatever it took to save or avenge her. But Mother's pronouncement of my punishment had annihilated my lovely dream. My visit to the MacPhails, two whole days and nights with that lovely family, the boat trip to Iona on Christmas Eve, finding out more about the Druids there - it was all gone, snatched away from me in a trice. I hated Mother as well at that moment.

So I said nothing and how long Father and The Dow were together in our house that afternoon I did not know. Whether anyone else had seen her go in – obviously Mother had not – I did not know either. And I was too absorbed in my own miseries to care.


We stayed at the Campbell house for a good hour. The cheerful, Christmassy atmosphere, with the rich smell of the mincemeat pies and the chatter about the forthcoming concert on Friday and party on Saturday, was like salt in the wound to me. Why did other families live in such carefree harmony when ours lived in a perpetual state of dread, walking on eggshells, unable to do things that were simply normal for other families without yet another horrible row? I thought of Catriona's family and, although I had never been in their home, I just knew that it would be like the Campbell house. It would certainly be nothing like ours.

Mother too was feeling the contrast, I am sure, for she looked miserable. Bridie Campbell noticed it at once.

'Maggie, m'dear,' she said in her lilting Irish voice 'you're not looking at all well yourself. 'Here . . .' She crossed her kitchen in three strides and took Mother's arm. 'Come over here and sit down. Is there something wrong? You've been overdoing it, have you? Got yourself into a state of exhaustion, I should think. You have to take care of yourself in your condition, sure you have, you know that yourself, for the babby's sake as well as your own.'

With gentle, cooing words, she guided Mother to the rocking chair beside the fire, evicting a large orange cat, which poured off the chair like warm marmalade, flicked up its tail and stalked out of the kitchen. Mother made no protest but sank down onto the cushioned seat which was still warm and hairy from the cat's occupation.

'I'm fine, Bridie. Fine. It's just . . . just . . .' Then, to my horror and Bridie's consternation, Mother's face crumpled and tears spilled down her cheeks. 'If we could just wait here for a bit . . .' Her voice failed her then and she bowed her head, her shoulders shaking.

'Liza, come over here and help your mother. She's not feeling at all well, so she's not.' Bridie looked over to where I was still standing in the kitchen doorway. I shook my head, quite sure that I was the last person Mother wanted at that moment. Bridie frowned and came to stand in front of me. 'What *is* going on, Liza? What's upset your lovely mammy so much? Her that's been looking so well these past few days, happy as a sand boy, looking forward to Christmas like us all.'

I shook my head and chewed my lip. Bridie bent down and looked full into my face. 'Sure, you've been at the weeping yourself,' she pronounced. 'Your bonnie wee face is all begritten. Are you going to tell me what's been happening?'

But I only hung my head and shook it. The other children had been absorbed in their own chatter and enjoyment of the food on the table, barely noticing our arrival, but now Gerry looked round and saw us. He wriggled himself free from the tightly packed bench, jumped down and ran over to Mother, launching himself at her lap as was his wont, ever sure of his welcome. The rocking chair bucked like a wee boat in a rough sea and Mother almost toppled out of it. Grabbing on to Gerry to save him from falling - and the effort to right both the chair and herself - startled her out of her misery and she even laughed shakily as the chair and its two occupants finally settled back down on the hearth rug.

149

'For God's sake!' Bridie pulled Gerry off Mother's lap unceremoniously, just as she would any of her own brood. 'Don't you be so rough, me lad. You could have hurt your mammy.'

Gerry looked as if he too would join in the family weeping session but Mother leaned forward and pulled him to her. 'It's all right, Bridie,' she said, her voice much stronger now. 'My wee man was just glad to see me. Weren't you, pet?' She stroked Gerry's hair and turned to Bridie. 'The smell of those pies is going round my heart. Can you spare me one? And maybe a wee cup o' tea? I'll be right as rain once I've had that. I was just feeling a wee bit shaky there. Nothing to worry about. No, really . . .' as Bridie made to stop her rising 'that's all I need. There's nothing wrong with me at all.' She smiled brightly, deceiving no one, but Bridie took the hint and simply pursed her lips as she went over to a cupboard to fetch a cup and plate.


It was gone half past five when we wound our way home along the dark path, torch-less, with only a pale, ghostly moon, playing hide and seek in a cloudy sky, and shadowy, second-hand lamplight from the cottage windows, to light our way. Bridie had finally wheedled me into eating two mince pies and drinking a cup of milk but my spirits were still at a low ebb. I dragged my feet behind Mother and Gerry but not so much that I lost sight of them. I might be scared of the retribution that awaited me if Father was still in the house but I was twice as scared of being alone in the darkness. Thoughts of the Druids and their fearful practices flitted through my mind, the words I had been reading by clandestine candlelight these past few nights leaping off the page to take shape in my overworked imagination. When the door of someone's 'cludgie' banged shut, I jumped and ran into the back of Mother's skirt, almost knocking her down.

Our house was silent and cold. Obviously Father had gone out without bothering to stoke the fire before he left. Mother exclaimed in annoyance and cast me another baleful glance. Everything was my fault that night.

She knelt down at the hearth and began raking the smoky embers into life. 'Go outside, Liza, and get some kindling from the shed. Bring it at once. Then get some more peats and bring them in.'

The last thing I wanted to do was go out into the dark night again and not only because of the cold. Gerry, of course, had disappeared into his room, keeping out of the way of such chores. Shivering, I picked up the empty peat basket and dragged my weary feet along the lobby to the back door. Erraid seemed to be alive with strange sounds – or so it seemed. 'Just the usual noises,' I told my jangling nerves. Then I heard it – a low laugh, a hissed exclamation and the sound of a key scraping in a lock. The shed had occupants, whispering ones who had just locked themselves in. My mind was doing cartwheels as possibilities spun round it. Ghosts? Tramps? Burglars? Children playing? All of these I quickly rejected. Ghosts were too fearful to contemplate - they only belonged in storybooks. Tramps and burglars belonged in my previous townie life – there were no such things in this remote place. And surely all the children were in their own homes, clustered round tables or fires.

'Liza! Are you bringing that kindling or not? This fire'll be out in a minute.' Mother's irritable voice floated down the lobby. It had no effect on me – I was too absorbed in my own speculations and fears – but it did have an effect on the occupants of the shed. The noises stopped abruptly and their absence seemed as loud as their presence of a second ago.

It struck me then like a thunderbolt. I think my head actually snapped back on my neck. I *knew* who was in the shed and I knew why. A couple of hours ago, I would have thought of the terrible insult to Mother and agonised over what to do. Now, I had but one priority and, in a flash, I saw how to achieve it. I marched boldly over to the shed door and knocked.

There was no answer. I had not expected one. I knocked again. Then I spoke.

'Let me in. I know you're both in there. Let me in or I'll go and get Mother.'

There was no response at first and I began to fear that my bold plan was not going to work. But, slowly, the key scraped in the lock and the door was pushed out towards me. I shot into the shed and pulled the door behind me. There was no light in there, of course, no candle, torch or lamp. But I was not afraid now of the dark. I had the scent of victory in my nostrils and a spirit of recklessness possessed me. 'Now or never!' I told myself.

'I know it's you in here, Father, and I know Miss Dow is with you. And I know you've been meeting up at The Lookout as well.'

There was an animal growl from a dark corner and a sharp movement which knocked a spade over with a clatter. For one dreadful moment, I thought Father was going to spring forward to attack me and my heart somersaulted into my mouth. Then, *she* spoke:

151

'Be quiet, Robert. Control yourself.' I heard a deep breath being drawn and a hoarse gurgle. The Dow spoke again. 'Liza, we have a perfectly good explanation for being in here. We . . .'

'No you don't!' I cut across her. There was no time to waste. Mother must surely come out into the back yard any moment or, at the least, send Gerry to find out what was keeping me. 'Don't waste your time explaining. I'm going to tell Mother all about what you two have been doing unless . . . unless . . .' I took a deep breath – this was it. 'Unless you let me go and stay with Catriona after the party. *And* you have to persuade Mother to let me as well, because she's mad at me for telling Catriona's mother lies and says I can't even go to the party. Promise me, Father, or I'll tell her about you and Miss Dow. I will! I will!'

Again, there came that animal growl but this time no movement. 'Bloody, conniving little bitch,' I heard a furious whisper. Then Miss Dow's cool voice:

'Yes, that's fine. Liza.' She might have been approving a sheet of sums in school. 'That will work well. Now off you go! Quickly, before your mother comes.'

'I want to hear Father say it,' I persisted. '*He's* got to say it.'

'Tell her, Robert.' The Dow sounded almost amused, as if I was entertaining her with my performance.

Father spluttered a few words to the effect that he would tell Mother to let me go to the party and the weekend visit to the MacPhail. He sounded as if the words were being choked out of him. I liked that.

'Now go, girl!' snapped The Dow. 'And keep your part of the bargain. Or else.'

I was tempted to taunt her with 'Or else what?' but settled instead for adding:

'And he's no' to belt me again – ever. Mother says I'm too old for it anyway. If he does . . .'

'Liza! Where are you? What are you doing?' It was Mother, patience exhausted at last, coming out the back door into the yard. 'Have you got that kindling? The fire's dying.'

I grabbed one of the hessian sacks in which we stored the twigs and skelfs of wood that we used for kindling. I had almost forgotten this part of my errand. Taking a deep breath, I pushed open the door of the shed and rushed out towards her.

'Sorry, Mother. So sorry. I was awfy needing the lav . . . the toilet. I just had to squat down in the bushes and go before I got the kindling and the peats. Here.' I thrust the hessian sack at her. 'You get in out of the cold now and get the fire breezed up. I'll no' be a minute wi' the peats.'

My voice was a cheery staccato. Well might Mother pause in surprise, for the bright, chirpy girl before her now in no way resembled the surly, snivelling one who had trailed unwillingly out the back door a few minutes ago. If it had not been so dark, she would have seen my ear-to-ear grin and been even more amazed, perhaps even to the point of suspicion. As it was, she simply took the kindling sack from me with muttered 'Thank goodness for that' and hurried back indoors.

I took my time filling the basket with peats, singing 'Oh, whistle an' I'll come tae ye, my lad' loud enough for the skulking pair in the shed to know I was still there. I was tempted to knock on the door again and say something like 'You can come out now. The coast's clear!' But some modicum of sense prevailed. After all, I still had to live in the same house as Father for the next four weeks and sit in school under *her* jurisdiction for another year or so. I had what I wanted. I was going to Fionnphort and Iona, to the Christmas party, to stay with the MacPhails and to find out about the ancient Druids of the sacred isle.

I contented myself with a final flourish of my song: 'Though *Father and Mother* and a' should gae mad, Oh whistle and I'll come tae ye, my lad!'

# CHAPTER NINETEEN

*I would rather have ten foes in front of me than one friend like you cracking pistols at my back.*
                                                  Robert Louis Stevenson, from 'Kidnapped'

I expected that Father would take his time to appear but he almost followed me into the kitchen. Mother was on her hands and knees at the grate, coaxing the fire into life, delicately building the peats into a pyramid on the flaming wood. He strode over to her, touched her shoulder and was almost knocked over when she sprang up in surprise.

'Let me do that,' he said, taking the fire-tongs from her hand. 'You're looking tired.'

Then, as Mother gaped at him in disbelief, 'Shut your mouth, Maggie. You'll catch flies in it.' He laughed and turned to drop on to his knees on the hearthrug.

I had wondered how he was going to behave, whether he was actually capable of swallowing his rage and keeping his promise and, if so, how he would make the sudden change plausible. I had reckoned without the arrogance of the man. He simply behaved as if the recent incidence of his violent temper, which had brought me such public degradation and threat of worse to come, had never happened. And he clearly intended to carry off this complete *volte-face* without any explanation, no questions asked or answered. I could only presume he had been thoroughly coached by The Dow. As noted before, she was an excellent teacher.

Mother was completely wrong-footed. She had been expecting more foul temper from him, probably a scene where he started to thrash me and she intervened, getting hurt in the process and even courting further violence towards herself. She was tightly wound up with dread, her face pinched and white, nothing like the bonny, bright, well-looked-after woman I had been looking forward to showing Father. Her eyes flickered over towards my corner and I gave her a big, encouraging smile which baffled her even more.

'You sit down, Mother,' I said, pulling out her accustomed chair. 'I'll see to the tea.' I was opening the smaller side oven on the range as I spoke and the aroma of warm tattie scones wafted into the kitchen.

Mother subsided on to the chair obediently, blinking in bewilderment. She actually looked quite frightened, probably thinking that this weirdly harmonious interchange could only be the precursor to an even bigger bout of unpleasantness than usual, that it was some kind of horrible cat-

and-mouse game. Only Gerry seemed unaware of the tension crackling in the room.

'Can we no' have mincey pies like Angus' house, Mother? Do you ken how to make them? They were that good.' He did not, however, scorn the tattie scones but helped himself to two as soon as I set the plate down on the table.

'There's cheese, too, son,' said Mother automatically. 'Take some cheese with your scone.'

For a few minutes, we all attended to the business of spreading butter, cutting cheese and spooning pickle out of the big jar. I went round the table, carefully pouring tea into cups, then passing sugar and milk to Father.

'Ladies first,' he said jovially, passing them to Mother, who almost fell off her chair in surprise.

It was strange beyond description to see Father buttering her up, working up to broaching a tricky topic. Role reversal indeed. Once again, I gave the credit for this performance – so completely outside Father's normal repertoire – to The Dow. She must have been working on him while I was piling the peats into the basket or, more likely, she had been coaching him for some time in the best way to keep Mother sweet and unsuspecting. I remembered the pleasant surprise of his uncharacteristic good humour the first two weeks of his last shore leave before he reverted to type over his jealousy of Arthur's compliments to Mother. Had The Dow already been working on him then? What game was she playing?

I was surely getting out of my depth, mixing it with such a consummate player. But it was done now and I was in it up to my neck.


'Well, Maggie,' Father began, not looking at me or Mother, keeping his eyes on the tattie scone he was buttering, 'I hear there's to be a Christmas Party on Friday.'

Mother looked wary and said nothing.

'Euan and Calum were telling me all about it when we were on The Rock. I gather we'll *all* be going.'

Mother still said nothing. She looked more afraid of his genial tone that she would have been of his bad temper. Father ploughed on. I heard the false heartiness and felt sure Mother would too.

'And then, when we got to Fionnphort and stopped to collect the post, we met up with Lachlan and he was talking about it. *And* it seems Miss Liza has got herself an invitation to stay on after it.'

155

Both Mother and I drew in a sharp breath and this time Mother did speak. 'Don't worry about that, Robert. Liza knows she did wrong to tell Catriona she already had permission to go and stay with the MacPhails. I've told her what her punishment will be. We don't need to say anything more about it. Please.' This last word was accompanied by a gesture of entreaty and a tremulous smile. 'No more upsets, Robert, please. It's not good for me . . . or the baby'.

Father nodded. 'That's what I was thinking too, Maggie. We'll say no more about it.'

For a horrible moment, I thought they were going to leave it like that with my punishment, as defined by Mother, still hanging over my head. I squirmed in my chair and cleared my throat loudly. It was the best I could do. I was too afraid to look directly at Father and I could hardly refer to his promise to me in the shed without rousing Mother's suspicions.

'Maybe . . .' he was definitely gritting his teeth now and the smile on his face was quite horrible, more threatening than any frown. 'Maybe we can let Liza off this time. It's not every day any of us get invitations like this one. It would maybe seem like an insult to the MacPhails if we stopped her going to stay with them. We don't want to get a bad name. For being ungrateful or rude, I mean.'

I recognised The Dow's coaching in this speech. Father would never have thought of such a thing. Mother gaped at him bewildered.

'You're not angry with her anymore? You don't think she deserves punishment for lying?'

I held my breath and willed Mother just to accept what Father was saying.

'Well . . .' Father was torn between wishing he could give me exactly what he thought I deserved and knowing that I held the power of life or death over his clandestine relationship with The Dow. 'Well, I *was* angry when Lachlan first told me that the visit had been agreed without my permission. That's why I marched her out of school and along the path. I was going to thrash her for it.' His voice had risen and he glared at me. For two pins he would have thrown caution to the winds and turned on me. From somewhere I found the courage to lift my head to meet his angry stare and he swallowed his rising fury with hard, audible gulp.

'No, Robert.' Mother spoke calmly, with just a slight tremor in her voice. 'I don't want you to belt her any more. She's growing up.' She gave him a meaningful look which I could not then interpret though I know now that she was thinking of my approaching womanhood, perhaps

156

more conscious of it because of the changes happening in her own body at that time.

Gerry had been paying no attention to the conversation, absorbed in drawing the cheese slice along the face of the block of cheese to produce wafer thin slices. But now, his head shot up. 'I'm growing up too,' he said peevishly. 'I shouldna get belted neither.'

'You pipe down or I'll show you whether you're too grown up for a leathering,' snarled Father, leaning across the table and spitting the words at his son. He had made no blackmailed promise to Gerry and all his frustration at having to keep that promise to me boiled over. Gerry squealed in fright, leapt up from the table and ran howling out of the room. Mother made to rise and follow him but Father spoke sharply.

'Leave him, Maggie. Let him go.'

She hesitated, torn between fear of Father and pity for Gerry.

'Let's finish this damned conversation about Liza visiting the bloody MacPhails.' His voice was clipped with an edge of menace. The whole business of backtracking from his earlier flare-up over my lie to Catriona was taking a lot out of him. Even with my future hanging in the balance, I felt a little glow of satisfaction over the struggle he was having. He had often made me say and do things I hated or was afraid of. Revenge is sweet.

Mother heard the menace in his voice and responded automatically with compliance. The three of us sat for a moment in silence, listening to Gerry's noisy sobs which grew noisier as he realised that Mother was not coming to comfort him.

'Shut that door, Liza,' ordered Father. 'Please,' he added, with an effort. I did so and Gerry's wails ceased to dominate the kitchen. 'Now listen,' he said, abruptly, clearly tired of the whole business. 'We will *all* go to the party on Saturday and Liza will go to the MacPhails after it and stay with them. Lachlan will bring her back on Monday. She did wrong telling her pal a lie and I was mad at her for embarrassing me. When Lachlan mentioned it and I knew nothing about it, it made me look like I wasn't master in my own household.' He grimaced and swallowed hard on his anger. It was obviously extremely unpalatable, for his face contorted horribly, but he ground out: 'She's learned her lesson now, after all this carry-on. Say no more about it. That's an end of it.'

Mother shook her head and looked baffled. She had thought she would be pleading with him not to harm me but instead he was pleading – well, as near as my Father could ever come to pleading – for her to show me mercy.

'But . . .' She frowned. 'I thought . . .'

157

Father tossed his head impatiently and I saw that his short supply of patience was nearing its end. I got up from my chair and slipped round the table to kneel at Mother's feet and lay my head on her lap. 'I'm so sorry, Mother,' I said, making a fine dramatic display of my repentance. 'I promise never to tell a lie again. Please can you find it in your heart to forgive me?' I sounded like a character in one of her favourite novels - Jane Austen or Charlotte Bronte, perhaps - and Mother could not help laughing. For once in my life, I had done exactly the right thing. The mood lightened and the tension slackened.

'Oh, Liza, Liza,' she said. 'What a lassie! What am I going to do with you?'

'You're going to let me go to the party and on to the MacPhails?' I suggested, standing up and leaning down to give her cheek a wee kiss.

'Oh . . . all right!' She gave me a playful shove. 'Just this once, mind. No more lies.'

'Never,' I promised with heavy mock solemnity and she laughed again as she rose from her chair. She made for the door intent on going to the howling Gerry. There never was a boy could keep up sobbing longer than him.

When she had gone, closing the door behind her, Father looked at me with narrowed eyes. He might have been appraising an opponent in a wrestling match and I realised that our relationship had moved on to a new level. I had never imagined that he loved me but at least his animosity had only been that of an impatient, bad-tempered adult towards an annoying child. Now he was looking at me as a man looks at his sworn enemy. I felt a cold shiver run through me. What had I done?

'You happy now, you devious little bitch?' He spat out the words. 'You better keep your part of the bargain or, so help me, I'll . . .'

'That's fine.' I did not want to hear the details of my fate should I break my side of our pact. 'I will keep my side of it. I promise.' I had eaten little more than half a tattie scone but I rose from the table, cleared my plate and cup into the basin and went quickly away through to my own room.


I kept out of Father's way as much as possible from then on. This was not difficult since he had as little desire for my company as I had for his. He lay abed until Gerry and I had left for school, his presence behind the bed-recess curtain a strong disincentive to any breakfast hijinks or squabbles. At noonday dinner and at teatime, he was absent so Mother put his plate of food in the warming oven at the side of the range. Where he was or what he was doing I did not ask and Mother did not offer an explanation. She looked tranquil enough, now that the upset I had caused was past, and I presumed Father was not being too harsh or demanding. The occasional times I did see them together they seemed friendly enough, even quite loving, towards each other and I felt a sick guilt as I watched them. I knew I was betraying Mother, selling my soul for two nights at the MacPhails and a day trip to Iona, but I was in too deep to pull back now. Whereas before I had been on the alert for any clues or signs that would feed my suspicions about Father and The Dow, I now made a conscious effort to ignore them.

I turned my attention instead to my quest for information about the Druids, reading more of the little book that Catriona had given me. The antiquity and spread of the cult was impressive - records of them being found in France and Britain as long ago as 300 BC – and the stranglehold they had on the common people likewise. They taught that ordinary people could not communicate with the gods; Druid priests were the only intermediaries. They kept their knowledge to themselves; no ordinary person could be any kind of leader in any field, whether medical, scientific, legal or astrological. It was the ultimate totalitarian society.

'What are you reading now?'

It was Thursday afternoon, the day before the end of term, and Mother and I had been making a batch of bread. She had slipped behind the recess curtain to have 'forty winks' while it proved. Gerry was along at Angus' house and I had been left alone. The bread would be another half an hour at least. I had slipped through to my bedroom, intent on reading more of Lachlan's book, but the bedroom was cold and the warm kitchen had lured me back. I held up the little book with its faded green cover and old-gold lettering on front and spine.

'Where did you get that?' Mother had been speaking through a yawn as she emerged from the recess, tucking her hair back up into its bun, but now her voice was sharp, accusing almost. She crossed the kitchen in two strides and snatched the book out of my hand. 'Is this the . . .' her voice tailed off as she read the title. 'Oh . . . no, it's not. I thought it was . . .'

'The one you had back in North Berwick?' I finished for her. 'The one you were looking at that day when I got in from school and you screamed and threw it on the floor.'

'I don't remember,' said Mother. 'At least,' she saw my incredulity, 'I know I had two books like this – I gave you the one about the Tales and Legends - but I don't remember what happened to the other one. Must have gotten lost in the flitting.'

There was something unconvincing about this statement. I pursued my quest for knowledge.

'This one's called *The Druids of West Scotland*. What was your other book called?'

'I don't remember.' For a book that had frightened the life out of her, it seemed to be extremely forgettable.

'Why did it frighten you so much?'

'What are you talking about?'

'That book.' I waved *Druids* impatiently in her face. 'You screamed and threw it on the floor.'

'Nonsense. You're being fanciful as usual, Liza. Now, put that book away before you get flour all over it. It's time to get the dough ready for baking.'

And that was all I could get out of her about the mystery book, twin to the one Catriona had lent me. But it occurred to me, as we kneaded the dough for the third and final time, that Lachlan might have a copy. Catriona had said the book was one of a collection – 'all about Scotland in the past' - and he had a whole shelf of them. The thought was yet another spurt of heat to my simmering impatience. Would Saturday never come?

# CHAPTER TWENTY

*It is one thing to stand in danger of your life and quite another to run the peril of both life and character.*                  Robert Louis Stevenson, from 'Kidnapped'

The big bothy had been transformed. Gone was the atmosphere of Sabbath gloom. Instead a cheerful buzz and lively movement among the gathered folk. The children sat in the front three rows, ready to file out and do their bit when their time came; the adults sat in the rows behind and there was much waving, gesticulating and calling messages between the two sides of the divide. Of The Dow there was no sign and her absence was no doubt contributing to the atmosphere of festive freedom.

Taking advantage of this, Gerry turned round and waved at me, wriggling and bouncing madly. He was in a high state of excitement because he had been chosen to sing a solo verse of The Bonnie Banks of Loch Lomond. Mother had ironed his white shirt twice and pressed sharp creases into his good tweed trousers. These had been rather too big for him before, drooping far below his knobbly knees, but, in just three short months, he had grown in both height and width. I waved back and blew him a kiss which he pretended to catch and tuck behind his ear – a little game we played.

He was about to stand up and possibly shout or mime some message to me when I saw The Dow's spare figure in the bothy's big, wide-open door. She was dressed in a long grey cardigan over a white blouse with a froth of lace at the neck. Her tartan skirt – she had many of these – was yellow and black today, of demure length, the pleats pressed to a knife-edge. Her green felt hat, however, set at a jaunty angle to display the arching grey feather, was quite at odds with the staid outfit and, under its brim, her dark eyes seemed to snap with life. I could not help contrasting her with the dreary figure I remembered from my first encounter with her on the ferry from Oban. Then she had seemed grey, gaunt and spinsterish but now, although she was as thin and proper as ever, there was about her a life-force and even a certain stylishness. I saw that she was actually a fine woman, with perfect bone structure, beautiful eyes and attractive carriage. Something – or someone – had happened to her to wreak this change.

The three rows of children quickly fell silent as they became aware of her entry and the adults behind followed suit, though not so quickly. I turned in my seat to look at Father who was two rows behind me but in an end seat, so that I got a good view of his intent profile. Unaware of my scrutiny, he was staring raptly down at the makeshift stage, a small smile tugging at the corners of his mouth. I did not have to guess what was putting that smile on his usually grim face and I knew for certain that it was not anticipation of Gerry's solo.

'Well done, Gerrard,' said The Dow, making a beeline for our family group among the throng outside the bothy after the concert. 'You were quite the best turn in the concert this year.'

'Oh, I wouldn't say that,' said Mother modestly but she looked pleased. Gerry had acquitted himself creditably, much to her relief as his last frantic practices in the house before we set out for the bothy had been fairly disastrous. He was of the species of performer which expends almost all its nervousness before going on stage, leaving everyone in the wings in a state of exhausted foreboding, and then going on to sail through the actual performance.

'And, Liza, too,' continued The Dow. 'Your class did extremely well. A beautiful rendering, I thought, of *Sweet Afton*. I'm positively looking forward to hearing it again tomorrow night at the party, aren't you, Mrs Galway?'

'Yes, of course, Miss Dow,' said Mother. 'It's kind of you to . . .'

'And I hear Liza has another treat in store after the concert. Going to stay for a few nights with the MacPhails. She will enjoy that. Such a lovely family. Delightful people. And Catriona and Liza have become such good friends.'

If her tone had not been its usual prim, patronising self, I might have suspected her of gushing. *She's buttering Mother up*, I thought. Guilty conscience, of course, or perhaps reminding me of our bargain. Or was there another reason she was so keen to have me away from home, right off the islet?

'Well,' Mother looked surprised at such enthusiasm. 'To tell you the truth, I almost put a stop to it. I'm still not happy about it. Liza didn't wait to get Robert's permission before she told . . .'

'Oh, don't worry about that, Mrs Galway. Liza has learned her lesson, I'm sure. Whatever it is she has done wrong. And Christmas is a time for forgiving and forgetting, you know. The season of goodwill! Isn't that so, Mr Galway?' As bold as brass, The Dow addressed Father directly, flashing her eyes imperiously.

'That's true, that's true, for sure, indeed.' Father sounded flustered. He shuffled his feet and rubbed his hands together in a play of warding off the cold. 'Let's get home, then.' He began to shepherd Mother, Gerry and me down the path.

'Goodnight, Miss Dow. Thank you for an excellent concert. And all your work with the children to make it so.' Mother remembered her manners as she was dragged away.

I looked back as we marched off. The Dow was standing looking thoughtfully after us. At that moment, the moon sailed out from behind a cloud and its silver light fell on her face. I did not much like the look on it. Gone was the cheerful expression of earlier or the smooth smile of a few seconds ago. Her eyes were narrowed, her expression one of brooding stillness. Not for the first time, I thought she looked predatory and sinister. Her gaze was fixed on Mother and I felt a stab of fear and a surge of fierce protectiveness.

If only I had paid more attention to that fear! But I was in the grip of my own fixation and nothing was now going to stop me having my weekend away from Erraid. I dismissed my feelings as daft imaginings and seized Gerry's hot little hand to skip ahead on the path to home.


Saturday morning dawned bright and cold. I was up first, making tea and toast, setting it on a tray and taking it to Mother and Father who were still abed. Mother had heard me in the kitchen, even though I had been as quiet as I could be, but Father was still snoring, his face to the wall and his broad back a hunched mound under the blankets. I set the tray down on her lap, smiled nicely at Mother's expression of gratitude and withdrew, letting the bed curtain fall back into place. I was out to keep in everybody's good books that day, holding my breath and praying that nothing would happen to spoil or put a stop to the prize that lay ahead.

The unaccustomed treat of early morning tea in bed worked well and both Father and Mother seemed in a mellow mood by the time we assembled for breakfast. I had the porridge made and the table set. Gerry had been wakened and coaxed into dressing, bribed with a spoonful of jam. Breakfast over, I set about my normal Saturday morning chores – blackleading the range, cleaning the windows inside and out, shining up the brass pots and lamps.

There was a boat due in later that day with special provisions from the NLB for all the lighthouse families. We had heard descriptions of past years' deliveries and were looking forward to some treats – Christmas puddings, tins of steak and kidney and boiled ham, bars of chocolate, bags of fudge, tins of fruit and cream, jellies, bottles of cordial, cheeses,

163

savoury and sweet biscuits, apples and oranges . . . the list went on as the wives remembered past years. The boat was expected early afternoon before it was too dark to unload and the NLB men on it would head back to Mull to stay overnight with the lighthouse people at Bunessan, who would also be looking forward to the seasonal largesse from 'The Board'.

In expectation of its arrival, Mother had decided to have just bread and cheese for noonday dinner and something special from our share of the goodies for tea. Nothing too filling, though, as we would all be feasting at the party later. This departure from our normal routine added to our mounting excitement and Gerry and I danced ahead of Mother as we joined the other families in the procession down to the quay. The cry had gone up, 'Ship Ahoy! Here comes the Board boat!' some ten minutes ago and we could all see the boat nosing through the waves towards us as we descended the path to the pier.

The Board regularly sent a boat with provisions for us but it was normally plain staples like tea and sugar, flour, oats and barley, sacks of potatoes, carrots and turnips. Fresh food like meat, fish, eggs, milk, butter and cheese we got either from Knockvolgan Farm, carried across the causeway in hessian bags, or from the general stores in Fionnphort, brought round the coast in the shop's delivery boat. The arrival of such provisions held little interest to anyone except the wives who had families to feed. The men and children were only interested once the stuff had been turned into meals.

But today everyone on the islet had turned out to greet the Board boat as it drew slowly into the pier. The entire population of Erraid, apart from the three men out on Dhu Artach, thronged on to the stone-built square that served as our landing stage. Euan and Calum stood back a little, smoking and exchanging banter, but keeping an eye on the proceedings all the same. There was always a Hogmanay bottle of whisky for each man and the landing of that particular box was eagerly awaited. The wives chattered, reminiscing about past years and talking of plans for this Christmas and Hogmanay. The children larked about, as children will, pushing and chasing each other, calling out playground names and insults.

I was standing on my own beside Mother because, this being Saturday, Catriona was at her home across on Mull and I had not really become friendly with any of the other girls yet. Besides, we were the top form and conscious of our dignity at times like this. We left the romping and larking to the lower forms. But Gerry was with Angus and that meant being in the thick of the action. The boys were playing what looked like

164

*Follow the Leader*, threading themselves through the crowd, turning and twisting, holding on to adult legs to swing themselves round, getting faster and faster. Several adults tried to grab them as they rushed past but none succeeded. I remember thinking that, if the boat did not hurry up and start unloading, there was going to be a disaster. The heavy, oily surge of the sea slapped against the sides of the pier and sucked greedily at its encrusted sides. Just looking at it made me feel queasy, remembering the misery of our crossing from Oban to Craignure a few months ago. How long ago that seemed now! Another life. But, at the same time as the sight of it repelled me, the sound of it exerted a strange, terrifying pull, as if it would suck me, along with the molluscs on the pier, out into its icy depths.

I was not thinking of The Dow or my father at that moment. He had made a sandwich of his bread and cheese and gone off muttering about meeting up with Euan. I had not seen *her* since the concert the night before. It was just as the first boxes began to be winched off the boat that he appeared. He was red in the face and seemed excited but he said nothing. Mother moved to accommodate him and I called out, 'Watch, Mother. You're awfully near the edge' – something like that, I cannot remember exactly. I only knew that she was now inches away from that greedy sea.

I started to move round with the intention of going behind and getting myself between Mother and the edge. At that moment, Gerry and Angus, in a final burst of hilarity, broke free from a tight clutch of wives, dodging hands that reached out to stop them, and careered towards us. Father stepped forward with a growl and would certainly have stopped them in their tracks had not Angus, who was behind Gerry, suddenly tripped and fallen forward, his head hitting Gerry's back and knocking him to the ground. Gerry fell at an angle, missing Father. His flailing arms caught Mother a glancing blow on her hip. It was not a heavy blow and, had she been expecting it, she would have braced herself against it with no harm done, except to Gerry's knees. But, at the very moment that Angus tripped, someone tapped Mother on the shoulder – so she said later – and she turned her head. Distracted, she was taken by surprise, knocked off balance and stumbled. Her foot caught in one of the iron rungs that were sunk into the flat stone of the landing stage. For a second, she wavered, almost regaining her balance, then she crashed down, going head first over the side into the sea.

I screamed. Gerry wailed. Father roared. All was noise and panic. I leapt forward – to try to stop her going into the sea, I suppose, though I could not have done so, her being a full-grown woman and me a mere twelve-year-old. But she had not plunged down into the water. Her foot was caught in the coil of the rope looped through the iron rung. The foot remained trapped and twisted and, although her body had swung outwards as she fell, she had been pulled back against the wall of the pier. She had made no sound as she fell and now she hung limply, like a rag-doll, the long skirt of her coat draped over her chest and head, her warm winter bloomers on show for all to see.

Now everyone surged around us, the boat and its cargo forgotten for the moment. Even the excited children stopped their play and came to the outer edge of the crowd, tugging at skirt hems, demanding to be told what was happening. Father knelt down and seized Mother's ankles.

'Pull her up! Quick!' Other people started forward but Father snarled at them.

'Can ye no' see that her foot's caught. If we pull, we'll twist it worse.'

'Can she no' hear us? Maggie! Maggie!' It was Bridie, kneeling at the edge, almost tumbling over herself as she leaned down and called to her friend. But Mother made no sound and her arms continued to flop below her head.

'Is she dead?' asked one of the children who had managed to wriggle through the crowd to the front. He was instantly hushed and given a 'thick ear', presumably by his own mother. But Gerry had heard and he became even more hysterical, emitting a series of ear-splitting screeches not unlike the gulls that keened overhead, only louder. The blood pounding in my temples accelerated with each of his screeches and I turned savagely on him, yelling 'Shut up! Shut up!' I must have sounded as hysterical as he did.

'It looks like she has struck her head on the wall when she swung back against it. She'll have knocked herself out.' The voice was calm and authoritative. The rabble of panic subsided and everyone turned to look at a tall man in naval uniform. He had obviously come off the boat. He moved to stand beside Father who was still kneeling and hanging grimly on to Mother's ankles. 'What we need is to get below her and take her weight. Then you can ease that foot out of the hook and lower her down to us. Can you hang on for a few more minutes? I'll bring the lifeboat round.'

Calum came forward. 'I'll take this ankle, Robert. You hang on to that one. Between us, we'll not let her go.'

Father acquiesced then and I breathed a sigh of relief. Several of the women had tried to take an ankle but he had refused furiously, not trusting any of us to keep Mother safe.

We all waited anxiously as the small lifeboat was lowered off the boat and two men shimmied down a short rope into it. They rowed the few strokes necessary to get the lifeboat round the corner of the pier to where Mother hung. We watched as they reached her, took her head and shoulders in their arms and stood up in the boat to lift her body up. Calum held on to one ankle, stabilising the body – Mother seemed like just a 'body' at that moment – and Father tried to work the foot free of the iron hook. But his hands were shaking, possibly from the effort of holding the body up for so long, possibly from panic or shock. He seemed to be taking a terribly long time. I stepped forward.

'Let me try, Father. You hang on to the ankle and I'll . . .'

'No, Liza. Let me. Stand back.' There was no mistaking or disobeying that voice. I whirled round as The Dow came to kneel beside Father. Within moments, she had freed the foot. I thought she jerked it quite callously to do so and wondered if she might have done more damage to it - and that maybe she even meant to. Then, I shook myself mentally. What mattered was getting Mother free and safe.

With the foot unfettered at last, Calum and Father leant over as far as they dared, still holding the ankles. Finally, they were able to let go and the men in the lifeboat caught her in their arms and laid her on the floor of the boat. The rescue was complete.

# CHAPTER TWENTY-ONE

*It's a kittle thing to decide what folk'll bear and what they will not.*
                    Robert Louis Stevenson, from 'Kidnapped'

The Board boat lost its place of primary importance for the rest of the afternoon. Once the lifeboat had completed its mission of mercy and delivered Mother on to dry land, the Board men were able to complete their unloading and depart for Bunessan. Indeed the boxes and crates – even the eagerly awaited 'Ne'er Day Bottles' one – remained stacked up on the landing stage for some time. The focus was all on poor Mother who regained consciousness whilst still lying on the floor of the lifeboat and was horrified to find herself lying with her skirts bunched up around her knees, sodden bloomers on show, in the company of two strange men.

She tried to sit up in the little boat but there was barely room and, in any case, as she later told me, her head was spinning and she was feeling very sick. Father rose in my estimation that day and I saw, for the first time, the person he must be at work and perhaps why his fellow keepers liked or, at least, respected him. Even before the lifeboat had turned the corner and brought Mother round to the iron ladder up the side of the pier, he had sprung into action.

'We need a stretcher,' he said. 'Quick now, folks. Has anyone got something that would do?'

Bridie spoke first. 'I've got a couple of curtain poles and some stiff calico. Come on!' She grabbed Jenny and the two of them went haring away up the path towards the cottages. They were back in few minutes with the makeshift stretcher. It was more like a hammock, really, the black calico sagging down between the poles to which they had nailed it. But there was no time for dissatisfaction. It was lowered down into the lifeboat and we all watched as Mother was rolled on to it. I caught a glimpse of her face and felt her horrified humiliation.

The stretcher with its sagging burden was lifted up. Father and Euan leaned over as far as they dared and took hold of it, pulling it up on to the stones of the landing stage. It was a bumpy business and more than once the watching crowd gasped in horror as Mother was almost tipped back into the lifeboat or even into the heaving, slapping sea. Poor Mother clutched at the poles and may have cried out in fear a few times but the crowd was making so much noise with shouts of advice and encouragement that she would not have been heard.

I did hear her 'Oomph!' as her body landed on the stones, more like a rush of air escaping from her lungs than a conscious cry, and I pushed forward to try to reach her side. But it was hopeless. Three men and six women, the entire adult population of Erraid, closed around the prostrate figure, all anxious to see what kind of state 'the poor woman' was in. The children were excluded although one or two of the tiniest began to squirm between legs.

Once again, Father showed his mettle. I heard him cry 'Stand back! If you please.'

I drew back and climbed up the path to get a view from above. I saw him extend his arms and push firmly backwards until he had created a space between Mother and the crowd. The Dow stepped forward then and shooed people to the right and left to clear the way. I saw Father lean over and speak to Mother, saw her try to rise and immediately fall back onto the calico. Father spoke again to her and then looked up at Euan who moved to stand at one end of the stretcher. Both men bent to the poles and lifted. They moved quickly through the space that The Dow had created. I saw her striding ahead, assuming command, beginning to ascend towards me, turning to beckon the stretcher-bearers on with an imperious gesture. And I felt the familiar spurt of anger. *What's it got to do with her?* Always, it seemed, she must be central and important to every event in our family. It had been thus from the moment we met her on the quay at Oban in September.

The other adults fell in behind Father and Euan, the children trailing after or trying to insinuate themselves into the crocodile – not easy for the path narrowed as it rose. As the procession drew level with my vantage point, I slipped in beside Father and was able at last to get a look at Mother.

She was huddled in a tangle of bunched, damp skirts, hatless with her hair hanging wetly about her face and, even from where I was, a few feet away, I could see that she was shivering violently. Her face was quite contorted by the chattering of her teeth and a drool of saliva bubbled from her quivering lips. I felt such an urge to run forward and put my arms around her, so pathetic a figure did she cut, so desperately in need of warmth and comfort. Even as I thought that, Calum, the third shore man that month, came running down the path towards us, waving a small, half-full bottle and carrying a blanket.

'Here!' he cried as he reached us. 'Give her some of this.' He waved the bottle at Father but it was I who darted forward before Father could lay down the poles of the stretcher. I almost got hold of the quarter bottle of brandy - and would have if only I had been a mite taller - but, before I could reach it, The Dow had snatched it from Calum and I had to be content with helping him to hap the blanket round Mother's shoulders and supporting her to sit up a little. The Dow unscrewed the cap and, crouching down, held the brandy to Mother's shuddering lips. The first mouthful was lost down her front as a violent shiver jerked her body. I heard her teeth clash off the rim of the bottle and pulled the blanket as tightly round her as I could. The second mouthful went in but was immediately sprayed back out in a spluttering cough.

'For God's sake!' Father, never long on patience, had lost his. 'Let's just get her up to the house. We can get her warmed up there.'

But The Dow ignored him and so did Calum. I took my cue from them and remained where I was, standing at the side of the kneeling schoolmarm, leaning down to hold the blanket over Mother's shoulders, indeed almost lying across her back in an effort to warm her up. And, at last, the shivering slowed a little and she managed to swallow the third mouthful, and then a fourth and finally the dregs. As The Dow straightened up and handed the empty bottle to Calum, I dropped to my knees and wiped Mother's mouth with the sleeves of my wool jersey.

'Don't worry,' I whispered. 'You're all right. We're almost home.'

For answer, she gave a weak groan and held out a trembling hand. I took it and at once felt her fierce grip. She did not let go, even as I rose to continue walking, but kept tight hold of it so that I was forced to walk by the side of the stretcher as we processed up and at last reached the path along the front of the cottages. Calum had run ahead and had the door to our house standing open to receive us. The Dow continued to lead, impervious to the resentful glares I was directing at her ramrod-straight back, and so she entered the house first and at once began giving orders.

'Bring the stretcher over here to the bed, men. Liza, take the quilt off and spread that blanket over instead. Now men, lift the stretcher up to the level of the bed. Mr Naughtie, you and I will roll Mrs Galway on to the bed. No, Mrs Galway, please lie quite still and let us move you as quickly and easily as we can.'

Such was her manner and tone that we all obeyed without question, even Mother subsiding and giving only a weak whimper as she was transferred to the bed by Calum and The Dow. I turned to see our kitchen-living room full of clucking women. Everyone had a suggestion to help bring Mother back from the brink of hypothermia and shock.

'Get those wet clothes off her.'

'Get a hot bottle at her feet.'

'No, better behind her knees. That warms the blood faster.'

'She needs hot, sweet tea.'

'She should . . .'

Father straightened from laying the now empty stretcher on the floor and erupted, all his pent up fear and shock fizzing out of him like froth from an uncorked bottle.

'What she needs is for all you busybodies to bugger off,' he yelled. 'Go on, get the hell out of here!' He took a menacing step towards the five wives and they gasped and retreated as one, with exaggerated looks of outrage, like a gaggle of minor actors in a pantomime.

I felt a nervous giggle rising in my throat at the sight of their faces and might have disgraced myself by letting it escape if The Dow had not stepped smoothly forward and laid a restraining hand on Father.

'Mr Galway is understandably upset,' she said to the women. 'You will excuse his unguarded language, I'm sure. But he *is* quite right. Mrs Galway needs peace and quiet now.'

'The poor lass needs a doctor; that's what she needs.' Bridie faced up to The Dow and I cheered inwardly.

'*I* shall examine her. I have medical training. I was a nurse during the war,' said The Dow and I at once pictured her in a white, winged cap and starched apron, carrying a lamp like Florence Nightingale.

That silenced the women, even Bridie, and they retreated reluctantly, the last two tripping over each other at the doorway, as Father shook off The Dow's hand on his shoulder and advanced towards them with a growl. Calum and Euan followed them equally reluctantly, assuring Father that, if there was anything else they could do, they were his men. Just ask. They could take the boat out and sail round to Bunessan for the doctor if that's what was needed. They could . . . But Father bade them go and get on with retrieving the Board's seasonal bounty from the landing stage. If they could just bring up our share, he would be grateful. They departed then, happy to have a practical task to complete, and the four of us were left alone.

'Where's Gerry?' Mother spoke up suddenly, startling us. We had all forgotten Gerry in the pell-mell procession of events. Father looked at me as if I was responsible for this omission and I cast around for an answer, coming up with 'He'll probably have gone to Angus' house. Bridie . . . Mrs Campbell . . . will look after him.'

Mother did not appear to hear me and repeated her question fretfully. Father took her hand and spoke as quietly as I had ever heard him speak, murmuring something I did not catch. It was clearly not effective as reassurance for Mother asked for the third time, her voice beginning to rise towards hysteria, 'Where is he? Where's my boy?'

The Dow swept into action. 'Liza, go at once to Mrs Campbell's house and get Gerry. If he is not there, find him and bring him to your mother. Off you go! Now.'

'But . . .' I wanted so badly to stay. I could still feel the pressure of Mother's hand in mine communicating its silent message, 'don't leave me'. I knew in my soul that she did not want to be left alone with Father and The Dow and, with my secret knowledge of their clandestine relationship, I wanted even less to leave her with them.

'Do what you're told, Liza,' barked Father. 'You're no use here anyway. Joan – Miss Dow – and I will see to your mother.' I heard his slip of the tongue and wondered if Mother had also. She had fallen back exhausted on the bed and I could not see her face.

With dragging feet, I crossed to the door, turning once before I went through it to look at the scene. The Dow was unlacing Mother's boots and Father was already at the stove, putting the kettle onto the hot plate.

'The hot water bottles are in the wee cupboard in the lobby,' I said, more as an excuse to linger than as useful information. Father glared at me.

'I ken everything I need to ken, Miss Smartie. Just get away and find that pest o' a laddie.'

There was no help for it. Mentally heaping undeserved curses on my little brother's head, I set off along the path to the Campbell house.


Those curses turned out to be not so undeserved after all as neither Gerry nor Angus were there. Bridie had no idea where they were and had not been bothered until I brought my searching enquiries to her door. Dusk was falling now and in half an hour or so it would be dark.

'Does your wee brother have his torch wi' him?' she demanded of one of the twins. Every child had a wee pocket torch – necessary in winter in a place with no street lights. But they had no answer save 'Dunno, Mam'. I was quite sure Gerry did not have his. He never did. Indeed it had been lost for weeks and he had been borrowing mine of late. I had only prevented *it* from becoming lost also by threatening him with all the legions of hell if he did not return it as soon as possible each time.

So, we had two nine-year-old boys wandering about in fast-falling darkness, on a cold winter's day, on terrain that was rocky, some covered in clinging crustaceans and others slippery with wet lichen. Bridie and I stared at each other, our eyes mirroring each other's rising panic.

'Come on.' It was Kirsty, one of the twins, and she was pulling on her coat as she spoke. 'We'll fan out, the three of us and search all over. You stay here, Mammy, in case they come back while we're gone. We'll come back in half an hour if we can't find them.'

'Take a torch each and – here! – take these.' Bridie thrust a walking stick at each of us. I had no heart for the operation and it was a kind of torture, setting off to walk further and further away from the house where Mother was at the mercy of that pair of cheats and liars. If I had felt ashamed of putting her through grief with my tantrums over going to stay with Catriona, I felt a hundred times worse now. But I had been ordered by the bossy Kirsty to climb the hill to The Lookout and check that the boys had not gone up there. I thought it unlikely but Kirsty insisted that Angus had used it as a hidey-hole in the past when in trouble over some peccadillo.

The climb, which I had so often done lightly and blithely in the autumn, now seemed pure travail. I was swathed in winter woollies, my climbing muscles unexercised of late. I was soon puffing and sweating as I made slithering use of the stick on the boggy hillside. Twice I slipped and slid back down several feet. It was like a nightmare game of Snakes and Ladders. By the time I was halfway up, it was becoming hard to see the ground. I stopped and fished my torch out of my coat pocket but it was of little help. I was 'down a snake' in no time, muttering the names I was going to call Gerry when I found him. The only thing was to hold the torch between my teeth and use one hand for my stick and the other to grab hold of patches of heather. I dropped the torch out of my mouth twice. I tasted mud and felt wet grass in my mouth as I replaced it there. My panting efforts were making me drool and I felt gritty saliva sliding down my chin. It felt like hours passed before I at last reached the door of The Lookout.

There was no light within and not a sound to be heard. Even before I wrenched open the door. I knew the little, circular room was empty. I had made my arduous climb for nothing. 'I told that bossy bitch they wouldn't be here,' I muttered as I sank down on to one of the benches and stared out the window.

Darkness was falling fast now but it was not having things all its own way for a great silver penny of a moon had appeared. The Sound of Iona was turning into a shimmering lagoon, seeming motionless in the windless, frosty air. I saw lamps beginning to flicker at farmhouse windows on the ancient, sacred isle and once again I empathised with David Balfour who had experienced those same lights as bitter taunts to a boy condemned (as he thought) to starve and freeze on Erraid. I

173

watched fascinated while, in the window of a house that stood on a rise in the middle of the island, a Christmas tree took shape as candles were lighted one by one at the end of the branches. A longing came over me to be in that safe, cosy, festive house, or one like it. I was cold, muddy and wet from my slithering climb and still in shock myself from the events of the afternoon. Above all, I was confused and fearful, a lassie of just twelve carrying knowledge about my father that I barely understood the significance of and full of concern for my mother on so many fronts: she was pregnant; she had had a terrifying accident; and she was being deceived by a man and woman, both of whom she trusted – the one to be a faithful husband and the other to be her children's teacher and mentor.

# CHAPTER TWENTY-TWO

*This is no' the kind of death I fancy.*

*Robert Louis Stevenson, from 'Kidnapped*

My downward journey from The Lookout was a tragedy in three acts. I slithered, sledging on my bottom for several yards, small, sharp rocks battering the end of my spine. I lost my walking stick but, at least, still had the torch. I struggled on with it between my teeth, grabbing at clumps of heather with both hands.

A rabbit broke cover and darted almost under my feet. I fell heavily, face down. The torch smashed against my chattering teeth, cutting my lip, and went out. Winded, chittering with pain and misery, tears streaming down my face to join the blood from my lip, I crept onwards. At last, I saw the lights from our row of cottages. Whimpering with relief, I broke into a run but had gone no more than five or six steps when the ground beneath my feet simply gave way and I plunged into sucking, squelching bog. Before I could even cry out, I was up to both knees in it. What little reserves of courage and strength I had left evaporated. I tried to pull at least one leg out but it was hopeless.

Time passed, my legs and feet grew numb and my thoughts freewheeled over all that had happened to us since arriving. I was dragged back to the present by the sound of shouting and, as I opened my gritty eyes, by the sight of three beams of light swooping and dancing around the terrain close to me. With a huge effort, I produced a squeak and then another, louder and more frantic.

'I think she's here, Euan. Bring your torch over here. You too, Calum.'

For the first time I could ever remember, the sound of my father's voice was a welcome one. I managed to raise my voice above a squeak and call out. Then two strong hands were grasping mine and, with a sound like a slobbery, smacking kiss, I was pulled out of the mire, leaving socks and boots behind. I stumbled forward, fell on my knees and was immediately scooped up by two strong arms. Quite forgetting how much I feared and hated him, I buried my face in my father's oilskin-clad chest and sobbed with relief.

By the time I had been carried in Father's arms down to the cottage, Gerry was already there, being stripped and towelled by The Dow. He and Angus, both in shock after the accident, had wandered off, paying no attention to where they were going. This would not have mattered, since Angus knew the islet so well, if they had not reached Erraid Sound as an unusually high tide was coming in and dared each other to race across and back, the winner being the one who managed the most crossings before it was too deep. They had ended up having to half-stagger, half swim back on to Erraid, with the swirling, icy sea up to their shoulders. Twice they had stumbled, feeling the terrifying tug of the current as the water closed over their heads and threatened to suck them out into the open sea. Kirsty and Allyson had found the boys and half–carried, half-dragged them up from the causeway

They had been brought into the Campbell house about twenty minutes after I had set off for The Lookout. Caught up in hearing the boys' tale of woe and getting them stripped of their wet clothes and wrapped in blankets, Gerry being then carried along the path to be dumped on our hearth rug, Bridie had not thought to wonder what had become of me until much later.

Meanwhile, Mother had been helped to change out of her own wet clothes and persuaded to get into bed. Casting around for someone to blame, Father had fixed on Gerry, whose lurch into Mother's side had unbalanced her and sent her tottering over the side of the landing stage. I would not have given twopence for Gerry's chances if he had simply wandered home unhurt but the sight of the pitiful, shivering lad that Bridie had carried in had melted even Father's stony heart. Mother, of course, had been horrified, this fresh calamity threatening to overwhelm her.

Only when Gerry and Angus had been seen to in their respective homes, had it occurred to anyone to wonder where I was. The twins remembered that I had been despatched up to The Lookout which immediately set Mother off again, bewailing yet another disaster, demanding that a search party set off at once.

I felt at death's door when Father carried me into the house. All thoughts of parties had gone out of my mind. I had had a bad fright and was chilled to the bone. Mother's cry of alarm when she saw me had echoed my own feelings of despair. She even tried to get up but her legs would not support her, the abused ankle being badly sprained. It was The Dow who took me through to my bedroom, told me to take off every stitch of clothing and handed me a big warm towel. The feel of it enveloping my icy, trembling flesh was like a blessing. She left me with a large jug of hot water to 'wash quickly and then come through to the fire for a hot drink'. I could not but be appreciative of this sensitive treatment, which acknowledged that I was no mere child to be stripped and washed in public as Gerry had been. She was not all bad, I reflected, as I sat on the hearth rug, wrapped in a blanket, sipping hot milk and honey and watching her slip out into the dark night.

'No, I want you all to go. I won't hear of any of you staying behind on my account.'

My brain, numbed by the terror and bitter cold of the past hour, had just been getting around to wondering what was going to happen about the party and what time it was. I had been almost aware of Father and Mother talking together in low tones in the bed recess, just at the edge of my consciousness, but Mother's declaration that we must all go to the party catapulted me right back into the imperative of the moment.

Mother was sitting up in bed looking pale but determined. 'It's bad enough that we've had all this carry-on – what with Gerry getting lost and half-drowned and Liza near-perished to death up that hill in a bog – but there's no need to make a mountain out of a molehill.'

'I don't know, Maggie,' said Father. 'I don't think ye should be on yer own. It . . . it wouldna look right. What would the other men say?'

Mother shook her head wearily. 'It's nothing to do with *them*. If I say I'll be all right, that's all that matters. I've no strength to argue about it. I just want to rest and I'll do that better if I'm left in peace. Please, Robert.' She sounded close to tears.

'There's no' time now. It's gone five and I'm no' even shaved. We'll never get ready in time. The boat goes at half past. Now, what the hell do you think you're doing?'

Mother had pushed back the covers and was making to get up. 'If you won't get the bairns ready for their party, then I will have to,' she said in a tight, quavering voice.

Gerry, who had been sitting quietly on the hearth rug, still wrapped in a blanket, suddenly piped up. 'So, we can still go to the party, then? Great!'

Father rounded on him. 'That's all ye care about, is it? Your mother near drowned and no' able to walk. You and that Angus playing bloody dangerous games – after all I've telt ye for years about the sea - and driving yer mother half-crazy wi' worry. And all you can say is "party". I've a good mind to belt some sense into you right now.'

He took a menacing step away from the bed towards the hearth and Mother cried out in protest. We were saved from another of those terrible scenes, still engraved on my memory after eighty years, by the door opening and The Dow sweeping in without so much as a knock on the door. She was carrying a stone pitcher, from which a delicious steam was rising.

'How is the patient now?' she enquired, her manner authoritative like a doctor or nurse. She crossed to the bed and set the pitcher down on the shelf beside it. 'Fetch me a bowl and spoon, Liza,' she ordered, not turning to look at me as she spoke but bending down to lift Mother's wrist and place two fingers on it, while taking a watch out of her pocket with the other hand. Father started to speak but she said 'Sshh!' very fiercely and concentrated on the watch. Father turned his attention on me then, nodding his head and jerking it at the cupboard where the bowls were kept. Clutching the blanket round me, I fetched one along with a spoon. We all watched in silence as The Dow finished her palaver with the watch and wrist – taking her pulse, I knew from having had my own taken once while in bed with mumps – poured some brown liquid into the bowl and began to spoon it into Mother's mouth. After a bit, Mother held out her hand, took the bowl and continued the spooning herself. Once it was finished, she smiled up.

'Thank, you, Miss Dow, you've been so kind. I don't know what we'd have done without you. So comforting to have someone with medical knowledge.'

I wanted to run over to the bed, then and there, and tell Mother about Father and The Dow. Then she would see how kind The Dow was! But I was afraid - afraid of Father and, yes, I blush to remember, afraid that it would spoil my chance of getting to the party, to stay with the MacPhails and to be taken to Iona. I said nothing, just hated The Dow and hated Father all the more.

Mother innocently enlisted the enemy's support. 'I don't want anyone to miss the party on my account, Miss Dow. 'Tell him that I'll be fine. Please.'

I watched The Dow appear to hesitate – I say 'appear' because I did not think it genuine hesitation then and I know now that it was not.

'Well,' she said, '. . . well . . . if you are quite certain, Mrs Galway.'

'But surely . . .' began Father.

'I think it will be better for Mrs Galway if we do as she wishes. Her pulse is settling down but she should not agitate herself any more. Her ankle will heal with bed rest and you should apply fresh witch hazel to the bandage when you come back from the party.' She indicated a bottle which stood on the bedside table and the matter seemed to be settled.

Father frowned. 'But there's no' the time . . .'

'*I* can get us ready,' I said, rising from the hearth rug where I had sat down again to continue thawing out my frozen feet. I could feel the throb of incipient chilblains but had no time to think of that now.

'Good girl, Liza,' said Mother. And then, to Father, 'You see. If the lassie feels able to go after what she's been through, then what's wrong wi' the men in the family?'

I scrambled to my feet holding the blanket round me with one hand and tugging at Gerry's with the other. 'Come on! Hurry up!'

I had him whisked through to his bedroom and was shoving him into his party clothes before he had time to protest. Leaving him to comb his hair and put on his shoes, I shot into my room and began throwing on my own outfit. Mother had lengthened my last year's party frock by adding a broad hem of purple satin to the pale lilac skirt and making a purple sash to cover the fact that the waistline was now halfway up to my armpits. She had also let out the seams of the bodice and put purple darts in each side. The effect was very stylish and I had been looking forward to wearing it but now I fairly threw it on without a glance at the mirror. When I hastened back into the kitchen, I saw that the Dow had gone, presumably to change into her own party clothes, and Father was sitting at the table, his lower face covered in shaving foam and one hand slowly beginning to scrape it off with his razor. Normally, I liked watching him shave – there is something very satisfying about it – but now I was focussed only on the time. Ten past six!

'Good girl, Liza,' said Mother again when she saw me all ready. 'Don't forget your overnight bag for the MacPhails. It's all ready in the lobby. Where's Gerry? Is he . . ?' She checked as he bounded into the room, laughing, looking smart and expectant, every inch a boy looking forward to a party in his well-pressed trousers and white shirt. No sign of the trauma of the past three hours.

'Oh, the resilience of youth!' Mother said, a quaver in her voice. 'Just look at the pair of you. Come and give me a kiss before you go.'

We went readily enough and Gerry knelt up on the counterpane whilst I stood at the bedside.

'Be good,' she whispered and I saw tears in her eyes.

'Never mind,' I whispered back. 'There will be another party next year. And we'll try and bring you back something nice off the table there.'

She shook her head, smiling through her tears. 'It's no' that, Liza, dear. I don't mind about going to the party. It's just . . . Liza, I'm relying on you to make sure Gerry doesn't get up to any nonsense. Mind you . . .'

But she was interrupted by the arrival of Bridie who hurried in, letting a cold draught swirl into the room. She was carrying her knitting bag and a tin of her famous gingerbread.

'I'm for staying here with you, Maggie,' she announced. 'I'll be looking after you.' She beamed approvingly at Gerry and me. 'Now, don't you two look a picture?' Turning to Father, she waved a hand at him. 'I'll clean up these shaving things. Get yourself into a clean shirt as fast as you can. Miss Dow says she'll tell Lachlan to wait his boat for you. Wasn't it her came and told me to make sure that you all got yourselves ready and down to the pier? I said you might no' be happy to leave the invalid but she had an answer to that right smart. She told me to come and stay here wi' poor Maggie while you're all out at the party.'

She took off her coat and hung it on the peg beside the door. She put her knitting down on the armchair beside the hearth and turned her attention to picking up the two mugs on the hearth rug and lifting the basin with its white, lathery contents off the table. Father made to protest but she cut across him in a way that had me holding my breath.

'Hurry up, Robert. You don't want to keep Lachlan waiting . . . or Miss Dow,' she added.

It was the magic formula. Within two minutes, he had wiped the foam off his face and swapped his rough, grey everyday shirt for crisp white linen. Then he dashed out into the back lobby and was back in less than a minute, wearing his Sunday-best suit and a tartan tie. *The Macleod*, I thought, having studied clan tartans only last week in school.

Mother, Bridie and I goggled and Gerry wolf-whistled. Having only recently learned the art from Angus, he was keen to show it off. Father hustled us out the door, his tongue sharper than ever.

We could hear the foghorns of the two boats chatting to each other and soon we saw the jolly scene on the landing-stage and heard carols being sung in defiance of the distaste in which they were held by the cheerless Presbyterians so common in these parts.

# CHAPTER TWENTY-THREE

*It makes a good enough dish for a hungry man*

*Robert Louis Stevenson, from 'Kidnapped'*

The two boats were both waiting, Euan skippering the NLB one and Lachlan standing on the landing stage ready to hand us down into his. As my schoolmates had predicted, it was a tight squeeze getting everyone in and obviously the NLB turned a blind eye to – or perhaps never knew about – the contravention of the safety sign that said 'maximum eight people'.

Gerry and I were bundled into Lachlan's boat and lost contact with Father. As we settled down, crowded into a corner of the tiny cabin, I thought I saw Father and The Dow huddled close on the other boat but I could have been mistaken in the fitful light of the lanterns which swung with the swell of the sea and cast swooping shadows across us all.

A cheer went up as we cast off and there were shouts and taunts of derision, as the occupants of each boat tried to encourage its skipper to outrun the other boat, but I took no part in this, still feeling heavy in my heart at leaving Mother and burdened with the responsibility she had given me. It took less than ten minutes before we were nosing side by side into the jetty at Fionnphort and I could not have said if either boat beat the other, although both sides claimed victory. The ferrybus was waiting and, as soon as he had tied up his boat, Lachlan was up into the driver's seat and gunning the engine in a way that had everyone jumping about and pushing to get on to the bus, as if he was going to leave without them. It was obviously all part of the fun and the mood began to affect me at last. I felt my spirits lift, especially when I saw Catriona sitting in the front seat waving excitedly to me. I kept a tight hold of Gerry's hand and we both squeezed on to the seat beside her.

Another cheer went up as the bus lurched forward and someone began to sing 'Jingle Bells, Jingle bells.' I looked round for Father but there was no sign of him on the bus.

'Look Liza! There's Father and Miss Dow. Down there.' Gerry was looking out the window against which I had thrust him. The bus was not big enough to take everyone and was going to have to make a second run. I leant across Gerry and peered out. There they were in the left-behind group, standing together with arms linked, as bold as brass. As I shaded my eyes to see past the reflections in the window, I saw The Dow raise an arm in mock salute as we drove away and, before I could stop him, Gerry waved back.

'Don't!' I snapped, pulling his hand back from the window.

'Why no'?'

It was a simple question but the answer was so far from being simple that I found nothing to reply.


Catriona's cheerful presence quickly dissipated my gloomy forebodings. She was full of chatter about the party and what we would find when we got to Fionnphort School. Living so close, she and her mother had been down there all day, setting tables, laying out the food that was provided by the local laird, blowing up balloons, wrapping packages with many layers for games of 'Pass the Parcel'. The musicians had arrived and begun tuning up and practising just before she and her mother had left to go home and change into their best frocks.

'The girls and boys that go to school there have been making decorations for weeks and it looks terrific,' she said. 'The decs *we* made are on the tree at the door as you go in. Dad collected them from Miss Dow yesterday morning when he brought me over. They look great as well. And I hope you're hungry. There's enough food to feed the whole of Mull.'

But it was the smell of spiced wine that thrilled me most when we finally disembarked from the bus and entered the building. It suddenly seemed a very long time since the 'push-past' bread and cheese we had had for midday dinner. The plan to have some goodies from our NLB bounty box had been completely lost in the turmoil of events and my empty stomach rumbled.

The school hall was a long room with a small stage at one end where a fiddler and an accordionist were sitting chatting, eating and drinking. Along one long side of the room stretched three or four tables, covered in white cloths and laden with plates heaped up with sausage rolls, pies and sandwiches. Along the short side under the stage, two more tables, one with bowls of trifle and jelly, one with plates of black bun and Victoria sponge. A serving hatch in the middle of the other long wall was dispensing cups of hot, spiced elderberry wine for the adults and tumblers of raspberry cordial for the children.

We had been among the first to arrive but as we moved along the tables, piling up our plates, more and more people came in, forming a laughing, jostling queue which snaked in a winding line into the middle of the hall. There was such an air of jollity and expectation, it was all so warm and welcoming and exciting, that I felt the tight ball of dread inside me begin to uncurl.

'It's amazing! It's beautiful! I love it!' I said to Catriona and she laughed and gave me one of her special smiles. She had a way of smiling that seemed to involve her whole face and upper body, her eyes crinkling, her mouth puckering, her cheeks puffing out, her shoulders rising almost up to her ears. If she had not been holding a plateful of food, I knew she would have rubbed her hands together. It was as if she was always hugging a wonderful secret to herself and could hardly contain her excitement.

'Look at the balloons,' she said. There was a great multi-coloured mound of them inside a sparkly net in one corner, promising high jinks when they would be released.

'Look at the other Christmas tree,' I replied. The one for our classroom-made decorations, a modest affair, stood by the doorway but a huge Scotch Fir filled one corner of the stage, beautifully decorated with glistening baubles and flickering nightlights, queened over by a large fairy, resplendent in a white gown with silver wings, tiara and wand. I had never seen anything like it. Some of the shops in North Berwick had put cheap little imitation trees in their windows the week before Christmas but they were as far from this glorious specimen as our bread-and-cheese push-past was from the banquet now laid out before us.

When I could get no more food on my plate, I made my way round to the serving hatch to collect my cordial, although I would much rather have had the warm wine which had, so I heard one woman say to another, a kick like a mule. I did not know what that meant but I knew it smelt delicious.

Gerry had found Angus and the two of them were already sitting on a bench stuffing their mouths as if they had not seen food for days. I suppose none of us had seen food like this for a long time, if ever. It was so fresh and rich and tasty, so attractively presented, so plentiful. I think we were all a little intoxicated by the whole experience, even without access to the mule-kick of the wine. I began to relax and let the cares and fears that had been besetting me for the past few days slide on to the back burner. *Sufficient unto the day is the evil thereof.* I remembered writing out that text fifty times as a punishment at my old school. It seemed as good a mantra as any for the evening that lay ahead.

The hall filled and the noise swelled. The food, which had looked enough for a large army, began to dwindle and the wine, which was being served from several big jam-making pans, began to run out. I had spotted

Father and The Dow coming in, looking, I thought, as much a couple as did all the other men and their wives. I marvelled that no one else noticed and did not remark on it. Now they were sitting some way from Catriona, Gerry and me and, although Gerry waved at them, they made no move to join us or to beckon us over.

'Should we no' go and sit wi' them?' he asked through a mouth full of trifle.

I was spared from answering by the arrival at our side of Marion and Lachlan. He had his arm round her waist and his other hand was stretched out to pull Catriona to her feet and into his other side. There came from them such an aura of safe, contented love that I felt a wave of longing sweep over me. My eyes prickled and my throat closed.

'Liza, my dear.' Marion MacPhail leaned down to take my arm and pull me into her other side. 'And little Gerry! So good it is to see you both again.'

Their warmth radiated, effortlessly including us both in their charmed circle. Out of the corner of my eye, I saw The Dow watching us.


Like Cinderella at the Ball, I threw myself into the party, enjoying every minute but always with a fearful eye, not on the clock like her, but on Gerry – as I had promised Mother – and on The Dow whose appropriation of Father seemed to me to be so glaring that I wondered no one else commented. All our practising paid off, for Catriona and I won the three-legged race for girls whilst Angus and Gerry won the boys' one. Races and games over, it was time for the entertainment. Each school stepped up on to the stage to present their well-rehearsed song and Erraid acquitted itself proudly, although I still could not like *Flow Gently Sweet Afton*. Gerry's solo was a triumph and he lapped up the applause. The tiny school from a place called Pottie (Angus and Gerry went into convulsive sniggers every time the name was said and earned a quelling stare from the Dow) stole the show with their rendering of *Coming Through The Rye*, executing a bewitching jig to the light, skipping tune while they sang.

A short break followed the schools' performances and many of the men, Father included, trooped outside. I had noticed this happening several times before and asked Catriona what they were doing out in the cold.

'Secret stash,' she said, winking.

'What of?'

184

'Half-bottles of whisky. The Laird will only provide the wine. He doesn't approve of hard drink. I suppose he thinks the men will drink too much and start fighting or such. So he just allows as much wine as he provides and no other booze. But he might as well no bother. The men have got loads of whisky in the shed out there. Dad showed me it earlier.'

I looked over at Lachlan who was sitting with his wife perched on his knee looking well content. 'But your dad hasn't gone out.'

'Naw. Mum would kill him.' She giggled. '*If* she sees him. Watch him slip out later, though, if he gets the chance. When she's not looking.'

I digested the amazing idea that there were marriages where the woman ruled the roost. I checked on Gerry – safely ensconced in a corner with a group of boys who were helping him and Angus to eat their three-legged prize, a box of Edinburgh Rock – and The Dow, who was standing alone, leaning against a wall, showing off to advantage her extremely smart outfit – a low-cut green velvet dress, very fitting over her slim waist with a soft, drooping skirt. Her hair was loosely coiled over her ears from which beautiful crystal earrings hung in long teardrops. Her matching necklace dropped an enormous crystal teardrop into her cleavage. She looked like a film star, quite out of place among the rosy-cheeked, ample farmers' wives with their simple, hand-made party frocks and sparse, cheap jewellery. Her face wore a calculating, brooding expression. Like a cat stalking a mouse, I thought.

The men came back in, noisier than ever, and it was time for the solo 'party pieces'. As Catriona had predicted, Lachlan was up first and sang *My Love is like a Red, Red, Rose,* looking doe eyes at Marion who blushed and shook her fist at him, crying 'Away ye big sap!' On cue, the audience roared and some quips were bandied about that I did not then understood and blush now to recall. Lachlan and Marion took them all in good part and gave as good as they got, Lachlan delighting the hall by seizing Marion round the waist and giving her a smacking kiss. Angus and Gerry pretended to be vomiting but everyone else cheered and stamped their feet.

After that, it was anything-goes and people were fighting for the chance to get up on the stage. Also as Catriona had predicted, everyone did what they always did every year and there were cries of 'Come on, Kate - Rothesay Bay' and 'We want Billy – It's a long way to Tipperary.' Eventually, it became a community sing-song with someone simply standing up and launching into the first line of a well-known song, whereupon everyone joined in lustily. It was late in the evening, during a maudlin rendering of *Roses are Blooming in Picardy* that I realised that I could not see Gerry. Angus had fallen asleep, huddled on the floor under the smaller Christmas tree. I suspected he had been secretly sipping dregs of wine from discarded cups. He looked like a fallen angel off the tree, his cheeky face smoothed into an expression of cherubic innocence and I could not help smiling until I looked around for Gerry.

I did not panic immediately, partly because of the relaxed, happy atmosphere all around, partly because I was on the verge of sleep myself as the exhausting day began to take its toll. I worked my way casually round the hall, exchanging banter, stopping now and then to sing with enthusiastic groups who insisted I join them. The wine (and whisky) had loosened tongues and manners; there were no strangers, no outsiders, no newcomers, tonight. I responded eagerly to such openness and felt that I belonged. It was a good feeling.

But, gradually, as the time passed and I went on circling the hall again and again, the dreadful truth began to dawn. Gerry was not here. I went outside to see if he had gone to the convenience but there was no sign of him. I shook Angus awake and demanded where his friend was. I might have saved myself the trouble. I circled again, this time asking if anyone had seen Gerry. This took what seemed like a very long time as I had to describe him over and over again and explain who I was and why I was worried.

Time passed and I became frantic. The jollity around me was like an insult. I wanted to scream. I saw Father coming back in again for the umpteenth time and saw too that he was very drunk. I should have been able to go to him and share my worries but I knew he would either take no interest and tell me to stop being a fusspot and leave him alone (probably with a few choice insults and curses for the benefit of his drinking cronies) or blame me for losing Gerry and turn on me. His temper when he was drunk was an unpredictable wild animal. If he caused a scene and turned violent in front of all these people, Mother would never recover from the shame and would blame me.

I saw him looking around, searching for something, someone. The Dow, no doubt. I had not been thinking of her, had never entertained the idea of asking for her help, but nor had I been keeping her in my sights. I had been too wrapped up in worry over Gerry. Father continued to look around and, spotting me, wove his unsteady way across the floor.

'You! Come here. I want to ask you something,' he said and leaned down to breath whisky fumes in my face. 'Where's yer teacher gone? Eh? Where is she?'

'I don't know, Father. And I don't care. I've not seen her for . . .' I stopped as a hideous thought sprang into my mind like a snarling tiger.

She was missing. And so was Gerry.

186

There was no point in expecting help from Father. He was too drunk. I cast around the hall frantically. Who could I ask to help me? Everywhere I looked, I saw family groups, wives sitting on their men's knees or both parents with children on their knees, some of the smaller ones drooping in sleep against mothers' bosoms or fathers' chests. I looked up at the big clock above the stage. It was almost midnight. Even as I dithered, the band struck up Auld Lang Syne and people were beginning to stand up, half-asleep children were being dragged to their feet and a ragged circle was forming around the hall. I saw Catriona bearing down on me, beaming, holding out her hand.

'Come on, Liza. Come over to Ma and Pa.'

'I can't. It's Gerry. He's missing.'

'What?' The band was getting louder and people were starting to sing. There was no hope of making myself heard. Unwillingly, I let myself be towed over to where Marion and Lachlan were waiting for us and, before I knew it, my hands were being held firmly by Catriona on one side and Marion on the other. The first and second verses were sung quite decorously but the third was another matter. The cue, 'An' here's a hand, my trusty friend' was the signal for arms to be crossed and the resulting, tighter circle began to run out and in to the middle, jumping up and down, keeping up with the music which became faster and faster. I was dragged back and forward, almost crushed each time we reached the middle and thrust our upheld, linked hands against those on the other side of the circle. In other circumstances, I would have enjoyed the good-natured rough and tumble of it all but, consumed with worry about Gerry and sick with apprehension about what The Dow was up to now, I was conscious only of burning impatience and frustration.

At last, it was over and the band was softly playing 'Will ye no' come back again?' as people began to gather their children and their belongings together. Tinies were being carried in parental arms, younger children were being dragged wearily out into the night and groups of older ones were being split up. There was much calling: to boys and girls who were dawdling; to the band to express appreciation; to Lachlan and Marion for all they had done getting the hall ready; and to each other, friendly banter muddled with the looseness of inebriation.

'Right, you two. Pa's gone to drive folks home in the bus so we three will have to walk home from here. It's not far, Liza. Just quarter of an hour – maybe twenty minutes - should do it. You're not too tired for that, I hope?' Marion bent down and looked me full in the face. She was smiling, the same full-bodied smile as her daughter, and I found it hard to spoil the moment. But spoil it I must.

'I cannae go,' I burst out. 'I dinnae ken what's happened to my wee brother. He's disappeared. And Mother told me to look after him. . .' I trailed off as tears of terror and impotence engulfed me.

It was my worst nightmare. The Dow had gone off with Gerry into the dark night, into territory that was totally unfamiliar to me.

# CHAPTER TWENTY-FOUR

*His mind was scarce truly human - the poor child still comes about me in my dreams.*
*Robert Louis Stevenson, from 'Kidnapped'*

Marion was caught up in replying to departing party-goers, thanking them for their thanks, wishing them Merry Christmas for Tuesday and 'safe home, now', while I hopped about with impatience, trying to find a gap to repeat my tale of woe. She had clearly not comprehended the gravity of the situation. In desperation, I looked for Father. Surely he would not get on the bus without making sure he had Gerry with him? But he might presume Gerry would be in a different bus and on a different boat, as we had both been on the way here. Father might not miss Gerry until he got to Erraid. In his present state, he would not be thinking responsibly. Mother had foreseen this, of course, which was why she had charged me with looking after her precious 'baby'. And I had failed.

'What's wrong, Liza? What are ye greetin' for? Yer no' homesick already, are ye? Here, I've got yer overnight bag. You were goin' to forget it.' Catriona was shining her torch on me and peering at my face.

I did not realise that tears were coursing down my face until I felt the salt smart the cut on my bottom lip. I shook my head miserably, unable to summon up the strength to make myself heard. I was deathly tired, all the events of the day crowding my mind and sapping my body. I could have dropped to the ground and given up there and then.

Marion became aware that Catriona was putting her arms around me and patting my shoulder. 'What's wrong wi' our wee Liza?' she said brightly. The moon suddenly sailed out from behind the bank of cloud that had been obscuring it and she examined my face. 'Worn out!' she pronounced. 'Let's get you two home before we have to drag you.' She seized our hands and began to walk briskly down the path from the school to the main road. Then she stopped and looked up into the sky. 'There's going to be moonlight for a while. We'll be quicker going straight over the hill. Here, Catty, change your shoes.' She took a pair of boots out of her bag. 'Have you boots in your bag, Liza? The hill path can be muddy and it's rough and rocky in parts. Those thin soles would be no good.'

She was opening my overnight bag as she spoke and extracting my school shoes – my boots had been rescued from the bog by Calum and cleaned by Bridie but they were so wet inside that it would be a day or two until they were wearable. Marion tutted when she saw the shoes and I had to explain. 'Well, they'll have to do,' she said. 'Just watch where you're putting your feet. The water in some of the potholes can be over your ankles before you know it.'

'Come on, Liza.' Catriona tugged at my arm. 'I love the hill road.'

I took a desperate look around. I saw Angus being wearily lifted on to the bus by his big sisters but of Gerry there was no sign. I saw Father lolling against the wall, cigarette in one hand, half-bottle of whisky in the other. He too was looking around, his head swinging from side to side, a look of puzzled infuriation on his face. But it was not Gerry he was waiting and looking for – I knew that. The Dow too was still missing. That was all he was interested in.

Nevertheless, I had to try one more time. 'Hang on, Catriona'. I conveyed my intention with gestures and hurried over to him before she could stop me. He was some distance from the noisy throng exiting the hall, so I could just about make myself heard.

'What about Gerry?' I yelled. 'There's still no sign of him.'

'He's gone on the bus,' he yelled back. 'The one that just left for Fionnphort. That's got Iona and Erraid folk on it.'

'Are you sure?' Was it possible I had somehow missed him in the melee? I hesitated but the thought that he was on the bus and would be looked after and taken home by our kindly Erraid neighbours was such a seductive idea that, in my burdened, exhausted state, I gave in. 'But what about you? How will you get home? What'll you do if you miss the boats?'

He shrugged and waved me away impatiently and I thought angrily: *If he doesn't care, why should I?* I rejoined Catriona and, hand in hand, flickering our torches ahead of us, we set off to climb the hill that lay behind the school hall and would, I presumed, take us up and over to the other side and the MacPhails' home.

I set my face to the hill and forced my weary legs to climb. Marion soon realised I was struggling, holding Catriona back, sometimes even letting her tow me up the steeper parts, although she was also carrying my overnight bag.

'Come on. Let's get you in the middle.' Marion stepped to my other side, took my torch, dropped it into her bag and took my free hand. 'Give us a song, Catty. Something we can march to.' She gave my cold fingers a reassuring squeeze. 'We'll be there in no time. Hot cocoa with marshmallows on top when we get there!'

Catriona struck up 'Pack up your troubles in your old kit bag' and Marion joined in loudly. I had no wind for singing and my legs increasingly felt like the promised marshmallows but between them they almost carried me up the hill to the ridge at the top where they halted for a well-deserved breather. We were looking down now into the disused Tormore quarry. The rails for the trucks, and two of the trucks themselves which had carried the stones down to the little landing stage, were still there. It had a ghostly appearance in the moonlight as if the spectres of the quarry workers, many of them dead in the Flanders trenches, could at any moment step out from behind the massive boulders strewn all around and take up their occupation again. I shivered, feeling a chill ruffle the hairs on my neck.

Marion and Catriona, of course, had the indifference of familiarity and simply leaned against the rusting trucks, breathing deeply to recover from the exertion of dragging me up the hill.

'Right, that's the worst over,' announced Marion after a minute. 'Nearly home, girls. What if we . . . What's that?'

We had all three heard it. A wounded animal in pain? Or two cats shaping up for a fight over a half-dead field mouse? It could not possibly be what it really sounded like, namely a baby or a very young child crying. We stared at each other, our appalled faces grotesque in the torchlights. On it went, without a break. Then it suddenly stopped and a moment later we heard what was for certain a human cry, although we could not make out the words.

Filled with dread, galvanised by fear, I started to run down the hill towards the sound, throwing away Marion's and Catriona's hard work to get me up there. Of course, I soon slipped and, in a replay of my earlier descent from The Lookout, found myself taxi-ing down on my bottom. This time, the back of my lovely party dress bore the brunt. Marion and Catriona pulled me to my feet and the three of us proceeded with more caution. The cry came again and this time we could almost distinguish words. I tried to call back but my voice came out in a strangled squeak. Marion stopped, drew a deep breath, cupped her hands to her mouth and shouted: 'Who's there? We're coming.' The response was encouraging: the cry of one word, clearly heard, 'Help!'

'It sounds like a child,' said Marion and Catriona agreed. I did not have to. I already knew who it was.


He was crouched in the lee of a rocky outcrop more than half way down the hill. Not the side of it we had climbed from the school hall but the one leading down to the row of houses that led away from the jetty at Fionnphort. The moon had gone into hiding again so that I could not see what lay between the bottom of the hill and the road along the front of the houses. Catriona told me later what lay there.

Once we drew closer, we were easily guided to him by the wailing. By this time, we all knew who it was. Marion dashed the last few yards and scooped him up into her arms. He at once accepted her substitute bosom and clung to this mother-figure, sobbing but faintly, as almost all his energy and most of his voice had gone. I caught up with her and put both my hands on his shoulders, whispering, 'Gerry, love. It's all right, pet. We're here now.'

At the sound of my voice, he turned in Marion's arms and threw himself on to me and would have knocked me to the ground if Catriona had not braced herself behind me. We hugged like long-lost friends. It was enough for me for the moment to know he was safe. But Marion was more practical and foresighted.

'I need to get this wee lad on a boat to Erraid right now,' she said, beginning to pull him from me. He clung like a limpet, whimpering. 'Tell him. Liza. Your mother and father will be out of their minds with worry if he is not on one of those boats.'

I privately reserved that anxiety for Mother alone but did not contradict her. 'It's true what Mrs MacPhail says, my darling wee man.' Unconsciously, I had dropped into the old baby-speak that Mother and I had used when he was a tiny and with which she still indulged him occasionally. I had long foresworn it, thinking it contributed to his eternal babyishness which was irritating me more and more these days. But my relief at finding him and my pity for the terrified, cried-out child had thrown me back on it.

'You've to come too, Za,' he snivelled, also falling back into baby-speak. Za had been his first attempt to say my name and it had stuck until he went to school and got ridiculed out of it by his schoolmates. 'I'm no' goin' on my own, no' past that place again.' His feeble voice began to rise towards hysteria.

I started to ask him what place he meant but Marion cut across us. 'I'll take him down to the jetty. You girls get away home. Come on, lad, There's no time to waste.'

'I want Za, I want Za, I'm no' goin' wi' you!' He was winding up for the kind of tantrum that had worked so well when he was a tiny, when Mother and I were bringing him up while Father was at sea. I felt a wave of sad resignation sweep over me. Of course I had been foolish to imagine that I would get away with having such a treat as my visit to the

MacPhails. What had I been thinking of? It was third time lucky for my personal devil: first the threat when my lie to Catriona had been uncovered and Mother had decreed my punishment; then Mother's accident, Gerry's disappearance and my misadventures on the descent from The Lookout; now it was the *coup de grace*, the knockout blow. I would have to take Gerry home.

'Come on, then, I said glumly, Then, remembering my manners, 'Thank you for your invitation, Mrs MacPhail, but I'll better take Gerry home as you say.'

Marion MacPhail shone her torch full in my face – and maybe saw the tears glittering in my eyes. 'Nothing of the kind,' she said firmly. 'Do as I'm telling you, girls. Get off home like I said. And put the kettle on, Catty. I'll be needing a hot drink when I get in.'

She spoke with authority and every well-drilled bone in my body responded, maybe encouraged a wee bit by my will which had been so set on this visit to the MacPhails. I allowed Catriona to pull me in one direction while Marion pulled Gerry in the other. He wailed a bit but was not able to sustain it as he needed all his failing breath to keep up with Marion's brisk pace which grew even brisker as the lights of the bus appeared in the distance, heading for Fionnphort. When the moon put in one of her fitful appearances, I turned back to see how they were faring and saw Marion running with Gerry in her arms.

Catriona watched too. 'Ma's going to try and get to the bus before it passes the graveyard. She'll maybe be able to get a lift down to the jetty or at least let them know to wait for her. There you are, Liza. Nothing to worry about. Yer wee brother'll soon be home safe and sound. Even if yer pa's not there, one of the other families'll see him all right. Come on, let's go. Yer wee holiday starts here!' She tugged at my arm but I had frozen, staring at her.

'What graveyard?' My voice was hoarse. I barely recognised it. 'What graveyard are you talking about?'


Catriona was striding ahead, no doubt desperate to get home, out of the bitter weather and the dark night, looking ahead to our cocoa treat. I lacked the strength to keep up easily with her and my efforts to do so left me without the breath to repeat my question. We scrambled to the top of the hill and tramped down the weedy path between the disused rails. Just before we reached the landing stage, which was even smaller than the Erraid one, she veered off to the left and I followed her along a narrow path that ended at a two-storey white house.

193

'Home at last!' she cried. 'Come on, Liza.' She was through the small gate – obviously this was the back of the house – and was throwing open the unlocked door with a flourish. 'Welcome to the home of The MacPhails of Tormore!'

She made it sound so grand that I half expected to hear a drum roll. I could not help giggling. Catriona MacPhail was to do many things for me in the lifetime of our friendship but never was any of them more important than her ability to make me laugh when I had almost forgotten how. It was not until we had divested ourselves of boots, coats, scarves, gloves, torches – all the paraphernalia of winter on the island – and were sitting at the big table in the cosy kitchen, waiting for the kettle to come to the boil, that I broached the subject again.

'You said something about a graveyard. Where is it? You said something about the road passing it. Were we near it? Would your mother and Gerry go past it on the way to the jetty?'

'That's a whean o' questions.' She grinned at my impatient tut. 'Oh, all right. You remember the day I told you about the Ghost of Erraid. I think it was the first time you were with us when we went over the causeway to Knockvolgan Farm wi' Miss Dow.'

'Yes, of course. You said Lady Maclean of Duart was drowned and her body washed up here. But the boy - her son - his body was never found. And she's still looking for him. That's the ghost.'

'Well done. Miss Dow would be right pleased if you remembered all yer lessons that well. So, do you also remember I said Lady Maclean was buried in the old graveyard here – well, just on the other side of the hill?'

'Mmm. I think so.' I had done so much reading of old tales about Jacobites and Druids lately that some facts were becoming jumbled.

'Well, that's the graveyard. Tormore cemetery. Lots of really old graves there and there a wee bit stone all covered wi' moss that some folk here say is Lady Maclean's. It could be, I suppose.'

'And she's looking for her son to bring him to be with her in that graveyard,' I finished slowly as the tale came back to me in full.

'Aye,' said Catriona, rising to cut off the piercing whistle of the kettle and carry it to the table where our two mugs and the bag of marshmallows were waiting. 'Aye, well, that's the legend. I think it's just a ghost story, someone's vivid imagination gettin' the better o' them.' She dropped three marshmallows on to the top of each cup of cocoa. 'Let's take these up to bed with us. I don't know about you but I'm falling asleep on my feet.'

I was deathly tired myself but, even so, as I lay in the truckle bed which Catriona had pulled out from under her own, I could not

194

immediately let sleep claim me. My mind gnawed at the loose ends: What had Gerry been doing there? How had he got there? Alone? Where was The Dow? Had she been with him? Why? What was the significance, if any, of his - or their - nearness to this old graveyard with its ghostly connections?

After a while, as Catriona slept sweetly, I heard Lachlan and Marion come home. There was the murmur of low voices downstairs in the kitchen and later on the stairs before a door closed with a click and silence fell. At last, I slept.

# CHAPTER TWENTY-FIVE

*The boat never turned aside and flew on, right before my eyes, for Iona.*
Robert Louis Stevenson, from 'Kidnapped'

'Let her go, lass.'

Catriona slid the last loop of rope off the bollard and jumped nimbly into the boat. Lachlan steered us out onto the open waters of the Sound of Iona and I felt a surge of excitement that matched the churning column of white foam our wash was creating.

Christmas Eve and a fine, crisp winter day, something of a miracle after the day before, which had been wild, wet and windy. Our hopes of the promised trip to Iona had teetered on the brink of disappointment and I had not had my nose outside the MacPhails' house all day.

'A morning in bed for you, lass,' Marion had decreed when I presented my wan face and drooping shoulders at the breakfast table in their large, homely kitchen.

'But it's Sunday,' I demurred, trying to blink the sleep out of my gritty eyes.

'Aye, so it is,' she replied.

'Isn't it a sin no' to go to church?' I asked, betraying my Catholic upbringing, quite forgetting Father's warning to Mother that first Sunday morning on Erraid.

Marion laughed. 'Well, Liza dearie, if it is, then there'll be a lot o' sinners on the Ross o' Mull this morning. Even more than usual that is! There's never many folk at the kirk on the Sunday after the Christmas party.' Obviously, she was happy to include the MacPhail family in the sinners as it was gone ten o'clock and none of them were making the slightest move.

So, once I had supped up my porridge and eaten warm oatcakes spread with homemade marmalade, I crawled back to bed and fell into a deep sleep, this time mercifully free of the turbulent dreams of the night before. Graveyards and ghosts, buses and boats, people singing and dancing, all had tumbled and chased through my subconscious that night. More than once, I had started awake, on the brink of falling – from cliffs, from high walls and once from the back window of a bus.

When I awoke, it was one o'clock in the afternoon and I felt rested at last, ready to enter into the family life that I could hear thrumming through the house. Catriona was singing somewhere upstairs, Marion was clattering pots and pans in the kitchen and Lachlan was sawing wood for the stove in the lean-to outbuilding at the side of the house. I washed my face, dressed and wandered along the landing, following the sound of singing. I found Catriona sitting on the bottom rung of a wooden ladder that led up into the attic of the house. She jumped up smiling when she saw me.

'Yer awake, Sleeping Beauty! How are ye feeling?'

'Good.' I nodded. Then I noticed what she had in her hand. It was a small, slim book, immediately recognisable. Yet another with the familiar faded green covers, the title and author's name on the front and spine in old-gold lettering, just like the Druids one she had brought to school for me, just like the *Tales and Legends* and just like the one I had seen Mother throw to the floor in the 'Good Room' of our North Berwick house. 'What's that you've got there?' I held out my hand and she gave it to me.

'*The Rise of Jacobitism in the West of Scotland*,' I read. Unlike on Mother's book, the lettering was perfectly legible.

'Is that the one your Ma had?' asked Catriona.

'I don't know. The writing on the cover of hers was all smudgy, worn away. I don't know what it was called.'

'Did you ask her? You said you were goin' to ask her if she'd brought it here.'

'No. I didna get around to it. Not yet,' I had forgotten about it in the pell-mell course of events ever since Father had come home and I had been pitched from one potential catastrophe to another.

'Well, take it,' said Catriona. 'No, go on' - as I hesitated - 'Pa won't mind ye borrowin' it and you can take it home wi' you and compare it with your Mother's one.'

Marion had called us for Sunday dinner then so I had thrust the book into the deep pocket of my winter cardigan and followed Catriona downstairs. It was still with me this morning as we sped across the Sound towards Iona, hard against my chest, in the inner pocket of the oilskin jacket which Marion had insisted on loaning me. *Just in case it turns,* she had said, meaning the weather, I suppose.

It had not been easy to get time and privacy to look at the book. With the wind keening round the house, rattling the windows, tugging at the gable ends, and the rain battering the sodden landscape, Marion had declared that it was a perfect afternoon for a game of cards. This was clearly a favourite occupation of the MacPhails for all three of them immediately leapt into action to prepare the room.

Marion whipped the pretty cloth off the circular table in what I took to be their Good Room. I had been overwhelmed to the point of embarrassment on descending the stairs to find that, in my honour, Sunday dinner was being served in this room. The fire had been lit and so too had the candles in their gleaming brass holders. Roast lamb with mint sauce, runner beans and roast potatoes had been served on delicate china platters and eaten with silver forks and knives. Apple pie had been served, not with the usual custard, but with real cream from a silver jug. When I had expressed my amazement at their doing this for *me*, all three had laughed and assured me that they had all been looking forward so much to my visit.

'We hardly ever get visitors, stuck away over here on the other side of the hill,' said Marion.

'Aye, it's out of sight, out of mind,' agreed Lachlan. 'Though they come soon enough in the summer when our strawberries are ready and in the autumn for our honey.'

Lachlan put more wood on the fire and Catriona fetched a pack of cards and a bag of buttons. That was the afternoon I learned how to play Blackjack. It was very similar to Twenty-One, a game I had played with my granny and grandpa on our occasional visits to their smallholding near Perth, except that a Jack of Clubs or Spades in a hand earned more from the banker. We took turns at being the banker, using the buttons as our betting chips. The short afternoon darkened and died without our noticing, so absorbed were we, and it wasn't until Lachlan rose to bank up the fire that we realised how dark the room had become. It was gone half past four. I could not remember spending a more relaxed, safe and happy afternoon ever. I think it was the novelty of being with a couple, man and wife, who were so easy and loving with each other and with a family so completely without tension in each other's presence, so devoid of the wariness that I had thought normal.

When the game was over – they let me win, of course, and I had to choose a button for my prize – I followed Marion through to the kitchen and at last managed to ask what had happened to Gerry, though she could tell me little enough. Lachlan had seen her running with Gerry in her arms and had slowed down in time to let her board the bus. Gerry had been handed over into the safekeeping of Euan, who had promised to see he was delivered into Mother's waiting arms.

'But did he tell you what he was doing there? How he got there? And why? Did he go alone? When did he leave the party?' I persisted but she only shook her head.

'I was too set on getting him down to the jetty and on to a boat for Erraid, I'm afraid. I didn't really ask him. Sorry. Liza, you'll have to ask him yourself when you get home.'

'What about Miss Dow? Was she on the bus? Or one of the boats?'

But Marion only shook her head and shrugged her shoulders. I was left with my questions.

It was not until a lot later that I had a chance to look at the book. Catriona and I were roped in to help Marion bake cheese scones for tea and then, of course, to help eat them. The evening was filled with more games, this time guessing ones – charades and such - and musical entertainment. Marion accompanied her husband and daughter on the rather tinny, elderly piano that stood in a corner of the good room and they sang a lengthy repertoire of songs: old Scottish ballads and duets; popular ones from the recent war; lively, comic ditties; even a couple of solemn, classical things that I had never heard before. It was such a polished performance that I realised they must have been practising, preparing to entertain me royally. As with the Sunday roast dinner served in grand style, this well-rehearsed concert touched me deeply. I felt more loved and wanted by this family who barely knew me than ever before in my life.

'Aw, look. We've drawn tears. Is she no' just the best audience?' said Catriona as their beautiful rendering of Robert Burns' *Ae Fond Kiss* came to an end. She came over and hugged me which made me snivel all the more. How could I explain to these three people who lived in such easy, loving harmony, and who were reaching out to draw me into their charmed circle, what it meant to me? And how it threw my own fraught family into such sharp relief?

I dashed away my tears and managed a laugh. 'You three would draw tears from a statue,' I said. 'You should be on the stage.'

And the day, so miserable outside the house and so wonderful inside it, drew to a close. I hoped for time to look at the book in bed before sleep but Catriona chattered away until Marion came in to kiss us both goodnight and turn out the oil-lamp that stood on a high shelf for safety in the bedroom.

'Say your prayers, girlies, before you fall asleep. Don't forget,' she said softly as she closed the door. I prayed that I would get a chance to look at the book in the morning, hastily adding the usual 'And God bless Mother and Father and Gerry and all my friends and everyone I know. Amen.'

God heard my prayer and I woke next morning when the room was still dark. I was sure it must be nearly morning for I felt well slept. Catriona was a hump in her bed, back turned to me, breathing slow and steady. I retrieved the book from under my pillow and inched out of my low bed, thrusting my feet into the slippers that Marion had tidily placed side by side and lifting my winter cardigan from the pile of clothes on the chair. Once out on the landing, I drew a long breath, shrugged on the woolly and wrapped it tightly round my chest for it was very cold. Every stair tread seemed to creak and each one louder than the last – or so it seemed to my taut nerves – but no one stirred and I reached the kitchen, still holding my breath. The warmth that greeted me as I opened the kitchen door had me letting out my breath on a long sigh. I sank gratefully down on the rug in front of the stove. It was still warm but not burning hot as during the day so I was able to lean my back against it.

The heat relaxed me, as did the continuing deep silence which assured me that I was undetected. I opened the little book and began reading. I soon came across mention of the Macleans of Mull.

*When the English civil war was over, the rule of Oliver Cromwell and his Parliamentarians got under way. Clan MacLean took sides with the Covenanters and fought on the royalist side at Inverkeithing in 1651. The MacLean chief, Hector, fell in that battle but not before he had inspired one of the Clan's enduring battle cries. In the heat of battle, Hector was covered from attack by seven brothers of the clan who, in an impressive display of devotion to their chief, successively sacrificed their lives in his defence. As each one fell, another rushed forward to interpose himself between Hector and the enemy, crying out in Gaelic, 'Bos air son Eachin', (Another for Hector) which has continued ever since to be a watchword whenever a MacLean encounters danger that requires immediate courage. Nor did the clan relinquish its loyalty to the exiled Charles II, despite losing heavily at Inverkeithing and the royalist cause being totally defeated soon after.*

*In Hector's memory, his brother, Alan, the new Chief, and all of Clan MacLean revered Hector's nine year old son who was also called Alan. They were as staunch supporters of the King as ever and this Scottish pocket of royalist support was a thorn in Cromwell's side. A fleet of five naval ships was despatched in 1653 with the mission to ransack Duart Castle and capture the young chief. But, as with the Spanish Armada in the previous century, the weather came to the aid of those being threatened. A terrible storm wrecked the hostile fleet as it lay in Duart Bay, sinking the ships. Some of the troops escaped and spread out over the island. The widowed Lady MacLean escaped with her son and made it to the south tip of Mull on the causeway islet of Erraid where, harried by Cromwell's soldiers, she rashly took a boat and headed, with her young son, out into open sea. The boat never stood a chance for the weather was wild and soon the boat was smashed on the vicious Torran Rocks which had seen an end to many sea vessels a great deal sturdier than the little boat. Her body was washed up in Tormore Bay near Fionnphort and she was buried in the*

200

*graveyard there. The boy's body was never recovered and a legend persists that Lady MacLean's ghost can sometimes be seen searching for him and that a bell rings out on the Torran Rocks when she appears.*

Most of this I knew already and I was beginning to feel sleepy again in the warmth when I turned the page and read: *It is said that she wants to take him back to her grave with her and that no nine-year-old boy is safe while the ghost is abroad.* Underneath this chilling statement, was a line drawing of Lady MacLean and her young son. It was strongly drawn and the features of both were very clear. I gasped. Now I understood why Mother had thrown the book down and screamed. The boy was the spitting image of Gerry. I stared in horror at the drawing, first at the boy and then at the woman. And felt the blood drain from my face and my throat close so tightly I could not swallow. The woman in the drawing was remarkably like The Dow.

'A penny for them, Liza, child. You're a million miles away,' said Lachlan, looking keenly at me as the boat turned against the strong current and headed for the jetty on Iona.

He was right. I had been lost in thought, picturing that drawing of Lady MacLean and her son. Incidents kept coming back to me, some of them I would have said I had forgotten, but now invested with sinister meaning. Mother's book and her reaction to it, of course, but also Mrs Forsyth's album on our last morning in North Berwick. But the photograph of the two figures, one much taller than the other, that she had wanted Mother to look at, could not have been of Lady MacLean and son. There had been no cameras in the seventeenth century, I knew that for sure.

Then there had been Mother's reaction to her first sighting of The Dow on Oban quay. I heard Mother's voice: 'What are you doing at that school? You're not a teacher!' Mother had recognised The Dow's strange likeness to the Lady MacLean of the line drawing in the book. The book on legends that Mother had given me had pages torn out – could these have been repeating what the *Jacobitism* book said about Lady MacLean, maybe cross-referencing the two books and maybe even reproducing the line drawing? Was that why Mother had torn them out? She had been upset when she first saw me with the Druids book then had calmed down – had she been afraid it was another copy of the *Jacobitism* book and that I would see the drawing?

And I thought too of The Dow's strange reaction to any mention of MacLeans and Jacobites. I saw again the taut expression on her face and the harshness in her voice as we sailed past Duart Castle that first day, on our way to Mull: *The MacLeans of Duart backed the losing side . . . Their estates were confiscated.* I remembered how she had choked me off when I had chosen to read an article about the forthcoming Gathering of Clan MacLean at Duart, during the newspaper exercise in class. Most of all, I thought about her interest in and attention to Gerry, sometimes so blatant that it bordered on unprofessional, as if she could not help herself.

And now, we had this latest escapade. Gerry, so like that long ago Alan, The MacLean of Duart, and just his age, had gone missing from the party last night at the same time as The Dow, and been found near the very graveyard that held the bones — and some said, the ghost — of the tragic Lady MacLean. I was desperate to get home and talk to Gerry.

With all these thoughts and remembrances chasing around my head, it was little wonder that I was 'a million miles away'. But time and tide wait for no man and our brave little boat was now nosing into the jetty.

Iona! If ever a place held an aura of the guarded secrets of centuries, then this was surely it. Lachlan bounded on to the landing stage, tied the rope and turned to me. I stretched out my hand and stepped reverently on to the ancient sacred isle.

# CHAPTER TWENTY-SIX

*Here was a man I would rather call my friend than my enemy.*
*Robert Louis Stevenson, from 'Kidnapped'*

Lachlan and Catriona strode up the short ramp from the small, wooden jetty with the nonchalance of familiarity. I straggled behind them, my eyes everywhere, trying to capture first impressions. I saw an uneven row of houses along a narrow street that lay to the right of the jetty and even a sign proclaiming 'Hotel'. Just as on Erraid, a path divided the houses from their front gardens. On this snell December day, these looked wind-harried and uninviting but wooden benches and tables proclaimed that it was not always so. On a fine, warm day, the street's residents might take their ease and admire the view, especially guests from the Hotel who would not have any work to do.

We climbed a slow incline of a road that led us straight up from the jetty into the heart of the island. I stopped frequently, falling further and further behind, as I scanned the horizon. I saw a few croft houses and, here and there, a rough attempt at fencing. Clusters of muddy, mournful sheep could be seen futilely nibbling at the flat, sodden ground.

'Come on, Liza. Keep up!' called Catriona. 'We're turning here.' She was standing at the top of the short rise, facing down towards me, waving her left arm up and down. I quickened my pace and saw, as I crested the rise, a small stone church, like a hundred other such in Scotland, and beside it a large house, presumably the manse. In a replica of the street, a path separated them from, not a garden, but a field which bore all the hallmarks of a vegetable plot in winter. This, I knew, to be the glebe, the plot of land given to the minister for his own pragmatic purposes. Some ministers kept a cow or a goat but most contented themselves with planting potatoes, carrots and the like. As I looked, a couple of bedraggled hens fluttered out from the far corner.

Catriona had turned away to follow her father but my attention was further caught by a square building on my left. It had three windows facing into the road and each had a pile of books on its inside shelf. Above the door was the legend: THE LEGH RICHMOND LIBRARY. I was drawn like a magnet, as always by the sight of books, and the idea that this remote place had a library amazed me for I had only ever seen or imagined libraries in town streets.

'Liza!' Catriona was now sounding exasperated. 'What are ye dawdling back there for? Come ON!'

'But look,' I called back. 'Look! A library.'

She reluctantly retraced her steps. 'Aye. A library,' she agreed drily. 'Have ye never seen one before?'

'Of course.' I was trying the door now but sadly finding it locked. 'It's not open,' I said disappointedly.

'Can ye no' read, you that's so keen on libraries?' she pointed to a small sign pasted on to one of the windows. I had been too entranced by the piles of books to see it. 'Open Tuesdays, Wednesdays and Fridays, 10.00 am – 4.00 pm. Closed Christmas Day and New Year's Day.'

'Ach, it's Monday,' I said sadly, abandoning my rattling of the door's handle. 'Can we come back another day? Do you think I would be allowed to borrow books, even though I don't live on Iona? Would being on Erraid be close enough?'

By this time, Lachlan had also retraced his steps and he joined us now. 'What are you lassies hanging about here for? I thought ye wanted to see the cathedral ruins? And I'm fancying a wee climb up *Dun I* for it's a bonnie day. We'll be able to see right up the Firth of Lorne, over to Staffa and the Treshnish Isles as well. But we'll see nothing if we don't get a move on. It's nearly noon and the light will start fading by half two.'

'It's her, Pa,' said Catriona. 'Fair tickled wi' Iona's wee library. She's book daft.'

'Sorry, Mr MacPhail,' I said, realising that I had done exactly what mother had told me not to – made a nuisance of myself. And the MacPhails my kind and generous hosts. For shame!

'If it's books ye're wanting' lass, ye should have said. I've got plenty of them up in our attic. My grandfather – my mother's father, that is – was a great one for the reading. He collected books everywhere he went. People knew how he loved them and were always offloading their old collections on to him. It drove my grandmother wild. Their wee house was full of them. When ye sat down at the table, you couldn't get yer legs under it for boxes of books.' He chuckled, reminiscently.

'I'd love to see them,' I said wistfully. 'So would my mother,' I added as an afterthought, realising for the first time where my passion for reading came from. 'She loves them too.'

'Then you must *both* come and visit soon and I'll let you loose on the attic,' he said generously.

'You'd better wear yer old clothes, then,' laughed Catriona. 'And a headscarf. It's dusty and cobwebby up there.'

'That's settled, then,' said Lachlan. He took one of my hands and firmly marched me away from the library, not letting go until we had crested another rise in the road, past a little cottage on our left, its outbuildings forming three sides of a square with two dull-eyed, incurious sheep in the middle of it.

I saw it then, on the right, lying in the lee of the slope between the road and the sea. I had looked over many times, sitting on the rock beside The Lookout, at the ruins of the ancient cathedral but to see them so close was thrilling. From Erraid, they looked no more than the derelict remains of rough buildings and a square tower. As we walked down towards them, I saw how much of the walls persisted, how clear was the shape, how real and somehow alive they were. I half-expected to see a line of monks, faces hidden by their cowls, chanting sacred song as they processed out of its doorway and wound their way down to the sea.

Lachlan was talking and Catriona was interjecting comments, both delighted to have an audience for their knowledge. 'In olden times, people believed that soil became sacred and magic if a saint was buried in it. So, if a person was buried next to a saint, the holy soil dissolved their sins.' That was Lachan.

Catriona chimed in. 'That's why the ancient Kings of Scotland were brought to Iona - to be buried near St Columba. This is the street of the dead.' She skipped on to a rough path, marked out by slabs of ancient stone. 'Once they'd had the funeral service in the cathedral, the coffin was carried along this path to the old graveyard.' She gestured vaguely and I looked to see a few old stones jutting out of the earth, mottled and moss-covered. I shivered suddenly as a strange feeling swept over me.

'Are ye getting too cold, lass?' Lachlan was remembering Marion's injunction to 'mind ye look after Liza and don't let her get chilled – she's no' used to being out in all weathers like you two.'

'No. I'm fine. It was just . . . I had a funny feeling.'

'Like somebody walked over yer grave?' asked Catriona. 'Well, that's no surprise. This place must be well haunted. Headless monks and the like.' She screwed her face up into a squint-eyed leer and began lurching around me, emitting hollow laughs.

'Ach, get away!' I said, giggling. But the feeling persisted even while we sat on stony ledges in the ruins to eat our 'dinner piece'. Marion had packed thick, crunchy bannocks, chunks of cheese and, wrapped in waxed paper, a slab of pale gold cake.

'That's Ma's honey-cake,' said Catriona, when I expressed my appreciation of its delicious moistness. 'She's famous for it. Makes it with our own honey. Sometimes she puts lemon peel or glass cherries in it but I like it best just plain.'

I sniggered. 'It's not glass cherries. It's glacé.' I pronounced it *glassey* as Mother had taught me. 'It's French. It means crystallised . . .' I tailed off, hoping she wouldn't press me on the point. I wasn't entirely sure what 'crystallised' meant.

'Fancy that,' said Catriona good-humouredly. 'Ye're a fund of useless information, Liza.' And she poked me in the ribs and ran off, challenging me to catch her. Lachlan was wandering about among the old graves, trying to read their weathered inscriptions. I swallowed the rest of my cake and leapt up to chase after her. She ran back the way we had come and then dodged through an open gate and up a muddy path to a cluster of trees at the far side of the manse. With a burst of speed, I reached Catriona just as she swung herself around the trunk of a silver birch. Our presence disturbed a clamour of rooks who rose into the air cawing indignantly. Startled, we both looked skyward. When we dropped our eyes, I got the fright of my young life. Walking towards us, emerging from the thicket of trees, was a ghost.

He was a tall, commanding presence, dressed in an off-white robe with a hood which was draped over his long red hair. Around his waist there was a heavy chain from which dangled several metal implements. I saw a tiny pick, a knife, a small pair of shears and various flat discs with ornamental designs wrought into the metal. Somewhere in my mind, I registered that there was no cross. A monk – which was what he looked like - would have had a cross, surely? On his feet were open sandals, caked with mud and dried leaves. In his outstretched arms, he carried a bundle of evergreen twigs, pale green foliage with white berries. Mistletoe, I knew.

Catriona's talk of hauntings by headless monks had fired my overwrought imagination and I stared at the apparition in terror. She, however, seemed unfazed. 'It's yerself, Mr Oran,' she said calmly. 'Not seen you for a long time. How are ye?'

The man – clearly he *was* a man and not a ghost after all, to my considerable relief – looked gravely at us. Then he lifted up his arms, bearing the foliage aloft, and declared something that sounded like a curse or, maybe, a blessing. It was not in a language I could understand – Gaelic, probably - but Catriona answered him quite gaily and I caught the word 'Lachlan' and guessed, from the waving of her right arm in the direction of the ruined cathedral, that she was telling him that her father was with us and he was just up the road. That made me feel safer. I would have backed Lachlan against this fey-looking creature in any fight.

Mr Oran turned, beckoning us to follow, and to my amazement Catriona did just that. I hung back, tempted to make a run for it and fetch Lachlan, but she signalled for me to follow. As I still hesitated, she stamped her foot and made impatient 'follow-me' gestures. I trailed behind them into the depths of the thicket until we found ourselves in a clearing. There was a white cloth on the ground on which lay more twigs of mistletoe and a small sickle. It was gleaming brightly against the white cloth and could have been of polished brass or even pure gold.

He bent to lay his burden of twigs on the cloth and then picked up the sickle. I tensed, feeling threatened, poised for flight. But he turned to the tree behind him which I saw was an oak tree, its trunk almost hidden by a thick covering of entwined mistletoe. With one swift stroke, he lopped off a large twig. It was a handsome one, the leaves glossy, the berries like fat pearls. He held it out to Catriona and spoke again in that weird, chanting voice, seeming to repeat the same words three times. It was as if he was conducting some kind of religious ceremony and I felt the now familiar shiver – someone walking over my grave, Catriona had called it – course through me.

'Thank you, Mr Oran,' she said with grave courtesy. Like she was acting in some strange play. She accepted the twig, nodded seriously, and turned to me. 'Would you like one too, Liza?'

I said nothing, just made saucer eyes at her, trying to convey my discomfort and bewilderment.

'It's for healing,' she explained.

'Healing what?' My voice came out as a hoarse whisper.

'Anything. It's ancient magic. Mr Oran is a Druid.'

'A Druid! But they don't exist any . . .'

It was her turn to make saucer eyes and they darted angry prohibition at me. 'Mr Oran is a Druid,' she repeated in a voice that brooked no argument. 'He is collecting mistletoe in the ancient Druidic way – with a golden sickle on to a white cloth. It must be the right time of year for it.'

'You mean Christmas?' I asked, still bewildered.

I was unprepared for the effect my words had on Mr Oran. He let out a deep growl and thrust his face out from the shadow of his cowl. His eyes were bloodshot and watering, the veins on his cheeks a red and purple lattice, his lips blue and cracked. If I had been fearful of fictional ghosts, I was ten times more terrified of this real-life apparition. I let out a howl and turned to run out of the pleasant little wood which had turned into a place of menace. I felt myself caught and pulled back by the wrist and thought it was Catriona. But, when I looked down, I saw a gnarled claw with bony knuckles that stuck up like clothes pegs on a line. I shrieked then, my terror spiralling out of control, and heard Lachlan's voice – oh, blessed sound! – 'Girls! Where are you? What's wrong?'

With a sob of relief, I jerked my wrist free, burst out of the wood and threw myself on Lachlan's broad chest, almost knocking him over.

'Steady, lass,' he said, staggering back. 'What's wrong? Where's Catriona?'

I waved a hand at the thicket. 'She's in there. With a Druid. He's . . . he's horrible!' I was trembling and my voice was high-pitched, near to hysteria.

'Ah!' Lachlan gently held me out from his chest and looked at me. 'Och, lass, ye've got yerself in a right state. Has Catriona been fillin' yer head wi' nonsense? That lassie's imagination runs away wi itself sometimes.'

'No!' I shook my head vehemently. 'There really is a Druid in there. In a white robe like one of the old monks. He's cutting mistletoe. She says it's for healing, magic healing from ancient times.'

'Ah!' said Lachlan again. 'Old Hector, is it? I've not seen him for a fair while. I was wondering if he was still here on Iona, still alive even.'

I shook my head again. 'She's callin' him Mr Oran.'

Lachlan laughed and I felt quite furious that he was not taking me seriously. His only daughter was in that thicket with the mad monk. And he had a weapon, the gold-bright sickle.

'That's what *she* calls him. It's just her nonsense, calling him after St Oran. *He's* supposed to have been the last Druid on Iona. They say he was buried alive as a sacrifice, right where the cathedral was built. When they opened the grave three days later, he was still alive. He said he'd seen hell and it wasn't too bad a place after all. So they buried him again for blasphemy.' Lachlan chuckled. 'How unlucky can one man get?'

'But isn't he dangerous? Should we no' go and get Catriona?'

'Och, she'll be fine. Old Hector is harmless. Lives in wee world of his own. Sometimes he's a Druid, sometimes a monk, sometimes St Columba himself even. He has a soft spot for Catriona. I think he fair likes it when she calls him Oran.'

As if to confirm Lachlan's relaxed assessment of the situation, Catriona emerged from the trees, smiling and obviously unharmed. She was carrying two mistletoe sprigs. Of Mr Oran – or 'Old Hector' - there was no sign.

'Here you are, Liza,' she said tranquilly, holding out a sprig. 'Take that back to Erraid with you. Rub the leaves on yer mother's ankle and get her to sleep wi' the berries under her pillow. That'll soon get it better.'

I did not want to touch it, still full of revulsion for him who had cut it, but neither did I want to offend her. Gingerly, I accepted and was surprised to feel how velvety the leaves were. It had a cluster of perfect, creamy pearls at its heart and was beautiful to look upon. Despite myself, despite the fear and misgiving I still felt, I felt drawn to it. I wanted to look upon it and touch it.

'Come on.' Lachlan took both our hands and began to march us briskly back towards the cathedral. 'No time to waste, now.'

So tight was his hold and so brisk was his pace that we did not manage to speak to each other until we reached halfway up Dun I, Iona's only hill. He let go of our hands then so that we could each find our own path to the summit. Our efforts to keep up with his long, strong legs left us without much breath for conversation. I wanted to know what all the palaver with the white robe, the white cloth and the gold sickle meant. Most of all, I wanted to know why the man had turned on me so suddenly and viciously.

'He's a harmless old soul.' Catriona echoed her father's words. 'He's been here for years. The farming folk look after him, give him food and let him shelter in their barns and such. I suppose you'd call him a tramp though no one ever says that word.'

'But where did he come from? Why was he wearing that white robe? What was all the mistletoe stuff about? And why did he go for me when I said that about Christmas?'

She laughed as best she could while panting up the hill. 'You and your questions! Well, he always wears that robe and that belt wi' all the dangly things on it. It's like his uniform – or *habit,* I think he'd say.'

'Like monks wear habits?'

'I suppose so. He can't seem to make up his mind if he's one of Columba's monks or a Druid priest. The robe seems to cover both.'

'Your father said he sometimes thinks he's St Columba himself.'

She giggled. 'Aye, probably.'

'But what about the mistletoe thing?'

'Ancient Druidic practice. They knew all about how plants and herbs could be used to heal illnesses – and some of them really work. But there was a lot of mystic stuff linked in with it. Mistletoe – a tea made from its leaves is good for stomach troubles - had to be cut with a gold sickle by a Druid in a white robe and laid on a white cloth. And it had to be done at the time when the moon was full, which it is at Christmas time.'

'That's what I said. Why was he so mad about me saying it?'

'We call it Christmas but the Druids called it the winter solstice. They hate any reference to Christianity.'

'Why?'

'Because the Christians persecuted the Druids. The Romans that invaded Britain were Christians and they hounded the Druid priests to death. Massacred them. Wiped them out, mostly. So those who escaped hated the Christians.'

'I'm not surprised,' I said slowly. 'So your Mr Oran, as you call him, just saw red because I said the word "Christmas"?'

'Oh, aye. Ye've to watch yer step wi him. He fires up quick as quick. But he wouldn't really hurt you. But then . . .' We had reached the summit and she turned to me with a wicked grin. 'A bonnie wee lassie like you might be just what he was looking for.'

'What for?' I asked warily, sensing mischief in her smile.

'Human sacrifice, of course. The fairer the maiden the better. Although a bonnie wee laddie will do just as well.'

I wanted to laugh it off but the creeping cold was upon me again. I turned thankfully to respond to Lachlan who was pointing out the Hebridean landmarks that lay all around.

## CHAPTER TWENTY-SEVEN

*With that kind of anger of despair that has sometimes stood me instead of courage.*
*Robert Louis Stevenson, from 'Kidnapped'*

All too soon, the short winter day began to slide towards its end. As we stood in the stark clarity and merciless cold that comes with a cloudless December sky, the rugged west coast of Mull slowly took on a warm, orange glow. I felt it drawing me towards it as a fire will draw chilled travellers to its hearth. Just looking at it made me feel warmer, comforted somehow.

'Sunset,' said Lachlan with a mixture of regret and homage. 'Shame we've no' time to go over to the *machair* and watch it but we'd never get there and back before it's dark.' He turned to me and smiled his kindly, untroubled smile. 'Yer mother will be startin' to worry if I don't get you back home soon.'

Catriona assumed her mentor role. 'The *machair* is . . .'

'I know,' I interrupted. 'I remember Miss Dow showing us the wild flowers in the Erraid one. It's a stretch of thick, short grass that all the farmers can put their sheep and cattle on.'

She laughed and tugged my hair. 'Top marks, missie. Aye, it's common grazing and full o' wee plants and flowers, right enough, but the Erraid *machair* is just a couple of wee bitties. The Iona one is huge. You can walk on it for ages and it's a golf course as well.'

'Aye, it's been a full eighteen holes since 1905.' Lachlan joined in with a note of pride in his voice.

'A *golf course?*' I thought of the golfers I had regularly seen in North Berwick with their tweed plus-fours and caps, great bags of clubs slung over their shoulders. They came down from Edinburgh in their big cars, sometimes chauffeur-driven, and brought wealthy custom to the town. I could not see them fitting into this remote, timeless place.

Lachlan broke into my thoughts. 'We'll come back in the spring, Liza, when the light nights come in and I'll take ye over to the *machair* here. It's on the west of the island.' He turned right around and gestured away from the Mull coast that we had been watching. 'If you think that orange light on Mull is bonnie, wait till you see a sunset over there!'

'Yeah. Looking straight out into the ocean - first stop America,' said Catriona.

'More likely Ireland,' corrected Lachlan. 'That's where Columba came from.'

'I ken that.' Catriona was indignant, 'But if ye steered or got blown a wee bit . . .'

I suddenly gave a huge yawn and shiver all at once and they both turned in concern.

'Ach, here we are blethering about sunsets and old saints and the lassie freezing half to death and exhausted. Time enough to talk about all that next time we come.' And, taking my arm, Lachlan began to steer me firmly down the hill, Catriona following close behind.

As we descended, I felt a rare glow of optimism suffuse my mind and body. Maybe it was the talk of coming back in the spring, the untroubled assumption that this would happen and a feeling that the girl who returned to Iona in a few months' time would be a different person. Like the warm glow that had softened and beautified the harsh landscape of Mull, my soul would be relieved of its burdens and my life would be softened and beautified. The anxiety over Mother's health and pregnancy; the worry over Father's relationship with The Dow; the fear of The Dow's unhealthy obsession with Gerry; and the longstanding, ever-present terror of Father's temper and brutality – all these would have been resolved and I would be a carefree girl - whatever that was. I had no experience to draw on but my imagination supplied the picture and the feelings so intensely that it felt like a prophecy of blessing. In this happy frame of mind, I boarded the boat and prepared to return to Erraid.


When we docked at Erraid, both Lachlan and Catriona insisted on walking all the way up to the house with me.

'We should pay our respects to your mother and enquire after her health,' was all he said when I protested that I could easily walk up on my own and they should head round the point to Fionnphort and get home before the night was pitch black.

As always, after an absence, I was in trepidation of Father's mood and, as the warm glow from my happy visit to the MacPhails and our day on Iona began to fade, the questions began to pile up in my mind once more. Had Father got home last night? Had The Dow? If not, what did they both do? Why had Gerry been at the old graveyard? Did Father know he had left the party without telling anyone? And, if so, what awful retribution from Father might have befallen him? What of Mother, her sprained ankle and state of shock? How did such things affect a pregnant woman?

But the one question I, in my ignorance, did not ask was to be more important than all of these. As the three of us turned into the path along the front of the houses, we saw Bridie Campbell coming towards us, her old woollen shawl clutched around her ample bosom, its frayed ends flapping behind her. As soon as she saw us, she broke into a trot and met us before we could reach our door.

'Thank God you're back, Liza. There's been no sign of your father since Saturday night, Gerry's been greetin' and bletherin' about the-Lord-knows-what, old graves and ghosts and nonsense like that. And your poor mother . . .' She hesitated, cast a quick glance at Lachlan and shook her head, obviously not wanting to talk about Mother in his earshot.

'Is my mother feeling better? How is her ankle? Can she get out of bed and walk on it?' I made to push past Bridie and head into the house but she caught my sleeve and moved to put her arm round my shoulder, drawing me away from Lachlan and Catriona. She beckoned with two fingers to indicate I was to lean in. She had something important and evidently secret, or at least private, to tell me.

'You'll have to be a brave wee lassie,' she began.

'What is it?' I cried, my imagination racing, as was its wont, where angels fear to tread. 'She's no' dead, is she?'

'Wheeest!' Bridie cast an agonised glance over her shoulder to where Lachlan and Catriona were standing hesitantly on the path behind us. 'Yer mother will be all right . . . I think . . . It will just take a bit o' time. But the wee babby that was to be yer brother or sister, well . . .'

'The baby's dead?' I clutched at the handle of our door. It was coated in a thin layer of ice but I barely noticed the cold. 'Dead? But how can the baby be dead if Mother's no' dead? How can it be dead before it's even born?' With these questions, I betrayed my ignorance and Bridie frowned.

'It happens, Liza. The babby lives inside the mother until it's born. It's got its own wee life in there but it can die in there too sometimes. It just happens.' Bridie's voice was rough and there were tears in her eyes.

'But why? How? Was it the accident? Was the baby killed when she fell?'

'We don't know. It could have just been the delayed shock that came over her yesterday night. She started shaking and crying, fit to break anyone's heart. Then this morning . . .' Bridie stopped and pursed her lips. 'Well, there's some blood – you've to prepare yourself, Liza. Be a big brave girl. Your mammy needs you.'

I pushed open the door and moved slowly into the lobby, calling 'Mother. Mother. It's me, home again.' I turned into the kitchen and saw a scene of frightful disarray. The table was a jumbled heap of clothing and wads of cotton wool, all splashed bright red. As I moved into the room, I saw a small basin among the jumble, filled with pinkish-red water and another smaller bowl containing some kind of red, bloody mess. I remembered the parcels of slimy offal we used to get from the butcher for the cat we had when I was little – 'liver-and-lights', Mother had called it.

I was dimly aware of Bridie barring the door to Lachlan. 'No place for a man,' she was saying. And Lachlan's steady, gentle 'Is there anything I can do? Has Mrs Galway taken a turn for the worse? Is she in need of a doctor? I can row round to Bunessan and get him. Where is *Mr* Galway - Robert?'

I did not hear Bridie's reply for I was now standing at the bedside. The sight of mother drove all other thoughts from my whirling mind. She was lying quite flat, without even a pillow for her head, although I could see that her feet were propped up on something under the covers. She was shivering, not violently but with such persistence that I knew she had been shivering like this for a long time. Her face was as white as the sheet she was clutching, her eyes closed but leaking tears, her teeth chattering in time to the dreadful shivering.

I put my hand on her arm. It was as cold as marble. She opened her eyes and turned her head to see me. 'Och, Liza, good girl . . .' was all she said – all she seemed capable of saying before she went back to shivering and chattering.

I suddenly felt furious. I was angry with Mother for sending us off to the party, angry with the three of us for leaving her, angry with Gerry for getting lost, angry with Father for not being here to take care of his wife, angry with The Dow for her pernicious presence in our lives, angry with the NLB for sending us to this place. Most of all, I was angry with myself for letting Mother down, for enjoying a happy visit to the MacPhails' home and a fascinating day on Iona in their company, while Mother was sinking into this dreadful state.

I whirled round on Bridie as she came into the kitchen, shutting the door on a protesting Lachlan. 'She's freezing,' I cried. 'Why have you let her get so cold? She needs to keep warm. She's shivering.'

Bridie came to stand beside me and looked down at Mother. Then she drew back the covers and I saw a bundle of what looked like small stones in a cloth lying on Mother's belly. Bridie took my hand and laid it on the bundle. It was icy cold and damp. I snatched back my hand in horror.

'Why are you freezing her with icy pebbles? She'll catch her death!'

214

'Her body – where the baby was - has to be kept as cold as possible for a few hours. I know it seems hard, lass but it has to be done. Your mother understands that.'

'But why . . ?'

It was Mother herself who answered me, her voice thin and high but quite distinct. 'I was starting to haemorrhage, Liza. The icy stones will help it to stop.'

'What's hem . . . hemur . .?'

'Just losing blood, dear. More than I should. Bridie is doing the right thing.' She gave a deep shudder and her features pinched even more sharply as her teeth began to chatter again.

'Come and help me clear up,' said Bridie. I moved unwillingly to take a bundle of bloodstained bedsheets from her. 'Take them out to the shed and put them to steep in the tin bath. Add some salt from the sack in the shed. And here, you'd better be taking this as well.' It was Mother's long, white nightdress the goriest thing of all, its lower half completely soaked in blood. The metallic smell of fresh blood filled my nostrils and I gagged. But Bridie had turned to her own tasks, lifting the bigger basin and carrying it over to the sink, ignoring me, leaving me to get on with it.

I hated her for expecting me to deal with all this. Why me? Always me! Then I suddenly thought of the horrible Christmas Eve that Bridie and Mother had had and felt a rush of shame. Tamping down my nausea, I gathered up the bloody pile and went out to the back yard.

And so it was that I learned about the messy misery that is miscarriage.


It was cold work filling pails of water from the rain-barrel and sloshing them into the tin bath that we all used for our weekly bathing. For that, of course, it was brought inside to the warm kitchen, placed in front of the fire and filled with kettles of warm water. I always enjoyed my weekly bath, especially as Mother now insisted I have it on my own, being 'too big to be sharing with your brother anymore.' I would luxuriate in the warm suds and imagine myself a grand lady in a marble tub with maids in attendance.

But this was a very different experience, out here in the icy darkness, with only the borrowed lamplight from the back of the houses to help me see what I was doing. Several times I stumbled with a full bucket in my hand and cold water splashed onto my legs and feet. By the time the bath was half full, I was soaked and shivering almost as badly as poor Mother. I thrust the bloody sheets and nightgown into the water, tamping them down with the handle of a shovel that was propped up against the coal bunker. I could see that it was going to require more water to cover them. I gritted my chattering teeth and fetched two more buckets from the barrel.

I was paddling my soggy way back into the house when I remembered about the salt. For a moment, I considered leaving it out and just lying to Bridie if she asked me about it. But some grim imperative that had to do with making reparations to Mother for leaving her, for failing to protect her as I had promised I would, made me turn back. I deserved this horrible penance and I should not shirk from any of it.

The shed door always tended to stick and, as winter progressed, had become worse. I prepared to take a run at it and shove with all my strength as I had had to do for the past few weeks when fetching oil for the lamps or potatoes, carrots and turnips from the sand-filled boxes. In my depleted, shivering state I made a poor fist of it and more stumbled than shoved against the door but found myself immediately, and most surprisingly, inside. The door had not been closed.

I tensed at once, distracted from my physical miseries by a rush of terror. 'Who's in here? Is there somebody in here?' My voice was squeaky with fear.

Something moved in the far corner and I almost screamed but the figure that straightened itself and came into the dim beam of light from next door's back bedroom was not big, not big at all, and certainly no threat.

'For God's sake, Gerry! 'I exploded, relief fuelling my anger. 'What the hell are you doing in here?'


I got it out of him there and then, the whole story, with the two of us standing in the dark shed, the one covered in dust and dirty sand, the other dripping and shivering. I had waited long enough and my anger at the whole horrible situation – so different from the calm, contented family life I had been part of for two precious days – found a target.

'Tell me what's been going on, you little shite,' I shouted and shook him viciously. 'What did you think you were doing on Saturday night? Going out of the hall on your own! Wandering to a graveyard, and *that* graveyard, for God's sake!' I was beyond reasonable thought now, forgetting that he had no knowledge of the significance of Tormore.

'You'd better stop using bad words or I'll tell Father,' he retorted with more spunk than I would have credited him with.

'Never mind that.' I shook him again. 'You'd make an angel swear, you would. Tell me why you did that on the night of the party. I was out of my mind worryin' about you until we found you. And Mrs MacPhail had to run with you to meet the bus. You made a right nuisance of yourself. I'll bet Father's furious.' *Making a nuisance of yourself* was a cardinal crime in Father's book and one of his favourite reasons for belting us. 'You'll get a right skelping.'

His cockiness disappeared at once. 'You won't tell him, Liza, will you?'

'Tell him? Does he no' ken already? Has someone no' told him?' Everyone on the bus must have known. They might not know the whole story, not the graveyard bit perhaps, but they would know that Gerry had somehow wandered off and not been at the hall when it was time to board the bus for the Fionnphort jetty, that Marion MacPhail had found him and run with him to catch the bus. The story would have been all over Erraid in no time.

'He no' here. He never came home after the party – or yesterday. I dinna think he's come back today, either.'

Something clicked in my chilled brain. 'What about Miss Dow? Has she come back?' But he only shrugged his shoulders and began to snivel.

I returned to my attack. 'Tell me what happened after the party before we found you. Hurry up! I need to get back inside and see how Mother is. Come on. Ye're no' leavin' this shed till you tell me.'

But, after all, it was a piecemeal, unsatisfactory account he gave. He had no memory of leaving the hall. His first realisation that he was not there had been when he opened his eyes and found himself at the gate of the old graveyard which had been bathed in bright moonlight. He had found himself held in the arms of The Dow. He had come awake and struggled to get down. She had taken his hand then and tried to pull him into the graveyard.

'She said there was something she wanted to show me, something awf'ly interesting, But I didna want to go in there. I was scared, Liza. It's a horrible, creepy place.' He gulped remembering his fear and his pathetic wee face in the half-light began to dispel my anger. I realised that he had not been to blame. He had fallen asleep in some corner of the hall, as several of the younger children had done towards the end of the evening, and The Dow had seen her chance. She had scooped him up and carried him, still sleeping, to the graveyard. What she had intended to do there I baulked at imagining. What was it she had wanted to show him – or was that just an excuse to get him to go in there? But why?

'What happened then?'

'I started screamin' and kickin' her. I couldn't help it. I was that scared. I thought she was goin' to drag me in but then we heard voices a wee bit up the hill an' I screamed louder. She ran away when she heard you comin'. I was that glad to see you, Liza.' He buried his face in my chest and gave a great sob.

I put my arms round him and stroked his hair. 'My poor wee man,' I said, all my anger spent. I thought of asking him if The Dow was back on Erraid, only one of the questions that were swirling around my head. But instead I gave into a few tears myself and for a few moments we clung to each other in the dark, dusty shed until we heard Bridie's call: 'Liza, where are ye, lass? Have ye finished seeing to those sheets?'

With that, I remembered the salt and hastily took a scoop of the rough grey granules from the sack that stood on a shelf near the door.

'Come on,' I said to Gerry. 'You can't hide in here. Neither can I.'

# CHAPTER TWENTY-EIGHT

*I had borne up well until this . . . but at that I threw myself down and wept.*
*Robert Louis Stevenson, from 'Kidnapped'*

'There you are, you little sh . . .'

I thought Bridie was going to echo my slip into bad language when she saw Gerry but she checked herself and cast a brief glance at Mother who, I saw, now had her head and shoulders slightly propped up although her legs were still humped up under the covers.

'Where have you been?' Bridie demanded, coming across the room to put her hands on Gerry's shoulders and turn him towards the lamp that stood on the table. 'Would you be looking at the state of you!' She began to bat her hand across the top of his hair but stopped as a cloud of dust arose from it. 'Where, in the name of all that's holy, have you been?' she repeated.

'I found him in the shed,' I said. 'When I went in to get the salt.'

Mother called faintly from the bed, something unintelligible, probably his name, and he started to go over to her but Bridie barred his way.

'Get yerself out of those filthy clothes and give your hair a good brush,' she ordered. 'Outside. Sure you could plant potatoes in it. And wash those hands. Thorough, mind, thorough. Ye're no' gettin' near yer poor Mammy in that state.'

He began to protest – when did he not? – but I saw the wisdom of this, knowing that sick people were always kept as clean as possible, as in hospitals.

'Come on.' I dragged him through to his bedroom and spent the next twenty minutes cleaning him up. We were almost ready to return to the kitchen when I heard voices raised and cocked my ear. Bridie's voice, yes, but not Mother's. Too strong for her but definitely female. I shushed Gerry who was in full flow, telling me about what he and Angus had got up to at the party before his abduction to the graveyard. As he stopped talking, I could make out Bridie saying: 'Well, I thought it best. It's what I've aye done when there's been a *miss* here but if you think . . .'

'I assure you I know what I'm doing. I have medical training.'

I was taken back at once to the scene two days ago – it seemed like months – when Mother had been stretchered up from the landing stage and our house had been full of curious neighbours, all offering advice. 'I have medical training. I was a nurse during the war.' Florence Nightingale – or what passed for her in Erraid – was here again.

219

'That's her,' I hissed. 'She's here. Come on. Let's see what she has to say for herself.'

'No! I cannae. I'm scared o' her.' Gerry began to whimper again and he hung back, refusing to be pulled out of the bedroom. I tugged at his hand but there was sand and grit on the floor and he slid backwards, falling on to his knees. I left him there, cowering like a caged animal, and went to confront The Dow.

She was kneeling at Mother's bedside, her arms thrust under the blankets. She seemed to be rubbing in a circular motion on Mother's belly with her right hand while her left was holding something between Mother's thighs. As I stared in a mixture of horror and fascination, Mother gave a cry and arched her back.

'What are you doing to her?' I screamed, terrified that the witch was hurting Mother. I made to lunge across the room at The Dow but Bridie grabbed my arm and deflected me off course.

'Get off!' I yelled. 'Can ye no' see that she's doing something terrible to her?'

But Bridie held on to me like grim death and I could only watch impotently as Mother convulsed and groaned several times and then fell back exhausted.

'Get those children out of here.' The Dow spoke sharply without turning her head. 'Now, Mrs Campbell. At once!' She had taken one hand out from under the covers, the one that had been rubbing Mother's belly, and was using it to stroke Mother's damp hair off her brow. The other arm remained hidden beneath the covers.

I might have insisted on going to Mother, or at least staying in the room, for Bridie was not a big woman and I think I could have stood my ground. But Gerry had appeared in the doorway and he began wailing noisily, incoherently, absorbing the atmosphere of crisis and fear without understanding what was causing it. Mother heard him and tried to sit up to see him but fell back on her pillow immediately, wincing. Whatever else she was going through, I could at least save her from Gerry's demanding presence. I allowed myself to be herded out of the room, collaring my whining brother as I went through the doorway and dragging him with me. Bridie shut the door firmly and Gerry and I were left in the lobby.

It was hard to think what to do, other than consoling and quietening Gerry. My words of reassurance sounded hollow in my own ears for I had no idea if Mother was 'going to be all right'. I was too old and too war-weary to think that saying it often enough would make it true but Gerry gradually accepted my reiterated false promises and lapsed into noisy hiccups.

'I want to go an' see Angus,' was the first thing he said when these subsided enough to let him speak. 'Can I go along to his house?'

Why not? It seemed as good a plan as any. 'We'll both go along to the Campbell house,' I said and he nodded with something approaching enthusiasm.

We found the twins, Kirsty and Allyson, crouched on the hearth rug by a roaring fire, toasting thick slices of bread on long-handled forks. The house showed every sign of Bridie's absence, dirty dishes piled up at the sink in the window and strewn amid a clutter of crumbs and crusts on the big table in the middle of the room.

Kirsty took one look at the two of us and rose from the floor. 'Come away in,' she said. 'What's been happenin' to you two? You look like ye've been drawn through a hedge backwards!'.'

Even as she spoke, I caught sight of Gerry and me in the mirror above the mantelpiece and recognised the truth of this. Despite my early ministrations, Gerry looked like a frightened scarecrow, his hair sticking up in dirty clumps, his clothes dishevelled, filthy, scabby knees poking out below his short trousers, his wee face peaked and scowling. As for me, I was still shivering from the soaking my skirt and shoes had taken from the buckets of cold water in the back yard, my hair was in a wild tangle and the face that looked down on me from the mirror could have been that of an old crone, so pinched and furrowed it was.

As we hesitated on the threshold, Kirsty came towards us and held out her hands, offering us one each. Her kindness did what her mother's brisk bossiness had not. I felt my lips quivering and a lump in my throat the size of a golf ball seemed to burst into hot, salty tears that scalded my wind-chafed cheeks. Gerry needed no excuse to join in, of course, and the pair of us were gathered into a hug. Allyson looked on with interest and, becoming aware of her bemused face, I pulled myself together and detached from the threesome. Gerry might have snivelled on but he was diverted by the appearance of his pal, Angus, who came bounding into the kitchen, ready as always to pick up their latest game. He paid no attention to Gerry's tears but simply grabbed his arm and pulled him across the kitchen and out into the lobby. 'C'mon see this, Ger! I've got a great idea for . . .' His words were lost as the boys disappeared into Angus' bedroom, shutting the door on their absorbing, make-believe world.

221

'Come and get a cup o' tea and some toast,' said Kirsty. 'How's yer poor mother?' She shepherded me over to the table and I sank down on a chair close to the fire, feeling the heat begin to thaw my frozen legs and feet.

The combination of the fire and her gentle concern melted my reserve. 'She's awf'y ill, Kirsty. She's freezin' cold. They've put these wee stones on her, still frosty they are, and she's just lyin' there shiverin' and shiverin' and . . .' I was about to launch into gory details which would probably have driven the poor girl into deep embarrassment, if not hysterics, but we were both saved by the sound of men's voices and tramping feet on the path outside. Allyson jumped up and crossed to the window.

'There's a boat just come in. I can see its lantern. It looks like Lachlan McPhail's boat.'

'But . . .' – I was confused - 'he was going away home after he brought me back.'

Kirsty was already in the lobby, heading for the outside door. For a moment I dithered between my hunger – it had been a long time since Marion's bannocks and honey cake – and my curiosity. I compromised by snatching up a slice of buttery toast and running after her. As we came out of the Campbell family's housse, I saw two men standing at *our* door, fiddling with the hasp. I recognised Lachlan at once. Even if the lamp he carried had not been throwing its light onto his face, I would have known that tall, upright figure anywhere. But his companion was a stranger, of that I was sure. Not one of the other keepers who were 'shore' that month – Euan or Calum – and certainly not Father.

Kirsty had no such hesitation. 'It's Doctor Sinclair,' she declared. 'He must have been sent for. To see to yer mother, Liza,' she added unnecessarily.

'But who . . .' – I was confused – 'who could have sent for him?' Bridie had said nothing about a doctor and, when I had left our house, The Dow had been occupied with her Florence Nightingale role.

We caught up with the two men as they waited for an answer to their sharp rap upon our door. Bridie appeared and her face registered blank surprise when she saw all four of us.

'I wasna happy just going home and leavin' things like this.' Lachlan's deep voice held the calm solidity that was already precious to me. 'I thought Mrs Galway had surely taken a turn for the worse. So, after I'd dropped Catriona back at home, I just nipped along the coast to Bunessan and called on Dr Sinclair. When he heard what happened to Mrs Galway on Saturday, he thought it best to come and see her.'

222

There was an awkward pause during which Bridie made no move to open the door more widely or step back to let any of us in. 'Just to make sure everything is a' right,' continued Lachlan. 'I'm sure you're doin' a great job of looking after her but . . .'

'It's not! It's not a' right!' A damn broke inside me and I screamed. 'It's no', it's no', it's no'! The baby's dead and my mother's goin' to be dead soon too.'

There was an instant of blank silence. Then the doctor, a small, stocky man in a tweed cap and heavy, waterproof coat, a large black bag clutched in his gloved hand, stepped purposefully forward and giving Bridie no opportunity to resist, strode into our house.


What happened after that was a bit of a blur for me. I finally broke down and gave way to a torrent of weeping, feeling all the horror of the gory scene that had confronted me in our house, the revulsion I had felt at my icy task in the back yard and, perhaps most of all, the contrast between the tranquil security of the McPhail family and the impossible demands of my own coalesce into such a sense of desolation that I sank to my knees right there on my own doorstep.

I was vaguely aware of strong arms lifting me up and carrying me back along the path and could hear a keening noise that went on and on until I realised it was me making it and stopped, subsiding into racking hiccups and shuddering sobs.

'There now, lass. There now. Dinna take on so. Yer mammy'll be a' right.' It was Bridie stroking my hair and I was back in her kitchen. I realised that I was sitting on Lachlan's lap, in the big armchair at the side of the fire, and that it had been his strong arms that had lifted and carried me.

He murmured something to Bridie and she rose and went over to the big jug of water standing beside the sink. In a moment she was back with a cool, wet cloth and was dabbing it softly at my face, cooling my burning eyelids, soothing my scalding cheeks. As my sobs and hiccups began to space out, I was dimly aware of a background noise of whoops and shrieks, alternating with heavy thuds that made the crockery on the dresser chatter.

'Would you ever be listenin' to those two tearaways? They'll be bringin' the house down, so they will!' Gerry and Angus were still immersed in their game and it was clearly reaching a noisy climax. As Bridie strode out into the lobby and began adding to the fracas with wrathful commands and threats to 'stop that bloody racket or I'll be skelpin' both yer arses, so I will', my bout of misery tipped over into hysteria and I began to giggle weakly, helplessly. Lachlan joined in with a guffaw. There was always something irresistibly funny about Bridie's bursts of crude and colourful language. In anyone else, they would have called forth shock and censure but in her they seemed not just a natural part of her character but a sort of gift, an injection of humour that might lighten the direst of situations. Grace comes in many forms and sometimes through the most unlikely people.

The boys took a telling and their voices dropped to a subdued murmur. The crockery subsided safely on its shelves. Bridie returned to the kitchen and began making fresh tea, abjuring the twins, who were back in their places on the hearthrug, to get off their lazy backsides and clear the mess off the table, wash the dishes and make more toast.

'What must Lachlan McPhail be thinkin'?' she demanded, as if he was not sitting right there at her table. 'The place like a pigsty. I've no' had a minute, so I've not, since early this morning, since that poor woman was took bad. Ye would think, would ye not,' she addressed the room at large, 'that two great *hulkit* lassies like them could be left to look after things? Ye would think that, so ye would. But ye'd be wrong, so ye would.'

Lachlan and I had almost got control of our laughter over her threats to the boys but this fresh onslaught on her daughters set us giggling again. Bridie Campbell was a tonic, pure gold in so many ways, but never more so than on that bleak Christmas Eve on Erraid.

Eventually, the work was done to her satisfaction and the five of us sat round the table drinking tea and eating toast while the enormous, unspoken *thing* ballooned in our midst. I wanted to ask why Bridie had been sent out of our house for I could not imagine that she had left of her own will. I wanted to ask where The Dow was. Was she still in our house with the doctor while he examined Mother? What would he say? What was going to happen to Mother now? And where, oh where, was Father?

At last we heard footsteps on the path; then a light tap on the door. Before Bridie could answer, the door was opened and a voice called 'Are you there, Mr McPhail? We're going to need your boat.' It was The Dow.

She came into the kitchen with her usual confident stride and haughty authority. I felt Bridie tense with resentment but The Dow seemed unaware of it. Or, if she was aware, she cared nothing for it. Lachlan was on his feet at once, scraping his chair back, brushing toast crumbs off the front of his jacket.

'What's happening?' he asked.

224

The Dow glanced at me with a slight hesitation. 'Where is Gerrard? Is he here too?'

'He and Angus are playin' in the bedroom,' said Bridie. Her tone was belligerent, as if she thought The Dow was accusing her of something. 'He quite safe here, so he is.'

The Dow ignored her and addressed Lachlan. 'Doctor Sinclair thinks it best if Mrs Galway is taken into hospital right away. He is down at the telephone right now alerting the cottage hospital in Tobermory. What do you think will be our quickest way to get her there?'

Later I would remember her calm assumption that Lachlan would act as transport and, even more irritating, the way she aligned herself with the doctor, almost as if they were a professional medical team, completely cutting poor Bridie out of it. But later too, I would acknowledge that it was a mercy Bridie's amateurish attempts to cope with the escalating crisis had been overridden, that Mother owed her very life to Doctor Sinclair and most of all to Lachlan who had followed his instinct and fetched him just in time. But at that moment, as The Dow pronounced the words that sounded like a death sentence to my overwrought imagination, I could only gasp and clutch at Lachlan's sleeve.

'Let me go too. I want to go with her. I must go with her. She'll want me with her.' My voice rose shrilly on the repetition.

'Nay, Liza lassie. You'd best stay here and look after yer brother . . . and be here for your father coming home,' he added somewhat doubtfully. I had forgotten about Father for the moment but, at Lachlan's words, my questions came back to me. Why had he not come home? Was he still at the school hall? But why? Or where else could he be? I hesitated and The Dow swooped on my indecision.

'Stay here, Liza,' she ordered in her best schoolmarm voice. 'Once we have your mother out of the house, you must go back and tidy it up, make a meal for yourself and Gerry, then get yourselves off to bed. I will tell you in the morning how your mother was when I left her at the hospital and what they are saying about her there.'

'Why are *you* goin'?' I burst out angrily.

'Doctor Sinclair has asked me to do so,' she said repressively. 'I have medical training. I was . . .'

'A nurse during the war – yes, we know.' My surly interruption made her narrow her eyes and for a moment we stared at each other. The atmosphere bristled with our mutual dislike.

'Right, Miss Dow,' said Lachlan, already out in the lobby and buttoning up his oilskin coat. 'Are you ready to go? I'll need to go round by my house and tell Marion what's happening. She'll be starting to worry where I am. But then, I'll just sail round the island to Tobermory. That'll be as quick as changing over to the taxi and less moving-about for the patient.' He paused and looked at me as I stood in the doorway, a sulky frown creasing my face. 'Keep yer pecker up, lass. Yer mother'll be in the best place and they'll have her right as rain in no time. It's a grand wee hospital.' There was a touch of island pride in his voice and he winked cheerily at me. I managed to respond with a tremulous smile and felt Bridie's arm about my shoulders. The sense of lonely responsibility and persistent failure that was my ever-present friend receded slightly.

'Can I come along and say goodbye to her?' It seemed little to ask.

'There is no point, Liza,' said The Dow. 'The doctor has given her a strong sedative and she is in a deep sleep. We must hope she will continue to be so throughout the journey to the hospital.'

I thought of Mother waking up in a strange place, not knowing how she came to be there, with neither of her children beside her. Not even her husband, though what comfort he would be was hard to imagine. She had already come through so much and was still so ill. I was letting her down yet again. I *should* be there. I opened my mouth to make one last desperate protest but, at that moment, Gerry burst out of Angus' bedroom into the lobby with Angus in pursuit. The two boys stopped when they saw the gaggle of people in the lobby and the doorway to the kitchen. Gerry's gaze raked over us all and stopped at me.

'What's happenin', Liza? Where's Mother? Where's Father? What's *he* doin' here?' He flashed a baffled glance at Lachlan and The Dow. Immersed in his make-believe world, he had completely missed the arrival of Lachlan and the doctor.

Before I could draw breath to reply, The Dow moved swiftly across the lobby and took Gerry's hand possessively, very much as I had seen her do on our afternoon school outings in the early part of last term. She bent down and spoke softly into his ear, drawing him back into Angus' bedroom, still whispering. Like a snake, I thought. And Gerry fell for it again, even after her abduction to the graveyard, even after the terror he had experienced at her hands only two days before. I could only watch helplessly and submit to being pulled back myself into the kitchen by Bridie, who looked as disgruntled as I felt but acknowledged when she was beaten.

# CHAPTER TWENTY-NINE

*Them that havenae dipped their hands in any little difficulty should be very mindful of the case of them that have.*

Robert Louis Stevenson, from 'Kidnapped'

I had no inclination to return to our house, imagining goodness knows what state of affairs there. I sat in Bridie's kitchen, hunched miserably over a cup of tea sweetened with honey by a solicitous Kirsty. I could eat nothing and the slice of toast I had grabbed on my way out, when we had first heard Lachlan and the doctor coming, had ended up trampled into the slushy path. I had thrown it down, I think, when the fit of wild weeping had come upon me.

We heard footsteps, voices, a door banging, more footsteps and voices. Allyson stood sentinel at the window and reported as much as she could see. There was a fitful moon so we got jerky bulletins reporting four men – we presumed Lachlan, Doctor Sinclair and the other two keepers who were 'shore' that month - bearing a stretcher out of our house and disappearing along the path. Probably the same makeshift affair that had been cobbled together when Mother had fallen over the side of the landing stage. That now seemed a lot more than two days ago. After a time, Allyson reported the light on Lachlan's boat moving out into the Sound and fading as it disappeared around the curve of the land towards Fionnphort. I thought of Mother, sedated and unconscious, lying on the open deck. There was a tiny cabin with a little table and a bench seat for two but no way would a stretcher fit into it. I hoped they had covered her with a warm blanket. Surely the doctor – or The 'medically trained' Dow - would have seen to that.

As soon as Allyson's bulletins ceased, Bridie stood up. I dragged myself to my feet, every fibre in my being cringing at the thought of going back into our house but feeling I had no option.

'Just you be stayin' here for now.' Bridie held out a flat, upraised palm, like a policeman directing traffic. 'I'll just be goin' along to see . . .' she hesitated, struggling to express her fears for what she might find. I thought of the bloody bedlinen and nightdress, the basins, the pink water, the 'liver and lights'. I sank gratefully back down on to my chair.

'Scramble eggs and fry sausages,' she instructed the twins. 'See to it. Enough for Liza and Gerry as well.' She went out the door muttering about 'expectin' that poor lassie to be makin' meals and lookin' after the wee fellow – after all that's just happened to her mammy'. I knew she was referring to The Dow's peremptory orders to me before she left to accompany Mother to the hospital. It was a comfort, even if, as I suspected, it came more from her dislike of The Dow than from pity for me.

Somehow we got through that evening. Relieved to be let off having to confront the aftermath of Mother's descent into serious illness, I found the smell of frying sausages made my mouth water. Gerry and Angus responded to it as well and ran through to climb up on chairs without being bidden. They were still in their fantasy world and addressed each other as Sir Hector and Clan Chief MacDonald, using a melange of old Scots dialect, Irish brogue and 'Boys' Own' slang. The twins and I laughed at them and I felt the block of ice inside me begin to melt.

Bridie was gone some time and Kirsty set a plate of food for her on top of a saucepan of simmering water and covered it with a bowl. When Bridie did return, her pale, freckled face was grey with exhaustion and her abundant red hair, normally tamed into a big bun on her neck, straggled greasily down her back. She accepted the warm food with a grateful murmur and drank two big glasses of water with it.

I expected her to tell me to go along and finish off the cleaning but she said nothing until she had finished eating when she surprised me by telling Kirsty to put some night things in a bag and go with us. 'Everything's shipshape, now,' she said with some satisfaction. 'I've changed the big bed so Kirsty can sleep in it and keep you company, so she can. I'll do all the washing tomorrow.'

'On Christmas Day, Mammy?' asked Allyson.

'Yes' was the short reply. And before I had time to thank her, Bridie had pushed both of us out on to the path and closed the door on us. When we entered our house, we found a scene of such welcoming warmth and orderliness that I almost wept all over again. The fire was burning steadily; the big bed was freshly made up and turned down ready for its occupant; the table was scrubbed and clear, except for a vase of bright-berried holly in the middle; the floor was freshly washed with only a couple of faint brown stains between the table and the bed bearing witness to the recent carnage. Even the dusty, muddy mess in my bedroom had been erased. Not even The Dow herself could have found fault with it.

That night I slept a great deal better than I had any right to. I was young and resilient so that even my self-pitying attempts to dwell on my orphan state – temporary but frightening nonetheless – failed to spoil my exhausted slumbers. Kirsty woke me with a cup of tea and a tiny bit of Mother's black bun and this unaccustomed pampering brightened what would otherwise have been a sad Christmas morning. I could not help thinking back to the shop on Oban High Street where Mother had bought the dried fruit and her concern to have the ingredients for her annual black bun. Would she even be back home with us in time to eat it with the traditional tot of whisky on Hogmanay?

Gerry was a great trial that morning. Mother's absence and illness had only finally sunk in. He had been too absorbed, once we got to the Campbell house, in his game with Angus to realise what had been happening last night and too tired to ask questions once we got back home. He had gone off to bed with barely a word.

This morning, he was badly in need of a bath but his smelly, unkempt appearance was outclassed by his foul temper. Neither Kirsty nor I could do anything to lighten his mood. She tried coaxing with promises of freshly made pancakes; I tried showing him the two Christmas presents that Mother and I had hidden under the big bed for him. He ignored Kirsty and told me to do something with the presents that made Bridie's salty language seem tame. I wondered where he had got such ideas from.

I never thought I would be glad to see The Dow but I was grudgingly grateful when she arrived at our door mid-morning, Gerry was in the act of tipping up the marmalade pot and smearing its sticky contents over the table whilst shouting abuse at poor Kirsty who, in an effort to get him to eat something, had set a piece of toast and the offending marmalade down in front of him. The Dow took one look at him and swept into action.

'Stop that this minute, Gerrard,' she said with full schoolmarm force. 'Get down from that table at once.' I held my breath as he stared at her for a moment but then, with a whimper, he obeyed. 'Come here,' she commanded and he slunk over.

She regarded him severely. 'In all my time as teacher on this island, I have not taken the tawse to any child. But that does not mean I do not have one.'

Gerry squirmed and whimpered some more. A schoolteacher's tawse came in different forms, sometimes a thin, stiff strap of leather, sometimes a soft, broad belt split into three of four fingers at one end. At our school in North Berwick, several of the teachers had had names for their tawses – Mr Chambers had called his 'Thomas the Tickler' and had used it from time to time on older, rowdier boys. Neither Gerry nor I had ever experienced its chastisement, our experience of corporal punishment being limited to Father's slaps and beltings. Mother only ever spanked me once in my life — for saying exactly what I was thinking about Father - and Gerry never.

The Dow took his hand in that possessive way she had with him. 'Liza, fetch clean clothes for Gerrard. I shall take him to my house and see he is bathed. He is a disgrace. And on Christmas Day!' She shook her head and made a disgusted sound, somewhere between sigh and a *tut*.

I went through to Gerry's room, unable to stop myself submitting to her authority even while I despised myself for it. But, when I returned to the kitchen with a bag of fresh clothes from Gerry's little wardrobe, I found my voice.

'What about my mother? You said you would tell me this morning what happened at the hospital. How is she?' I tried to sound self-possessed and grown-up but my voice betrayed me and the questions ended on a squeaky tremble.

She played with me, flexing her power, and I hated her. I wanted to erupt like a maddened cat and fly at her, scratch her eyes out. Somehow I kept my temper and waited while she found delaying actions to take up her attention: bending down to brush Gerry's hair out of his eyes; flicking invisible specks off her coat lapel; glancing out the window as if she had heard a sound when there was none. But I refused to plead and I would not even ask again. I waited. And eventually, she tossed her head and spoke as if it was nothing important and I was a minor nuisance for asking.

'Mrs Galway has lost a great deal of blood and is very weak.' She turned as if to leave, tugging at Gerry's hand.

I moved to stand between her and the door. 'Will she be all right? What is the hospital saying?' Desperation made me bold. I had confronted this harridan before and I could do it again. 'Tell me. Tell me everything you know.'

'Really, Liza, how dramatic you are!'

I said nothing, just continued to bar her way and challenge her with a bold stare. She pursed her lips and narrowed her eyes but I think she too was remembering how I had stood up to her and Father after finding them together in the shed and had wrung a bargain out of them.

'Oh, very well, miss.' She spoke slowly and wearily, as if she found it all nothing but a bore. 'Your mother was taken into the women's ward and a doctor there examined her. Mr McPhail and I waited to hear what the doctor would say before we set off back home.'

'And?' I interrupted. Her bored manner mocked my frayed nerves.

'*And* they treated her according to what they found. She underwent a . . . a surgical procedure. They were giving her a blood transfusion when we left.'

Surgical procedure. Blood transfusion. The terms meant nothing to me but they filled me with dread nonetheless.

'Did you speak to her before you left?'

'No. That was not permitted.'

'Will she . . . will she . . . is she going to be all right?'

'That depends, Liza. On a number of things.'

'What things?'

'Things you would not understand. And it also depends on what you mean by all right.'

'Will she die?' The question that had been burning inside me from the moment she came into the room burst out of me and at once I regretted it. Gerry had been listening wide-eyed, swivelling his head from one to the other of us during the interchange, clearly understanding nothing. But at the bald word 'die', he let out such a wail that Kirsty, who was out in the backyard fetching water for washing the breakfast dishes, came running through in alarm.

The Dow at once jerked his hand and shook him. 'Stop that at once! Liza, get out of my way. Now! Your mother is being well looked after and we must just wait for more news. Now - move!' And she barged past me with such force that I struck my shoulder on the door jamb and sustained a painful bruise. Gerry was dragged out still howling; Kirsty and I were left staring at one another, speechless.

News of Mother's plight had, of course, spread throughout our little community and our Christmas Day, which I had expected to be lonely and miserable, became busier and busier as the day progressed. The other four wives all came by, accompanied by various children and bearing gifts. Everything from little bars of home-made soap, smelling of lavender, to chunks of cake and paper pokes of sweets. Gerry escaped The Dow's clutches by the end of the morning and returned looking almost unrecognisable, his face scrubbed and shining, his freshly-washed hair trimmed and combed into submission, his perpetually scabby knees disinfected and anointed with *Vaseline*.

'Did you ask her if she kens what's happened to Father?' I asked him, without much hope, as we walked along the path to Bridie's house to join them for Christmas dinner. He looked at me vaguely as if the word, 'Father', was new to him, and ran towards Angus who was standing at the Campbells' door, waving a big red fire engine and shouting, 'C'mon see what Santa Claus brought me!'

It was to be Lachlan McPhail – how often that dear man was to intervene in the roll of events! - who brought the news. Just as dusk was falling on the short winter afternoon and we lolled replete on Bridie's hearthrug after a huge dinner, came the shout from Allyson at the window: 'Here's a boat coming in – it's Mr McPhail's, I think.'

'He'll be bringing news of yer mother, for sure,' said Bridie. 'Put yer coat on, Liza, and go to meet the boat.'

I did not need a second telling, I was running along the path towards the landing stage, tugging my coat on as I went, before she had finished talking.

As the boat coasted in, Catriona emerged from the cabin and leapt ashore to catch the rope her father threw to her, loop it into the iron rung on the stones and tie it into a big knot. I had a clutch of dread remembering Mother's foot caught in that very rung and her body hanging upside down, head almost touching the water. What was happening to her now? She seemed so far away, in this unknown hospital in a place called Tobermory. I felt tears prick my eyelids.

'Happy Christmas!' As soon as the boat's rope was secured, Catriona threw her arms round me and Lachlan jumped ashore to put his long arms around the two of us in a tight hug.

'Come up to the house and have some tea,' I said as the three of us walked away from the landing-stage. I remembered Mother's black bun. I could at least attempt the role of hostess.

'Aye,' said Lachlan, nodding thoughtfully. 'Aye, that will be best. I have something to talk to you about, Liza.'

'And I've got a Christmas present for you,' chimed in Catriona. 'Well, it's from Ma, really. She said to give it to you from us all.'

I realised that I had not opened my Christmas present from Mother – the label on it said 'from Mother and Father' but I was under no illusions about how much Father had been involved in choosing and wrapping it. I had found it when fetching Gerry's two presents out from under the big bed. He had been too deep in ill-tempered tantrums to open them so I had left my one parcel under the bed, unopened.

The house was not exactly cold but the fire was low. Coming in out of the snell, rimy wind, we would have welcomed it warmer.

I threw off my coat, moved the kettle on to the range and began to poke at the fire to stir up enough hot embers to make fresh coal burn.

'Let Da do that,' said Catriona. 'You open your present.'

'I'm sorry. I've nothing for you, I didn't think . . .'

'No matter. Open it!' She wriggled out of her coat and unwound a long wool scarf from round her neck so rapidly that I thought it might tangle and choke her. I could not help smiling at her impatience. I had almost no experience of giver's glee myself but I recognised it in her. I sat down in Mother's fireside chair, carefully untied the glittery red ribbon, rolled it up into a little ball and slowly unwrapped the snowflake-spangled paper, taking care to tear it as little as possible, smoothing and folding it neatly, Catriona knelt on the hearthrug and jiggled up and down, bobbing her head, setting her red-gold curls bouncing.

Inside was a flat, oblong, grey box. Getting excited myself now, I lifted the lid and pulled apart the overlapping leaves of fine, pale pink paper. Nestling inside, was a small, leather-bound book, It was the colour of autumn leaves, burnished to a soft sheen. On the cover, tooled in beautiful gold lettering, was the legend: *Liza's Journal*. I gasped with pleasure and lifted it reverently from its nest. It seemed to take on the warmth of my hands immediately and I felt that I did not ever want to put it down.

'Open it!' Catriona prompted. It seemed there was one more surprise for me. Inside the front cover along the spine was a thin leather sheath, encasing a red and gold propelling pencil. I slid it out and felt its slight, satisfying weight in my hand and noted the clear cylinder attached to one end, full of graphite refills. This lovely book, with its matching pencil, was the finest article I had ever held in my hand, let alone possessed. I could not believe it was really mine.

'It's so beautiful, so fine, so lovely.' My voice trembled and a tear slid down my cheek. 'Thank you so much. I'll treasure it . . . always.'

'Ma says you've to start using it right away. She says you're always asking about things. You need a book to write down all you find out.'

I blushed. Had I been 'making a nuisance of myself' asking too many questions? But how like Marion MacPhail to respond not with annoyance or dismissal but by giving me this lovely book to write the answers in. I might have become quite maudlin over such thoughtful kindness but Lachlan brought the moment to an end abruptly. Rising from the fireplace and rubbing the coal dust off his hands onto his trousers, he dropped his bombshell.

'We've found your father, Liza. We saw him in Tobermory hospital when we took your mother there last night.'

# CHAPTER THIRTY

*Ye may keep a man from the fighting but never from his bottle.*
*Robert Louis Stevenson, from 'Kidnapped'*

I dragged my delighted eyes away from the beautiful present and stared up at Lachlan. My brain, cluttered with the recent helter-skelter of events and experiences, struggled to take in what he was saying. For a few moments, the three of us seemed immobilised, frozen in time. I could swear even the clock stopped ticking.

The kettle was first to come back to life and its rising shriek startled us all. Lachlan put a big hand out to lift it off the hotplate on to the side of the range, nodding to Catriona as he did. She took his drift and went to fetch three cups and saucers from the dresser.

'Why?' I found my voice although it was barely above a whisper. 'What's he doing there?'

Lachlan spooned tea leaves into our old brown derby teapot and poured boiling water on them. My mind registered that he had forgotten to warm the pot first.

'What happened to him? How did he get away up there? Is he ill? How long. . ?'

'There ye go again,' Catriona said. 'Ma's right. You do ask an awful lot o' questions. You'll have that wee notebook full o' answers in no time!' Her teasing words and kind smile brought me gently out of the fog that had descended at Lachlan's blunt words and, despite my racing heart and rising panic, I smiled back. She squeezed onto the armchair beside me and put an arm round me. We both looked expectantly up at Lachlan and there was such comfort in having her beside me as I faced this fresh development.

'It was the doctor himself that told me on the boat up to Tobermory. Miss Dow was sittin' beside yer mother, makin' sure she was warm enough, and he and I fell to bletherin'. I asked him if there was anyone else in the hospital – it being Christmas, I thought maybe it would be empty - and he said there was just one very old lady from Salen and a mystery man who had been found at Fionnphort on Sunday afternoon. He said no one knew who the man was and the man himself seemed to have lost his memory. He had a head injury and a bit o' hypothermia.'

'What's hippo . . ?' asked Catriona.

'It's what happens when someone gets too cold for too long,' replied Lachlan.

I thought of those long minutes I had spent in the freezing bog on my way down from The Lookout on the afternoon of Mother's accident. *Hypothermia.* Although I had never heard the word, I felt I knew the feeling: the creeping paralysis, at first painful but gradually yielding to blessed numbness, drowsiness and finally sleep.

'Will he die?' For the second time on that Christmas day, I asked this question about one of my parents. I had no doubts that the unknown man was Father. I saw him standing outside the schoolhouse that night after the party, lolling against the wall, cigarette in one hand, whisky bottle in the other, making no move to get on the bus to the Fionnphort jetty. He had been drunk and probably more concerned about where The Dow had got to than whether Gerry was safely on the bus - or even how he himself would get home.

Lachlan dropped down onto his haunches and took both my hands in his. 'No, no, lass. It's no' as bad as that. He's just being looked after until he gets better and remembers who he is.'

'Did you see him? Did you tell him who he is? Who found him? How did he get to Tobermory?' The questions in my head tumbled over one another on their way out.

'I went through to the men's ward after we'd seen your mother settled. I had a hunch the mystery man was your father as soon as Doctor Sinclair told me about him. The matron was mighty relieved that I kent who he was. Him bein' new around these parts, no one else did. She said the man that found him was just walkin' his dog on Sunday afternoon near Fionnphort School and he heard a noise in the shed. He went to see what it was and found your father lyin' on the floor, half-unconscious and groanin'. The man went home and got his bike. He cycled to Doctor Sinclair's house in Bunessan and the two o' them went in the doctor's wee car back to the shed. Doctor Sinclair took your father to the hospital right away.'

A horrible thought struck me. 'Did The - I mean *Miss* - Dow go to see him? Does she ken it's him?' Somehow this seemed more unbearable than any of it.

'The matron wouldna let more than one of us see him. He's to be kept very quiet just now, she said.'

'But did you tell Miss Dow? Does she know that it's him there?'

'No, I didn't, Liza. It didna seem right her knowing before you or your mother. Your mother's in no fit state to be getting news like that but I thought you should know first. That's why we came over today.'

I breathed more easily and for a moment my stream of questions dried up. Or perhaps there were just so many of them that the outlet was clogged. Lachlan poured three cups of tea and put two big spoonfuls of sugar in mine. 'Drink this, lass. Ye've had a wee shock.'

'There's black bun.' Suddenly, that seemed important. 'It's in that tin there.'

The three of us sat silent for a few minutes, drinking our tea and nibbling at Mother's black bun. They gave appreciative murmurs but I could taste nothing. It was Catriona who spoke first.

'Can we take Liza home with us, Da? She canna stay here on her own.'

'Of course we can,' said Lachlan. 'If that's what she wants. Wee Gerry too.'

'An' it'll be easier to get them up from our house to Tobermory to see their Ma and Da in the hospital,' she said.

'I dinna think they let children in to visit,' he replied doubtfully. 'Well, maybe Liza . . .'

I imagined Gerry's reaction to a situation where I got to see Mother and he did not. My heart sank. But first things first. I pulled myself together and became the responsible big sister again. I put my empty cup down and rose. 'Come on,' I said. 'We'd better go an' tell him – and Bridie – what's happened.'


'But I want to stay here. I dinna want to go to *their* house. I want to stay *here!*'

I looked helplessly at Gerry's stubborn, tear-streaked face and then, in appeal, at Bridie.

'Och, Liza, dear, ye know I'd be havin' the wee man if I could but I promised Jenny I would be lettin' her sister and her man have Angus' bedroom for the week. They're arriving this night, so they are, and they're stayin' until the day after New Year. Angus will be sleepin' on a shake-doon on the floor in here beside Arthur and me.' Bridie's face was a picture of perplexity as she tried to juggle these competing demands on her hospitality.

'Liz and Gerry must come over to Tormore with us,' said Lachlan for the sixth or possibly seventh time. To his credit, he did not sound impatient, though there was a tiny muscle trembling in his cheek as if he was clenching his jaw.

'But I want to stay . . .' began Gerry again and stopped as there came a sharp rap on the door. Bridie nodded to Kirsty who went to answer it. A moment later, she led The Dow into the crowded room.

236

'I saw you coming up from the pier, Mr MacPhail. Is there news of Mrs Galway?'

'Not any more than we had last night, Miss Dow. It was about her father that I came over to speak to Liza. He's . . . Are you all right, Miss Dow?'

She had let out a small gasp and put her hand to her mouth. With her other hand, she steadied herself on the back of a chair. I watched her thin lips tighten and her eyes narrow as if in concentration. She straightened her already erect spine and seemed to grow in height a little. 'I'm perfectly all right, thank you, Mr MacPhail. A touch of indigestion – such rich food at this time of year, you know. You were saying about *Mr* Galway. Has he come back yet?'

Her voice was controlled and very calm. Indeed, as I watched her, I thought there was an unnatural stillness about her, as if she was holding her breath or taking only very shallow breaths. Lachlan did not pursue the topic of her well-being but I thought he gave her a searching look from under his black brows.

'He's in Tobermory hospital as well. He's had an accident.'

'An accident? When?'

I could have sworn there was relief in her voice and a slight relaxation in the set of her shoulders. I was puzzled as to why the news that Father had had an accident would cause these changes.

'Yes.' Lachlan was not about to tell her any more than he had told Bridie. 'Possibly a fall. They'll be keeping him in for a while to see how he recovers.'

'I see. I'm sorry to hear that.' She paused and I could see the wheels of her mind turning as she evaluated the implications of this news. 'So poor Liza and Gerry have no one to look after them?'

'Not at all. I am taking them over to stay with us at Tormore. Marion would not have it any other . . .'

'But I don't want to go there. I *won't* go! You can't make me. I want to stay here with Angus. I'll no' see him all the holidays if I'm stuck over there wi' *them*.'

I opened my mouth to rage at him for being so cheeky and ungrateful - I was more ashamed of him at that moment than I had ever been – but The Dow was quicker.

'Then Gerrard must come and stay with me. I have plenty of space. He can have his own room. And he can see as much of Angus as he wants.'

Again I opened my mouth to protest but again I was pre-empted.

'That's great! Thank you, Miss.' Gerry crossed the room in a flash and stood at her side, slipping his treacherous little hand into hers, his terrifying experience at Tormore graveyard on the night of the party apparently overshadowed by the need to be near Angus.

'But . . . but we should stay together,' I protested. 'Should we not?' I appealed to Lachlan but he only shrugged. He had obviously had enough of Gerry's stubborn awkwardness and was glad to be presented with a solution.

'If he wants to stay on Erraid, Liza, that's his best option. It'll only be for a few days, we hope. Your mother or your father will soon be home. Maybe even the both o' them.' He made a good stab at sounding convincingly optimistic and I could see that he was running out of patience as he added: 'Let's be getting on our way now. There's bad weather forecast later and I dinna want to get caught in the boat.'

There was no arguing with that. The weather and the sea were two tyrants that ruled our lives in that remote island corner. I ran back to our house to pack a bag for myself, Gerry and The Dow close behind. They were still there, discussing which toys and books he would take to her house, when I joined Lachlan and Catriona in the boat. It *should* have felt like a safe situation to leave him in.

The week between Christmas and New Year is always a strange one, a no man's land between a religious feast full of tender sentiment and a pagan feast full of riotous celebration. In those days, Christmas was a low-key affair in Scotland, barely even a holiday except for schoolchildren; New Year and especially its eve, Hogmanay as we called it, was the highlight of the year when drunken revelry was expected and even accepted, if not condoned, by the pious and godly.

I remember that very week of 1924 hardly at all because it was dwarfed by the events at its end. I settled happily back into the truckle bed in Catriona's room and into the easy hospitality of the MacPhail household. The days slipped by in a happy trance. I missed Mother, of course, and worried about her. Lachlan faithfully tramped over the hill to Fionnphort to make the daily phone call to the hospital and returned bearing bulletins that meant little: 'comfortable'; 'stable'; 'responding well to treatment'; and so on. None of them gave us any clue as to whether she was in any danger or how long it might be until she was well enough to come home.

I did not ask – and Lachlan did not say – how Father was doing. As the days passed with no mention of him, he receded into the background, just as he had always done during his absences at sea or on The Rock. It was all too easy to forget about him – I had had a lifetime of willing practice - even if, somewhere at the back of my mind, lay a sense of dormant menace.

The weather was bad, that I do remember: heavy, freezing fog for several days, clearing only at the behest of wild gales and bitter, drenching rain. It was no time to be travelling, either on the rough, winding road by motorised transport or by sea in a small boat. The possibility of going from one end of Mull to the other, to visit Tobermory hospital, was never even mooted. And so, the old year rolled towards its end as Hogmanay approached.

'We always go to first-foot my Aunty Jeannie just after twelve,' said Catriona, as we lay in bed that morning. Marion had said we might have an extra hour or two since we would be up beyond midnight to see in the New Year. 'Did ye do first-footin' back in Berwick?'

'*North* Berwick,' I corrected. 'They're two separate places, one in Scotland and one in England.'

'Ta for the geography lesson. Well, did ye first-foot on Hogmanay?'

'Yes, of course,' I replied. 'Everyone in Scotland does, don't they? Mother always wrapped a bit o' her black bun in waxy paper and took that and a lump of coal next door to Mrs Forsyth.'

I suddenly felt homesick for those days when Father was hardly ever at home, when Mother, Gerry and I had been a tight little trio. Last year, the three of us had practised a song about a farmer's boy for our party piece. We had been outside Mrs F's house by a minute to midnight, holding our breaths as the town clock struck the hour and rapping on the door before the second note sounded. Gerry had been thrust forward with the lump of coal since tradition demanded that, to bring good luck, the first foot inside the house in a new year must be a 'dark, handsome man' and he was our nearest equivalent. Then it had been hugs and kisses, warm good wishes for a 'Happy New Year' all round. Mother handed over the black bun which was added to a table already groaning with food and drink. Within minutes, more neighbours arrived and the party got underway. Our song was applauded when our turn came, Mother had a few sherries and became quite pink and giggly, Gerry and I gorged ourselves on goodies and drank too much raspberry cordial.

'Well, it'll be a bath for us tonight and hair washed. Boots polished and clean clothes from the skin out. All ready for 1925. Then we walk over the hill to Tormore. Aunty Jeannie lives in a wee cottage just down the road from the graveyard. We have to leave here at quarter past eleven to be sure of . . . What is it, Liza?'

I had clutched her arm and my eyes were wide with alarm. 'We're no' goin' near that graveyard again, are we?'

239

'Well, we walk past it. Dinna worry. Pa will have the big lantern with him, the one on a pole. It makes enough light to . . .'

'I dinna want to go near it. Please. I can't bear it. I dinna want . . .' I stopped, suddenly aware of how like Gerry I sounded. Petulant and demanding. I was thankful Catriona could not see my scarlet face.

She was saved from thinking of a reply to my outburst by the sound of Marion coming up the stairs, calling: 'Time to get up now, lassies. Ye've had a fine long lie. I've got your breakfast nearly ready.'


Like all Scottish housewives in those far-off days, Marion went into a frenzy of cleaning on Hogmanay. Catriona and I were set to one task after another and we worked our way through the short daylight hours and into early evening, scrubbing floors, changing beds, cleaning windows, blackleading the range and even cleaning out cupboards.

It was while doing this last that I made a discovery. I was on my hands and knees emptying a wee cupboard under a set of four stairs – the old house rambled on several levels – and, reaching right into the poky back corner, I found a small, slim book. When I pulled it out, I saw at once that it was another in the now familiar series: faded green cover, title and author's name on the front and spine in old-gold lettering. In fact, it was another copy of *Tales and Legends of the Highlands and Islands*. But, unlike the one Mother had given me some three months ago, this book had no missing pages. A quick flick-through established this and I remembered my suspicion that the missing pages in Mother's copy had been torn out, rather than having fallen out. I remembered too that I had Mother's book with me – my hasty packing had included a quick sweep along the top of the tallboy in my bedroom - but I had no time to begin a comparison of the two books to find out what was missing from Mother's copy. I slipped the book into my apron pocket and hoped I would find a quiet moment to compare the two.

As the hours passed and the MacPhail house became cleaner and cleaner, the tension mounted - that special Hogmanay tension that invests the beckoning hour of midnight with magical promise. In spite of, or perhaps because of, all that I had gone through in the past week, I found myself buzzing with happy excitement. I was just a young lassie, after all, even if I did not often feel or act like one, and I could not help responding to the escalating anticipation. Even the dog was too wound up to eat his dinner properly and kept returning to his bowl for another mouthful, in between trailing around after each member of the household in turn and occasionally darting to the dark windows to bark at nothing.

The ritual of the 'last bath of the year' began at eight o'clock in the evening. Marion went first. A delicious perfume seeped out under the barricaded kitchen door, wafted by the steam from the jugs of hot water she was emptying into the big tin bath.

'That's the bath crystals I gave her,' said Catriona with satisfaction. 'They cost me two weeks' pocket money. Pa got them for me when he went over to Oban a few weeks ago.' Lachlan went next, using the same water, and we giggled as we thought of him smelling of the flowery bath salts. He sang loudly as he splashed in the tub: *The Crookit Bawbee*, practising for his 'turn' at the forthcoming party. When he was finished, dressed only in a huge black towelling robe, he carried the tub outside and emptied it in a far corner of the garden. He was still singing as he filled it up with fresh hot water for Catriona and me.

I had left my Christmas party frock at the MacPhail house because it had been streaked with mud after my wild descent down to Tormore cemetery when we heard Gerry's cries. Marion had steeped it to loosen the dirt gently and had dried and ironed it carefully so that its lilac-and-purple glory had been restored. I had time now to enjoy putting it on and twirling before the mirror – I had been too distracted in the rush to get ready for the boat to Fionnphort the previous Saturday.

I had a pang thinking of Mother and her dress-making skills, appreciating the stylish flair – not to mention the loving care - that had gone into the alterations. How would she pass Hogmanay? Would she even notice it? Did the hospital do anything special for its inmates on this most special of nights? And Father, what of him? Had he regained any of his memory yet? Would he even know what day of the week it was, never mind what day of the year? Would he ever remember what had happened to him? And what about Gerry? What was *he* doing tonight? What had The Dow been doing with him all this past week? How safe was he in her clutches? He was bound to be spending most of his time at the Campbell house, playing with Angus - surely she wouldn't get up to anything under Bridget's nose?

I thought of the pretty journal, my Christmas present from Marion. Later, I must record all these questions and maybe even have some answers by then.

'Are you ready, girls? It's nearly time to leave.' Lachlan's voice boomed up the stairwell.

'Come on!' cried Catriona, seizing my arm. 'Let's go and have some fun.'

I shook off these gloomy thoughts about my family. I was here on Hogmanay on the Isle of Mull, renowned for its Highland hospitality, with three people I had come to love. I could have a night off from my worries. It was time to party.

# CHAPTER THIRTY-ONE

*The sea runs deep into the mountains and winds about their roots: it makes the country difficult to travel, full of prodigious wild and dreadful prospects.*

*Robert Louis Stevenson, from 'Kidnapped'*

As Catriona had predicted, Lachlan had a huge lamp on a long pole which he held aloft as we set off to climb the hill up to the old quarry. We made a merry little band, laughing and singing, arms linked, all four at first and then, as the path narrowed, Catriona with Lachlan in front, Marion and I close behind. I was dreading the cemetery but we were down the hill and past it before I really noticed, so absorbing were the singing, the jokes and the banter. Besides, Lachlan's lamp cast a wide circle of bright golden light within which I felt contained and shielded from danger of any kind, natural or supernatural. The cemetery, as we rollicked past it, lay in deep shadow and seemed far removed from this night of happy celebration. I half-expected Catriona to make melodramatic ghost noises, and was preparing myself to rebuff them, but either Marion had had a word with her or she had worked out for herself that this would not be a good idea.

And so, in fine fettle, we found ourselves outside Aunty Jeannie's cottage at ten minutes to midnight. It was a chill, cloudy night and sleety rain had been threatening on the icy wind for the past hour. We waited in the road, stamping our feet and blowing on our hands, these extremities feeling frozen despite thick socks and woolly gloves. I looked around me and saw pinpoints of light here and there, isolated cottages and crofts. The cluster of houses at Fionnphort was out of sight for we were down in a dip but it was less than half a mile, I knew, to the jetty for the Iona crossing.

At last, we saw the front windows of the cottage being flung wide to let the old year out and in less than a minute we heard the village clock start up the ding-dong tune that would end in the first stroke of midnight. As it pealed out, I found myself wrapped in a tight hug.

'Happy New Year, Liza,' said Catriona. 'I'm so glad ye came to Erraid. It's just great havin' you as my friend.' And she kissed my cold cheek with a wriggle of delight that endorsed her words. I felt hot tears slide down my face and dashed them away with a gloved hand.

'Dinna greet,' she said anxiously. 'Are ye awful missin' your own family? It's right hard to be away from them on Hogmanay.'

But it was not missing my parents and brother that was making me cry. I could not have articulated exactly what it was. I was caught up in an emotional maelstrom: gratitude and relief; uncertainty and fear for the future; and a longing so strong that it bordered on jealousy.

'Happy New Year yerself,' I managed to say. 'I'm no' greetin'. It's just the cold.'

Then Marion was hugging us both, Lachlan too, and their kisses and good wishes were as warm to me as to their daughter. I was very close to breaking down. Why does kindness threaten our façade of courage so much more than cruelty does?

'Come on,' cried Lachlan, seizing the lamp-pole from the tree that he had propped it against. 'Time to first-foot Jeannie and Michael. Have you got the lump of coal, Marion?'

He strode up to the cottage gate, pushed it open and was up the short path and hammering on the door before I had even dashed the fresh tears from my chafed cheeks. The door was flung wide and the cries of 'Lachlan! It's yourself!' sounded full of delighted surprise, even though, as Catriona had told me, he had been their faithful first foot for many years.

The next hour passed in a scrum of handshakes, hugs, kisses and 'Happy New Year's as neighbours from all around poured over the hills and down to 'the hoose in the dip', as everyone seemed to call it. Clearly, it had been the Hogmanay rendezvous for many years and I soon saw why.

Jeannie and Michael were a middle-aged couple, both of comfortable girth and cheery manner. Childless themselves, they poured affection upon every child for miles around and spoiled them outrageously. Jeannie was a legendary cook and baker, as the wondrous table of seasonal fare testified, while Michael was a raconteur without parallel. No one could tell a joke or a tall story like him. He was endlessly amusing and fascinating. This combination of amazing food, unstinting childcare, first class entertainment and warm hospitality had earned them their rightful place as king and queen of the Ross of Mull party scene, of which their Hogmanay gathering was the highlight.

Before I knew it, it was two o'clock and I was drooping with the lateness of the hour and the amount of food I had consumed. There was no sign of our leaving any time soon, indeed the crowd was just moving from community singing and dancing to calls for individuals to perform. I waited just long enough to watch a maudlin Lachlan duet *The Crookit Bawbee* with a dewy-eyed Marion before I sneaked through to the back bedroom where the coats were piled on the big double bed. I made myself a nest among them, rolling up a couple of scarves to make a pillow; then I curled up and was soon sound asleep.


I screamed. I was in the grip of a nightmare in which first my pillow and then my covers were being snatched away. My bed was bucking like a ship in a storm and all around me clamoured loud, frantic voices. As sleep began to loosen its grip, I struggled to breach the barrier into waking.

'Hurry! Hurry!'

'Are ye ready?'

'Come ON!'

'Ach for pity's sake, man, get a move on.'

'I just want to get that scarf . . .

'Great God! There a bairn in here. Among a' the coats. Would ye look at her?'

'Get her out o' there. Quick, now.'

I felt myself being lifted up in strong arms and carried through the house. I was laid – well, dumped, really – in an armchair. I watched, dazed, as what had been a boozy party turned into an emergency station. Aunty Jeannie's front door lay open to the frosty night as men rushed in and out. I heard the sound of the ferrybus which had been parked down at the jetty and, as it slowed to a halt, Lachlan's voice, sounding unusually sharp.

'Get on, all of ye. There's no' a minute to lose.' He revved the engine and the clutch of men in the doorway and garden began to disappear from my view.

'What's happening?' I caught the sleeve of one of the women who were clucking about, trying to be of help to the men and being either ignored or pushed out the way. Obviously, whatever the excitement was, it did not include them.

'The lifeboat's goin' out. As soon as the men can get there.'

'The lifeboat? What lifeboat? Where is it?' My fogged brain was clearing and I had a hazy memory of the boat that had transported us from *MV Lochinvar* to the quay at Craignure when we had first come to Mull in September. It seemed such a long time ago. But the woman turned away to respond to the thumb-sucking child who was pulling at her skirts and whining.

Suddenly, the excitement was over. Standing up, I saw the last man running down the path in his socks, boots in one hand. Before he had got his second foot on the running board, the bus was lurching forward, tyres screeching as Lachlan hit the accelerator. The women who had been thronging around it, running up and down the short garden path, calling out their wishes and prayers for 'Good luck' and 'God speed' and 'Come home safe, now', leapt back and fell silent as they watched the bus disappear over the hill. They trailed slowly back into the cottage, drooping, the frenetic excitement of the past minutes draining away. I saw one woman cross herself – the first such gesture I had seen since leaving North Berwick – and then saw her bite her lip and glance furtively around. Clearly, she had been told - as we had been by Father on our first Sunday on Erraid - that any sign of the Roman Catholic faith had to be suppressed here.

'Liza! There ye are.' Catriona pushed her way through the knot of women in the doorway and ran over to me. She turned her head as she came, calling 'She's here, Ma.' And, in a moment, Marion too was at my side.

'Oh, thank goodness,' said she. 'I was looking for you before the shout went up. Wondered where you'd gone to. Then it was panic stations once we heard the bell, of course, and all the men were rushin' about like hens wi' their heads cut off. A shout on Hogmanay – can ye believe it? The men are all half-fu' At least, they'll no' feel the cold the same. That's something.'

I stared at her, baffled. 'What shout? I never heard a bell.'

'You've been sleepin', you! You still look half asleep. Where were you? We looked everywhere, didn't we, Ma?' Catriona chimed in.

'I was on the big bed among the coats.' I felt sheepish now, ashamed of once again 'making a nuisance of myself'. 'I'm really sorry.'

But Marion only laughed. 'We looked through there at the bed but you must have been hiding under the pile. Never mind. We've found each other now.' But, despite her customary easy manner, I saw anxiety in her face.

'What's happening? Where have the men gone? Why do they need a lifeboat?
What .. ?'

'And away she goes wi' her questions! Liza, do you ever ask just one at a time?' teased Catriona. But I was fully awake now and in the clutch of a familiar feeling of dread. 'Mrs MacPhail, Marion, please tell me!'

Marion took my arm and drew me a corner. 'Go and get a glass of cordial for Liza,' she bade Catriona, who went off obediently but looking disappointed to be excluded from the moment of revelation.

'We call it a "shout" when the men are called out to man the lifeboat. The nearest station is at Bunessan and they ring a bell when the boat needs to go out. A loud bell. I'm surprised you didna hear it.'

Cocooned in the pile of coats and scarves, I must have sunk into a sleep so deep that not even a loud bell had penetrated my consciousness.

'But why? What's wrong? Is someone drowning?'

'I hope not, Liza, I do hope and pray not,' she replied solemnly and I felt a chill in my heart.

'So why . . ?'

'We dinna ken, Liza dear. No' yet. But it'll be someone in trouble out on the sea, that's for sure.' She shivered. 'God help them, whoever they are.'

And so we waited, as has been the lot of women over the centuries, when their menfolk go off into danger. Some prayed, a few sang a hymn softly, the same one over and over again: *Eternal Father, strong to save*, a great favourite on the island. At the end of each verse, they raised their voices:

> *Oh, hear us when we cry to Thee*
> *For those in peril on the sea!*

The time dragged by. Being women, we fell to household chores as a way to calm – or, at least, find an outlet for – frayed nerves. By half past three, you would never have known there had been a party. All evidence was cleared away, every last crumb and dreg. Most of the children had found nooks and crannies to curl up in and only the older ones like me, anxious to be part of the adult drama, remained awake. From time to time, one of the women would say she really ought to go home and the others would agree, maybe even begin to make half-hearted preparations for departure, but soon they were all back in the rough circle of chairs and cushions on the floor, staring gloomily at the fire, on to which Aunty Jeannie kept throwing more logs and coal.

Conversation lagged or went round and round in circles but always hovering like a carrion bird over the burning questions: Who or what was in danger? Why? Where were the men now? When would they return? And, unvoiced but loudest of all in everyone's head, *Would they all return safe?*

Eventually, despite their best intentions, everyone else under the age of fifteen had succumbed to sleep of a kind, slumped in chairs and corners, a couple under the table leaning back-to-back against each other like bookends. But, unlike earlier in the night when I had done my burrowing-mole act among the coats on the big bed, I was wide awake now, my brain charged, my body restless. Catriona had succumbed to sleep on a floor cushion, propped up against her mother's chair; Marion was absorbed in listening to a lengthy tale about someone's demented old granny who had almost set the house on fire last week. I slid off my own floor-cushion and leaned back under the chair above me, settling down as though to sleep. No one had commented after several minutes so I risked wriggling slowly back until only my legs were under the chair and I could sit up behind it. I waited again to see if I would be noticed but no comment came. In a moment, I was creeping on all fours round the back of the chairs and escaping from the stuffy room into the chill of the lobby.

It took a minute - which seemed like an hour to my straining nerves – to locate my coat among the heap on the bed. At last I had it. I opened the bedroom door cautiously and almost yelped as one of the women came bouncing through the back door, returning from a visit to the 'wee hoosie' at the end of the back garden. I hastily ducked behind my door as she hurried past, keen to get back to the warmth of the fire.

By the time I gained the garden path, closing the outside door very gently behind me, I was in a high old state of excited self-congratulation. If I had broken out of a medieval dungeon after a long imprisonment, I could not have felt more pleased with myself. I almost skipped down the path to the gate and out on to the road. I was still warm from my hours by the fire and heated up still further by the last few minutes' tension so that the frosty cold only felt exhilarating. The moon over Mull was enormous as always, sailing behind banks of clouds and reappearing, it seemed, bigger than ever each time. I moved away from the house, more from a sense of self-preservation than from any idea or purpose.

Truth to tell, I had wanted only to be up and moving. The dragging wait around the fire, the endless rehashing of the same anxieties and regrets about a Hogmanay spoilt had begun to feel like a rasp on my raw nerves. The need to get out and go somewhere – anywhere – had been overwhelming. Now, here I was, out of the house. What was I going to do?

If I had been asked, I would have said that the last thing I wanted to do was go near the graveyard. Yet, somehow, that is where my steps took me. What I expected to see there, I do not know to this day. I found nothing, just the big, rusty gate creaking in the cold wind and the black shapes of the graves picked out here and there by fitful moonlight.

Then I heard it. Not the loud, summoning Bunessan Lifeboat bell that I had not heard in my soundproofed nest of coats but which the women had described to me, marvelling that I had slept through it. This was a high, sweet sound with a melting, seductive quality as it drifted over the sea toward the land. And, in a flash, it came back to me. Catriona telling me the story of 'The Ghost of Erraid' that afternoon in late September when The Dow had taken the school over the causeway to Knockvolgan Farm: Lady Maclean of Duart fleeing Cromwell's soldiers with her son, desperately launching a boat off the south tip of Erraid and smashing it on the Torran Rocks; her body washing up here, at Tormore, and being buried in this very graveyard that I was now fearfully surveying; the child's body, the nine-year-old boy, never recovered. I heard Catriona's teasingly sepulchral voice: *'They say she is still looking for him. Still seeking. Still calling for him. Wanting to find him and take him to the graveyard to be with her. We never ken exactly when she'll come . . . but we ken when she's on her way. A bonnie, tuneful bell rings way out at sea and, sure as God, there'll be a boat wrecked on the Torran Rocks that day.'*

I thought back: to The Dow's tense attitude whenever anything came up about the Macleans of Duart; to her unhealthy, monopolising interest in Gerry; to the pictures and photographs in the series of little green books; to those torn-out pages in Mother's copy of *Tales and Legends*; to Mother's discomfort when she first saw The Dow on Oban quay; and lastly, with a little choking cry, to that line drawing of Lady MacLean and her son in *'The Rise of Jacobitism in Scotland'*, its likeness to The Dow and Gerry.

Every hair on my body prickled as I finally made the connections that had been dancing at the edge of my consciousness ever since I first set eyes on The Dow. With a hoarse scream, I began to run up the hill, desperate for a sight of whatever drama was being played out right now in the swirling currents of the Sound of Iona.

# CHAPTER THIRTY-TWO

*Her voice had risen to a kind of eldritch singsong . . .*

*Robert Louis Stevenson, from 'Kidnapped'*


I stood panting on the top of the hill among the strewn rocks of the old quarry, staring out to sea. At first, I saw nothing for the moon had sailed behind a large bank of cloud and there was only the regular, faint twinkle of Dhu Artach as its light turned round and round. I strained my ears to hear voices which would surely carry on the frosty air. Nothing. I felt like the last, lonely person left alive. As the heat generated by my mad dash uphill faded, I began to shiver and to contemplate the miserable prospect of trailing back down the hill to Jeannie's house and facing the scolding that would be waiting for me. Running away in the middle of the night in perishing cold - and from a house where I was a guest – constituted making a *very* big nuisance of myself. Perhaps there was even now a search party of cold, tired women out looking for me, anxious for my wellbeing but extremely irritated at my behaviour. Thank goodness Mother – or, worse still, Father - was not among them: I would have been 'for it' for sure.

Suddenly the scene flooded with silvery light as the heavy clouds rolled away. The sheer beauty of it had me catching my breath, momentarily diverted from my pressing concerns. The Sound of Iona was turning into a shimmering sheet of purest silver. The sacred, magical island, cathedral ruins rearing up behind the little street and white croft-houses studded like pearls into the rise and fall of the land, was truly the 'faery isle' I had read about in the books Mr Chambers had pressed on me before we left North Berwick. Over the scene, seeming only inches above the water, hung a great white globe of a moon.

Now I could make out the lifeboat, its flag fluttering slightly, in the piercing, icy light. It seemed to be quite near the lighthouse and stationary, as far as my eye could tell - I knew distances and speeds would be distorted to my view. Then, to my right, I saw another, smaller boat making its way from further up the coast towards the lifeboat.

I forgot my shivers and apprehensions of a moment ago as I watched the drama unfolding before my eyes as clear as a play on a stage. I saw the smaller boat approach the lifeboat, draw alongside and rest still. Two tiny figures appeared on the lifeboat, standing one at each end of what looked like a board. Another two figures stood up in the smaller boat.

The board was transferred across the parallel sides of the two boats. There was a long, black bundle on the board – I thought I saw it move before it was lowered out of sight on to the deck of the smaller boat. A short parley ensued between the men on each boat and then both were moving away from each other, the small boat heading back towards a point on Mull north of where I was standing – Bunessan, probably – the lifeboat moving towards Iona but very slowly. I saw a beam of dancing yellow light playing upon the water this way and that as it moved. Searching for something – or someone?

I stood for a few more minutes, watching, wondering. The small boat disappeared from view as it rounded the curve of the land on my right, the lifeboat grew smaller and smaller, the flickering search-beam fainter. An enormous bank of thick cloud began to roll down The Sound and Iona slowly disappeared from view, the iridescent water turned black and the moon conceded defeat once again.

'Liza! Liza! Is that you?' Catriona puffed her way up the old wooden steps and appeared on the top of the hill. I turned slowly, uncertainly, and saw Marion too, toiling up from some way below.

'Where have ye been? What are ye doing out here on yer own? We've been frantic!' Catriona flopped down on a large boulder and winced as a sharp point found its way through her winter coat into her thigh.

'I couldna sit in the house any longer. I just had to get out and walk somewhere. It was drivin' me daft just waitin' and waitin'. . .' I broke off as Marion came over the top off the steps and onto the flat stretch where I was standing. She was out of breath from her attempt to catch Catriona's much younger legs and said nothing at first.

'I'm sorry if I worried you,' I said. It sounded lame and even a little surly. I made more effort. 'Really sorry. I didn't think about it. How it would worry you, I mean.'

'Why didn't you tell me you were going for a walk?' Marion found her voice but only enough to frame the blunt question. No gentle, easy kindness now.

'I'm sorry,' I said again. What else could I say? I had a flash of brilliance: I could divert the attention away from myself and my behaviour. 'I saw the lifeboat out there. The moon came up and it was quite clear. And another wee boat came out from up there.' I gestured northwards. 'It went over to the lifeboat and there was something on a long board that they passed over from the lifeboat to the wee boat. Then the wee boat turned and came back.' Again I waved my hand up the coast towards Bunessan. 'The lifeboat went the other way towards Iona. It was flashing its lamp on the water all the time, like it was looking for something.' I stopped, slightly out of breath for the words had tumbled out of me in my attempt to divert attention from my sins.

'Well, that's as may be, Liza' said Marion. She was regaining her customary benevolent authority with her breath. 'What's happening out there is happening and there's nothing we can do to help or hinder it. We'll find out all about it soon enough. And you getting your death of cold up here - *and* driving me and your wee pal here mad with worry – won't change anything. It's back home now with you, my lass. We're halfway there already. There's no sense in trailing away back down to Jeannie's again. It's time you girls were in bed.'

'But I need to know what – who – was on that board, the one that got passed over from the lifeboat. It might be . . .' I could not bring myself to articulate my fears, partly because I did not think they would give them any credence, partly because I did not myself want to give them any.

But neither Marion nor Catriona were listening to me. A silent message had obviously been conveyed between them and, like well-drilled soldiers, they sprang into position on either side of me, took my arms by their elbows and frogmarched me down the hill towards the faint orange light that could be seen at the MacPhails' kitchen window.

'The stove hasn't gone out yet,' said Marion. 'I'll liven it up in no time and we'll get the kettle on. Hot drinks and hot water bottles for us all.'

Half an hour later, despite my outspoken conviction that nothing as trivial as hot cocoa and a warm bed interested me, I was sitting on the kitchen rug, huddling into one of Marion's big woolly cardigans, sipping scalding cocoa, while she filled the red rubber bottles and sent Catriona to put one in each of our beds. To my feeble demand to be allowed to wait up until Lachlan came home and told us what had happened, she simply said: 'I'll wake you whenever he comes in. I promise.'


She did not need to. To my surprise, the soporific effect of regaining warmth after being thoroughly chilled triumphed over my anxiety and my determination to stay awake. I plummeted into sleep as one anaesthetised by chloroform, deep, dreamless unconsciousness. And yet, some part of my brain must have stayed on call for I woke with a start and sat up in my narrow truckle bed, ears straining, sure I had heard a voice. And yes, there it was: deep and strong, Lachlan's low, urgent tones. He was back!

Without stopping to think, I slipped out of bed, thrust my feet into slippers and was on the stairs in a flash. The kitchen door was open and, by the time I was halfway down, I could make out his words:

'The woman's clean out of her mind. Ravin' like a lunatic. Going on and on about her son. *Her* son, mark ye! Her that's been a spinster all her life. Insistin' that he was with her in the boat - that she was takin' him home. "Home with me where he belongs" she kept sayin', over and over. And shoutin' at them to get back out there and find him before he drowned *again*.'

'Again? What did she mean "again"? What was she talking about? Who does she imagine she is?' Marion's voice was lower and I had to creep down on to the bottom tread to catch what she said. Her questions exactly voiced my own and I held my breath for Lachlan's reply.

'God alone knows. She's in the care o' the doctor now. He'd been called out and was waitin' for the reserve boat when it got back to Bunessan. He'll likely have taken her up to the hospital right away. She'll need checked over. Apart from her wild mental state, she has a bruise on her forehead and a cut over one eye. Must have hit her head on something when she jumped over the side.'

'She *jumped*? Are you sure? I can't believe anyone . . .'

'Oh, aye. She stood up in the boat when she saw us comin'. She was screamin' but we couldna make out what she was sayin'. Then when we started to draw alongside, she ran to the other side of her boat. She was screamin' still and one o' the men said he heard it quite clear, said it was that old Gaelic thing: '*Bos air son Eachin*!' It's a sort of war cry, I think.'

I screwed up my eyes in concentration. A memory of something I had read recently was stirring in my brain but I could not quite grasp it.

'I ken it,' said Marion. '*Another for Hector*. Something to do with the Chief o' Clan Maclean being defended by his clansmen in a battle – they all died trying to save him, one after the other. Didn't do him any good, though. The English army – it was Oliver Cromwell's lot, if I remember my history – won in the end and Hector was killed anyway. But why was Miss Dow yelling that? She's no' a MacLean . . . is she?'

'Maybe. Could be related from way back in the past, I suppose,' replied Lachlan.

'But, even if that's true, how does it account for her jumping – and all this raving about having a son. I canna imagine it, her that's always so prim and schoolmarmy.'

'It's strange, all right, but, when we finally got the lifeboat back to Bunessan, they told us she been goin' on and on like that all the time she was there. Of course, she'd gone away wi' the doctor by that time – they said he had to restrain her and give her an injection to quiet her down - so I didna see her again but they said she was mad wi' worry – frettin' just like a mother for her son.'

'And the boat she was in has been found - but it's empty?'

'Aye. We saw it soon after the reserve boat took her away. The moon came back out for a minute and the lad using the binoculars up in the prow spotted it, beached on the sand at *Druim Dhugail* - that wee bay below the ivy cliffs on Iona.'

'Is it the lighthouse boat, then? I suppose it must be. What else *could* it be?'

'Aye, it was beached for the night round at David Balfour's Bay, 'cause it's needin' a few repairs. This month's shore keepers were goin' to be workin' on it before it's needed to bring the men back from The Rock at the end o' the week.'

'So,' Marion's voice was slow, considering, 'she must have climbed over the hill to get it and pushed it out. Could she do that? Would she be strong enough?'

'There's no other explanation. The tide was on the turn so there'd have been the pull o' the sea to help her. It's a short wee beach. She must have given it a couple of good shoves and jumped in to get the engine goin' right away. I've seen it bein' done from there by just one man.'

'Then she'd have been heading straight out to The Rock. Was she trying to get to the lighthouse, d'ye think?'

'Don't think that was her intention, no. When we got her out of the water into the lifeboat, and she kept goin' on about takin' her son "home", she seemed to mean somewhere near here. She was yellin' and wavin' her arms in this direction. Towards Fionnphort or Tormore, it looked like.'

'Did no one ask her?' Marion's question sounded reasonable enough but it drew forth a bark of harsh laughter from her husband.

'Ask her? She was listenin' to no one, that lady, never mind answering their questions. Just rantin' and ravin' like a . . .'

'Lunatic. Aye, you said. *Was* there a boy on board with her? Or was that just a figment of her imagination?'

'There was no boy in the boat when we found it at Iona. And we searched the water all around, of course, and called and called, in case there had been one and he'd fallen overboard as well. But there was no sign of anyone.'

'Just her imagination, then?'

'I hope so, Marion. I dearly hope so. I'd hate to think we failed to find him and left him to perish out there.' Lachlan suddenly sounded deathly tired and there was silence from the kitchen for a few moments. I imagined Marion putting her arms round him and the two locked in a mutually consoling embrace. Then Lachlan spoke again.

254

'Thing is, Marion, love, if there *was* a boy with her – I'm just saying *if* – how could she have persuaded him to come with her. He'd have had to walk all the way to Balfour's Bay in the pitch dark and freezin' cold. Why would any boy do that?'

'And what boy could it have been?' Marion took up his train of thought. 'It would have to have been one of the lighthouse families' boys and they'd all have been safe in their own homes, either bringing in the New Year with a party or tucked up in their beds by the time she was settin' out . . . What is it?'

'No' *all* o' them, Marion, my love. No' all. She had wee Gerry Galway stayin' with her this week. Mind I told you he wouldna come wi' me when I brought Liza over on Christmas Day.'

'I thought he was stayin' at the Campbell's house - with Bridie?'

I could bear it no longer. All my worst fears were confirmed. I leapt up and rushed into the kitchen. 'It *is* Gerry! It *is*. She got him to stay with her just so she could do this. She's been plannin' it ever since we came here. I *knew* she was goin' to do something terrible. Oh, poor Gerry! And I was supposed to be lookin' after him. Mother will kill me!'


The grey blur of impending sunrise was spreading along the horizon by the time Lachlan, Marion and I reached some sort of conclusion. My repeated assertion that: 'It's the pictures in those books, I ken it!' were at first met with blank stares. In frustration, I bade them 'Wait here!' and rushed upstairs to fetch both the book I had found the day before, during the Hogmanay cleaning spree, and the one that Mother had given me weeks ago, when I had been asking for books about Duart Castle and Clan MacLean. There had been no time to compare them and find out what the torn-out pages in Mother's book had been about. But, as I raced feverishly upstairs, I had a growing conviction so strong that I paid no heed to Marion's cry of 'Don't you be waking Catriona – the wee lamb's fair worn out.'

I found Mother's book easily at the bottom of my travel bag – without disturbing the comatose Catriona - but became increasingly frustrated as I searched for the other until I remembered that I had thrust it into my apron pocket and left it there. I was downstairs again in a flash, throwing Mother's book on the kitchen table and rushing over to the big hook upon which hung several aprons.

'Tales and Legends of the Highlands and Islands' read Marion aloud as she picked up Mother's book. 'What about it, Liza? It's just one from that old collection up in the attic, isn't it?' She handed it to Lachlan who was looking equally bemused.

'Got it!' I exclaimed as I pulled the apron I had been wearing down off the peg. The little green-and-gold book tumbled out of the capacious pocket along with a clothes peg and some screwed-up sweetie papers. Marion had bribed us from job to job with chocolates from a Christmas-present box.

I seized the book off the floor and left the apron to lie there. 'Look! It's the same, except this one has pages missing.' The three of us compared the two books.

'Yes, Liza, they are the same apart from the missing pages. So what?' Marion said. 'What's this got to do with Miss Dow nearly drowning and saying she had a boy with her? Or your wee brother?'

I took the complete book and opened it at the place where the pages were missing in Mother's copy. I riffled though it desperately. I had not had time to read these pages yet and was not sure exactly what I was looking for. I was too frantic to concentrate on text but I did not need to: within seconds, the book fell open at a full-page picture of an old portrait. I gasped. It was the same portrait I had seen in the book Catriona had given me on the Sunday before Christmas, *The Rise of Jacobitism in Scotland*.

I thrust the book at the startled Marion and Lachlan. 'Look!' They looked, at first doubtfully – perhaps they thought The Dow's madness was catching – but then with sharpened gaze and intake of breath. The portrait - Lady MacLean of Duart and her nine-year-old son, Alan – struck them as it had me when I had seen it in the Jacobitism book. There was no mistaking Lady MacLean's likeness to The Dow and Alan's to my brother, Gerry.

'And I've remembered something else,' I said triumphantly. 'The other book – the one Catriona gave me when I was stayin' here before Christmas – it had that story about Hector and the men jumpin' in front of him in battle and gettin' killed. The cry that Miss Dow gave – it's all in there as well. It was all about the Clan MacLean and *her*.' I stabbed my finger at the woman in the portrait. 'How her ghost comes back lookin' for her son.' Again I stabbed at the portrait, this time at the boy in it. 'Can ye no' see? She *is* the ghost of Erraid! And she's been livin' here, posin' as the teacher, waitin' to find her son so she can take him to be with her in the graveyard. She's found him. It's Gerry – ye see how alike he and that boy in the picture are? She was tryin' to take him in the boat over to the graveyard but she must have  lost control of the boat and let it wander out towards The Rock. Then you stopped her wi' the lifeboat. That's why she jumped. That's why she shouted that stuff about Hector.'

I ran out of breath and stopped on a squeak. 'But Liza,' began Lachlan. He stopped and sighed, looking helplessly at Marion as if to say 'you're the one that knows how to deal with hysterical girls'.

Marion said nothing. She went on staring intently at the portrait; then she spoke in a thoughtful voice that carried an air of quiet sanity. 'We'll not worry too much about the ghost story – everybody on Mull kens that's just a daft old legend - but I think Liza may be on to something. What if Miss Dow really is under the delusion that she's this Lady MacLean – the one buried in the old graveyard? They're certainly quite like each other if that picture's anything to go by. What if she has gone mad and thinks she has to find her son – or at least a boy of the same age who looks like him? What if she did have a boy in the boat with her and was trying to take him to Tormore graveyard?'

Lachlan nodded slowly. 'I see what you're sayin', love. She was certainly havin' delusions when we picked her out of the water and it sounds like she got worse. You think she might have been actin' out the ghost story? Thinkin' she really was the old Lady Maclean?'

'And, if she was trying to take a boy to the graveyard, what do you think she was planning to do with him there? If she thinks she's a ghost – dead, that is – and she wanted the boy to join her . . .' Marion's voice had lost its calm and was rising on a note of horror.

I had been listening to them with mounting terror. I had thought I wanted them to agree with me but now I realised that I had not. I had really hoped that they would talk me out of my nightmare suspicions with some reasonable explanation. Now I faced the truth. Whether Joan Dow was a ghost or simply a mad woman, there was only one conclusion to be drawn: she had taken Gerry with her in the lighthouse boat last night, intending to take him to the graveyard and murder him – and possibly kill herself too - so that they could be united at last in death.

But her plan had misfired and she had jumped out of the boat, leaving him on it. That boat was now beached on Iona but of Gerry there was no sign.

# CHAPTER THIRTY-THREE

*A darkness of despair, a sort of anger against all the world that made me long to sell my life as dear as I was able.*

*Robert Louis Stevenson, from 'Kidnapped'*

I grabbed frantically at Lachlan's arm and pulled. 'Come on! We've got to get over to Iona and find him. Please! Come on!'

They stared me for what seemed like minutes but was likely only seconds. Marion spoke first across my babbling. 'We don't know for sure that there *was* a boy on board with her and, even if there was, *was* it your brother? Mind you,' her brow furrowed, 'if there *was* a boy. .'

'There's only that mad bitch's word for that,' said Lachlan. 'Sorry,' he added as Marion made saucer-eyes of disapproval at his language. But I had more to worry me right then and, in any case, had often heard a lot worse from Father.

'That's what we need to find out,' said Marion, coming to a decision. 'Take the boat, Lachy, and go round to Erraid and see if there's a boy missing.'

'That'll take ages,' I cried. 'Gerry could be drowned or worse by the time we do that. We need to go to Iona now. Come on!' I pulled at Lachlan's sleeve. Ineffectually, of course - I had as much chance of moving Ben More. He stood his ground, barely seeming to notice me.

'Trouble is,' he said, 'everyone will be sleepin' off the Hogmanay party. There'll be no one around to ask. I dinna fancy knockin' folk up that have only just gone to bed a couple of hours ago. An' most of them havin' taken strong drink – an' plenty o' it.'

'Well, try Miss Dow's cottage first. If she didna have wee Gerry with her, he'll be all alone in that house. He might wake up an' be frightened. If he's there, ye can bring him back here and then we'll think about what to do next. Ye would think, would ye no', if she took any other boy, his folks would have surely noticed by now?'

'Aye, normally,' said Lachlan 'but ye ken what Hogmanay's like. Bairns just curl up and sleep where they can find a corner. No one worries about them until the next morning – or afternoon, more like. Especially on Erraid where everyone kens everyone else. It's such a safe wee place . . .'

'A safe wee place, is it?' Marion's voice was sombre. 'No' as much as we thought, it seems. A mad woman looking after the bairns all this time. Oh, Lachy . . .' She sounded close to tears.

Her words, or perhaps her tone, galvanised Lachlan. 'Right. I'll get round there and find out what's been going on.' He began pulling on his oilskin coat. He was still wearing the breeches and boots. 'You two wait here. I'll come right back and tell you what I find out.'

I did not waste precious time arguing with him. I slipped out of the kitchen into the back porch where the outdoor coats and boots were kept. I had my thick coat on top of my nightgown, stout shoes replacing slippers, a woollen hat stuffed on my head, gloves in my pockets, and was out on the path down to the jetty before he had taken his leave of Marion who insisted on preparing a knapsack of bread, thickly spread with butter and honey, and flask of hot tea. 'No knowing how long you'll be,' she said. 'Eat this in the boat on the way round.'

He was for objecting to me accompanying him when he saw me waiting beside the boat but I forestalled him. 'If Gerry's on his own in her house, he'll be frightened when we wake him up. Maybe he's already awake and terrified. It'll be better if I'm there. Ye ken what he can be like when he gets upset.'

It was a telling shot. Lachlan could very well remember Gerry's tantrum on Christmas Day which had resulted in us leaving him in the care of The Dow. Perhaps he was reproaching himself with having done so, now that we knew what kind of person she was. Or perhaps he had simply run out of energy to fight my insistence.

'Get in,' he said and within minutes we were moving through the steel-grey water out of Tormore Bay and, breasting a rolling swell that had me shaking my head at the offer of bread and honey, we rounded the south tip of Mull towards Erraid's little landing stage.

It was a ghost place indeed on that bitter cold, pre-dawn, New Year's morning. Not a soul was stirring as we docked. Lachlan gave me the rope and bade me jump out and tie it to that fateful iron loop. I had never done this before – I think he forgot I was not Catriona – but I made no protest, just crossed my fingers and jumped with my eyes shut and my heart pounding. I felt a wee glow of pride as I managed to tie the rope securely and heard Lachlan's 'That's it. Good lass.'

Up the familiar path towards the houses, all of them we saw, as we drew level with the row, shuttered and silent. Whatever jollifications had welcomed in 1925 on Erraid, there was no sign of them now. We crept along in front of the houses, past the school and down the short path to The Dow's cottage. It looked as dead as all the others, curtains drawn, no light to be seen, utterly silent. If Gerry was in there, he was either asleep or . . . My stomach, already churned up by the boat journey, gave a sickening lurch. Lachlan knocked on the door and tried the handle. It turned easily. She had not locked it on her departure. But then no one on Erraid ever locked their door and why would she have done so last night? She had no intention of returning alive. That thought made me feel more nauseous than ever.

It took only a minute to ascertain that there was no living being there. What was obviously her bedroom was chillingly neat, as if she had known that it would be other people who next entered it. The bed was made up with not the slightest rumple or crease in the counterpane, the pillows smooth, the corners knife-edge perfect. On her bedside cabinet, a candle, a bible and a black spectacle case. Beneath the one chair, a pair of slippers side by side and, on the back of the door, a green dressing gown on a single hook. These were the only signs of occupancy. The chest of drawers had nothing on its top, the mirror above it very clean, no smudge or finger-mark. The narrow wardrobe was tightly closed. There was a faint whiff of rosemary and lavender, a sharp, herbal scent that I immediately recognised although I had never really noticed it before.

By contrast, the other, smaller bedroom, which Gerry had been sleeping in, was a tumble of clothes, shoes, books and the clutter that he created wherever he went. I tramped upon a painted metal figure as soon as I stepped into the room and stooped to pick it up, my eyes filling with tears as I recognised one of the toy soldiers that he and Angus loved to play with. The bed was unmade, the covers drooping to the floor at one side, not even pulled back to air. One pillow was on the floor, the other askew. My racing imagination saw him being dragged out of bed, half asleep, maybe even drugged.

'Well, that answers one question,' said Lachlan grimly. 'He no' here. Hasna been for some time. This bed's stone cold and the candle's guttered out.' He turned and pulled open the curtains, letting the grey light of pre-dawn sneak in. He looked over at me as I stood with the toy soldier in my hand, biting my lip, tears on my cheeks. 'The question is: do we knock up the other houses and see if he's in one of them or do we . . .'

'He no' here!' I burst in vehemently. 'I *told* you we should have gone straight to Iona. He was on that boat with her. I know it.' I started to cry in earnest then, all my worst fears confirmed. I was beyond panic, all hope gone. It was as if I was already grieving for my lost wee brother.

Lachlan had his big, strong arms around me in a flash, holding me close into the stiff oilskin of his jacket, removing my woolly hat and stroking my hair. He murmured words in Gaelic which I could not translate but sensed their comforting intention. My sobs soon lessened. I had not been brought up to indulge myself in orgies of self-pity. And Lachlan's next words – in English this time – pulled me right out of this one.

'Iona it is, then lass. If the wee lad *is* in one of the other houses here, then he's safe and we dinna need to worry about him. If he's not, we'd better get on wi' finding him. We'll just be wastin' precious time, tryin' to knock all these dozy folk up after their Hogmanay party. That could take us a helluva a long time, explainin' the whole story to them all. We've nothing to lose. The lifeboat'll be out again too, once it's proper light. Between us, if he's out there, we'll surely find him.'

He spoke briskly as if there was nothing to worry about: we would find Gerry; it was just a matter of time. I nodded, rammed my hat on again and followed him down the stairs. Neither of us said what was in our minds: we might well find him but would he be alive or dead?

As we moved towards the front door, I glanced once more into the empty kitchen and noticed for the first time a book on the table. It was small and, as I turned into the room, instantly recognisable: faded green cloth cover, its title a gold-tooled inscription on the front and spine. I darted to the table and snatched it up, disturbing a piece of paper which fluttered out from the pages it had been marking. I caught my finger in the page and opened it.

It was another copy of the book Catriona had brought to school for me: '*The Druids of West Scotland.*' The page I was now looking at was the start of a new chapter headed '*Human Sacrifice*'.

'I thought ye were desperate to get on the way to Iona.' Lachlan stood in the kitchen doorway, frowning, but I barely heard him. I was reading the opening sentences of the chapter: '*Druids were said to conduct horrific human sacrifice and this more and more as they were hounded to extinction by the invading Christian Romans in the early centuries AD. It is said they hated the way that Christian celebrations had been substituted for their ancient pagan festivals, e.g. Christmas for Winter Solstice. They would resort to human sacrifice at such times to assert and preserve their ancient celebrations. They favoured a boy child for the sacrifice at Christmas, perhaps because of the Christian emphasis on the birth of Jesus.*

They favoured a boy child for the sacrifice at Christmas! I was back on the summit of Dun I, Iona's only hill, on Christmas Eve, listening to Catriona telling me about Druids and teasing me about the strange, demented old man – Mr Oran, she called him, although Lachlan's name for him had been more prosaic: Old Hector.

261

'*A bonnie wee lassie like you might be just what he was looking for.*'

'*What for?*'

'*Human sacrifice, of course. The fairer the maiden the better. Although a bonnie wee laddie will do just as well.*'

'Look!' I thrust the open book at Lachlan. 'Look what she was reading.'

He sighed heavily as he took the little book from me. I really was trying his patience to the limit. He glanced at the text. 'So?'

'She must have been worried about that old man on Iona, the Druid one. Maybe she was thinking he would come for Gerry, to sacrifice him at Christmastime. Maybe she thinks that's what happened to Alan.'

'Who's Alan?'

'The boy in the picture. The son of Lady MacLean who drowned with her. His body was never found. Maybe she thinks he was taken by Druids to be sacrificed. And, with it being Christmastime, maybe she was afraid that Druid man on Iona would come for Gerry. Maybe she thought she'd better get him over to the graveyard before that happened. Maybe . . .' I ran out of breath as my wild thought processes outpaced my speech.

'That's a lot of "maybees", Liza,' said Lachlan. He shook his head as if to clear it of such wild conjecturing. 'Come on, lass. We'll no' find out the truth o' the matter, standing here. Let's get back in the boat and head over to Iona.'

Dawn was breaking at last as we sailed up the coast of Iona towards *Druim Dhugail*, the little beach where, Lachlan said, the NLB boat lay grounded in the sand. If ever a time and place lent itself to thoughts of ghosts and foul deeds, that first dawn of 1925 surely did. Pale wraiths of mist floated, now obscuring, now revealing the land. My eyes ached with the effort to see something – anything – among the brown bracken-clad earth and black-grey rocks. I dashed away the tears that were partly from eyestrain and partly from exhausted fear and despair. At the back of my mind, a drumbeat insisted: *too late, too late, too late.* I was shivering uncontrollably from a combination of searing cold and frayed nerves.

We had just skirted *Port na Curaich* – 'The Bay of the Coracle' or 'St Columba's Bay' where the saint was said to have landed in the sixth century - and were heading northwards towards *Druim Dhugail*, when there came a sound that would have frozen my blood if I had not already been so cold. A scream so high that it was almost a squeal, except that it went on and on, like a slate pencil being drawn across a huge glass window. And behind it, just discernible, a deeper, broken sound, a sort of roar that could have been a man's voice.

'What the hell . . .!' said Lachlan, taking his hand off the tiller and letting the boat slew round in the current to face the island.

I jumped into the prow and leaned far forward in a precarious attempt to see but a swathe of mist lay thick along the shore, obscuring the land behind. There was a brief hiatus and then the scream resumed.

'It's heading back down the way we came,' I cried, as Lachlan came up behind me and pulled me back into the boat, muttering 'Get back in. Do *you* want to end up in the sea as well?'

I ignored this. 'Turn the boat round, Lachlan. We've got to follow it. I'm sure it's something to do with Gerry and that madman.'

'If you mean Old Hector, you're barking up the wrong tree there. He's harmless, for sure. He likes to pretend he's some fierce character from the past but he wouldn't hurt a fly really. You shouldna listen to my Catriona. She just likes to make up tales to . . .'

'Come on!' I stamped my foot with impatience. 'Turn the boat.'

The screaming could still be heard, fainter now, higher up perhaps but definitely heading round the coast towards St Columba's Bay. Lachlan hesitated and for a moment we rocked on the waves, their steady movement seeming to reflect his indecision.

'Whoa! Come back, laddie!' The sudden clarity of this shout was accompanied by the mist abruptly tearing apart like a torn veil to reveal a man standing on a grassy knoll above a tiny pebble beach. He was dressed in a long white robe, the hood pulled back off dishevelled long red hair. He was tall, his presence, even at this distance, commanding. And he was bellowing like a stag in rut, pausing between each cry to bend over and gather his breath for the next bellow. There could be no doubt. It was Mr Oran, the Druid, and he was in pursuit of some helpless victim whose screams could still be faintly heard.

'It's him!' I cried. 'The Druid. And he chasing Gerry. I'm sure of it. We've got to get round the coast before he does. We've got to save my brother.'

But Lachlan was now standing up on the wooden bench that ran across the centre of the boat. When the old man bent double for another breath, Lachlan cupped his hands over his mouth and shouted: 'Hector! Hello, Hector. Hello!' His voice hung on the mist, seeming to fade away up The Sound, and I thought that it was hopeless: the Druid man would not hear. But I was wrong. The man's shouting ceased and, as the mist parted yet again, we saw that he was coming down on to the little beach and waving.

'Ach, we canna take the boat in there,' said Lachlan, stepping down off the bench and screwing up in face in frustration.

263

'Look, he's running again,' I said. 'And waving to us to follow. Come on. Maybe he'll lead us to Gerry.'

'Maybe, maybe, maybe,' grumbled Lachlan but he was already turning the boat and setting a course to the south of the island. We lost sight of the Druid several times, partly due to the mist and partly due to the terrain which necessitated him going inland and upward above the old quarry where – I remembered The Dow telling us during a local history lesson – beautiful grey-green marble had been hewn up until ten years ago. But he hove into view again as we came into St Columba's Bay. He was running down to the sea, his sandalled feet slipping on the myriad multi-coloured stones.

Lachlan cut the engine to let the boat drift gently aground and settle into the pebbles and sand. 'Stay here,' he bade me. 'I've got waders on. You'll just get soaked.'

He leapt out of the boat into water that reached his groin, grimacing as the icy water closed round him and the chill penetrated even the thick rubber of his breeches. Dancing with impatience, I wanted so much to go with him but the thought of that deathly cold, oily swell around my body deterred me. I was not even wearing knickers under my nightdress, after all.

So I had to watch as the two men met on the stony beach. There was no hope of hearing what passed between them but I saw the Druid man gesturing several times, back to where we had come from. At last, after what seemed like hours to my tortured nerves, Lachlan waded back out to our boat and climbed aboard.

For once, I did not bombard him with questions. I was quite dumb with dread as I lifted my face to him. He sat down heavily on the bench and took a small hip flask from a pocket in his jacket and swigged it with shaking hands. I realised that he too was suffering badly from the cold – not to mention a total lack of sleep after a gruelling six hours, most of these spent at sea - and felt a brief moment of compunction.

'He's here. He's alive. He's not hurt.' The three sentences jerked out between gulps of the fortifying spirit in the flask.

I let out a long shuddering sigh and dropped to my knees in a puddle of seawater. 'Thank God.' A heartfelt prayer, not an expletive. 'Oh, thank God!'

# CHAPTER THIRTY-FOUR

*I was grateful to God, as I trust I have often been, though never with more cause.*
*Robert Louis Stevenson, from 'Kidnapped'*

'He's running away from Old Hector. Seems that mad bitch has filled his head wi' tales about the harmless, old fellow.' The contents of the hip flask were doing their job and Lachlan was able to frame longer sentences.

'Tales about D-Druids? About them m-m-murdering wee b-boys at C-Christmastime? Like it s-s-said in that b-book.' My teeth were chattering so hard I was having trouble speaking. The sodden hems of my nightdress and coat were dripping icily into my shoes. I wished I too could have a drink from that magic hip flask.

Lachlan came to the same conclusion. 'Here, lass,' he said, holding it out to me. 'Just take wee sips. Dinna choke.' As I complied and felt the whisky burn its way down into my core, he spoke again, thoughtfully. 'Likely she was reading it to him last night and scared the livin' daylights out o' the wee man. That's why it was lyin' on her kitchen table. That'll be how she persuaded him to go wi' her, over to Davy Balfour's Bay to get the boat. Maybe she told him she was goin' to bring him to us at Tormore. She was planning to head to the graveyard there so it would've fooled him nicely.' His voice was grim and I shivered still more.

'So when the b-boat he was on got b-beached on Iona, he was terrified of being c-caught by Old Hector?' I realised I had slipped into Lachlan's name for the old man. I had accepted that he was no more of a murdering maniac than Lachlan himself. Hector was as much a victim of The Dow's terrifying fantasies as Gerry had been.

'Aye. Exactly.' Lachlan took a last swig from the flask and handed it to me. 'Ye can finish the wee drop that's left. Dinna tell Marion I gave ye strong drink, mind.' He winked and I felt a miniscule glow deep inside me that was not from the whisky. It was from a glimpse of a world beyond this nightmare, of a normality where people joked lovingly with each other.

Lachlan was speaking again as he returned the empty flask to his pocket. 'Old Hector was bedded down for the night in the cave behind the beach at *Druim Dhugail*.' He waved a hand back up the coast. 'He uses it a lot in winter. Keeps piles o' furs there - and plenty o' this stuff.' He patted his hip-flask pocket and chuckled. 'No' such fine stuff, mind you. The home-made variety. Take the skin off yer mouth, it would!' He was starting up the boat's engine now and seating himself at the tiller. 'The lad had got himself out o' the boat and was wanderin' in the dark. Greetin' sore, Hector says. That's how he heard him.'

I had a picture of poor Gerry, lost, probably soaked and shivering like myself. And terrified - out of his young mind with terror, indeed - of being caught by the murdering Druid that The Dow had warned him of. I should never have left him with her. All my instincts about the 'mad bitch' had been right. I had been so glad to get off Erraid and back to Tormore with the MacPhails, to be once again part of that safe, loving family, that I had ignored my premonitions. I felt a spurt of guilty self-loathing. What was Mother going to say when she found out? I had failed her completely, broken that promise made on the night of the Christmas party in Fionnphort School. I heard her weak whisper: *I'm relying on you to make sure Gerry doesn't get up to any nonsense.*

'So the old man went out to see who it was makin' such a racket and came upon yer wee brother. Tried to speak to him and find out what was goin' on, what the lad was doin' out here in the dark on his own. But he just screamed all the louder, Hector says, and started runnin' away.' Lachlan raised his voice above the noise of the engine. 'Hector was right worried about him – seems he has a cut on his head wi' blood caked all over his cheek and ear – so he started to run after him. But the more Hector ran, the more Gerry ran. And the more Hector shouted at him to stop - that there was no need to run away and Hector wouldna harm him - the more the lad screamed and kept runnin'. That's what was goin' on when we came.'

'Gerry's injured? His head's bleeding?' I felt panic begin to tighten in my chest.

'Well, he canna be that bad if he can run this far. Likely he banged his head in the boat – maybe when the bitch jumped - that would rock it some. That would account for the time between the boat getting stranded on *Druim Dhugail* and when Hector saw him. He was maybe knocked out for a bit.'

'Knocked out?' I could hardly bear it. Everything Lachlan retold of Hector's account simply piled fear upon fear in my frantic mind. 'Is that serious?'

'No' necessarily,' replied Lachlan, soothingly. 'We can take comfort from the lad getting out o' the boat and runnin' all this way. He'd no' have been able to do that if he was in any kind o' a bad way. The main thing now is to find him and take him home.'

I knew he was speaking of his own home at Tormore, not my own empty, motherless and fatherless house. 'Yes. Oh yes! Please. Come on.'

I joined him on the seat beside the tiller and he put his free arm round me.

'That's what we're goin' to do, lass. Hector's goin' overland – but I told him to stop shoutin' so much. It's just makin' matters worse. We're heading to meet up at *Port Aoinidh nan Struth.*'

'Where?'

'It means "Port o' the Cliff o' Streams." It's just a wee way round the coast. There a good inlet there that I can take the boat into.'

'But how will that help?'

'Hector's goin' to try and herd the lad down onto the beach there. I said he can shout just a wee bit to get him there if he has to. Then, once the lad gets down onto the beach there, he'll see our boat and we can shout to him, wade in to get him and bring him out here wi' us.' He patted the tiller. 'Then we can all get away back home.'

As always he made it sound quite simple, a foregone conclusion. And I wanted it so much that I decided to believe him.


A weak morning sun was straggling through the last shreds of mist as we drifted towards the sliver of inlet that is *Port Aoinidh nan Struth.* To this day, I can never think upon that scene without a visceral throb somewhere in my spiritual depths.

At first, as we glided to a shuddering halt in the pebbly sand, I thought it was to be yet another dead end in this frantic quest. All was silent and still as we waited. I saw that Lachlan had his eyes closed, though whether he was praying or just snatching a moment's rest I could not have said. My own prayers were half desperate supplication, half melancholy despair.

Then we heard Old Hector's rough shout, followed by a keening shriek that set my pulses racing. In a moment, a small figure could be seen scrambling down the cliff, sending scree flying before it. The figure stopped when it reached the top of the inlet and seemed to execute a weird dance before running again, this time down one side of the gully. It was the side that rose gradually up from the sea and would lead up to the top of the cliffs and away around the coast back towards St Columba's Bay.

I could not bear to lose him again. Not when he was so close. Without asking Lachlan, with no thought for my own comfort or safety, I leapt out of the boat and into the knee-high water. Yelling at the top of my voice, I drove myself through it, hampered by my trailing, dripping garments, but still managing a fair pace.

'Gerry! Gerry! Stop! It's me. Liza. Come back. You're safe.' On and on I shouted, over and over again, waving my arms. I thought I saw him pause but then he ducked his head down and drove himself forward, stumbling, not screaming any more. The terrain he was so painfully covering was taking him higher and higher.

In one last desperate attempt to reach him, I let out a piercing, ear-splitting shriek that I sustained as long as I could. And it worked. Gerry stood quite still for a moment, like a hunted gazelle poised for flight, and then he turned and looked back down at the little beach where I stood. I snatched off my hat, remembering that it was made of pale cream wool, and waved it. 'It's me, Gerry,' I yelled. 'Liza. Come down. It's all right. You're safe.'

There was a moment suspended in time when it seemed that he would turn and run still higher up the incline away from the beach. And then, he seemed to crumple and drop down on to the heather. He was on his knees, silent now, immobile.

'I'm coming, pet,' I yelled. 'Hang on. I'm coming.'

I started to run towards the incline, feet slipping on pebbles, toes stubbing painfully. I sensed rather than saw Lachlan behind me. Then his big hands were on my lower back, pushing me very fast up the hill. We reached the crouching Gerry in a matter of seconds and his head shot up, eyes like big, glassy marbles. I was on him before he could make a sound, gathering him into the sodden folds of my tweed coat, hugging him so tightly he might have suffocated if Lachlan had not intervened, lifting him out of my clutches and beginning to carry him back down to the boat.

By the time we reached the beach, Gerry was gibbering incoherently, clearly still in the grip of the terror that had driven him, running and screaming, over a mile and a half of rough, hilly terrain. He continued to quiver and gibber as Lachlan set him down, escalating abruptly into jerking, hysterical shrieks as he saw Old Hector coming towards us.

'It's all right, Gerry. It really *is* all right.' I told him over and over again but he was past hearing or responding. I wondered if I should slap his face. I had read about people doing that to break the spell of hysterics. But I hesitated. It seemed so cruel — the poor wee soul had suffered so much already.

Even as I dithered and Gerry went on blubbering and jerking, trying to evade Lachlan's grip, a strange thing began to happen. Hector came up to the boy and dropped down on his poor old knees, there and then in the wet sand. Lachlan, still pinioning Gerry's arms, did likewise. As if by a pre-arranged signal, they both began to chant words in Gaelic, at first

268

gently and slowly but then getting faster and louder until they were a strident command, repeated over and over again. I watched fascinated as Gerry's jerking body gradually stilled and his cries subsided. As the Gaelic chant slowed to a halt, he flopped against Lachlan, who scooped him up and held him close to his chest. Gerry was sobbing softly now, hiccupping a little.

Lachlan nodded to the old man who held up both hands, palms towards us, in acknowledgement of something – I knew not what. Then he bowed, a strangely formal gesture, before he turned and left us, striding away up into the hinterland of the island. I wanted to urge Lachlan to carry Gerry on to the boat – quickly, before he started screaming and struggling again. But something stopped me and I stood with Lachlan to watch Old Hector until he was out of sight. It felt something like a mark of respect.


We met the lifeboat on our way back round the coast. It hailed us with its megaphone and Lachlan steered over to draw alongside. The three men aboard, all Bunessan men, expressed delight when they saw Gerry, still quiescent, snivelling softly into my neck as I held him tightly.

'We'll tell the police and the coastguards,' said one.

'Aye, if we hurry back, we'll just be in time to stop them launching the search again,' said another.

'The police will be wantin' to talk to the boy. Seems they canna get any sense out o' that schoolmarm. They need to know what happened.'

'And the NLB need to be told about their boat. It's in a bonny mess.'

'Aye, they'll need to send another one down soon and tow that one away for repair.'

Despite having noted the need to hurry back, they seemed more interested in speculating on the consequences of the incident.

Lachlan brought their discussion to an abrupt close. 'I need to get these two bairns back. They're shiverin' wi' cold and the wee lad is in shock.'

'*Me too*,' I thought as he revved up the motor and surged away from the lifeboat, out across The Sound towards Fionnphort.

Marion had been watching from an upstairs window, keeping an anxious vigil ever since we had set out. Incredibly, we had been gone for less than two hours. We saw her running down towards the landing stage at Tormore Bay. I stood up in the boat, Gerry in my arms, and saw her snatch the scarf off her neck and wave it – in acknowledgement and relief, I suppose.

'Thank God, Oh, thank God.' She echoed my own words from half an hour ago but, wisely, without soaking her knees and clothes in seawater. She leaned across and took Gerry from me, freeing me to jump out of the boat and tie it up – I was becoming quite smart at this basic island skill. The four of us must have made a funny group as we straggled up the short incline to the house, a tangle of embracing arms and heads angled to rest on shoulders, none of us wanting to let go.

Catriona had not heard her mother leave the house. Marion had been so desperate to see if her straining eyes were telling her aright – that I did indeed have my brother alive and safe in my arms – that it had not occurred to her to waken her daughter and tell her that the boat was coming in. But Catriona did hear us as we came clattering into the kitchen, making all the noise that four people will, especially when three of them are frozen to the marrow and two of them in a state of excitement. Lachlan and I were talking through and over each other, trying to answer Marion's questions, but Gerry was slumped silent and heavy in Lachlan's arms.

Catriona came flying downstairs with only her nightdress on, feet bare, her mop of bouncing red curls making a halo round her head in the pale morning light. She stopped short in the kitchen doorway when she saw us, 'What's happened? Where have you been? Is that . . . wee Gerry?' Then, 'Och, so it is. Thank God!' The Almighty was being well thanked that night.

Lachlan laid his burden down in the big rocking chair by the stove. He opened the largest door in the black range and the blast of heat that wafted over me was something I would never forget. It did what an hour and a half of bitter cold, soaking clothes and searing dread had not. I sank down on to the floor beside the rocking chair, covered my face with trembling hands and burst into tears.


January the first, 1925, was a day lost to me. There was a blur of being stripped of my wet nightdress and coat, of sodden boots and socks being tugged off with a sound like pulling an animal out of squelching mud, of being wrapped in a heavy woollen blanket. A big, steaming china mug appeared in my shaking grasp. Something very hot and very sweet burned its way down my gullet as I was dimly aware of Gerry being lowered into the tin bath - which was also steaming – in front of the stove. Next I was being gently helped into the tub myself by Marion and Catriona. Of Lachlan, by then, there was no sign. I expect he had gone to bed, poor man, utterly exhausted by the most unforgettable Hogmanay of his thirty-nine years. My last hazy memory was of sinking into my truckle bed in Catriona's room.

When I woke up, eight hours later, it was pitch dark outside. Night-time again! I lay in the soft glow of a tiny nightlight, cocooned in comfort, my brain in freefall as images from the night before played in my mind like flickering magic lantern slides. I watched the show sleepily with a growing sense of wellbeing and deep relief. Gerry was safe. The Dow had been exposed for what she was: crazy, predatory and dangerous – especially to nine-year-old boys like my wee brother. The nameless unease, which had dogged me ever since Mother's first cry of horror when she saw a picture in one of the little green-and-gold books – the books that had led me, bit by bit, towards the truth, towards the terrifying climax of events last night – that unease had been justified after all and had at last been explained.

I was on the point of dropping off again when the one piece of the puzzle that remained unsolved jumped into focus on my mental screen. I saw again the scene on the beach at Lachlan's 'Port o' the Cliff o' Streams'. Gerry in Lachlan's arms, thrashing about like a thing possessed, gibbering hysterically. Old Hector dropping to his knees on the sand. Lachlan following suit. That weird Gaelic chanting, getting faster and louder, the same thing over and over again. Gerry's jerking body stilling and his shrieks fading to low sobs and hiccups. And thus he had stayed, as if in a trance, all the way back on the boat and through the palaver of stripping, bathing and presumably being bedded down somewhere to sleep off his adventures.

And I saw that strange but – I now knew - harmless old man, hands held up, palms towards us, bowing quite formally, before he strode away to let Iona swallow him up again. What had that been about? Some kind of spell they had been casting on Gerry to calm him down or take away bad memories? I remembered Mr Chambers, back in the old North Berwick days – which now seemed like another life although less than six months ago – calling Iona 'the magic isle'. Had Lachlan and Old Hector been invoking some of that magic there on that bleak strand in the grey January dawn? Whatever it had been, it had worked for good - that was for sure. Poor wee Gerry had been through a terrible ordeal and it had been no surprise that he was beside himself. If he had carried on in that state, we would have been struggling to get him on to the boat, let alone keep it afloat while we crossed The Sound to Tormore. Whatever they had done or said, whatever powers they had invoked, the result had been the calm, docile wee fellow that Marion had received so thankfully into her arms down on the landing stage.

271

I resolved to ask *her* about it. Lachlan might just laugh at me and call me fanciful. Catriona would probably use it as the starting point for a new skein of scary tales – I was getting wise to her now. But Marion would tell me the truth with compassion and gentle wisdom; she would help me understand and accept. With a sigh of relief at reaching this satisfactory conclusion, I drifted off to sleep again. It was seven o'clock in the evening when next I awoke.

# CHAPTER THIRTY-FIVE

*You have none such friends . . . They would have died for me like dogs.*
*Robert Louis Stevenson, from 'Kidnapped'*

I found the whole family, Gerry too, preparing to sit down to a meal, the traditional 'Ne'er Day Dinner' of steak pie and trifle. As soon as the smell of the pie hit my nostrils, I realised I was ravenously hungry. It had been a long time since the feast at Jeannie and Michael's Hogmanay party.

Gerry ran to me as soon as he saw me and we embraced as if we had not seen each other only eight or nine hours ago. I suppose, for both of us, the events of the night before seemed to belong in some weird and terrifying parallel universe, from which we had miraculously escaped; and now we were met up again, back in the normal world.

Marion insisted on all of us sitting down 'in a civilised manner' and enjoying the lovely food she had prepared. 'We can talk about it after the meal,' was all she would say, repressing questions and reflections about what had happened. Lachlan loyally backed her up and, although it seemed a terrible effort at first to put it all to one side, we had a very pleasant celebration meal. Lachlan and Marion toasted '1925 at Tormore' and 'Bless this house' in tumblers of whisky and water, Catriona, Gerry and I joining in with glasses of elderflower cordial.

At last, replete with sherry trifle and cream, we gathered around a roaring log fire in the rarely used parlour – it *was* New Year's Day, after all – and Marion conceded: 'We'll do the dishes and clear up later. Now! Let's get all this nonsense out of the way. Then we can enjoy a nice game of Blackjack.'

There was something enormously comforting in hearing all the fears and horrors of the past months – and their terrifying climax on Iona in the early hours of the morning – described as mere 'nonsense'. The tight ball inside me began slowly to untangle. I began to dare to hope that it was all over and somewhere, on the other side of it, lay a life free from haunting fear.

Towards the end of the meal, there was a knock on the door and there stood a rather wet police constable. He apologised for disturbing our 'Ne'er Day Dinner' but wondered if the wee lad was fit to be asked a few questions. He was at once welcomed into the MacPhails home, being

273

someone well known to them all, although a stranger to me and Gerry. Once he had had a cup of tea and a slice of Christmas cake pressed upon him, Lachlan suggested we all adjourn to sit around the fire and hear Gerry's story. The policeman agreed, realising that he would have his best shot at hearing the full story if Gerry was feeling relaxed and safe. We gathered comfortably around the blazing hearth and Marion took Gerry on her knee, wrapping her arms around him and whispering that all the policeman wanted to hear was the story of what had happened in Gerry's own words.

'I'm no' in trouble, am I?' he whispered back and she shook her head and hugged him.

'It's not you that's in trouble, lad.' The policeman had heard the whisper and he smiled kindly at Gerry. 'We just need your help to understand what happened.'

'Will *she* . . . will Miss Dow . . .'

'Don't you worry about her, lad. She'll no be troubling you – or anyone else – for a long time. We just need your help to make sure she doesn't. You're our key witness.' He said 'key witness' with great solemnity and a portentous nod. Gerry sat up a little straighter and tried to look important. Then he began to talk.

He was at first hesitant and inclined to pathos, his bottom lip trembling as he recounted how The Dow had at first spoiled and indulged him in the week between Christmas and New Year, feeding him titbits and treats, letting him have Angus down to play in her house for hours each day. But, somewhere around the twenty-ninth or thirtieth of December, things had begun to change. Angus' time with him had been cut shorter and shorter until, on Hogmanay itself, she had turned him away at the door.

'She said we had things to do that day, we'd no time for playin',' he recalled. 'Then she made me read to her, out of this wee book about Druids. She'd been readin' bits of it to me all week and tellin' me other stories – about Iona and Druids. She said there was an old man on Iona, one of the last o' them. The bit she made me read that day was about them killin' people. No' in a fight or anythin' – just doin' it like it was some kind o' thing they *had* to do. In a serra. . . serra . . .'

'Ceremony.' I put him out of his misery and he nodded enthusiastically. He was warming to his role now as the centre of attention.

'Last night,' he continued, 'I wanted to go to Angus' house 'cause they were havin' a party but she wouldna let me. She gave me this funny stuff

274

to drink at bedtime. It was quite nice, though. Really sweet. And she sat on my bed and read the same bit again to me – about the Druids killin' people. Then . . .' His voice tailed off and he frowned. 'She must have woken me up but I dinna remember. Next thing I knew we were out on the hill and she was draggin' me. I was feelin' right bad. I was sick a couple o' times but she just kept draggin' me.'

I could visualise it as clearly as if I too had been there and my heart went out to him. 'Did she say where she was taking you?' I asked.

'Aye. She said we had to get away off Erraid because the Druid man that lives on Iona was goin' to come and get me and kill me. Like it said in the book. What they did to people for their . . . their *serramunnies*.' He glanced at me to confirm he had got the right word and I nodded, my heart wrung for my poor wee brother. 'She said she was goin' to take us both in the boat round to this place here.' He waved a hand around the room. 'Said she was takin' me to where you were, Liza, at Catriona's house.'

Lachlan nodded at me with some satisfaction. 'That's what we thought, was it no', Liza?'

'Was it?' My memories were a vague jumble. 'Yes, yes, I remember,' I added quickly, to please him as he looked affronted at my doubtful reply.

'So we got to that bay away over there.' He waved a hand in the direction of Erraid. 'The one we went to that mornin' the inspector mannie was here, Liza.'

'David Balfour's Bay,' I said.

'An' she made me get in the boat. I didna want to, 'cause I was still feelin' sick. Must have been that funny drink she gave me at bedtime. I tried to run away from her but she picked me up and threw me into the boat. I fell an' hit my head an' I must've cut it - there was blood running down my face at the side. Then we were out in the sea and the boat was jumpin' about all over the place. She was shoutin' at it, pullin' at the stick thing . . .'

'The tiller,' I supplied and he nodded

'It wouldna do what she wanted it to and she was screamin' and the boat was, like, goin' round in circles . . .' Gerry's childish voice quavered to a halt as he relived those dreadful minutes. Marion put an arm around him pulled him into a maternal cuddle and he responded as if she had been Mother.

'That's likely what was wrong wi' the NLB boat,' said Lachlan. 'Why it was up there in Balfour's Bay waitin' for the men to fix her. There must be something wrong wi' the steering.'

'What happened next,' I prompted Gerry, although I think we had all guessed by now.

The boat had been spotted in its erratic progress by the men on lighthouse duty on The Rock and they had sent a distress signal to the coastguard at Bunessan who had scrambled the lifeboat crew. The rest of it we knew: that The Dow had finally gone berserk when she realised that her plan to get Gerry over to Tormore graveyard had been foiled; that she had jumped into the water – possibly intending to drown herself – but had been fished out by the lifeboat men and taken back to Bunessan; that the boat with Gerry still in it had been swirled away on a turning tide, miraculously missing the Torran rocks, and had ended up stranded on the shores of Iona. He had not known what to do then and had waited, hoping someone would come. When no one did after some time, he had climbed out of the boat and waded ashore.

'I was that cold,' he said, shivering at the memory, despite the fire that leapt up the chimney only a couple of feet away from where he sat on Marion's lap. 'I thought maybe there'd be a house an' I could knock at the door and ask if I could come in for a wee while.'

But he found none and his bleeding head was throbbing sore. He had given way to loud sobs and this was what Old Hector had heard as he lay snug among his furs in Pigeon's Cave.

'Then the Druid mannie appeared and I thought he was comin' to kill me, like she said,' sniffed Gerry. 'I was awfy scared.'

The rest Lachlan and I knew, having been a part of it, and we soon had Catriona, Marion and the policeman caught up with events. A short silence fell as each of us reviewed the tale, piecing together the bits each of us had guessed at or been a part of. Then the policeman snapped his notebook shut and rose.

'Well done, lad. I'll write that all out and bring it round for you to read in a couple of days. Then you can sign and have one of these good people' –indicating Lachlan and Marion – 'witness your signature. I understand both your parents are in Tobermory Cottage Hospital?'

'Yes.' I confirmed, thinking how forlorn it sounded.

'Good. Thank you for your hospitality,' he said, bowing a little to Marion and shaking hands with Lachlan. He nodded at me, smiled at Gerry and was gone.

'But there's one bit I still don't understand,' I said, turning to Lachlan.

'I think I can guess,' he replied with a slow smile. 'You're wondering what Old Hector and I were doing on the beach at *Port Aoinidh nan Struth* when Gerry was like to go fair mad, screamin' and foamin' at the mouth.'

He glanced over at Marion. She tightened her grip on Gerry who had stayed in her embrace.

'Yes,' I said. 'I thought he was going to go on like that for ages and we'd never get him into the boat and back across The Sound, the way he was thrashing about.'

Gerry whimpered a little in Marion's arms, whether from embarrassed shame or relived terror I could not tell.

'Ah, well. That was a little bit of Iona magic,' said Lachlan with a smile.

'Magic? What kind of magic?' I had had well and truly enough of strange tales and legends. I wanted hard facts.

'Did you never hear tell that Iona is a thin place?'

'Ye-es, 'I said slowly. 'My old teacher in North Berwick said that the veil between heaven and earth is thin there, that you can reach God easily.'

'And he wasn't far wrong,' said Lachlan. 'But where ye can be close to God, ye can always bet that the devil is lurkin' close by too, tryin' to stop you. Folk can get possessed if they're no' careful.'

'Ach, Lachy, stop frightening the lassie,' said Marion.

'So we had to pray away the evil,' continued Lachlan as if she had not spoken. 'That was the ancient Celtic prayer that wards it off and drives it far away. Best said by two people together. More powerful. Old Hector and I both ken that.'

Gerry was staring at him wide-eyed and open-mouthed. I realised that I was doing likewise.

'So there we have it,' said Marion briskly, as if we had not just heard a tale of: a mad, suicidal woman; a kidnapped child; ancient human sacrifices; a shipwreck; a demented old man; a headlong chase; an enchanted island; and what amounted to exorcism on a beach at dawn. 'Now, let's have a game of Blackjack.'


'Bairnies, bairnies! Come here.'

Mother was sitting up in bed, holding out her arms, smiling and looking better than I had seen her look for many months. It was the second week in January and the weather had at last allowed us to travel up to Tobermory. Lachlan had brought us in the ferrybus. Quite a number of the inhabitants of Fionnphort, Bunessan, Pennyghael and Craignure had been with us, getting on at the various stops as we headed to 'The North End'. By the time the bus chugged down the hill into Tobermory High Street, it was quite full and noisy with the chatter of islanders agog with rumour and speculation.

Of course, the tale of what had happened on Hogmanay night and in the wee small hours of New Year's Day had quickly spread throughout the Ross of Mull and over the causeway to Erraid. After a couple of days, Bridie and Angus had trekked across at low tide to visit us at the MacPhails' house – Bridie full of remorse that she had not kept Gerry with them in the Campbell house, however great the squash - and had heard the whole story, blow by blow. In turn, she was able to update us on the NLB having been told the story by telephone and a replacement boat being on its way in time to fetch the men whose spell out on The Rock was ending, take them back to Erraid and transport the next trio out to the lighthouse. The Board was also sending a replacement keeper for Father who should have been ready to go out to Dhu Artach but was still here in Tobermory Cottage Hospital.

Lachlan and Marion had both come with Gerry and me to visit Mother. Catriona too since, lacking a teacher, Erraid School had not yet opened. The matron of the small hospital was a formidable little woman. She reminded me of those little dogs who, lacking the stature and gravitas of larger breeds, assert their presence by belligerent yapping. Even though Mother was the only patient in the four-bed ward and was clearly well on the road to recovery, Matron still informed us that there was a strict two-visitors-only rule and visiting time was one hour a day between three o'clock and four o'clock in the afternoon. Not a minute earlier or later.

This being the case, the MacPhails left us in Matron's care and took themselves off to enjoy an hour sampling the delights of Tobermory which was little more than a village but represented 'town' to the *Muileachs* – the inhabitants of Mull.

Gerry ran into Mother's embrace, jumping onto the snowy white bed in a way that had Matron tutting and shaking her head. I followed at a slower pace, taking Mother's hand and leaning down to kiss her cheek. We had been well warned not to dramatise the tale of all that had happened, so as not to set Mother's recovery back by delivering such a shock. But, needless to say, Gerry immediately forgot his promise to Marion and began a garbled, excitable account of his adventure so that poor Mother soon began to lose the healthy glow that I had been so glad to see in her cheeks. Her eyes wide with incredulity, she looked at me over Gerry's shoulder. 'What in the name of God is all this?' she demanded.

'Och, he's just laying it on thick,' I said quickly. 'We're both fine now. And *she's* gone well away. There's nothing to worry about. Come on . . .' I pulled Gerry off the bed, out of her arms, and plonked him in the chair at the side of it.

Shushing his protests and interruptions, I gave Mother a brief rundown of events, playing down The Dow's possibly murderous intentions, touching lightly on the fear of Druids she had instilled in Gerry and doing my best to make it sound as though the mad dash around the coast of Iona in Lachlan's boat had been no more than a bit of a lark. I painted Old Hector in the colours of a lovable old eccentric and made no mention at all of the 'exorcism' on the beach. Luckily, Gerry's memory of what had happened once we found him was too hazy for him to contradict or seek to embellish my version of events.

'Lachlan and Marion have been so good,' she said. 'And Bridie, too. They're right good folk here on Mull. I wasn't too keen to come here among strangers, so far from North Berwick, but I see now I was wrong. They've hearts of gold. They barely know us, and we've been nothing but a bother since we came, but they've all been so kind . . . so kind . . .' Her voice faltered and her eyes filled with the ready tears of convalescence.

'They're here today,' I said. 'All three o' them. But Matron would only let two visitors in.'

'Where are they? Outside?' Mother craned her neck towards the ward door.

'No. They said they would let us three have the whole hour to ourselves this time. They're going to bring us back in a few days' time and they'll come in then.'

'And, after that,' said Mother, reaching out a hand to stroke Gerry's cheek and frowning at the scabbed scar on his cheekbone – legacy of that dreadful night – 'I might be back home. Matron said this morning that if my blood pressure keeps steady and . . . well, a few other things . . .' she coughed and glanced at Gerry. The 'few other things' obviously included delicate matters unfit for the ears of a nine-year-old boy. 'I'll get out, hopefully, next week,' she concluded triumphantly and Gerry and I both hugged her in relief.

Later in the hour, when I had steered the conversation round to a description of the Christmas party in Fionnphort School and other cheerier topics, watching her carefully for adverse reactions, I said as lightly as I could: 'Do ye ken how Father is? Is he still here as well? Lachlan told me he'd lost his memory. Has it come back?'

She sighed and shook her head. 'I'm afraid not, Liza, dear. He was quite ill for several days and I gather they feared for his life. They didn't tell me that till later, of course, because I was too ill myself.'

'Is he better?'

'Better in body, I think, but not, I'm afraid, in mind.' She sighed. 'They even tried bringing him in here, in a wheelchair, to see if he would

279

remember me. But he didn't seem to even notice me, let alone recognise me. He was just staring away into the distance and muttering something.'

'What about?'

'Nothing that made any sense.' She hesitated and leaned forward to murmur in my ear – Gerry was amusing himself picking the petals off the red geranium that Marion had sent in with us – 'He was swearing a lot. Something about a bitch, 'a bloody bitch' and other foul words that I won't repeat.'

'Who was he talking about?' I knew, of course, but wondered if Mother did.

'Well, not me, that much was clear. He looked straight through me as if I wasn't here and kept going on about "the bitch".' She took my hands and held them both inside hers. 'You're a big girl now, Liza, and you've had to grow up fast these past few weeks. You understand me when I say that your father sometimes . . . sometimes shows an interest in other women.'

So The Dow had not been his first unfaithful dalliance. I hated him all the more. 'He was talking about some other woman? One he'd been . . . *showing an interest in?*'

'It seems so. But how he ended up in the state he was in when he got here to the hospital is a mystery. Maybe some other woman that he was . . . *friendly with* had something to do with it. Maybe they quarrelled and she hit him with something. He had a huge bruise on his head and a lot of swelling in his brain, the doctor said.'

Should I tell Mother that he had been 'showing an interest in' The Dow? Could it have been her doing that he had ended up in this state? That *she* had no real interest in him was now clear. She had simply been using him to get close to Gerry.

'Mother,' I said slowly, taking her hand, 'I think it's *her* - Miss Dow - that he's raving about.' I glanced at Gerry but he was on to his third flower now and absorbed in laying the petals out in a pattern on the table at the foot of the bed. It had a white cloth on it and the red petals looked like splashes of blood. Leaning forward, talking in as low a voice as possible while still being audible to Mother, I began the tale.

# CHAPTER THIRTY-SIX

*I have seen wicked men and fools, a great many of both; and I believe they both get paid in the end; but the fools first.*

*Robert Louis Stevenson, from 'Kidnapped'*

The old kirk of Torosay was a favourite place for funeral services. Its proximity to the equally old Craignure Inn meant that mourners, once the last metrical psalm - *The Old Hundredth* was a great favourite – had finally died away, could warm themselves at the roaring peat fire in the horseshoe grate and partake of the inn's famous scones and tea. Over the centuries, the inn had often benefitted from this trade.

Mother, released just for the day from the hospital, was playing the role of bereaved widow and hostess with her usual calm dignity. Gerry and I found ourselves the objects of pitying curiosity and we struggled to find a response to it.

The news of Father's death had come the day after our visit to Mother at Tobermory. He had suffered a huge stroke – always a strong possibility for a man exhibiting all the signs of a serious brain injury, the doctor had said. Because of Mother's own state of health, the danger had not been explained to her and Gerry and I had been considered too young. His continuing amnesia had been accompanied by several convulsions – something else we had not known – and, had the weather been better, he would have been conveyed to the larger hospital in Oban, and maybe to the even bigger one in Glasgow, where more sophisticated diagnostic equipment might have established the extent of the damage and the prognosis. But the ferry had not been running for the best part of a week before the final, fatal seizure. Indeed, it was still making only spasmodic voyages between Oban and Mull, often getting held up at one or other side of the Firth of Lorne for long hours before being able to make the next crossing. The timetable was 'all to pot', as Catriona said.

The NLB had been wonderful. As soon as they were told – by Arthur or Bridie, I think – what had happened, they had telephoned the Tobermory hospital and spoken to Mother, expressing condolences and assuring her that they would pay all funeral expenses, including the rather sumptuous 'purvey' at Craignure Inn. This had been a great relief to her as her first worry had been how she could organise the funeral from her sick bed and offer hospitality after it to all who attended – as was the custom. In normal circumstances, people would go back to the house of the bereaved family and expect to be fed and supplied with beverages ranging from strong tea to whisky and sherry. With Mother still in hospital – the shock of Father's death had set her recovery back considerably – and our house unoccupied for the best part of a fortnight, the Board had suggested the inn, overcoming Mother's feeble protests easily, and made all the arrangements.

In a brief committal service, Father had been buried in Tormore graveyard. As I had stood shivering in the January sleet, Gerry and I propping Mother up like bookends, I had reflected on the irony. The Dow had pursued Father in a flirtatious, flattering relationship, with a view to getting close to Gerry. All to try and bring my wee brother to this very graveyard with the bereft ghost of Lady MacLean, as she had believed herself to be when in the grip of her demons. What would have happened if she had succeeded? Would she really have gone ahead with murder? We would never know now but the thought of it – so believable there, on that cold, grey morning – had added the icy shivers of pure horror to the bitter cold of the weather.

The minister, his short, fat body straining the buttons of a heavy black coat so long that it brushed the frozen ground, reached new heights of pomposity as he intoned '. . . we commit his body to the ground . . .'

We had made a sad little band that morning in the graveyard – six solemn adults, including Mother, one tearful wee boy and one dazed lassie trying to come to grips with her emotions. As a community, we were in shock, not least because there had still been no explanation of the cause of Father's fatal fall and head injury.

The lighthouse families had each been represented by one adult: the three 'shore' men that month, Arthur and the other two men on his rota, Thomas and Hamish; and the wives of Calum and Euan who were out on The Rock, Jenny and Etta. A new keeper had arrived to replace Father in time to join Calum and Euan out on the lighthouse, thinking he was simply covering for a sick man but, with Father's death, the job had become permanent. His family, however, could not join him until a house – *our* house – became available. With the January rota due to end in a fortnight's time, temporary arrangements were in place for him to board with Calum and Jenny during his 'shore' period, until Mother was well enough to organise our removal from Erraid. All this I had heard Jenny explaining to Mother as we waited drearily for the hearse to arrive. I had not given any thought to what would happen to us, now that we could no longer be called 'a lighthouse family'. I felt a jolt of distress as this dawned on me. Despite the besetting anxiety of the past four months, I had come to look on Erraid as home. Perversely, now that the twin causes of my anxiety – Father and The Dow – were both gone and I could have looked forward to a happier existence there, it was going to be snatched away. We no longer belonged. Not only was our little family bereft of the man of the house; it was to be bereft of the very house itself.

Lachlan was waiting with the bus at the graveyard gates, with Marion and Catriona sitting in the front seat. Marion immediately took charge of Mother, tucking a blanket over her knees as she settled her into the seat behind her. Catriona hugged me as if we had not seen each other for weeks when, in fact, I had been staying with the MacPhails ever since Christmas Day and had had breakfast with her only two hours before. Gerry clung to Mother's hand and was lifted on to her knee once Marion's blanket was in place. The others filed sombrely in and there were only hushed murmurs as the bus wound its slow way to Torosay Kirk for the memorial service and an hour of dreary hymns and droning prayers. It was times like these that I missed the colour, the 'smells and bells', of the Catholic Church.

The only cheerful thing about the service was the presence of the remaining members of the lighthouse families: Bridie with Kirsty, Allyson and – to Gerry's delight – Angus; the other two wives, Kitty and Mhairi; and the whole gaggle of Erraid children. They had all come up the coast in the new NLB boat which had replaced the damaged one still stuck in the sand of *Druim Dhugail* beach on Iona, awaiting better weather when it would be towed to the boatyard at Tobermory for repair. It was Erraid School minus its teacher and, as we bobbed up and down to sing psalm after psalm, I was acutely aware that this would be the last time I would be one of them. I had not wanted to go to school when I arrived on Erraid, thinking myself too old for it, and my term there had been fraught with tension, blighted by suspicion and a nameless dread that had turned out to be only too well justified. And yet, as I exchanged suppressed grins and giggles with my schoolmates – pompous solemnity was having its usual contrary effect upon us – I felt a sadness as if I was already missing them and missing being one of them.

'Had your husband no family? No brothers or sisters? Of course it *is* a long way to come – and the ferry so unreliable at present. I was fortunate to get the last one over yesterday. I would not be here otherwise.' The speaker, addressing Mother from his considerable height, was a severe-looking man. He wore a starched white collar and a charcoal grey suit with a black armband. The NLB in person he was that day and very aware of it.

'Robert came from a large family,' replied Mother. 'He was the eldest of ten children.'

It was the first I had heard of it. No aunts, uncles or cousins had ever appeared in my short life. Mother had been an only child, a fact she had told me long ago when I first compared our sparse extended family with that of my schoolmates. I suppose I had somehow in my mind just extended this state of affairs to Father and had had no expectation of having any wider-family relations.

'My goodness!' The minister had come to join us and had heard Mother's words. 'Of course, he *was* a Roman Catholic. They are known for their large families.' He sniggered. I had no idea what he found funny about that and felt the urge to tell him to leave Mother alone. 'Did none of them want to come today? Not even one?'

Mother drew herself up haughtily. 'He had three brothers who were all killed in the war.'

'Oh dear,' said the Mr NLB and the minister looked taken aback.

'And six sisters. Three of them died of the Spanish flu shortly after the war. He'd lost touch with the others, I'm afraid, and I was in no position to start trying to find them, being in hospital myself when he died.'

'Of course, of course. Yes. How sad.' Both the minister and Mr NLB looked chastened, as well they might, by this crisp summary of Father's tragic family history. The minister turned hastily to talk to Lachlan who was warming his backside at the inn's roaring fire. I thought of Father as one of a large family, none of whom I had met or even heard of. To me he had always been a lone figure, fearsome, and unapproachable.

As the tension and repression of the past three hours in graveyard, bus and kirk began to thaw, responding to the warmth of the fire, the mouth-watering aroma of hot, savoury pies and freshly baked scones and the congenial atmosphere of the inn – not to mention the tots of whisky and sherry being offered around – the conversation gradually escalated from a subdued murmur to a cheerful buzz. Bonnets and gloves were doffed, neckties loosened, buttons undone. The children occupied one of several large alcoves in the L-shaped room and happily stuffed as much food as they could get into hungry jaws. Gerry and Angus were already absorbed in one of their games in another smaller alcove, having first heaped their plates and carried them there.

But I was restless, not inclined to join my schoolmates. In truth, I no longer felt part of them and their chatter seemed childish. I had come through so much in the past month; I felt that I had left childhood behind. With Father dead and Mother still not fully recovered from the miscarriage and subsequent haemorrhage that had almost killed her too, I was acutely aware of the adult concerns of taking care of my wee brother, finding somewhere for us to live and something for us to live *on*. Without Father's wage, how would we manage? I had heard about the Mull Poorhouse, near Tobermory, but had never dreamed that its shadow might so soon loom over my family. What went on in such places was the stuff of terrifying, cautionary tales: families split up and only allowed a few hours a week together; adults and children worked to the bone, fed on the roughest of diets and housed in the most austere of accommodation. I had no idea if anyone ever came out of such places alive. The spectre of such a fate had begun to haunt me although I had articulated it to no one as yet. And so I prowled around the room, slipping unnoticed among the knots of adults.

'It's a terrible shame, so it is. Those twa wee bairnies fatherless and Maggie – a nicer, more ladylike lassie ye'd never meet – left a widow. What's tae become o' them? Pair wee things, the three o' them!' That was Mhairi, speaking with her mournful Highland lilt and lapsing into Gaelic as she shook her head and wrung her hands.

'Aye. An' the worst o' it is they canna find out what happened to Robert. What happened to him after the Christmas party at the school? We can all remember him there and some folk say they saw him outside at the end but none o' us remember him getting on the bus for the jetty,' said Kitty.

'Then the next we hear he's been found in the shed beside the school, near dead. Never recovered his memory so he couldna tell us what happened – whether he tripped and fell, drunk as he was, or whether there was someone else there. Some kind o' fight, maybe, and he was pushed or knocked down - hit his head as he fell,' Etta speculated

'It's a mystery, so it is,' agreed Jenny. 'None o' the other men stayed behind after the last bus run. My Calum says Robert wouldna' get on the bus just kept saying he was waiting for someone – though who it could have been nobody can think. Everyone had gone by then.'

'Maybe he meant Liza; maybe he forgot she was going to stay with Lachlan and Marion,' suggested Kitty. But the other three women looked doubtful, as well they might: the idea of Father caring tuppence about me when he was drunk or even caring enough to wait and see that Gerry and I had got on the bus, was unlikely. They had only known our family for four months but they had seen enough, in that tight-knit, little community, to know just *how* unlikely.

285

I moved on round the room. Conversely, as the women talked of Father, the men were talking of The Dow.

'It's right hard to credit,' Thomas was saying, rocking on his heels and sipping a little more whisky with every third tilt forward, a process I watched in some fascination before tuning in to what was being said. 'There she was, as prim as my granny's lace-trimmed Sunday bloomers, walking about like she was floating on air and her nose twitching like there was a bad smell below it. Like she was something special, a cut above the rest of us. And, all the time, she was a lunatic, only fit to be locked up in an asylum! Mad, ravin' mad.' He took a particularly large swig of whisky and set his empty glass on a tray which was passing in the hands of a waiter, deftly lifting up a new, full one without breaking his rocking-sipping rhythm.

'Aye, and us putting our precious children into her care. Trusting her with our little treasures,' intoned Hamish who was inclined to become sententious after his third dram. 'It beggars belief.'

'Well, she never did them any harm – other than wee Gerry Galway, that is. She was a fine teacher, so she was, anyone could see that. The bairns respected her and they learned a helluva lot from her. Credit where credit's due,' said Arthur, always a fair man who liked to see the best in people.

'That's as maybe. When she was in her right mind - I'll gi'e ye that,' said Thomas. 'But she damn near drowned wee Gerry on Hogmanay. And there's talk that she was trying to take him to Tormore graveyard – where we were this morning burying his father – and that she might have murd . . .' He caught sight of me lurking behind Arthur with my ears flapping and stopped abruptly.

Arthur, however, had not seen me and he plunged on. 'They say she thought she was the ghost of Lady MacLean way back in the 17th century, the one that drowned and her body washed up at Tormore. When she was in the grip o' her *obsession'* – Arthur rolled the word round his tongue with satisfaction – 'she was lookin' for a wee laddie the same age as the ghost's son, him that was wi' Lady MacLean in the boat when it smashed on the rocks. *His* body was never found. So she was wantin' a wee lad to take to the graveyard to be with her – she was goin' tae murder . . .' He stopped as the other two men made frantic hushing gestures and gesticulated.

But I was already turning away. If only the men had realised it, I had known – or at least suspected – the full horror of The Dow's intentions long before they had, indeed before anyone had. I took a glass of raspberry cordial and made myself up a plate with two sausage rolls, two

286

scones and a generous dollop of blackberry jam. I slipped out into the hotel lobby and sat down on a small chair beside a coat rack.

As I ate, I thought about Joan Dow, sedate and dignified spinster, learned and gifted teacher, but harbouring an obsession that drove her to the point of maniacal murder. Two seemingly irreconcilable characters within one person. I thought back to our first encounter on Oban quayside: Mother's immediate sense of danger, recognising the likeness to the picture of the doomed Lady MacLean. I remembered Mother's 'What are you doing at that school. You're not a teacher.' Mother's instincts had been right. The woman before her had been a terrible threat to her children, especially her precious son. But Father and The Dow had already been in cahoots and Mother was powerless to stop them appropriating Gerry for the rest of our journey to our new home on Erraid, side-lining her - and me.

I thought back to my altercation with The Dow up in the Lookout when I had first suspected the meetings between her and Father, the vicious way she had slapped me and had almost knocked me out. After that, she and I had watched each other, cat-and-mouse, culminating in the day I found the two of them in our shed and struck an uneasy bargain with them: I would keep their secret if Father would ensure I was allowed to go to the Christmas party and stay with the McPhails after it. Of course, the Dow had encouraged that: it had suited her purposes to get me off Erraid so that she could get closer to Gerry. I burned with shame as I thought of that. If I had not been so fixated on being allowed to go and stay with Catriona, if I had gone straight to Mother then and told her what I knew, maybe the whole business might not have happened. Maybe. But Mother would still have been pregnant, might still have had the accident on the landing stage and miscarried, haemorrhaged and fallen deathly ill. She would still not have been there to stop The Dow taking Gerry while she was in hospital.

I remembered my suspicions: had The Dow distracted Mother on the landing stage just as Gerry fell towards her, causing her to trip, catch her foot in the loop of rope and fall over the side? Had she tugged unnecessarily hard on Mother's ankle as she freed it from the rope, making the injury worse? Had it all been planned by The Dow to ensure that Mother would not be at the party in Fionnphort that night, that it would be easier to get hold of Gerry and take him to the graveyard? If Gerry had not woken up and struggled, if Catriona, Marion and I had not heard his cries and run down the hill to the graveyard, would she have murdered him there that night? And killed herself as well? Thus, to her crazed mind, Lady MacLean and her son would have been united in death at last.

Instead, she had tried again, crazier than ever, on Hogmanay, filling Gerry's head with horror stories of Druid human sacrifice, but, failing again and demented, had thrown herself into the freezing waters of the Sound of Iona. I munched my way through the purvey food, lost in thought, puzzling over the loose ends and worrying about our future.

# EPILOGUE                    2007

*Home is the sailor from the sea*
*And the hunter home from the hill.*

                    Robert Louis Stevenson, from 'Requiem'

'I was an awful worrier as a lassie.' The old woman smiled at Jen. 'Maybe it was all those years with my father before he died, living with his moods and tempers. But I needn't have worried after all: it all worked fine out in the end. More tea, dear? I'll make a fresh pot.' She rose and made her slow way through to the kitchen.

Jen rested her head on the embroidered antimacassar and thought back over the long story, sifting through it, making the connections, marvelling at her own connection to it all. She had always known that somewhere in her family history was a bit of a skeleton: a great-grandmother who had been the result of a classic scion-of-the-family and servant-maid coupling, somewhere in the north west of Scotland. But, until now, she had never been much interested – not until the strange events on Mull two years ago.

An afternoon's research in Register House in Edinburgh and many hours on genealogy websites had uncovered the family tree and her links to a family called Galway, a lighthouse keeper's family in the 1920's.

Jen's great-grandmother, Rose, born 1888, had been the illegitimate daughter of one Ailsa Robertson (no record of the father – presumed to have been a son of the grand house where Ailsa was in service). Rose had been given away in adoption, as was customary in those days, and had grown up to marry and have five children, the youngest of whom had been Jen's late grandmother, born in 1922.

Ailsa meanwhile had gone down the respectable route after this, marrying and having only one more child, a daughter called Maggie. Rose and Maggie had thus been half-sisters, though unaware of each other's existence.

Maggie had married Robert Galway in 1910. Another afternoon's research, with help from interested staff in the National Library of Scotland, had revealed that Canadian author, Liza Connolly, had been Liza Galway, the daughter of lighthouse-keeper Robert Galway and his wife, Maggie. The family had been living on Erraid in the 1920s.

289

It had seemed a long shot that Liza might still be alive or, if so, contactable. But, thanks to the internet, it had taken only a few minutes to establish her Toronto publisher's website and contact them. The answer that came back a few days later had stunned her. Liza Connolly, née Galway, was alive and as well as a body of 94 years old can be. *And* she was once again living on Mull, having returned after more than seventy years exile.

'I've made us some lunch,' Liza called through from the kitchen, interrupting Jen's reverie. It was adjacent to the cosy, little sitting room where they had been sitting while she told the story of 'The Ghost of Erraid'. Those had been the old lady's own words, her pale old eyes achieving a twinkle as she said it. 'Would you be a dear and carry the tray for me?'

Jen jumped up with alacrity, imagining tiny, frail Liza trying to lift a laden tray.

'Now, dear. You have questions,' said Liza, once they were settled back by the fire, fresh tea poured and plates charged with dainty, crustless sandwiches.

'Yes.' Jen took a sandwich. What to ask first? It seemed only polite to start by enquiring about the Galway family – or what had been left of it after Robert's death. 'You stopped your tale at the point where you were worrying about what would happen to your Mother and brother – and yourself, of course. How did your future . . . well, *pan out?*'

'It "panned out" pretty good.' There was a trace of Canadian accent in the way she pronounced 'purty'. 'We found another way to stay on Erraid. Mother wanted to - she said that, right away after the funeral. Like me, she'd come to love the place and the people, even in the few short months we'd been there. We'd all made good friends, Gerry with Angus, me with Catriona and herself with Bridie and the other wives.'

'But didn't the Lighthouse Board make you leave their Erraid house? You said your father's replacement was going to bring his own family to live there.'

'The NLB were very kind. In those days, big companies like that tended to be philanthropic. People were poor and there was no welfare state or health insurance. So it was down to the big employers to take care of workers and their families. They saw it as their Christian duty.'

'The Board let you stay on in the Erraid house?'

'For a few weeks, until my mother was fully recovered and strong enough to organise a move. Father's replacement – a big man with a red

290

beard, I remember – stayed with Calum and Jenny on his first shore month. Then Lachlan and Marion – God rest their lovely souls – took us in for a couple of months. Then . . .' she paused for effect. 'Guess what happened!' Her sharp, old eyes twinkled.

'What?' Jen sat forward on her seat. Liza, the successful author, was reeling in her listener.

'The NLB couldn't find a new teacher. While they were advertising the post, Mother offered to take the classes until they did. She had to go through a sort of interview – well, a man from the Board came over to Mull to talk to her. She must have impressed him because The Board accepted her offer during the weeks we were staying with the MacPhails. Lachlan rowed the four of us – Catriona, Gerry, Mother and me – round to Erraid each morning. It was early spring by then and those wee morning trips were lovely. The dawn light on the water and the seabirds keening overhead.' Liza's eyes softened and focused on a long-ago scene. 'After about six weeks and still no sign of a new teacher, The Board sent an inspector to see how Mother was doing. She charmed him, of course, and impressed him with her knowledge and results. Mother was always such a reader, right from her girlhood. She'd only ever done it for pleasure or self-improvement but now she had a chance to use it. The inspector recommended that Mother be appointed officially as an 'unqualified teacher'. There were some stipulations – I think she was officially employed for only a year at a time on the understanding that, if a qualified teacher became available, she would not be re-employed. In practice, the job was hers for as long as she wanted it. But much more important was the schoolhouse that went with the job. We could stay on Erraid!'

'You must have all been delighted.'

'Indeed we were. It was like a miracle. I stayed at school for another three years until I was fifteen – most unusual at that time, but Mother had progressive ideas about the education of women, it turned out – she had just never voiced them while Father was alive. I helped with teaching the younger children and she and I took on learning things together. We studied Greek and Latin. *And* French – that came in useful later when we moved to Montreal.'

'What took you there? It sounds like you were all so happily settled in Erraid.'

'Well, I could not stay there forever. There was no work for me there and I was well past the age when I should have started earning. I started to look at positions in service but they were all far away on the mainland and, although I would have gone to one of them happily, Mother did not want to let me go. She and I had become like partners, bringing up Gerry and running the school. I talked it over with Marion and Bridie, two of the wisest, most practical women I knew. They both said the same thing: Mother must find another husband – she was too young and too attractive to remain single. Then I could be free to get on with my own life.'

'And did she? Find another husband.'

'Eventually.' Liza chuckled. 'We had a few false starts and a couple of total non-starters. But Marion and Bridie stuck to it and finally produced a winner.'

'They played matchmaker?'

Liza chuckled again. 'They certainly did. It took them just over a year. I think they were quite sad when Kingsley came along and swept Mother off her feet. They'd been enjoying themselves!'

'Kingsley?'

'My stepfather. It was just about love at first sight. And they so nearly missed each other. He was just about on his way to Canada. He was emigrating from the border farm where he had grown up – near Melrose, it was – and he had just come over to Mull for a couple of weeks to say goodbye to his granny who lived in Salen. He and Lachlan knew each other – they been in the navy together during The First World War – and Marion pounced as soon as he came to call. He and Mother never stood a chance against Marion's wiles.' Again Liza chuckled. 'Not that they wanted to resist.'

'What happened?'

'He stayed on Mull for many more weeks. Managed to transfer his place on the emigration ship to another one three months later. By that time, he and Mother were engaged and she had agreed to join him in Montreal once she gave notice to the NLB and packed up.'

'You and your brother went too?'

'Yes. It was hard for us leaving all our friends here. In those days, there was little chance you would see again for years, if ever.'

'So you all left Erraid?'

'In 1928. I remember that voyage like it was yesterday. Gerry was beside himself with excitement. That helped him accept losing his best pal.'

'Angus?'

'Mmm. And it was hard for me to part with Catriona. I didn't see her again for over ten years. She came over to Canada in the summer of 1939, meaning to stay just a few weeks – a holiday – but then war broke out and Lachlan wrote to me asking if I could keep her there until it was over. Of course, I said "yes". I was married by then with two wee tots to look after and it was great having her to help. Joe, my husband, liked her as much as I did. So much so that he found her a husband to keep her in Canada even after the war ended. By that time, she was mother herself and settled in Hamilton, Ontario.'

'And your mother? Was she happy out there? I hope her second husband treated her better than your father did.'

'That wouldn't have been hard.' Liza grimaced but then softened. 'She and Kingsley had a long and happy life together.'

'Did she ever talk about your father, about him and Miss Dow?'

'She never really spoke of my father again. The Dow wasn't the first woman he had run after during their marriage. But I think she felt that his death at The Dow's hands — even it was an accident - was a kind of poetic justice.'

'Did she and Kingsley have children?'

'Mother couldn't have any more children. She'd had to have a hysterectomy after the miscarriage. Kingsley knew that when they married but he never seemed to mind. He took on being a father to my brother and me and we adored hm. He taught us what a father should be. He was so good for Gerry. Turned him into a fine young man.'

'A happy ending, then, after all those fearful events?'

'Aye.' Liza sounded very Scottish again. It was fascinating how she dipped in and out of the two accents. 'A happy ending. Another sandwich, my dear? Or are you ready for a bit of this apple pie?'


It was late in the afternoon and the shadows were lengthening on the pretty garden outside Liza's cottage when all Jen's questions had finally been answered. She felt a little guilty as she took her leave. The old lady looked tired and frail as she stood in her doorway, waving the car away. Jen had a strong sense that she would never see her again. So strong, in fact, that she stopped at the little post office and asked the plump, cheery woman behind the counter a favour.

'If I can, lass. What is it?'

'If I leave you my card - here, it's got my phone numbers, landline and mobile, and my email address. If anything happens to Liza - Mrs Connolly — will you let me know? Please.'

Jen's business card joined others on an overcrowded noticeboard and she left the ramshackle little shop without much conviction of ever hearing about Liza again.

But she was wrong.

'That is quite a story, Jen.' George put his empty glass down on the bar. 'But there's still a lot of unexplained stuff.'

Jen nodded. 'I had lots of questions too,'

'And did she answer them?'

'Mostly. Some loose ends.'

'I'm glad,' said Sarah dreamily. 'Some things should be left to the imagination. 'Let's go outside. The rain's stopped.'

It was a mild late-spring evening. They ordered another round of drinks and settled back to admire Edinburgh's incomparable skyline as sunset cast a pale orange glow over the castle ramparts and turned the old tenement roofs into a black, higgledy-piggledy humpback.

'Where does the bell come in?' George picked up the matter as soon as their drinks were served. 'We heard it that day and Liza said she heard it the night of the Hogmanay party – after she left the house and went up the hill.'

'And it was part of the "Ghost of Erraid" legend that Catriona told Liza,' added Sarah.

Jen nodded. 'Liza said it was a delayed echo from the lifeboat summons bell that they used to sound to rouse the men when they were needed. Nowadays, of course, telephone and radio contact does the job but, up until the 1940's, the bell was rung at Bunessan whenever the lifeboat was being called out. Seems the sound sort of bounced out over the sea and ricocheted off the rocks, making that high-pitched, tuneful sound we heard.'

'But you just said . . .'

'I know: that they stopped ringing the bell in the 1940s. Liza didn't have an explanation for the day *we* heard it so I went to Bunessan lifeboat station. I spoke to the skipper. He was able to tell me about the shipwreck that day as well.' She paused to take a sip of her Pinot Grigio. 'They had a party of schoolchildren that day, visiting the station and learning all about it. The old bell is still there, preserved in pride of place. The children wanted to hear it being rung so the man on duty that day obliged. Of course, I asked what time that was.'

'And?' George and Sarah spoke in unison.

Jen smiled. 'Yes. It was around the time that we heard its echo.'

'So that's that mystery cleared up.' George was getting bored. 'Where do you girls fancy eating tonight?'

But Sarah was loth to leave it there. 'What about the shipwreck that day? Just at the time the bell was ringing?'

'Well,' said Jen slowly. 'Well, that's one mystery you can keep, Sarah. They know who and how and when - and probably even why - but the link to the bell isn't clear at all.'

'So who was it?'

'Well . . . there's a family living on Erraid now. It's their job to look after it for the Dutch owners, including the row of cottages where the lighthouse families lived. Anyone can book in for a stay – it's perfect for artists, writers, musicians, anyone looking for peace and quiet in a beautiful location. They do some guided retreats and self-sufficiency holidays as well. Inevitably, I suppose, they occasionally get someone looking to find relief from mental distress or to escape from their problems.'

'And there was someone like that when we were there on holiday?'

'The body recovered was a woman in her thirties. The folks from Erraid confirmed that she was in a depressed state of mind but was trying through meditation and other mind therapies to come off years of anti-depressant medicine. They had been supporting her in this but were concerned that she was trying to come off the medication too quickly.'

'So she flipped completely and committed suicide?' asked George in his matter-of-fact voice.

Jen shook her head. 'Not proven. No suicide note was found and she had seemed fairly stable that morning when she took the boat and set out. They thought she was just going round to Fionnphort, maybe up the coast to Ulva. She'd done that before, during her fortnight on Erraid, and was competent at handling the motorboat, so they hadn't worried.'

'So what happened?'

'No one knows for sure. One theory is that she went further out from shore than usual and got caught in a strong tide on the turn. Another theory is that she fell asleep – it was a very hot day, you remember – and the boat drifted, got caught in a swell and was dashed on to the rocks. The skipper at Bunessan Lifeboat Station thinks that she might have been reading about the Ghost of Erraid, about the shipwrecks and the connection with the strange bell. Then, in a bad state of mind, she took the boat out, not intending anything particularly, but when she heard the echo from the bell that was being rung for the party of children that afternoon, it tipped her mind. She took it for a sign and drove the boat right at the rocks.'

'You mean she took the sound of the bell to be a sort of signal that a shipwreck was underway and decided to be that shipwreck?' said Sarah, in a hushed voice

'Something like that. It's only his theory, of course.'

295

'It could just have been a coincidence,' said pragmatic George.

'Yes,' Jen conceded, grudgingly. 'Just an accident – the tides are very strong in The Sound of Iona - and the bell just happened to ring at the same time.'

They fell silent, contemplating the possibilities.

'I'm sticking with the power of the bell legend,' said Sarah at last.

Jen grinned. 'No such thing as coincidence, eh? "There are more things in heaven and earth than are dreamt of in your philosophy." Shakespeare, isn't it?'

'Hamlet,' said Sarah. 'To Horatio.'


'As far as I can make out, the whole bell thing is a testament to the power of legend.' Jen poured herself a large glass of water and downed half of it. They were in an Indian restaurant now, waiting for their food to appear. 'The first time the ringing coincided with a shipwreck was in 1874, not long after the completion of the lighthouse. A nine-year-old boy and his mother were shipwrecked on the rocks. The lighthouse keepers saw it was about to happen and alerted the lifeboat station; the bell was rung to summon the men and the phenomenon of the bell echoing out at sea happened. *Her* body was recovered but *his* never was. It was probably an old newspaper clipping about it that Mrs Forsyth, Liza's neighbour in North Berwick, had in her album. Possibly a retrospective on the anniversary of the shipwreck: "the never-solved mystery of what happened to the boy." Over the years, this shipwreck must have got linked to another one that had happened in the eighteenth century – a boy and his nanny – on the same rocks. Of course, there was no lighthouse and no lifeboat station then.'

'So, no bell to ring,' said George. 'Where did the bell story come from, then?'

'Well,' Jen said, 'that clipping not only referred to the boy and his nanny in the eighteenth century, it linked back to the seventeenth century one – Lady MacLean and her son. It implied the legend of one boy-and-woman shipwreck on the Torran rocks occurring every century. It also made much of the strange bell out at sea at the time of the nineteenth century wreck. I suppose it was only a short step from there to the bell becoming part of the story in all three centuries.'

'The power of legend,' said Sarah dreamily.

'Power of lies, more like,' snorted George.

'Liza had a theory about that.' Jen smiled as she recalled the sharply intelligent old face. 'She said that legends are formed by stories from people's imagination – yes, lies if you like, George – rolling down the decades and centuries and gathering up other stories as they go, like snowballs gathering more and more snow as they roll until they become huge and turn into snow sculptures. Then everyone looks at them and thinks they were all part of the story all along!'

'So the bell phenomenon got tied in with the woman-and-boy-shipwreck legend after the nineteenth century one,' said Sarah. 'Then it got extended backwards to the eighteenth and seventeenth century ones.'

Jen nodded. 'The ghost of Lady MacLean looking for her son was one legend and the bell heralding the shipwrecks was quite another but somewhere along the line they joined up. Just like Liza's snowballs. Oh good! Here comes the food!'


'What about the little green-and-gold books that kept turning up? What was in the one that made her mother scream before they even set out for Erraid?'

They were replete now, waiting for coffee.

'It was of a painting of Lady MacLean and her nine-year-old son.'

'But what made Liza's mother scream when she saw it?'

'Liza said the boy, Alan, was the spitting image of Gerry but she never found out if there was a family connection. It would be a good genealogy project for someone.' Jen paused, struck by the thought that, if a connection were ever established, then she too would have Chief of Clan MacLean blood in her veins. A long-ago shadow from another world falling across her path.

'How strange! And then, when she saw Miss Dow, she thought she looked like the Lady Maclean in the book?'

'To be fair, the chances are that Joan Dow purposefully cultivated a look similar to Lady MacLean. After all, she half-believed she *was* her when she was in one of her strange moods.'

'Did Liza ever find out what happened to her father the night of the Christmas party? Did he fall or was he pushed?' Sarah giggled. 'And what happened to Joan Dow? Did Liza ever hear any more about her?'

'Convicted of kidnapping a minor and sentenced. There was some talk of attempted murder or manslaughter but that didn't stick. She was clearly unhinged so she was sent to a secure mental hospital. Nothing was heard of her for decades and then Liza's mother got a letter from her. Sometime in the fifties, I think.'

'What did it say?'

'Joan had had modern psychiatric treatment and was rehabilitated to some extent, although still living in an institution. Part of this rehabilitation was to make amends to the victims of her mad behaviour – as far as was possible anyway. Her doctor traced us to Canada and Joan wrote to Maggie apologising for the terror she had afflicted on the family. And she cleared up the mystery of Robert's - the father's - fatal head injury.'

'So it *was* her?'

'Yes, but not intentionally. When she got back to the hall after the party, she heard a noise in the shed and went in to see. It was Robert looking for more booze. He tried to force his drunken attentions on her and she pushed him away. He staggered and fell and she left him there. She stayed overnight with the Fionnphort schoolteacher and walked back over the causeway next day when the tide was out. She didn't know that he had struck his head and lain unconscious in the shed all night.'

'She probably didn't care,' said George. 'She was going off her head by then. It was only a few days later that she tried to take Gerry to the graveyard and murder him. And then, when she was stopped by the lifeboat, she tried to drown herself. I don't suppose she was sparing much thought for a violent, drunken letch like Robert Galway.'


Jen had misjudged the Mull postmistress. Nine months later, an email dropped into her inbox from one, Betty McNeil. It was short and to the point: Liza had died peacefully in her sleep two days ago and the funeral service was in three days' time in Torosay Kirk at Craignure, and thereafter to Tormore cemetery for burial. That had been Liza's own request, lodged with her solicitor, and she had her plot there purchased and waiting.

Sarah had begged to come with her and Jen was glad of the company, never more so than when she stood shivering by the graveside in the January sleet and biting wind. The connection was not lost upon her and Liza's description of Robert's burial, eighty years ago in this same cemetery, played in Jen's mind. The ceremony over, the scattering of funeral guests, many of them Canadian, hastened towards their warm cars.

'Just one minute,' said Jen as Sarah began to pull her away. Sarah stood back as Jen moved to a far corner of the little graveyard and stopped beside a small, not quite upright gravestone. 'Here it is. Robert's grave, still here.'

Sarah joined her and the two stood in silence, reading with some difficulty the weathered stone face: Robert James Galway, 1894 – 1925. Husband of Margaret Galway, father of Elizabeth and Gerald. R.I.P.

Then, without a word, they turned away.

'*Will* you write it all up, Jen?' asked Sarah, as they drove north along the narrow winding road towards Craignure. It was not the first time she had suggested it. 'I'd love to help you, even if it was just proof reading. It would be a crying shame to let such a good story just die with Liza.'

'Yes,' said Jen as she slowed into a passing place. 'I think I must try, at least. You're right, Sarah – I owe it to Liza. And I'd love your help!'

'What shall we call it?' Sarah wriggled excitedly in her seatbelt.

'I'll let Liza choose,' said Jen. 'She had a name for it.'

'And that was . . ?'

'The Ghost of Erraid.'

## THE END

# THE JEN-AND-LIZA CONNECTION

```
HECTOR  ---- m------ AILSA -----son of house where Ailsa
            l                          worked
            I                            l
            I                            I
            l                            l
            I                            l
            l                            l
ROBERT GALWAY ---m----MAGGIE (b 1890) >>> half sisters <<<ROSE *
            I                            l
            l                            l
            I                            l
            I                            l
   LIZA (b 1911) and GERRY (b 1914)        youngest daughter,
                                           Agnes, (born 1922)
                                                   l
                                                   I
                                                   l
                                                   I
                                    eldest child Kate (born 1947)
                                                   l
                                                   l
                                                   I
                                                   l
                                            JEN (born 1977)
                                    Great-granddaughter of ROSE *
```

# REFERENCES AND SOURCES

*Kidnapped.* Robert Louis Stevenson. First published in 1886. The edition used was published by Canongate Books Ltd, Edinburgh 2006

*Strangers to the Land.* Ruth Dickson. Published by GSG Ltd, British Columbia 2013

*The Lighthouse Stevensons.* Bella Bathurst. Published by HarperCollins 1999

*Kilcaraig.* Annabel Carothers. Published by William Heineman Ltd 1982

*Four Ducks on a Pond.* Annabel Carothers. Published by Birlinn Ltd, Edinburgh 2010

*As It Was - An Ulva Boyhood.* Donald W. Mackenzie. Published by Birlinn Ltd. Edinburgh 2000.

*Tales and Travels of a School Inspector.* John Wilson. First published in 1928. The edition used was published by Birlinn Ltd, Edinburgh 2007.

*Island Wife.* Judy Fairbairns. Published by Two Roads 2013

*Island of Wings.* Karin Altenberg. Published by Querus 2011


*The Hebrides.* W.H. Murray. Published by William Heineman Ltd 1965

*Iona - a Book of Photographs.* Published by The Iona Community c 1949

*Old Mull.* Guthrie Hutton. Published by Stenlake Publishing Ltd. Ayrshire

*Walking North with Keats.* Carol Kyros Walker. Published by Yale University Press, London 1992

*A Guide to Walks in the District of Fidden.* Published by the Ross of Mull Heritage Centre 2004

*Mull and Iona 40 Favourite Walks.* Paul and Helen Webster. Published by Pocket Mountains, Dumfries and Galloway 2012


*Duart Castle - Where Eagles Dare.* Jarrold Publishing

*Death or Victory – Tales of the Clan Maclean.* Fiona Maclean. Published by White and Maclean Publishing 2011.


*Scotia Nova Poems* edited by Alistair Findlay and Tessa Ransford. Published by Luath Press Ltd. Edinburgh 2014


*www.pantheon.org:* an internet encyclopaedia of mythology, folklore and religio

Lightning Source UK Ltd.
Milton Keynes UK
UKOW03f2253170417
299324UK00001B/48/P